David Foley was born in Dublin, where he still liv   ʟ
and he has worked there as a solicitor for nearly thiɪ   ᴇ
to write murder mysteries but making the time to ᴄ   .
Fortunately, the passing of the years has brought with it an easing of commitments and
given David the opportunity to pursue his literary interests. This is his first novel.

*

Praise for *The File Note*

"An impressive and charming murder mystery which entertains and keeps
the reader on edge throughout by combining clever plot twists with witty
observations. Its humour and characters, who inhabit delightful corners of
Dublin and small-town Ireland, hark back to a gentler time. I enjoyed every
word and can't wait to read about the many more adventures that I am sure
are in store for Hadfield, a country solicitor who lives life at his own pace and
is the understated hero of *The File Note*."

—*Rachel Fehily*

"Where there's a Will there's usually a body, but David Foley manages to serve
up a few more for good measure in this thoroughly enjoyable old-style murder
mystery. Drawing on his own legal background, the author deftly fashions a
tale of family intrigue and village suspicion with a cast of characters as well
drawn as some are loathsome, set against the usually unexceptional backdrop
of succession law. Part Agatha Christie, part *Midsomer Murders*, *The File Note*
is a welcome and refreshing throwback to the days of well-crafted and leisurely
paced mysteries – which, in the era of high octane and rarely credible thrillers,
seemed to be gone forever."

—*Eugene McCague*

"Quick, witty, good fun – an excellent debut novel. This page-turner will keep
you reading late into the night, and looking forward to its successor."

—*Victoria Browne*

"I would happily recommend this book to anyone who likes murder mysteries.
It is an enjoyable and entertaining read with a clever and intriguing plot."

—*Richard Bennett*

"Hadfield and FitzHerbert are a winning combination in this rural murder
mystery."

—*Sinead Farrell*

The File Note

First published in 2019 by
Liberties Press
1 Terenure Place | Terenure | Dublin 6W | Ireland
Tel: +353 (0) 86 853 8793
www.libertiespress.com

Distributed in the United States and Canada by
Casemate IPM | 1950 Lawrence Road | Havertown | Pennsylvania
19083 | USA
T: (610) 853 9131 | E: casemate@casematepublishers.com

Copyright © David Foley
The author asserts his moral rights.
ISBN (print): 978-1-912589-08-1
ISBN (e-book): 978-1-912589-09-8

2 4 6 8 10 9 7 5 3 1
A CIP record for this title is available from the British Library.
Cover design by Roudy Design
Printed in Dublin by Sprint Print

The File Note

David Foley

For Aisling, Stephanie and Charles

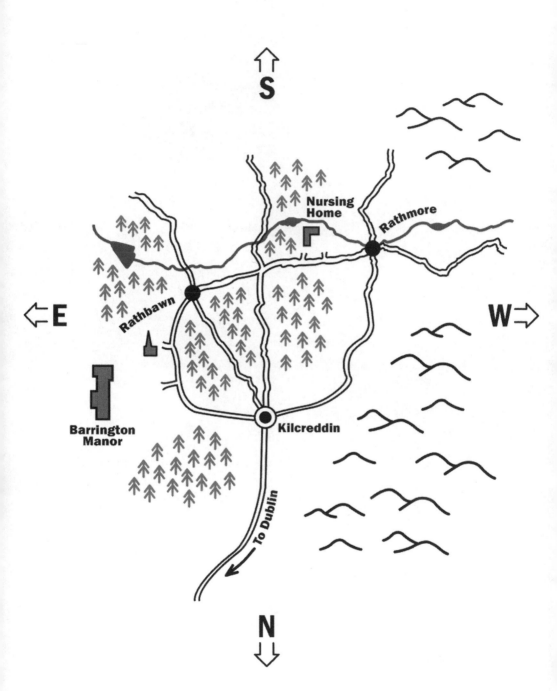

CHAPTER 1

It was a particularly cold day for October as Hadfield pulled up outside the office, where his boss was waiting for him. He hopped out of the car to open the passenger door and take the old man's briefcase.

'Damn this arthritis,' said Mr Timmons, as he eased his way in.

'Straight to the Manor, then?' asked Hadfield.

'Yes, and as quick as you can. I'm running a bit late as it is.'

Andrew Timmons was the principal of Timmons & Associates, a small legal practice in Kilcreddin, and, as a bachelor all his life, was well used to his independence. Hadfield wasn't entirely sure of the older man's age, but reckoned he had to be in his seventies. Until recently, Timmons would have driven everywhere himself, including the odd outing on his Harley-Davidson, which was a particular hobby.

As the only other solicitor at the firm, and still an associate, despite the fact that he was approaching forty, it had fallen to Hadfield to assist with transport arrangements as the arthritis worsened.

'Can't you go any faster?'

'I'll try, but it is quite a tight road' replied Hadfield.

They were on their way to the family home of the Barringtons, which was situated on a large estate about five miles from Kilcreddin. The route was a winding one, and not without its dangers.

Mr Timmons (or 'A.T.', as he was known in the office) was not renowned for his patience. Hadfield reluctantly increased the speed, while keeping his eyes firmly fixed on the road ahead.

'Terrible business this,' said Hadfield.

'Yes, certainly. A terrible business indeed. Poor George.'

Timmons was referring to George Barrington – or Lord Barrington, to give him his proper title – a longstanding client of the office. He had died a few days earlier while visiting his sister, Greta, at the nearby nursing home. Initially it was thought he had suffered a heart attack, but it was not long before rumours began to spread. Poisoning was now suspected, and an arrest was even being talked about.

'I hear Robert Staunton was arrested,' continued Hadfield.

'I'm not sure it was an arrest. Just in for questioning. Apparently he was seen in the nursing home at the time. Hello, what's this?'

They had arrived at the entrance to Barrington Manor, to find a number of people holding placards. On seeing the car, the crowd began to chant.

'I think it's the protesters, over the tree-cutting near Rathbawn,' said Hadfield.

'How could they even think of it, at a time like this! And Lord Barrington laid out in the Manor. Scandalous! No doubt Simon Armstrong is behind this. Look, there he is: roll down your window.'

Hadfield stopped the car, and nervously did as he had been asked.

'What do you think you are at, Armstrong? Have you no respect for the dead?'

'Did he have any respect for the living?' came the angry reply, from a skinny bearded youth in scruffy clothes.

'It's outrageous. Let's see what the police make of it.'

'It's not us who are breaking the law.'

'You can explain that at your leisure down at the station. Let's go, James.'

Hadfield quickly shut the window and passed through the entrance on to the driveway up to Barrington Manor.

The Manor, and the surrounding lands, had been in the Barrington family for centuries. In fact, the estate had originally stretched all the way to Kilcreddin and the neighbouring villages of Rathmore and Rathbawn. The house itself was an imposing structure in the Gothic style, topped off with various turrets of differing heights.

There were a number of cars in the gravelled area to the front of the house. Hadfield parked as close to the arched porch as he could manage. After being helped out of the car, Timmons checked his attire to ensure all was in order. He was a small man, slightly rotund, and quite fussy about his appearance. Only the best three-piece suits would do.

'Will you need your briefcase?' asked Hadfield.

'I'm not sure. You can leave it in the car for the moment.'

'I'll wait here, so.'

'You'd better come in, seeing as you're here.'

Hadfield had met Lord Barrington briefly on a number of occasions and was on nodding terms with some members of the family, but was not sure that attending the family wake was entirely appropriate. Timmons noticed his reticence, and added: 'I won't always be here to handle the Barrington matters. You might as well get to know them a little better – and now's as good a time as any.'

Hadfield had his doubts, but accompanied his employer up the steps to the large front door, where a person who appeared to be a butler greeted Mr Timmons, enquired as to the name of his companion, and then escorted them across the large, marbled hallway to the wood-panelled library. The room was empty, save for a raised coffin and a woman arranging flowers.

'Sad day, Mr Timmons.'

'Yes, Agnes. A very sad day.'

'Shocking really, isn't it, Mr Hadfield. To go like that.'

Hadfield nodded his agreement. Agnes Goodbody was the local florist, and supplied flowers to the manor house. She also looked after Timmons & Associates, and was a constant source of information on local matters. The word 'gossip' was never too far away when describing her.

Hadfield followed Timmons to the coffin. Lord Barrington looked much as Hadfield remembered him: well built, and with the distinctive handlebar moustache. His complexion was not quite as ruddy as would have been the norm, but that was perhaps to be expected. Thirty seconds was enough for Hadfield, who retreated, to leave his boss alone with his thoughts.

'Seems he was poisoned . . . ' whispered Agnes.

'Yes, I have heard mention of that.'

'And Rob Staunton the suspect!'

Hadfield nodded, but made no reply.

'They are like a bag of cats in there,' she continued, looking towards the adjoining drawing room, from which could be heard the sound of muffled voices.

'Oh. Why's that?'

'His Lordship was supposed to be making an announcement this weekend. They think it was about the wills. Nobody is sure where they stand. Although I'm sure Mr Timmons will know.'

'What's that, Agnes?' enquired Timmons, as he turned away from the deceased. Hadfield noticed that his eyes were a little red, and that he was replacing a handkerchief into his pocket.

'Nothing, Mr Timmons. Just warning Mr Hadfield that there is a bit of an atmosphere next door.'

'Hardly surprising, really. In the circumstances. We should join them, James.'

Heads turned as they entered the drawing room. Hadfield himself had quite a striking appearance. He was a tall man, and quite thin, but still athletic for someone fast approaching forty. His sandy brown hair was offset by dark, straight eyebrows and a long, aquiline nose. Most distinctive were his eyes, which were a deep green, with tiny flecks of varying shades of brown. He stood behind Timmons as Lady Barrington approached. She was quite tall herself, and slim, with long black hair, and although she was likely to be approaching seventy, she looked well on it. Indeed, she was very beautiful, with porcelain skin and clear blue eyes.

'Andrew. Thank you for coming.'

'Of course, Lydia. You know my colleague, James Hadfield?'

'Yes. I think we may have met at the office.'

'My condolences, Lady Barrington.'

As Timmons commiserated with his client, Hadfield looked around the large room, and the various people who were present. Lord Barrington had three children from his first marriage. The eldest was Richard, who was about the same age as Hadfield, followed by Samantha, who was about a year younger, and Jasmine, who was in her mid-twenties. Their mother had died in a horse-riding accident two years previously, and Lord Barrington had married Lydia the following year.

There was a young, good-looking couple, whom he did not know, talking to Jasmine. He *did* recognise Reverend Devereux, but not the two rather strict-looking women to whom the Reverend was holding forth. One of these women looked somewhat similar to Lady Barrington: she was tall and thin, with long black hair. While she might have been described as beautiful, somehow Lady Barrington appeared to be the more attractive. Perhaps the strictness of the stranger's demeanour was the difference.

Albert Boyd, the local bank manager, was deep in conversation with Richard's wife, Margaret. The one other person in the room was Samantha's husband, Denis Russell, who was now making a beeline towards him. He was considerably shorter than Hadfield but quite dapper, with the little hair he had, sleeked back to such an extent that it created something of a sheen. He wore black-rimmed 1950s-style spectacles. These must have been quite strong, because they made his eyes appear to protrude a little disconcertingly.

'Hadfield, isn't it. With Timmons?'

'That's right.'

'Used to dabble in it myself.'

'Oh?'

'Yes, in Dublin. Corporate, primarily. Gave it up when I married Samantha and moved down here.'

'You weren't tempted to go into practice locally?'

'Not a bit. Found my true vocation in the arts. There's the musical society, of course: a lot of my time needed for that. You don't sing yourself, do you? We could always use an extra man. Our next production is *The Mikado*!'

'Er . . . no. Singing wouldn't be one of my strengths.'

'Oh well. But you *will* attend one of the shows. Not long now until opening night.'

'Er . . . .'

A raised voice prevented Hadfield from replying. 'Well, they won't be here a minute longer, as far as I'm concerned. They've long overstayed as it is.'

'That's not your decision to make. I can have any of my friends for as long as I like.'

'Not when the estate comes to me.'

'Assuming it does. And anyway, Daddy always said I could stay here as long as I wished.'

'But not with any spongers that happen to be in tow. He was going to give them their marching orders soon enough. Wasn't too impressed finding the three of you in bed last weekend. I'm sure that was to be part of the "Announcement".'

'I explained all that to him. It was . . . .'

'Please,' interjected Lady Barrington. 'Richard, Jasmine. Really!'

'I can't take any more of this!' exclaimed Jasmine, sinking back into a couch and sobbing loudly. She was a striking young girl who tended to catch attention wherever she went. Her dark bobbed hair, pale visage, full red lips and sparkling blue eyes were difficult to ignore. Although at the moment most of these features were covered with a handkerchief as she dabbed her eyes.

Richard turned away and went to refill his glass. He was similar in appearance to his father: tall, broad-shouldered, and with a ruddy complexion – although he didn't sport a moustache. His temperament was known to have much in common with his father too, with a tendency to be gruff – not always helped by a short temper.

'I'll introduce you to the interlopers,' said Denis. 'Actually,' he added, in a low whisper, 'before I do: a question. Do you know if George actually signed a new will?'

'No idea, I'm afraid. You'd need to ask Mr Timmons on that.'

'No matter,' he replied, leading Hadfield over to the young couple, who appeared to be the subject of the earlier contretemps.

'Scott. Penny. Might I introduce you to James Hadfield.'

The couple were of a similar age to Jasmine – in their mid-twenties – but were dressed much more casually than her. In fact, perhaps a little too casually for the occasion. The girl was svelte: she wore her blonde hair in a pony-tail, and had an almost angelic face. Her counterpart was a good-looking, clean-shaven, sallow-skinned fellow. As they greeted each other, Hadfield noted that they did not seem at all put out at being the centre of the squabble between the siblings. He also noted Scott's distinctly English accent, and enquired about it.

'Yes, Eton does that. Cambridge too I suppose,' came the reply.

'Oh. What did you study there?'

'This and that. Didn't finish. Decided to go travelling.'

'That's how we met,' added Penny.

'And what's your line of business?' enquired Scott.

'The law. I'm a solicitor with Timmons & Associates.'

'Ah. Did you know anything about the announcement this weekend?'

'Er . . . no. What exactly was to be announced?'

'The old boy's new will, I gather.'

'It was supposed to be revealed weeks ago,' added Penny, 'but he kept put-ting it off.'

'Why was that?'

'He wanted Lydia to sign a will at the same time. I think they were having a disagreement over that.'

'George was definitely not in the best of form lately,' said Denis. 'Might explain his grumblings about the, er . . . accommodation arrangements.'

'He didn't seem overly fond of you either, old chap,' retorted Scott.

'Well, I wouldn't agree with that. We didn't see eye to eye over my theatrical career but . . . .'

Scott sniggered at this – which prompted Penny to have a barely suppressed fit of giggles.

Denis gave the couple a disdainful look. 'At least I have a career. Come with me, James. I will introduce you to the other *temporary* residents. Reverend Devereux appears to have abandoned them.'

The similarity of one of these residents to Lady Barrington was soon explained: she was her elder sister, Letitia, having recently arrived from Paris for a visit. She was accompanied by Clarisse, who, although considerably younger, did not quite have the looks of her friend, being short, plump and rather plain. But the grimness was about equal.

'A terrible tragedy,' said Hadfield, after the introductions had been made.

'I dare say,' came the laconic reply from Letitia.

'Yes,' added Clarisse.

Silence descended.

'You knew Lord Barrington quite well?' suggested Hadfield.

'We hadn't met before. I only really came to see Lydia. He seemed civil enough, the few times we engaged.'

'I only spoke to him once,' added Clarisse.

A further pause ensued.

'It must be a great support to Lady Barrington to have her sister here at such a difficult time.'

'I'm sure.'

Another lull.

'You . . . er . . . are staying here? At the Manor?'

'Yes,' replied Letitia.

Clarisse nodded.

Hadfield felt he had taken the conversation as far as he could, when Denis came to the rescue.

'I took the liberty of getting you the two first-night tickets we talked about,' he said, fishing two gaudy pieces of paper out of his pocket.

'Ah'

'I expect you will still be here then.'

'Difficult to say,' replied Letitia. 'Nothing has been finalised yet.'

'Well, take them anyway, and we can fix up as and when.'

'Very kind.'

'Hmm . . . ' was as much as Clarisse had to say to that.

Hadfield decided to move on and join Albert Boyd: the one person present whom he knew quite well. He made his excuses and approached Albert, who was now talking to Samantha, Margaret having joined her husband to start what seemed to be quite a heated discussion.

'So, if you could organise that as soon as possible, I would be very grateful.'

'Of course, Samantha. Ah, James, good to see you.'

As the local bank manager, Boyd interacted with Timmons and Hadfield quite regularly. He was a tall, skinny man of about sixty; his usual attire consisted of a brightly coloured suit with contrasting dickie bow. Not very bank-manager-ish, but no longer worthy of comment in Kilcreddin. Today he had dressed more soberly, as befitted the occasion.

Although not unattractive, Samantha had not been blessed with Jasmine's good looks. Her appearance was of the no-nonsense, businesslike kind. This could be a little offputting for people, but as she was a GP by profession, it was probably no harm. Chatty patients were not always good for business.

Samantha seemed a little startled when Hadfield first joined them, but quickly regained her composure.

'You've met the gruesome twosome then,' she commented,

'Er . . . .'

'Letitia and Clarisse,' added Albert.

'Yes. We had a brief few words. Denis brought me over.'

'Handing out more tickets, I see. The thing will never make any money.'

Samantha checked herself for a moment, but seemed to be unable to hold back her emotions.

'Daddy was right all along,' she said, searching in her bag for a tissue and excusing herself as the tears began to flow.

'Samantha, dearest,' exclaimed Denis, rushing over to help her to the nearest couch.

'All a little fraught today,' whispered Albert.

'I can see that,' replied Hadfield, as he noted Richard knocking back another drink and raising his voice once more.

'Enough! Can we at least wait until the old fellow has been buried? Everything will be fine!'

Margaret could not be heard, but whatever she was saying seemed to quieten her husband. She was a slight but pretty woman who had done her duty of producing three children – including the male heir to the Barrington dynasty – but it was common knowledge that their relationship was in a little difficulty.

'Being forced together over this might not be helping matters,' added Albert quietly. 'I think I might slip away before there's any more drama. I'll just have a quick word with Andrew before I go.'

'Good Lord! Of all the nerve!'

This exclamation had come from Richard, and seemed to be directed at the two people who had just entered the room, one of whom was in a wheelchair.

'Outrageous!' added Samantha, who seemed to have recovered – with the aid of a brandy.

'Indeed, my dear,' added Denis. 'Quite scandalous.'

Jasmine looked up briefly, but then began sobbing once more.

CHAPTER 2

The newcomer in the wheelchair was Greta, Lord Barrington's sister.

Miss Greta, as she was generally known, was a spinster who had lived at the Manor until Lord Barrington's first wife arrived. She had then moved to a pleasant cottage in Rathbawn, just outside the Manor. In later years, as her mobility had reduced, she had moved to the nursing home – the scene of her brother's demise – which was a little further up the road leading to Rathmore, the larger neighbouring village which was due west of the Manor. She was quite frail but well preserved, and still retained a brightness in her eyes and a sharpness of mind. In particular, she was very proud of her long hair, which was always styled immaculately, and she never failed to have her fingernails painted in the latest colour. She was an important client at the Rathmore beauty parlour.

The protestations were not, however, directed at Miss Greta but rather at Robert Staunton, the person pushing the wheelchair. He was of medium height, with close-cut dark hair and an athletic, muscular body: there were few single (and some not-so-single) girls in the locality who did not consider him attractive. He was not a relative of the family but was the son of a couple who had worked for Lord Barrington. They had died quite young, and their employer had to some extent taken their only child under his wing, arranging for his schooling locally and then employing him at the estate. He had very dark eyes which were hard to capture, partly due to being overshadowed by his dark eyebrows, but also due to his tendency to avoid direct eye-contact. He was now looking firmly at the floor of the drawing room.

'What do you mean, Richard?' asked Greta sharply.

'What I mean is perfectly obvious: Staunton has some nerve, coming here to pretend to pay his respects to the person he murdered!'

'Take that back, Richard!' interjected Lady Barrington, becoming obviously upset and, aided by Timmons, reaching for a chair. 'Robert wouldn't do any such thing.'

'I will *not* take it back. And everyone here agrees. Isn't that right?'

There was a momentary silence as Richard waited for affirmation from those present.

'Speak for yourself,' said Letitia, as she lit a cigarette.

'Well, I agree,' replied Samantha. 'Haven't the police arrested him?'

'Clearly not. He is here, isn't he.'

This last remark from Scott produced a giggle from Penny, who turned away to get a fresh drink.

'It's no laughing matter, miss,' came the quick retort from Samantha. 'The police had him in custody for ages. He was the only one at the nursing home. They are just preparing their case. Isn't that right, Denis.'

'I'm quite sure that's right, my dear.'

'But I was at the nursing home too. Perhaps I'm the murderer!' exclaimed Greta. 'Or Reverend Devereux. Or Albert Boyd. They were there too.'

There was an awkward silence as Albert looked intently at his shoes and the Reverend contemplated the ceiling. Finally, Richard responded in exasperation. 'Nobody suspects you of anything, Greta. Or the other two. Staunton had a clear motive.'

'Oh?' enquired a newly interested Letitia. 'What was that?'

'The will, of course. He was afraid that George was going to cut him out because of the new business.'

'There was a greater chance of him cutting *you* out,' replied Greta. 'What with your great new plans!'

'Why would he do that? I'm family. Staunton was going to set up in competition with the shoot. The old man was not happy with that, as well you know.'

Robert spoke for the first time. 'I explained all that to George. It was never going to be in competition with . . . .'

'Exactly, Richard,' interrupted Samantha. 'And the only way to get his hands on the money was to stop father changing his will by killing him!'

Samantha burst into tears again, and was comforted once more by her husband. 'There there, my dear. All will be sorted in due course. I am only an ex-member of the junior profession, but I don't believe the law allows one to profit from their crime . . . .'

Lady Barrington seemed to recover somewhat, and spoke up again. 'I don't know what you are all trying to say, but George would not have cut Robert out. He was more worried about you three.'

'What do you mean by that?' Jasmine asked indignantly.

'You all know very well. George was not happy with how you were conducting your affairs. No financial restraint. No business sense. No work ethic.'

'That's not true,' replied Samantha. 'I work very hard at my practice.'

'Perhaps, Samantha, but is it making any money?'

'And what business is that of yours?' shouted Jasmine, jumping up from the couch. 'Who are you to say what we can or can't do? We all know that you didn't have a penny before you married Daddy.'

'I won't rise to that, Jasmine. I'm just saying that Robert was not necessarily exercising George's mind when he was changing his will.'

'I thought it was *your* will that was exercising his mind . . . .'

This last comment was from Letitia, whom Lady Barrington now fixed with a steely stare.

'That's right,' piped up Richard, 'we all know he kept putting off the "announcement" because of you. Whatever it was you were doing.'

'Or not doing,' added Samantha.

'I don't propose to discuss this with you now. All I am saying is that I don't believe Robert had anything to do with the poisoning. In fact, I think I know who did.'

This was greeted with various exclamations and outbursts around the room.

'I am not saying anything further,' said Lady Barrington, when the hubbub finally subsided. 'I will see you all at dinner. We'll say eight – a little later than usual – as I will need to meet with Mr Timmons beforehand. Drinks at seven. Everyone is welcome to stay, or to join us later. Oh, and I've decided that this evening would be a good time to make the "announcement" that myself and George had planned. Andrew, you might join me in the study.'

'Making sure everything is legitimate, I hope,' said Letitia, as her sister passed by. This received no response from Lady Barrington, but Miss Greta could be heard muttering 'Really! That woman!' in the background.

Silence descended on the drawing room as Lady Barrington and Timmons left the room.

'I say' said Scott, once the door had closed, 'does anyone actually know if George did change his will?'

Nobody responded.

'Well, if he didn't, where does that leave Lydia? Denis, you'd know.'

Denis looked at him disdainfully. 'Not my area, really. Perhaps James might.'

Everyone turned to Hadfield, who tried to keep a calm façade as he inwardly cursed Timmons for bringing him here.

'Well, I'm not sure that . . . er . . . it would be appro-'

'Oh come on,' interjected Greta. 'It must be a simple enough question.' She paused before glancing at Denis and adding, 'For any solicitor.'

Hadfield thought it better to answer than face further pressing on the subject.

'Well, the Succession Act would apply, I guess. If there is a will already in existence, she would be entitled to a third of the estate at a minimum.'

'Good for Lydia!' chirped Penny.

'What do you mean "at a minimum"?' asked Scott.

'Well, if the will provides for more than a third, she can take that. If it provides for less than a third, then she can still elect to have a third.'

'Oh, enough of all this,' said Jasmine. 'I need some . . . fresh air. Penny, Scott?'

The three finished their drinks and headed out.

Reverend Devereux coughed and smiled his beatific smile, which was accentuated by his baldness and round, clean-shaven face.

'Well, I'd better get back. Check on the preparations for the funeral and all that.' He waited a moment in contemplation, before adding: 'I will be back for dinner, of course.'

'It might be best if we headed off ourselves,' whispered Albert to Hadfield.

'I have to wait for Andrew. I'm driving him back.'

'Of course. You could just . . . .'

'Albert!'

'I've been summoned. You might join me.'

They walked over to the most recent arrivals.

'Miss Greta. Rob. You know James Hadfield.'

'Yes. With Timmons, I think,' replied Greta.

Hadfield shook hands with Robert, although he felt sure that at least two pairs of eyes were boring into him. He knew Robert to see, and to speak to briefly at social events, but as Robert was about ten years younger than him, their paths rarely crossed. Hadfield was aware that he had become Miss Greta's minder – which seemed to have grown out of a friendship that had developed between them over the years, rather than due to any imposition from Lord Barrington. Miss Greta had taken an interest in Robert after the death of his parents, and it was likely that she had a significant say in the decisions to have him schooled locally and employed by Lord Barrington on the manor estate. When she left Rathbawn for the nursing home, she had let Robert stay at the cottage she owned in the village for a nominal rent – an arrangement that still continued.

'My condolences,' said Hadfield.

'Thank you. Now, Albert I need to talk further on that matter we last discussed. Perhaps . . . .' Greta looked askance at Hadfield.

'Yes, of course. I was . . . er . . . just heading outside.'

*

It was very cold as Hadfield descended the front steps of the Manor, but he felt that it was preferable to the atmosphere inside. He walked around the driveway for a while to keep warm. Eventually, Albert emerged.

'That was certainly entertaining,' he said as he approached Hadfield.

'You could say that. Some interesting characters, for sure. Who are Penny and Scott?'

'Penny was in school with Jasmine. Arrived a good few weeks back with Scott, and they have stayed at the Manor ever since. George was not too impressed with Scott. In fact, he asked myself and Andrew to make enquiries. Not much of a credit-rating, as far as I could tell. Andrew was waiting to hear back from Dockrell..'

Albert was referring to Superintendent Dockrell of the Special Branch, whose niece, Lucinda, had just joined the office as an apprentice.

'Nothing yet, then?'

'Not that I have heard. But I would think Dockrell is a bit busy at the moment.'

Albert raised an eyebrow as Hadfield looked at him a little blankly.

'Oh. Of course. The murder. Yes. I see. What . . . er . . . what's the story with the "gruesome twosome", as Samantha called them?'

'Letitia is Lydia's elder sister. I'm told they weren't in touch for years. Lydia marries George and she arrives on the scene from Paris. I don't know anything about Clarisse except that she's a woman of few words. And she's French. Well, I'd better be off and get some work done before the dinner this evening. Tell Andrew I couldn't wait but we can talk later. Cheerio.'

And with that, he strode over to his vintage VW Beetle, bent his tall frame awkwardly into the car and headed off noisily down the driveway.

Hadfield had to wait a while longer before Timmons came out.

'Ah! There you are. Didn't know where you'd got to.'

'Thought I'd just stretch my legs a bit.'

'Hmm. Must have been a long walk. They said you left an hour ago. Can't say I blame you, I suppose: it was a little bit fraught in there. Anyway, let's go. A lot of work to do, and I need to get changed for the dinner this evening. As good a way as any to see George off, all things considered. He'd have wanted the cellar to be opened in his memory.'

Timmons lived for his practice, but outside the office he enjoyed the finer things in life: food, wine, travel. As a bachelor, he was well positioned to indulge these interests – which possibly explained his rotund figure and convivial, if sometimes irritable, manner.

As Hadfield drove away from the Manor, he could not resist broaching the final comments Lady Barrington had made before she had left the drawing room.

'I . . . er . . . couldn't be sure but . . . er . . . I thought that Lady Barrington seemed to think that she might have an idea who poisoned his Lordship. And that it wasn't Rob.'

'She has her suspicions. I might need to look into a few matters for her. Maybe have a word with Dockrell.'

'Oh, I meant to say. Albert wanted to speak to you but had to head back to the office.'

'Is he going to the dinner?'

'Yes. He said he would see you there. Actually, he mentioned that Dockrell was looking into Scott's background at the moment.'

'Unsavoury character, that fellow, if you ask me. Seems to have had some brushes with the law. Drugs, I gather. Bernard is checking further into it. Look, those damn protestors are still here. Slow down.'

Timmons rolled down his window.

'Apart from the complete lack of moral decency, you are trespassing, causing an obstruction and creating a traffic hazard. There are legal means by which you can make a protest, you know.'

'These are the only means those type of people understand. They think they are above the law. Come on, everyone.'

And with that, Armstrong and his fellow protestors began chanting and waving their various placards around the car, one of them catching Timmons on the shoulder through the open window.

'And you can add assault and battery to that, Armstrong! Drive on, James.'

Hadfield eventually got out onto the road.

'Bloody hell. That was a bit much.'

'Nothing but trouble, that fellow Armstrong.'

'Straight back to the office?'

'Yes. A call to the police first thing, obviously. Then I have to prepare Lydia's will for signing before dinner.'

'Oh. Is that the "announcement", then?'

'Hmm. I will leave that to Lydia. You will find out yourself this evening.'

'Am I expected to go?' asked a panicked Hadfield, who had thought his duties as regards the Barringtons had been completed for the moment.

'Well, Lydia did invite you. It would be rude to refuse. And, as I said, I can't be their legal advisor forever. You need to build a relationship with them for the future.'

'Of course. Quite right,' was the crestfallen reply. Little else was said until their arrival outside the office in Kilcreddin a few minutes later.

'Thanks, James. I'll make my own way to the Manor. I said I'd be there for seven thirty, for the paperwork. See you at dinner.'

*

Hadfield left his house at a quarter to eight. He planned to arrive at eight on the dot. And leave as soon as was feasible. He still felt a little uncomfortable being at the Manor at all. And having a grand dinner while Lord Barrington was lying in repose in a nearby room did not sit too well with him either. He was musing that perhaps that was how things were done in these circles, when he heard a loud siren behind him and a police car flashed past.

Ah, he thought, *Timmons must have persuaded the guards to remove the protesters. Good old A. T.!*

There was no sign of the earlier protest when Hadfield arrived at the entrance to the Manor. He drove straight in and up the driveway to the house. He saw the police car that had passed him parked outside the house. To his surprise, there were two other police cars there as well.

Must have been some job getting rid of Armstrong and his gang, he thought.

He parked his car well away from the activity, and walked towards the front door. He saw Albert sitting on the steps with his head in his hands. As Hadfield approached, he noticed that the bank manager was crying.

'Albert. Is everything all right?'

'James. I can't believe it!'

'What?'

'Andrew. And Lydia.'

He started to cry again

'Tell me, Albert. What is it?'

'They . . . . They . . . .'

'They what?'

He started to sob even more loudly, before shouting: 'They're dead!'

CHAPTER 3

Hadfield was cold and dejected as he approached his offices on High Street. The funeral for Andrew Timmons had been a muted affair, and the continuous drizzle at the graveyard ensured he was wet right through. With no near relatives, it had fallen on Hadfield to say a few words – although he had felt that a more prominent member of the locality might have been appropriate. Lord Barrington could have been relied upon to do the necessary, but that had proved out of the question. Reverend Devereux had done his best to speak to the tragic circumstances, but the imminent joint funeral of George and Lydia Barrington, and the circumstances of the recent deaths, was evidently something of a distraction for him, and the ceremony had been a little low key.

The offices of Timmons & Associates were a small but quaint affair, with a whitewashed front and pretty latticed windows on either side of a fine mahogany door. Hadfield stopped in front of the door and stood for a while reflecting on his fifteen years with the firm, becoming a little uncomfortable as he caught himself considering the brass nameplate to the right of, and just above, the matching doorknob. The old fellow was barely in the grave, and he was already wondering about the signage for the venerable, and indeed only, legal practice in Kilcreddin.

The situation was not how he had wished it. Despite his employer's impatience and intermittent irritability, Hadfield had been fond of Timmons. However, he had to accept that the reality was that Timmons would have continued as the principal of the business until mental or physical incapacity intervened – and even then he might have tried to struggle on. While his death was undoubtedly tragic, it nonetheless brought with it a significant opportunity for the junior associate. For good or ill, it was Hadfield's responsibility, as the only solicitor now practising with the firm, to continue the fine tradition of

Timmons & Associates. Or possibly 'Timmons Hadfield & Associates' – just to make matters clear for clients and colleagues.

Hadfield turned around and faced towards the other side of High Street. The offices were closed for the day, as a mark of respect, and he had arranged to meet Hilary, Mick and Lucinda for a late lunch in the Riverside Inn, just across the road, to raise a glass to Timmons' passing.

Hadfield entered the inn, trying to look as composed and thoughtful as the circumstances required. People were always interested in others' business in Kilcreddin, and were certain to have a good gawk whenever the front door sounded. The locals at the bar turned and stared, as usual. Hadfield nodded in their general direction.

The composure with which he had entered the establishment quickly dissipated, however, as he realised that he had forgotten to book a table. He anxiously checked the immediate vicinity for Morton, the proprietor. As a regular for lunch, Hadfield would have no difficulty securing a spot, but he needed a discreet location to discuss the recent extraordinary events without interruption or ear-wiggers. As an old client of the firm, Morton could be relied upon to do the necessary. The same could not be said of the young, and often surly, waiting staff the owner employed.

Morton was nowhere to be seen. This did not bode well, as the lounge was very busy. Hadfield was just on the point of throwing himself on the mercy of Fiona, the nearest member of staff, when he heard his name being called.

'James! We're over here.'

He turned around and saw Hilary and Mick in the best corner-table of the lounge.

'Ah, there you are. I was looking for Morton to organise a secluded little area, but you seem to have managed all right.'

'I booked it as soon as you suggested the lunch here,' said Hilary, 'but we can look to move if you wish.'

'No, no, this seems fine.'

Hilary Byrne had been Mr Timmons' personal assistant since Hadfield had joined the firm, and for several years before that, from when old Mrs Roberts retired. Although a few years Hadfield's senior, she still retained a certain youthful beauty, with her dark black wavy hair, wide sensual lips and clear blue eyes, all helped with the minimum of make-up. She also ran the show at Timmons & Associates, having long since managed most matters for Mr Timmons and, more recently, for Hadfield as well. Michael Flanagan (everyone called him 'Mick') was the office clerk: he was younger than Hadfield, and not as long in the job. A loyal sort, but needing minding.

'Here's to old Timmons,' said Mick as he raised his empty pint of Guinness.

Hadfield took the hint, and tried to catch Fiona's attention. Eventually she wandered over.

'What can I do for you today, Mr H,' the waitress asked in the flirtatious manner which she tended to adopt when in his presence – although it was never clear whether she was looking to attract or fluster him.

'Two pints of Guinness, Fiona, and er . . . ' – looking at Hilary – 'a glass of sauvignon blanc?' Hilary nodded.

'And some menus as well, please.'

'Is that all, Mr H?' the waitress responded, somewhat suggestively.

'For the moment, Fiona. Thanks.'

'Here's to A.T.,' said Hadfield after the drinks arrived.

They raised their glasses in unison.

'Poor old Mr Timmons. Such a tragedy,' said Hilary, wiping tears from her eyes.

'Yes, a terrible loss.'

'It's more than a tragedy, Hilary,' replied Mick excitedly. 'It was murder!'

'Now, Mick,' said Hadfield, looking around anxiously, 'nothing has been officially confirmed. Let's not jump to conclusions just yet.'

'Mr Timmons and Lady Barrington found dead in the study at the Manor – and all the family around? That seems pretty suspicious to me.'

'Yes, but . . . .'

'And Lord Barrington gone hardly a week: that was murder too!'

'We don't know that for sure, Mick.'

'Rob Staunton was brought in for questioning about him: we know that!'

'Keep the volume down, Mick. We don't want to start any rumours. You know what the locals are like.'

'I think the horse has bolted on that one, Mr H.'

It was true, Hadfield mused, as he drank a little more from his pint. The whole village had been discussing recent events, with the story getting more outlandish with each telling. Very little involving the Barringtons passed unnoticed in the village, and it was usually the subject of considerable gossip. The family were an important part of the community – but they were also an important client of the office, and Hadfield did not want to be involved in any unseemly village chat in relation to their circumstances.

'Well, what do you make of it all, James?' Hilary enquired in a low voice. 'They say all three were poisoned.'

'I have heard that.'

'Linda at the station says it looks bad for Rob: he was there at each murder.' Hilary paused as she noted Hadfield's frown. 'Er . . . if it *was* murder, of course,' she added.

'It does look bad for Robert, I have to say,' he conceded – although at the same time he was recalling Lady Barrington's last words in the drawing room. 'But being in the vicinity of a crime does not make you a criminal.'

'If crime it be,' Mick interjected, before taking a long draught of his pint.

'The police must think there's been a crime: they have been all over the nursing home, and they are still up at the Manor,' replied Hilary.

'But they have released Staunton,' said Hadfield.

'For a second time,' added Mick.

'The presumption of innocence, Mick; the presumption of innocence. Let the law take its course. Now let's see what Morton has on the menu for us today.' Hadfield hoped that referring to the possibility of food might deflect discussion from the amateur detection of murderers.

'I'll have the beef,' said Mick.

'I'll have the chicken,' said Hilary.

'By the way, where's Lucinda?' asked Hadfield.

'She's meeting with her uncle for lunch. She said she would try and join us later.'

'Don't you think,' continued Mick, 'that all these deaths being caused by poison, and Staunton being the only person present each time . . . . Don't you think that makes his innocence look a little shaky?'

'It may, Mick, it may, but can I peruse the menu for a moment, please, before deciding what I am going to have for lunch.'

'It's always the same,' said Mick.

'I am sure they have a special or two available. I will ask Fiona if I can . . . er . . . .'

Hadfield looked around to locate Fiona, but she was not to be seen in the vicinity. He thought he might have to revert to further discussion of the 'Nursing Home/Manor Murders', but just then Morton came into the lounge and noted his pained expression.

'Mr Hadfield. I'll be with you in one moment.'

'Ah, good,' said Hadfield, as he turned back to his fellow diners and took a sup of his pint. 'Morton will look after us. After all, Timmons & Associates are long-established patrons of the Riverside Inn.'

'I've never noticed *that* bringing any special treatment,' replied Mick.

'Well, perhaps not you, Mick, but . . . .'

'A terrible tragedy, Mr Hadfield,' interjected Morton, as he approached their table. 'Poor Mr Timmons – and his best years still to come.'

'Oh, yes, thank you, we were just discussing that before you came.'

'Our solicitor for many a year. He arranged the conveyancing of this estab-lishment himself when Morton senior decided to hand over the reins.'

19

'Yes, I remember it well. I had a hand in the drafting . . . .'

'Of course, it got quite fractious in the end. The old bugger didn't really want to hand it over. Started to claim he should be paid for a freehold title when it was only a long lease. Wasn't that right, Mr Hadfield? Never quite sure that we got to the bottom of that . . . .'

'Well, it all worked out in the end,' Hadfield quickly responded, trying to move things on.

'It's true; I enjoyed the six months we didn't speak.'

'He's enjoying his retirement at the nursing home, I hope,' said Hilary, with one of her winning smiles.

'I think so, Hilary, though he would never admit it.'

'Good. Good. I was . . . ' started Hadfield.

'Of course, Lord Barrington's murder had all the tongues wagging up there.'

'Now Peter, please, we can't say . . . .'

'They were worried where the finger would be pointed for a while. But the manor murders changed all that. Seems they have their man now. You were there, Mr Hadfield: you probably know more than all of us'.

'Peter, please. It really isn't right to be getting into all that at the moment. Mr Timmons is hardly buried a few hours.'

'You're right of course, Mr Hadfield. I was at the funeral myself for a short while. Can I get you another round of drinks – on the house. In honour of Mr Timmons.'

'That would be very kind, Peter . . . .'

'You probably have no appetite for a bite to eat with the day that's in it . . . .'

'Well, actually Fiona had left a couple of menus. We were wondering if . . . .'

'I'll send her over to see if there's anything you need. I'll organise the drinks.'

Before Hadfield could make any further enquiry on the food front, Morton had turned and headed for the bar.

Eventually Fiona arrived.

'Have we decided what we're having?' she asked, looking straight at Hadfield.

'Well, before we decide, could we have a quick run through your specials please, Fiona.'

Fiona put on a shocked expression. 'Mr H., I don't know what kind of girl you think I am. I just bring the food and drinks.'

'I meant the food, of course. Your food specials. That you have on today.'

'Oh,' she replied, feigning disbelief, 'the soup's pea and ham, and the main is lasagne. Apple tart and cream for afters.'

'I think Mr H. was hoping for something a little more special than that,' suggested Mick.

'Not necessarily,' said Hadfield in a low voice, looking towards the bar. 'It's just that I was thinking of something a little different. Beef, or something like that.'

'There's plenty of beef in a lasagne,' said Fiona, smiling coyly.

'And in roast beef – which *is* on the menu,' added Mick, while trying to stifle a laugh.

'I think,' said Hilary with a firm voice, 'that a steak is what Mr Hadfield has in mind. It is always available to regular clients of the inn. So that will be one chicken kiev for me, the roast beef for Mr Flanagan and a sirloin steak, medium, for Mr Hadfield. Mr Morton is bringing us another round of drinks himself, on the house, as a gesture to Mr Timmons' recent untimely passing. So that should be all for the moment, Fiona. Thank you.'

Fiona left without further ado.

CHAPTER 4

'Here we go,' said Morton as he arrived with the drinks. 'Two Guinness and a white wine. And a snifter for myself to raise a glass to old Mr Timmons.'

'To Mr Timmons,' they all said, as Morton knocked back his brandy.

'I suppose you'll be in the driving seat now, Mr H.'

'Well, er, yes, I think that's likely. Subject of course to . . . .'

'You'll probably have to take on a new solicitor to deal with all the cases. Maybe make a few changes. Put your own stamp on the place.'

Hilary and Mick started to shift in their seats, with Mick looking particularly uncomfortable.

'We'll take things a step at a time. A solicitors' office doesn't change much over time. Bringing in a new solicitor would be a fairly radical move.'

And an expensive one, thought Hadfield. The reality was that he was quite familiar with the office caseload, and most of it was on his desk. He would have to review Timmons's files to see what needed to be done there. Hilary could review those and let him know the position. In fact, Hilary could probably run the files herself. Of course, Lord Barrington and his affairs were always handled personally by Mr Timmons. Taking on these matters would very much depend on the attitude of the successors to his interests. He might have to free up some time for a charm-offensive. Maybe a short-term locum would be in order.

'Will you keep the firm name?' asked Morton.

'I, er . . . I haven't thought about that at all, Peter. Far too early for those considerations.'

'You'll take over his office, though.'

'I really don't know. But yes, I suppose that would make sense, with the bigger caseload and everything.'

'What do you reckon, Peter?' Mick cut in. He was becoming a little anxious around the topic under discussion. 'Is Rob Staunton in the frame for the . . . murders?' Mick looked at Hadfield, expecting a rebuke, but the latter was more than happy for the conversation to move on.

'Looks that way. He was the only one there at each murder. And I heard they found some pretty incriminating evidence at his cottage. Seems he's broke too. He must have been hoping some money might come his way.'

'But why Lady Barrington? And Mr Timmons as well?' asked Hilary. 'What did they have to do with anything?'

'Maybe he thought they knew something,' replied Morton, 'and had to cover his tracks. You spoke to the police, surely. Did they have any ideas?'

This last question was directed at Hadfield. He had indeed been interviewed at the Manor, and had given a full account of everything he had done, seen and heard that day. However, he did not plan to get into that with Morton.

'They just asked me some routine questions. They certainly weren't telling me anything about their own thoughts on the subject.'

'I think it's pretty clear who did it,' said Mick. 'Just a matter of forensics now, I'd say. Although they may want to check on Lord Barrington's will. Word has it, that might be relevant.'

'And maybe Lady Barrington's as well,' added Hilary. 'Do you think they can ask for them, James?'

'Er, well . . . criminal law isn't one of our areas, so I wouldn't want to say. But if they are allowed to, and they need them . . . I suppose we would have to consider making them available. So as not to be obstructing the course of justice.'

'Have you seen the wills, Mr H.?' asked Morton conspiratorially.

'No, I have not. Mr Timmons handled all matters of that nature for the family. And even if I had, I couldn't tell you. Client confidentiality is paramount in a solicitors' practice.'

'There was talk of new wills for both of them, but that there was a disagreement holding it up,' suggested Morton, trying a different tack.

'I've heard his Lordship was not too happy with her plans for the money,' added Mick.

Morton nodded sagely. 'That's right, Mick. None of it going to the family, I was told. Can't say I'd have been too happy in his Lordship's shoes myself.'

'And Lady Barrington can't have been too happy being told what to do with her own inheritance, either.'

'That's right, Hilary. Some said Lady Barrington did it when word first got out about the poisoning.'

'What!' exclaimed Hadfield. 'And then she goes and kills herself and Mr Timmons, while she's at it?'

'Well, the events at the Manor have put Lady B. a little out of the picture,' Morton conceded.

'Unless,' Mick piped up, 'Timmons had rumbled Lady Barrington. And she had to poison him as well.'

'This is getting a little out of hand,' interjected Hadfield. 'We should let the law take its course. Here comes the food, thank God. Anyway, how did Lady Barrington manage to die while killing Mr Timmons?'

'Maybe the poisoning went wrong. Or she realised it had all gone too far, and killed herself.'

'Hmm…. Peter, could you bring me the wine list. I think a good claret would be in order. I'm sure you'll partake of the red?' Mick nodded enthusiastically as Morton retired to the bar.

'You'll stick with the white, Hilary?'

'Yes, thank you, James. Of course, if Lady Barrington was the guilty party, it means Rob Staunton couldn't have done it.'

'Exactly, Hilary. You see, Mick, you are proving my point. Your very own theorising is exonerating Staunton – the very man you said was the murderer.'

'A murderer, you say,' remarked Fiona. She had been waiting for her customers to make room for the plates, but decided to take matters in hand herself. 'Who are you accusing of that?'

'Absolutely nobody, Fiona. It's everyone else here who seems to be doing that. I have been trying to uphold the presumption of innocence in these matters.'

'But you said there was a murderer.'

'No, I said that *Mick* here said there was a murderer. In fact, he has in the space of a few minutes suggested two murderers – the second of which precludes the first.'

'But,' replied Mick, 'what if Lady Barrington had engaged Staunton to bump off His Lordship? And Staunton then got worried that she was going to stitch him up?'

'You can't possibly . . . . Now Fiona, I don't want you to . . . .'

'Fiona, you can put mine down here,' interrupted Hilary. 'The gentlemen will make room for theirs once they have moved their pints.'

There was a hurried downing of pints, and the table was cleared. Fiona put Hilary and Mick's dishes down first. She delayed slightly before putting the steak on the table, adding: 'Your meat, Mr H. With the two veg coming shortly.'

Mick snorted, a little too loudly, and reached for his handkerchief as Fiona retreated from their table.

'What, pray tell, is so amusing?'

'Er . . . .'

'I think Fiona might have taken a shine to you, James,' whispered Hilary.

'Well, she has a damn strange way of showing it. Never around when you need her, and full of nonsense when she's here. Now where the hell is Morton with that wine list?'

'Right here, Mr H. Here's the peas and mash for the steak. And the wine list.'

'Good. Now if you could hold on there . . . . Hilary will have the same again. And I'll order a bottle of . . . the St Emilion 1990: a good year, I believe. It should be drinking now.'

'We're out of the 1990. But we have the 1991, if that will do. I believe that was a good year too.'

'I see. And the price for the 1991?'

'Exactly the same.'

'Er. . . . hmm . . . oh, all right then. And you might bring two glasses with it. Mick is developing a taste for fine wines.'

'On its way, Mr Hadfield.'

'Very kind of you, Mr H.,' said Mick 'but just to finish off the point: you must accept that it is possible that Rob could be guilty and that Lady Barrington may also have been involved.'

'I accept no such thing,' said Hadfield. Although, on thinking about it, could Lady Barrington have been trying to shield Rob when making her declaration in the drawing room that day? He decided to change topic. 'What I do accept is that we will have to have a full review of office matters.'

That shut him up, he noted with satisfaction, as Mick focused on his roast beef.

'What do you have in mind, James?' asked Hilary, excitedly.

'Well, I haven't given too much thought to that just yet. And of course it wouldn't be appropriate so soon after Mr Timmons' passing. But we will need to review his cases. Just to see if there is anything requiring urgent attention. Perhaps you might . . . .'

'Of course, James. I could do that. I'd have a good idea of what's current.'

'Excellent. And I suppose Morton's suggestion on the office makes sense. I will probably need the bigger room to deal with the added files.'

Hilary nodded helpfully.

'And we might need to think about a change of name – a minor one, of course – so as to clarify matters for the world at large.'

'Like what?' enquired Mick with an arching eyebrow.

'Oh, I don't know . . . maybe . . . Hadfield Timmons Solicitors. I always felt the reference to associates slightly undersold the practice.'

'You might be *over*selling it,' responded Mick, 'unless you want to change it to Hadfield Timmons *Solicitor*.'

'The Law Society might have a concern on that too,' added Hilary. 'Possible misrepresentation there.'

'Hmm . . . yes. Maybe "Hadfield Timmons & Associates" shows a degree of continuity.'

'But isn't it normal for the succeeding partner's name to come after the original name?' enquired Mick.

'Times move on, Mick. I've seen many different descriptions cropping up in recent years. It's all about branding, you know. The twenty-first century is fast approaching. A practice must be seen to be at the cutting edge to remain successful.'

'In Kilcreddin?' asked Mick.

'What would existing clients think?' asked Hilary.

'About what?'

'Putting your name ahead of that of the founder of the firm.'

'Well . . . they will recognise that I am now the principal of the firm.'

'Or would they see it as belittling the work Mr Timmons did to get it to where it is today?'

'Hmm.'

'And the Barringtons might not take too kindly to it either.'

'Yes. I see. Might need to think that over some more . . . .'

'How about Timmons Hadfield & Associates?' interposed Mick.

'Possibly, Mick,' replied Hadfield, somewhat tersely, 'but what if I take on another solicitor? That could change the name.' He paused for effect. 'And possibly personnel requirements.'

This time it was Hilary's turn to snigger, with Mick looking distinctly uncomfortable as he finished the last of his beef.

Hadfield sat back after his dessert and took a small sip of the brandy he'd ordered with it. Mick hadn't the nerve to ask for one, and had said he would prefer a Guinness. Hadfield had no intention of letting Mick go from his clerking position, but felt it would do no harm to let him stew for a while and appreciate the job he had.

His mind turned back to the afternoon at the Manor, and the last time he had seen Andrew Timmons. What had actually happened? Did Lady Barrington really know who poisoned Lord Barrington? Perhaps that was a ruse of some kind. Or was the killer in the room when she left to speak to Timmons? Why the need to meet him before everyone else?'

'Afternoon, all.'

Hadfield's musings were interrupted by the arrival of Lucinda Dockrell, the trainee who had recently joined the firm. She had a pleasant, you could even say good-looking, face, but came across as quite plain: she always had her brown hair in a simple ponytail, used no make-up, and wore quite large, thick glasses.

'Good afternoon, Lucinda,' replied Hadfield. 'Can I get you something to drink?'

'No thanks. I've just had lunch with Uncle Bernard, and I can't stay long. I've a project I have to get finished this evening.'

'Hmm. The workings of the mind, no doubt.'

'Something like that.'

Although Lucinda had studied law and was training to be a solicitor, Hadfield knew that she also had an interest in psychology, and was taking a correspondence course on some aspect or other of it, as a hobby.

'What are you researching at the . . . .'

'Has he any ideas yet?' asked Mick eagerly.

'Uncle Bernard? He doesn't tend to say too much about his cases. Unless he's sure. Or he has a reason.'

'I see,' said Mick, a little crestfallen. 'Nothing to report, so.'

'No. Except what they found at Staunton's cottage.'

'Oh? What did they find?'

'Empty medicine bottles and stuff. Seems they were stolen from the nursing home the day Lord Barrington was killed.'

'When were they found?' asked Hilary.

'Just after the murders at the Manor. While they were interviewing him. They hadn't found anything the first time they searched, but they turned up in his bin the second time.'

'That's pretty damning, isn't it?' said Mick, feeling fully justified in his initial assessment of the case.

'I suppose,' said Lucinda. 'But it appears that Robert Staunton might not necessarily be the only suspect.'

'Oh? Who else have they in mind?'

'He hasn't said. And I don't think he knows. But it seems Lady Barrington said she knew who murdered Lord Barrington, and that it wasn't Robert Staunton.'

'Crikey!' exclaimed Hilary. 'When was that?'

'On the afternoon of the murders at the Manor.'

There was silence for a while before Hilary spoke again.

'James, you were there that afternoon. Did you hear her say that?'

'Er . . . I did, yes. And I told the police as well.'

'Why didn't you tell us?' came the aggrieved query from Mick.

The truth was that Hadfield may well have told Hilary the details of the visit to the Manor, but there were certain risks inherent in imparting information to Mick. The principal one being his propensity to talk.

'I, er . . . I wasn't sure if it was appropriate. With a police investigation under way and all that.'

'Who else was there when she said it?' asked Hilary.

'Everyone.'

'Meaning?'

'Well, the family. Some friends of Jasmine. Lady Barrington's sister and her friend. Reverend Devereux. Boyd. Even Rob Staunton was there.'

'How did they react to what she said?' This time it was Lucinda asking the question.

'Well, there was a bit of a clamour, I suppose.'

'But nobody acted . . . ' – Lucinda paused while searching for the right words – ' . . . out of character at the time?'

'Not that I noticed. Except Robert, who said nothing at all. But that's probably very much in character.'

'Did Mr Timmons have anything to say about it?'

Hadfield was starting to feel as though he was being questioned by Lucinda's uncle rather than his young niece.

'Well, I did actually ask him about it on the way back to the office. Didn't say much. Although I think he mentioned having to look into some matters for Lady Barrington. And perhaps speak to your uncle as well.'

Hadfield wasn't sure whether it was the effect of the alcohol or the realisation that the conversation in the car was the last contact he had had with his boss, but he felt tears coming to his eyes as he remembered the journey back from the Manor.

'I'm sorry, James,' said Lucinda, putting her own hand on his. 'Not very sensitive of me to be asking all these questions at such an emotional time. He was a lovely man. I'll miss him too.'

'Yes, we all will,' said Hilary.

'Hear hear,' said Mick.

There was a quiet moment as they all remembered the reason they were there.

'Well, I'd better be off,' said Lucinda after a while. 'Er . . . would it be OK if I went to the Barrington funerals tomorrow? Uncle Bernard is going to be there, and I'd . . . like to be with him.'

'Of course, Lucinda,' replied Hadfield, composing himself again. 'We will see you in the office afterwards.'

'See you then.'

All three were silent as they watched Lucinda leave. Each of them were thinking of their future. At the office. And maybe beyond.

'Actually, Hilary,' said Hadfield, 'would you mind doing something for me first thing after the funerals tomorrow?'

'What's that?'

'Could you check to see whether there are any wills there for either of them?'

'No problem.'

'And any current files.'

'Sure. I'd say there are about ten.'

'Thanks. Er, Mick.'

'Yes,' came the slightly nervous reply.

'Had you intended going to the funeral?'

'Well, I'd never met Lord Barrington in the office, and I don't know any of the family to speak to.'

'Then you can man the fort in the morning, while we're out.'

'I'd be happy to, Mr H.,' replied Mick, with a noticeably perkier tone.

Hadfield paid the bill, had a brief word with Morton, avoided eye-contact with Fiona and headed out into the cold, damp evening air of Kilcreddin.

Mick lived at the lower end of the village but was loitering with intent (to suggest another drink in his favourite hostelry a little further down the road) until he suddenly realised he was supposed to be home before teatime to let his wife escape to her weekly bridge game.

'I don't think you'd see me in the morning if she missed that,' he said as he started off down High Street at a trot. 'Thanks again for lunch.'

'Not at all. See you tomorrow,' replied Hadfield.

There was a slightly awkward silence for a few moments. Hilary lived quite close to Mick, and should have been heading in that direction herself.

'Fancy one more before we turn in?' she suggested, as off-handedly as possible. 'Bellamy's is next down, and shouldn't be too busy.'

Hadfield looked up the street towards his own house. It was a nice country-style cottage at the top of the hill, but it did not feel that comforting at this early hour. At the same time, they had drunk quite a lot already, and to go on again might be asking for trouble.

'We have a busy day tomorrow, I suppose. The funerals, and then catching up with work. It might be as well to call it a day.'

'You're right. A lot on tomorrow.'

Hilary looked away slightly, and this was followed by another short silence. 'I suppose you think of her often.'

Hadfield paused. She was referring to his fiancée, Deirdre, who had been killed in a car accident a little over two years previously.

'I do. At times like these, it's hard not to.'

'I can understand. A tragedy like that will take a long time to get over . . . if you ever can.'

'Yes. Thanks, Hilary. It hasn't been easy. But we have to keep going.'

'OK, see you tomorrow, then. Thanks for this afternoon.'

'Thanks for being there. See you in the morning.'

Hilary slowly walked down the street towards home.

Hadfield watched her as she left. She had been very supportive throughout his time in the office. Especially the last few years. But he had always kept a distance, even though he enjoyed her company. Office life separate from love life. Was it wrong to be attracted to her? Did Andrew's passing change that?

Many thoughts went through his mind. He looked across the road at the office, and thought about the day's events. And the future. Maybe 'Timmons Hadfield & Associates' was about right.

He then turned and made his way up High Street towards home . . . and a quiet brandy.

CHAPTER 5

Hadfield approached the Church of St Martin's a little gingerly the next morning, the one brandy having stretched into three – or was it four?

St Martin's was a small, quaint structure with a tall spire and an old-fashioned clock. It was located very close to the entrance to the Manor estate; this was no doubt related to the fact that its original construction had been substantially funded by Lord Barrington's predecessors. Its continued maintenance had been heavily dependent on his lordship's donations in recent times.

The bells were tolling for the funeral service as Hadfield entered the grounds of the church. As a Catholic himself, although not a particularly fervent one, it was not often that he found himself here. To be attending for the second time in a matter of days was disconcerting. He looked over at the graveyard, which was in clear view to the right as he approached the front door of the church, and thought of Mr Timmons, who had been laid to rest there only yesterday.

It had been good of Timmons to take on a Catholic apprentice in what had always been considered a Protestant firm. Having said that, it was not unlikely that he had had an eye to the future at the time, with the Protestant population dwindling and Catholic prosperity increasing. Either way, it had got Hadfield a job and secured his future, and he was grateful for it, even if the question of 'partnership' had never seemed to come up.

As he entered through the front doors, he realised that the church was already quite full. Just as he was on the point of resigning himself to standing at the back, he noticed a small flurry of waves from near the front which appeared to be directed at him. It was Hilary, of course; she had kept him a seat. Hadfield walked as slowly as possible up the central aisle – there being no access ways to the side of the small church. He noticed Lucinda in one of the pews at the back. She was sitting beside her uncle, Detective Superintendent Dockrell.

He also noticed Letitia and Clarisse sitting not far away from them. *Obviously not attending with the family*, he thought.

Hadfield continued on to the front of the church, keeping his head down as he went. He begged his pardon a number of times as he joined Hilary on the inside of the pew. She had obviously arrived early and secured a seat, just behind those reserved for the immediate relatives of Lord and Lady Barrington, in the front three pews on either side. The rest of the congregation comprised the great and the good of the village and surrounding areas – although most were likely to be those either employed or supported by the Barringtons. Anxious times ahead for many present, no doubt.

'Suffering a bit this morning?' Hilary enquired.

'No, not at all. Fine, thanks.'

'Few brandies at home?'

'Er . . . just a small drop. To help me sleep, what with all that's going on.'

'Of course. I dropped in to the office on the way. Mick was proud as punch to be in charge for the morning. Not too many calls, it seems.'

'Good, good,' Hadfield replied. He remembered that he had intended to drop in earlier himself to check on Mick – and the office in general. The brandy had put paid to that.

Just then, the congregation began to shuffle in their seats, and Hadfield and Hilary turned to see two coffins, each held aloft by four black-suited undertakers, make their entrance into the church. One by one, the family members slowly followed the coffins up the central aisle.

Leading the way was Richard. He was followed – not joined – by his wife. Their two daughters and the younger son accompanied her as they progressed slowly up the aisle.

Following Richard's family was Jasmine. She looked well, but the best of make-up could not hide her emotional upset. Or her tiredness.

Jasmine was very closely followed by Samantha, who seemed distinctly irritated. No doubt family etiquette dictated that Samantha should follow Richard behind the coffins, but Jasmine had managed to step into that position, and left her elder sister to take up the rear. Denis, and their son, Bartholomew, were close behind.

'Someone doesn't look too happy,' said Hilary as she nudged Hadfield and nodded towards Samantha.

'I noticed. I'm not sure if it is the coffins or Jasmine which is the greater cause.'

The coffins had now arrived in front of the altar, and Reverend Devereux descended to greet the grieving family. He was effusive in his condolences: each member of the family received a sober, mournful and pained handshake – as well as a lengthy address. This forced the procession to wait before being seated, and after a while gave rise to a degree of disquiet.

It soon became clear that this was not entirely due to the Reverend's unhurried greetings, but was instead caused by Miss Greta, who was seeking to join her nephew and nieces at the front of the church.

The disquiet may have been fuelled somewhat by the presence of Robert Staunton, who was assisting Miss Greta up the aisle. The general murmuring in the pews suggested some surprise that he had attended the funeral – and possibly that he was not still 'assisting the police with their enquiries'. Robert seemed not to notice the animated whisperings, and manoeuvred Miss Greta's wheelchair to the front pew, where he joined Samantha and her family, placing the wheelchair immediately in front of the seat he had taken.

There was no perceptible acknowledgment of Robert from Samantha or her husband. Miss Greta received short greetings from both. As Richard and Jasmine were on the other side, any awkwardness they would have felt in dealing with Robert's presence was avoided.

'Not exactly an outpouring of grief,' Hilary pointed out as the family took their places.

'There is etiquette in these matters,' Hadfield interjected. 'Important to maintain a degree of decorum in adversity.'

'At least until the wills are read,' replied Hilary.

Silence descended on the congregation as Reverend Devereux began what proved to be a very lengthy sermon, with continuous references to the generosity of Lord and Lady Barrington and their predecessors in the development and maintenance of the church. The need for this generosity to be continued was implied on a number of occasions, particularly in relation to matters of roof, clock and organ. The subsidy for the annual fête, which generated proceeds which were of critical importance when it came to keeping 'the religious show on the road', got a mention too.

After a while, Hadfield's mind began to wander. If Robert was innocent, who was guilty? He did not know the details of the children's financial status, but a lot was common knowledge.

Richard had already been provided for with a substantial house and lands at Rathbawn, and was gainfully employed at the estate.

Samantha had received a gift of their house in Rathmore on her marriage to Denis, and ran a well-known GP practice in that village. Jasmine had been given a property in Dublin by her father when she started her studies, and had the use of the manor house whenever she wished. Her lifestyle suggested she also had his continuing financial support while he lived.

Was that why Robert Staunton was the only suspect? Even though Lady Barrington thought otherwise? Or so she said. Of course, she had mentioned Lord Barrington's unhappiness about how the children were conducting their affairs. Could there be financial difficulties affecting any of them which might have been behind her suspicions? She had certainly suggested that Samantha's practice was not making much money. And there was Richard's foray into the stud-farm business. Everyone knew that was costing a fortune, but with no obvious success as yet. And Jasmine was not known for her frugality, despite having no obvious source of income.

As these thoughts were going through Hadfield's head, he slowly comprehended that the voice that had sent him in this direction was no longer speaking. It was in fact Richard who had taken the pulpit and was delivering the eulogy for his father. The congregation seemed a little nervous, and there were audible mutterings around the church.

'Have I missed something, Hilary? Reverend D. had me dozing.'

'Richard is pretty worked up. He seems to be making accusations. Listen.'

' . . . and furthermore I think the police need to step up their efforts and tackle the tragedy that has befallen us head-on. I have no doubt but that the deaths of my father and my stepmother, and that of Mr Timmons, were premeditated, and I have no doubt who is guilty of these crimes.'

With this, Richard turned his head and looked pointedly at Robert Staunton for what seemed a very long time.

'But today is not a day for righting the wrongs that have been done. Today we are here to say farewell to Lord Barrington: a father, a grandfather, a brother, an employer, a benefactor, and a central part of this community for most of his life. Our prayers are with him on his journey to a better place.'

Richard stepped back from the pulpit, to a stunned silence. After a few strained seconds, Samantha started a lone, timid clapping. Her husband, Denis, and Jasmine followed soon after, and this eventually had the effect of prompting a general, if confused, putting-together of hands. Hadfield noted that Miss Greta and Robert did not join in. Hadfield and Hilary had felt obliged to accompany the throng – primarily as Richard appeared to be looking closely about him before retaking his seat.

'That was a bit pointed,' whispered Hilary.

'And perhaps a bit rash. DS Dockrell is down the back. With Lucinda. Wonder what he made of it.'

*

As two of the people closest to the top of the church for the funeral service, Hadfield and Hilary were among the first to meet the family and offer their condolences outside.

Normal hierarchy appeared to have been restored with Richard, Samantha and Jasmine waiting in order to meet the exiting attendees.

'Sorry for your troubles, Mr Barrington.'

'Thank you . . . er . . . Hadfield, isn't it? The solicitor chap.'

'That's right. James Hadfield. And this is Hilary Byrne – who works with us in the office too.'

'Very sorry for you, sir. I am sure it is a very difficult time for you.'

'Yes, yes. Indeed. Of course, one has to continue as best one can.'

'Well . . . ' started Hadfield, with a view to moving onwards.

'Er . . . Hadfield. Obviously now is not the time, but we will need to meet up. Fairly soon . . . to discuss how best to manage matters. That sort of thing.'

'Of course! Absolutely. Delighted to!' replied Hadfield, realising as he said it that he was perhaps expressing a degree more excitement over this Barrington retainer than the circumstances warranted. 'Er . . . please feel free to get in touch when you think it the appropriate time to do so.' *That sounded a little better*, he thought.

'Very good,' said Richard, and with that he turned to the next in line after Hilary.

As Hadfield moved on, he noted that Letitia had walked away to a far corner of the churchyard. She was joined by Clarisse, who seemed to be trying to comfort her. He also noticed that Samantha had turned away and was holding her son, Bartholomew. She had been replaced by Denis.

'My condolences,' Hadfield offered.

'Thank you,' he replied. 'Unfortunately Samantha is too upset to speak to anyone at the moment.'

'Of course. I understand. Er . . . this is Hilary, who is also part of the firm.'

'Ah yes. You must of course be grieving for your own loss. Poor Mr Timmons.'

'Yes. A great shock for all of us.'

'Indeed. A well-respected member of the community.'

'He certainly was,' replied Hilary.

'I can imagine you will all be quite busy for the next while. Wills, probate, that kind of thing.'

'I should imagine so.'

'Just as well I am so busy myself. The upcoming *Mikado*, of course. Remaining occupied should help us all keep the mind off our terrible losses.'

'Yes. Hopefully. Er . . . perhaps we'd better not hold up the others, James,' Hilary suggested.

'Of course. Please pass on our thoughts to Samantha.'

'I certainly will,' replied Denis. 'Thank you.'

Jasmine was next in line, and was being consoled by Albert Boyd. She seemed to have recovered some of her energy, and had perhaps added a little make-up. Scott and Penny were smoking in the background. They looked a little strained.

' . . . I will be sure to drop by, Albert. Thank you for coming today.'

Jasmine's attention turned to Hadfield. She gave him a sweet smile and a demure fluttering of her eyelashes.

'Mr Hadfield. How good of you to come.'

'Yes . . . of course,' said Hadfield, a little taken aback by the warmths of the greeting. 'Er . . . very sorry for your troubles.' He had had limited contact with Jasmine in the past – generally confined to witnessing documents Mr Timmons had prepared which required her signature, or very brief greetings at local events supported by the family.

'Thank you. You're very kind.'

After a short pause, Hadfield ventured: 'I am sure this has been very difficult for you. You are probably still in a state of shock.'

'Yes. That's probably right. It is hard to know what to think at the moment.'

'I suppose the grieving process will take some time.'

'That is true. And then I will have to think about my own future . . . with Daddy gone.'

'Yes . . . of course.'

'I expect I will be seeing a lot more of you.'

'I'm sure . . . erm . . . that, er . . . .' Hadfield, a little confused as to what she meant by this, was finding it difficult to formulate an appropriate response.

'With poor Timmons gone. Doubtless we will be calling on your services at the office.'

'Ah . . . yes. Absolutely,' Hadfield replied. 'Can I introduce Hilary, who works with us at the office.'

'Please accept my condolences, Miss Barrington,' added Hilary, who had been waiting patiently.

'Thank you,' replied Jasmine, before turning back to Hadfield, with: 'I know Hilary, of course. I think she pretty much ran matters for Mr Timmons. And probably does the same for you.'

'Yes . . . indeed. Perhaps we are holding up the others here? Again, we're very sorry.'

'Yes, thank you both. We'll meet again soon,' replied Jasmine, with a gloved handshake for each of them.

As Hadfield and Hilary walked slowly away, they noticed Miss Greta and Staunton at a remove from the Barrington siblings, at the entrance to the graveyard. Hadfield dithered.

'Do you think we should go over? Perhaps they don't want to meet people.'

'Maybe they are not happy with the eulogy and just want to be separate from Richard,' replied Hilary.

'Well, in that case . . . .'

'Actually . . . Robert seems to be coming this way.'

Hadfield turned and noticed that Hilary was indeed right.

CHAPTER 6

'Mr Hadfield,' said Robert, as he approached, 'Miss Greta would like a quick word, if you wouldn't mind.'

'Oh . . . I see. Of course,' was the slightly alarmed reply.

Turning to Hilary, Robert added: 'She asked for Mr Hadfield alone.'

'I understand, Robert,' said Hilary. 'My condolences on Lord and Lady Barrington's death. I believe you were quite close.'

'Yes. Thank you.'

Robert accompanied Hadfield back to Miss Greta, who was immaculately attired in her wheelchair, with a large black shawl to keep her warm and her nails painted black to match. She was in fact capable of walking but preferred to use the wheelchair if standing for long periods was likely to be required.

'My condolences, Miss Barrington,' Hadfield said as he approached, unsure what else he could add.

'Thank you. A terrible state of affairs.' She readjusted her shawl and looked straight at Hadfield. 'Now, I understand you worked with Timmons.'

'That's right, ma'am.' (*Probably not the right form of address*, Hadfield thought, but nothing else came to mind.)

'And you are a solicitor.'

'Yes.'

'And you attended the service for my brother.'

'Yes.'

'Did you listen to the eulogy by Richard?'

'I did.' (This was not quite a lie: after all, he did catch the end of it.)

'Then can you confirm to me that Robert here was defamed by Richard in that speech?'

'Er . . . .'

'Well . . . was he, or wasn't he?'

'Er . . . how might he have been defamed?'

'By being accused of murder!'

'I . . . erm . . . I'm not sure if his name was actually . . . .'

'It didn't have to be. He was looking straight at Robert when he made the accusation.'

'I see . . . or . . . I'm not sure if I actually did see. How can you be sure?'

'The whole congregation had to have seen it. Did you not follow Richard's eulogy?'

'Of course I did. Very . . . er . . . heartfelt. I just can't be sure he was actually accusing . . . .'

'The accusation was blatant. Does the law of defamation require that you actually name Robert, so that you have a case?'

'Well . . . that would of course . . . er . . . depend on the facts of the particular case.' The reality was that Hadfield didn't actually know.

'But you were there, for God's sake. You said you heard and saw everything. You're a solicitor, aren't you? Has Robert been defamed, and what can we do about it?'

'Well . . . that would have to be decided by a court, you see.'

'And you can't tell if Robert has a case or not?'

'He might have a case, of course, but in these matters, er . . . one would normally . . . perhaps consult Senior Counsel.'

'And why in the name of heaven would you have to do that? You're a lawyer, aren't you?'

'Well . . . you see . . . if litigation is being contemplated.'

'Of course litigation is being contemplated: Robert has been grossly defamed by that jackanapes Richard!'

'Well, if you are going that route, then it is . . . considered prudent to consult a Senior Counsel specialising in court cases in that area . . . to get some guidance on the likely . . . .'

'I think it would be prudent to consult a solicitor who actually knows something about the law!'

'Of course, Timmons & Associates are fully familiar with the law. It's just . . . .'

'Enough, enough. Here comes busybody Boyd. We may have to make an appointment to meet with this "Special Counsel" to have this matter properly dealt with.'

'Certainly, Miss Barrington, I would be more than . . . .'

'Good day, Albert. I see you commiserated with your most important clients first.'

'Not at all, Miss Greta. It was only . . . .'

Hadfield retreated from his summary dismissal with as much decorum and dignity as he could muster, finally linking up with Hilary on the fringes of the crowd.

'Christ, that was tricky! Sorry, I meant . . . . Crikey! I mean . . . You know what I mean.'

'I think so. Why "tricky"?'

'She thinks Richard has defamed Robert. She might want to bring a case.'

'Does she have one?'

'How the hell would . . . ? We'll have to look at the textbooks on that but, er, the bigger question of course is: can we act against Richard?'

'Hmm . . . it looks like Timmons *Hadfield* and Associates could be busy for the next while!'

*

After the burial, Hadfield and Hilary headed back to the office in their separate cars.

Hadfield arrived first, to find Mick at reception, reading the paper. 'Anything to report, Mick?'

'No, quiet enough on the phones. Post is in: nothing too urgent. Charles FitzHerbert rang – just a social call. Asked if you could ring him back whenever suited.'

FitzHerbert was an old pal from Hadfield's student days in Dublin. A barrister who had done quite well for himself in the Four Courts. They met up in Dublin occasionally, Hadfield usually staying at the club, where they could meet for dinner and catch up on the news over a good bottle of wine. Or two. He hadn't been to Dublin for a while and was definitely due a visit.

Just then, Hilary came in.

'Afternoon, Hilary,' said Mick.

'Afternoon, Mick. Everything under control?'

'Sure. I've left the post there on your seat.'

'Thanks.'

'The funeral went off OK?'

'It did. It seems that James will be busy with Barrington family matters for a while. Richard and Jasmine seemed keen to get in touch to discuss "legal" matters. And Miss Greta wants to sue Richard for defaming Robert at the church. Samantha was too upset to talk, but I'm sure she'll be in touch in short order. Or her husband will, at any rate, if she sends him instead. Assuming his rehearsals allow him the time.'

'What's that about defamation?' asked Mick.

'Richard accused Robert of murder, and was putting pressure on the police to get on with the investigation.'

'Yikes!'

'Well,' interjected Hadfield, 'he didn't actually name Staunton. He just said he believed that murder had been committed.'

'While looking straight at Robert the whole time,' added Hilary.

'Is that defamation, Mr H.?'

'Well . . . as I advised Miss Greta, we will have to look into all that. Maybe consult Counsel. You might get out the texts on that, Mick, and any relevant case law, and we can look at it further.'

'Will do.'

Although only a law clerk, Mick was sharp enough when it came to legal issues, and was very adept at sourcing the necessary texts and precedents.

'My difficulty with all of this is that I don't want to be seen to be acting against Richard in any way. It's likely he'll be running the show up at the Manor soon enough. And I can't act for both Richard and his aunt in the same matter.'

'Although in a defamation case it would be Robert who would be the plaintiff. Maybe he would have to go elsewhere to be represented?' suggested Hilary.

'Yes, but I think it likely that Miss Greta will be funding the case, and won't take too kindly to being dropped so we can act for her nephew,' Hadfield replied.

'Don't act for either?' proposed Mick.

'We might never see them again in that case. And God knows how the others would take it. I think we'll just have to wait and see how things develop. With a bit of luck, the whole defamation thing will blow over.'

'If Staunton's guilty – that should end it!' added Mick.

'Hmm. Hilary, I think I might start the transfer to Mr Timmons's office, in case I need to meet clients in private. That sort of thing.'

'Of course, James.'

'You might drop the wills in at some point when you get a chance, and leave them on the meeting table in the room.'

'Lord Barrington's is already there.'

'Oh.'

'Along with the current Lord Barrington files.'

'Ah.'

'There is no record of any will for Lady Barrington.'

'I see,' said Hadfield. 'Maybe she didn't have one. That's what A.T. said he was drafting when he came back to the office.'

'Possibly, but he didn't ask me to do it. I checked the file dealing with the wills. There are drafts there that were prepared a few weeks back for both of them on Lord Barrington's instructions. A.T. may have drafted a new one for

Lady Barrington himself. He often did his own paperwork, particularly for urgent matters.'

Hilary had obviously been using her time productively before attending the funeral. The same could not be said for Hadfield. His energy levels had started low and were fast approaching empty at this stage. He had suggested the moving of offices so as to limit his exertions to some physical activity, but even that might now be beyond him.

'Suffering a bit today, sir?' enquired Mick.

'Well, I have been better. In fact, I think I'll head across for a late bit of lunch, actually. A toasted sandwich . . . something like that.'

'And the hair of the dog!'

'Bit early for brandy, Mick, but the principle's not a bad one. Maybe a pint . . . .'

Just then Lucinda came in through the front door.

'Afternoon, all. That was certainly a funeral with a difference,' she said. 'It's not everyday you get an accusation of murder in the eulogy.'

'We were just talking about it,' replied Mick. 'Maybe it's defamation.'

'Unless it's true.'

'Fair point.'

'What did your uncle make of it?' asked Hilary.

'He didn't say much, but he did shift in his seat when the police were mentioned. A sure sign of discomfort. Sorry for being late, but I had to wait for him after the funeral. I think he wanted a word with those friends of Jasmine.'

'Oh?' enquired Mick. 'Are they suspects now.'

'I'm not sure. But I don't think it was going to be a friendly chat.'

'Is that Mr Timmons' briefcase you have there, Lucinda?' asked Hilary.

'Yes. It was in the study when they found him and Lady Barrington. They've checked it for fingerprints and contents, but it doesn't seem to have anything of relevance. Uncle Bernard thought you might want it back. To remember him by.'

'That was most thoughtful,' said Hilary. 'A.T. was very fond of it.'

They went quiet for a while as they all thought of their old boss. It was just them now.

CHAPTER 7

It was a crisp, clear morning as Hadfield left his cottage at the top of the hill and walked towards his office. He had managed to stay on long enough the previous afternoon to get his new surroundings into some sort of shape. When he got home, he had gone straight to bed, and slept well. He wanted to get in early, to read Lord Barrington's will uninterrupted, and felt reinvigorated as he listened to the birds singing on his way down. Not much else was stirring on the street as he approached the front door. He looked briefly at the brass plate and decided that, yes, 'Timmons Hadfield & Associates' was the way to go.

As he settled into Mr Timmons' plush armchair behind the large mahogany desk, he felt a little shiver run down his spine – as though somebody might be in the room with him. After a careful look around, and a good listen, he felt sure he was alone. Perhaps it was just the spirit of Andrew Timmons saying farewell.

He noted a plastic folder on the meeting-room table and went over to inspect it. The folder contained an envelope which referenced that the contents were Lord Barrington's will. The date was a little under two years previously: some time after his first wife's death, but well before he had remarried.

The document was lengthy, dealing with the usual legal requirements initially, and followed by a number of relatively small individual bequests. A more sizeable sum was given for the upkeep of the church and graveyard at the Manor. Reverend Devereux would be pleased! A lump sum was also to be put aside to invest in a bond which would provide an annual income for his sister, Greta.

Hadfield noted with surprise that a bequest of IR£250,000 was given to Robert Staunton. Those who thought him guilty would have a field day with that!

The main part of the will dealt with Lord Barrington's property, investments and residual assets. The manor house and estate lands were bequeathed to Richard but subject to a right of residence for Jasmine until she should marry.

Lord Barrington's second property, a quite substantial house and lands near the coast in west Cork, was granted to Samantha. An investment property in Dublin was given to Jasmine.

The will then directed that the remainder of the assets, comprising another investment property and various stocks and shares, be sold. The proceeds, which clearly would be a very large sum, together with any cash remaining, were to be split evenly between Richard, Samantha and Jasmine.

The executors of the will were named as Andrew Timmons and Albert Boyd. The will also provided for a situation where an executor could not, or would not, act. With a degree of trepidation, Hadfield noted that he himself was the nominated replacement for Mr Timmons.

Hadfield sat back and considered the terms of the will. If one was looking for a motive for the murder of Lord Barrington, you could argue that each member of the family, as well as Robert Staunton, would benefit from his death. Indeed, on that basis, even Reverend Devereux could be in the frame!

Hadfield looked at the various Barrington files that were piled on the meeting-room table. He remembered Hilary mentioning the draft wills that were there, and his curiosity made him look at these before anything else.

He read Lord Barrington's first. It was similar to the one he had signed, but a number of changes had been made, so as to provide for his new wife, Lydia.

Firstly, the manor house was subject to a right of residence for life in her favour. The estate was also made subject to a fixed annual sum for her lifetime.

The house in Cork, which had gone to Samantha, was subject to the exclusive use of Lydia during her lifetime, for any eight weeks of her choosing in each calendar year. Jasmine's investment property had the caveat that 50 percent of the income be paid to Her Ladyship while she lived.

Hadfield had expected the substantial residue to be split four ways, between the children and their stepmother. Instead, he noted that each was to receive 20 percent, with the final fifth going to Robert Staunton. Hadfield scratched his head. What was going on here? He was a bit surprised to see Robert in the original will at all. But why would His Lordship decide to give him a 20 percent share of a very large residue? And what would the others think of that? Hadfield could see how relations in the Barrington household might have become quite fraught in recent times, if there had been any inkling of these changes. The first will could be said to have provided the children with a motive to kill, so as to acquire the individual bequests. But an even stronger reason might have been the wish to prevent a new will being signed and the bequests being seriously reduced.

If Lady Barrrington had known of this intended new will – which, it seemed, she did – it would explain why she thought Robert an unlikely suspect. And why the very children who were accusing him were much more obvious candidates for the crime.

Hadfield turned his attention to Lady Barrington's draft will. There was a specific bequest of her jewellery to her 'old friend' Greta. Various charitable bequests were made, the largest of which was IR£50,000 to Reverend Devereux, to be used for the benefit of the annual fête which was held at Rathbawn each year. The remainder was to be split equally between the three children. *And Robert Staunton!*

Hadfield was incredulous. He could possibly understand Lord Barrington making provision for Robert, because of his guardianship over the years, but why would Lady Barrington want to make a bequest? He remembered what Hilary had said about the wills having been prepared on Lord Barrington's instructions, and decided to check the file. He noticed that there was a letter preceding the drafts which came from Lord Barrington. It set out the details of the bequests to be included in his own will. But it also went on to set out the terms for Lady Barrington's will. All of these had been faithfully included in the drafts which Mr Timmons had prepared, and which, he noted from the file, had been sent on to Lord Barrington for his review.

Was this the reason for the dispute between Lord and Lady Barrington? Was she unhappy with the terms of her will, as directed by her husband? Was this what was delaying the 'announcement'?

Just then, Hadfield heard the front door open.

'Is that you in there, James?' asked Hilary loudly.

'Yes.'

She put her head around the door. 'Cup of tea?'

'Lovely. And a couple of biscuits too, please. I've been here for a while.'

'Right-o.'

She returned shortly with a tray for two.

'How do you find your new office?'

'Fine, thanks. Fine.'

'Had a chance to look through much yet?'

'Just the wills.'

'Wills?'

'Well, Lord Barrington's. And the two drafts on file. I'm still trying to work out what it's all about.'

Hadfield summarised what he had read.

'I see what you mean,' Hilary said, once he'd finished. 'Although George looking after Robert isn't a huge surprise. There were rumours.'

'Oh?'

'Well, more gossip really. People thought that he may have been Rob's father. That the Stauntons came to work on the estate with a young child as part of some arrangement.'

'What arrangement?'

'I don't know. To keep the thing quiet.'

'That Lord Barrington had a fling with Mrs Staunton?'

'Maybe. Although there was some suggestion that Rob may have been adopted by the Stauntons, and Lord B. would look after all three himself.'

'Curiouser and curiouser. Although it would explain the bequests.' He paused for a moment, as he thought further on it. 'But why would he make such a big change in Rob's favour in the new will?'

'I think that's obvious, James.'

'Oh?'

'The arrangement was to keep his first wife from finding out. Once she had died, he was willing to acknowledge that he was Rob's father.'

'That must have been the "announcement" he had planned. Once the new wills were signed.'

'Quite likely.'

'Except Lady Barrington wasn't happy with what he wanted in her will.'

'Looks that way. Anyhow, I had better get to work. Plenty of files there for you to look at, as well.'

They finished their tea, and Hilary left him alone again.

Hadfield went over to the meeting table to look at the Barrington files which Hilary had left out. He noticed Mr Timmons' briefcase in one of the chairs. His thoughts began to wander again.

Timmons had said he was going back to the office to draft Lady Barrington's will. But if there was already a will on file, could he not have used that? Unless she had given instructions for a new will. If she did, presumably it was this new will he was bringing to the Manor before dinner. For signing.

He lifted up the briefcase. It was exactly the same as the one his boss had given him as a present, to mark Hadfield's first ten years with the firm. Timmons had got one for himself at the same time: his old briefcase had worn itself out. The initials 'A.T.' were engraved on the front in the same way as 'J.H.' had been marked on his.

He opened the briefcase and looked inside. Nothing of any real note – and certainly no will. Why would he go to the Manor to sign a will and not bring one? Unless it had been signed. And perhaps kept by Lady Barrington. But that would be unusual. A signed will would normally be kept at the solicitors' office. Where there would be a fireproof safe. Could it still be at the Manor? As Hadfield mulled over the possibilities, he remembered something about his own briefcase. On one side, there was a zipped compartment, which could hold a file or two. But hidden under the zip flap was a second, smaller zip, which opened a much slimmer section. He opened this part of Timmons' briefcase and looked inside. There was a document, and it seemed to be on deed paper – a special type of yellow, durable paper used for legal documents. He took it out very carefully.

His heart-rate began to increase as he looked it over. It was a will! Signed and dated by Lady Barrington. On the day she died. Hadfield's surprise only increased as he read through the terms.

Greta was given the jewellery, as before. The same charities were also mentioned, except this time Reverend Devereux was given IR£250,000 for the annual fête. How extraordinary. As he read on, he could not believe his eyes. The entire balance of the estate was to be divided up equally. One half to be given to her sister Letitia. The other half to be given to her son, Robert Staunton.

Hadfield sat back, shaking his head. Her son! It must have been Lady Barrington who had persuaded her husband to give Robert 20 percent under his will. And more than likely she wasn't happy with His Lordship's proposed split of her own estate. If her signed will was the one she had always intended to make, he could see why Lord Barrington was having difficulties. Half to Robert. And half to a sister she hadn't seen in years. And a quarter of a million for the annual fête!

Hadfield looked at where Lady Barrington had signed and noted two witnesses. The first he recognised immediately as being the scrawl of Andrew Timmons. The second witness had a very clear, legible signature. It was Clarisse Benoit.

*

Hadfield went straight out to the reception area.
'Hilary. You won't believe what I've just found.'
'What?'
'Lady Barrington's will. In A.T.'s briefcase.'

47

'What does it say?' asked Mick, sticking his head around the door of his office.

'Anything interesting?' added Lucinda, as she came out of the small kitchen behind reception with a cup of tea.

'Well, on the basis of the strictest confidentiality, of course.'

'Of course,' everyone replied.

Hadfield summarised the terms of the will.

Mick gave a low whistle.

'Rob. Lady Barrington's son. Who would have thought?'

'And Letitia getting half,' added Hilary. 'That is strange. I heard they haven't been in touch for years.'

'Maybe she knew about Rob,' said Mick excitedly. 'And was blackmailing her!'

'What was in Lord Barrington's will?' asked Lucinda.

Hadfield sighed. He wasn't entirely sure of the wisdom of imparting all this information at this stage.

'In the utmost confidentiality. Absolutely no gossip or insinuation. With anybody.'

'Of course.'

Hadfield filled them in on the terms of the signed will, and also the drafts which had been left on file.

'Hmm,' pondered Lucinda. 'Lady Barrington must have told Lord Barrington that Rob Staunton was her son, if he was going to make such a big change in his favour.'

'He may have known all along,' suggested Hilary.

'Oh?'

'There were rumours way back, Lucinda. That His Lordship was the father.'

'I see. Well, that would explain a lot.'

'Including the planned "announcement",' added Hadfield.

'I suppose that means Letitia could not have been blackmailing her sister,' replied Mick, a little deflated. 'If she was going to announce Rob as her son anyway.'

'You could say it makes Rob a less likely suspect,' observed Hadfield.

'But if not Rob, who did kill them?'

'That fellow Scott Hargreaves, if you ask me,' came the unexpected answer from a new arrival.

Everyone looked around, to see Agnes Goodbody, who had just come through the unlatched front door with some fresh flowers.

'Why do you say that?' asked Hadfield.

'He hasn't been himself at all since the funeral. After Lucinda's uncle collared him. Very excitable, so he is. Wouldn't be surprised if an arrest is imminent.'

'Would they not have arrested him already if they thought he was involved in the murders,' asked Mick.

'Maybe. Well, if it's not him, it's that one Letitia. She's a fright. Barely spoke to her sister. Nobody else could stand her. Especially Greta. Don't know why she was there at all. Unless she knew something. Or wanted revenge.'

'Why did Greta especially dislike her?' asked Lucinda.

'I was never told anything specific, of course, but she reckoned Letitia . . . ' – there was a pause – 'and her *companion* . . . were up to no good. Greta and Her Ladyship were lifelong friends, and she would have known both their histories. She has her suspicions, if you ask me.'

'So that would mean Scott didn't do it?' asked Lucinda.

'Unless they were in it together,' replied Mick breathlessly. 'He was her henchman.'

'I think we might be getting ahead of ourselves here,' said Hilary..

'Agreed,' replied Hadfield. 'There is plenty of work to be done. I'll just . . . .'

'Is that a will in your hand?' interrupted Agnes. 'Is that His Lordship's? When did he . . . ?'

'As I said, Agnes, we are very busy at the moment. Goodbye.'

*

Having retreated to his office, Hadfield decided it might be about time he got down to some work. First up was a review of the current Barrington files. A number comprised agricultural letting agreements in respect of various lands within the estate which had either been exchanged or were due for signature. A few related to supply agreements for the produce. There was an insurance claim in respect of an injury on the farm. An unfair-dismissal case which seemed close to settlement. Some hire-purchase agreements for machinery. All seemed relatively straightforward and well in hand.

One file which would need some input concerned a lease being negotiated in respect of a shop unit at one of the investment properties. The solicitors for the tenant had sent some comments on the draft lease the previous week – and he noted that the comments ran to six pages! He decided that the reply to that one might be best left to another day.

The final file was a general file for Lord Barrington, which seemed to deal with miscellaneous queries and issues of a minor nature. Hadfield perused the more recent correspondence but all matters appeared to have been addressed or resolved, one way or another. As he turned the final page of the file, he saw with surprise that this comprised some short, handwritten words on a plain page of the firm's headed notepaper. Hadfield recognised the writing as that of Mr Timmons.

His former boss's writing had never been good, and this particular scrawl was no exception. As best as he could decipher it, the note was an attendance of some kind, recording details of a client meeting for the file. It seemed to read as follows:

Lady B affiliated –
Abide Robert –
Client backyard –
Farm mates –
Refer 5120 –
Wills charge

There was a date at the top of the page – the very day Mr Timmons and his client were murdered.

It seemed likely that Timmons had written these notes when he returned from the Manor. It was possible that Timmons was noting down Lady Barrington's concerns as communicated to him that day, before following up when time allowed.

Unfortunately, the actual words made no sense at all to Hadfield. What was Timmons trying to say? Was it some kind of shorthand or aide-memoire? He looked at the page again for a number of minutes but could not find any useful meaning in it.

He looked at the old wooden clock on the mantelpiece over the fireplace and noted that it was after 1 PM. He popped his head out the door:

'Hilary?'

'Yes.'

'Fancy a spot of lunch?'

'Sure.'

'And . . . would you mind making a couple of copies of the top page on this general file.'

'No problem.'

'You might stick the copies in an envelope. I want to bring them with me.'

'OK.'

'And let the others know we'll be back in about an hour.'

CHAPTER 8

'Let's go to the Arms,' said Hadfield, as they left the office. 'We'll grab tea and sandwiches in the foyer. Should be able to get a quiet spot there.'

'Any time-bombs waiting in A.T.'s files?'

'Not that I could see. Just a letter making a meal out of our draft lease for one of the shop units. That's Dublin solicitors for you.'

'I suppose you will be dealing with that now until the probate is sorted.'

'I guess. Probably need to get Boyd in the loop sooner rather than later. Make sure he's up for being executor.'

'That makes sense. . . . Anything else?'

'How do you mean?'

'On the files.'

'Well, actually . . . that's part of why I suggested lunch. I'll explain when we get there.'

The Kilcreddin Arms Hotel was just a little down the road from the Timmons & Associates offices, on the same side. It was firmly of the 'old world', with all the hallmarks of faded grandeur. The bedrooms were rarely used, but it did a reasonable bar and restaurant trade. Afternoon tea could be had in the foyer just off reception, where the chairs were comfortable and the space between tables was generous. The sandwiches were not the most exciting, but were usually fresh. It was a family-run business, with Mrs Stokes in charge, her husband having passed on about a decade before. Her children were all actively involved, but Mrs Stokes's word was always final.

As they went through the front door, they were greeted by the hostess herself, who was standing just behind the reception counter.

'Afternoon, James. Afternoon, Hilary.'

'Good afternoon, Beatrice,' they both replied.

'How is everything in the legal world?'

'Kept going, at any rate,' replied Hadfield.

'People still dying, of course. Always good for business – for undertakers . . . and solicitors.'

'Well, yes . . . but the world must go on . . . .'

'Are you in for lunch?'

'Thought perhaps tea and sandwiches . . . just over there?' suggested Hadfield, pointing to a low table with two armchairs in the corner, and which also benefited from a lampshade immediately behind it.

'I'll have someone drop over to you in a moment.'

'Thanks.'

'So,' enquired Hilary, after Mrs Stokes turned away, 'what is it you wanted to talk about?'

'Oh . . . yes . . . it's something I noticed on one of the files you dropped in.'

'Which one?'

'The most recent general file for Lord Barrington.'

'Didn't think there was anything too extraordinary on that.'

'Well, no . . . there wasn't. Except there was a handwritten note: some kind of attendance by Mr Timmons.'

'From when?'

'It's the last page on the file – the one you copied – and it's dated the same day as . . . well, his last day . . .'

'I see.'

'The problem is, it doesn't really make any sense. Of course it's quite difficult to read, but . . . .'

Hadfield's explanation was cut short by the arrival of Hugh, Mrs Stokes's son, who had general responsibility for the waiting staff at the hotel. He was about the same age as Hadfield, and similar in height, but dark haired, with sallow skin and brown eyes. Still a bachelor, he would be considered what some ladies might call a 'good catch' in the town.

'Afternoon all,' he said chirpily to both of them, but with his eyes focused particularly on Hilary. 'Would you like to order something?'

'Yes please, Hugh. A ham sandwich on white for me,' said Hadfield.

'And for you, Hilary?' enquired Hugh

'Er . . . chicken on brown please, Hugh,' she replied.

'And a pot of tea for two as well,' added Hadfield.

'Is that everything?'

'For the moment anyway, I think.'

'Terrible business with the Barringtons,' Hugh added, seeming keen to continue the conversation.

'Yes indeed. Terrible,' replied Hadfield.

'And poor old Timmons, caught up in it all too.'

'Yes. Hard to know what to make of it, really.'

'I suppose things have been very busy for you all up at the office.'

Hugh seemed to be directing this query to Hilary, who was showing a degree of reluctance to engage in the conversation.

'Yes, Hugh,' replied Hadfield. 'Quite a few . . . er . . . balls in the air, so to speak, but we are managing as best we can.'

'Of course,' replied Hugh.

There followed a slightly awkward pause, which finally ended with Hugh turning directly to Hilary and saying: 'Didn't see you at the social the other night, Hilary.'

'Er, no . . . what with the funerals and all.'

'Of course.'

'It didn't seem right.'

'Understood. Well . . . maybe next time. I'll get this order organised for you.'

'Thanks, Hugh,' replied Hadfield.

'Thanks,' added Hilary.

'Was that the Horse Club social he was talking about?' asked Hadfield, after Hugh had left.

'Yes.'

'But you're not a member.'

'No, but . . . er . . . Hugh had asked me to come along if I was free.'

'Ah' was as much as Hadfield could muster.

He was aware that a number of locals were interested in Hilary. And that she would date from time to time. Mick could be relied upon to spill the beans – albeit when the fling had run its course. He hadn't known Hugh Stokes was a possible suitor. And for how long?

'I suppose the evening of A.T.'s funeral would not be the best night for heading out,' he added finally, just to break the silence – although slightly embarrassed to think they were close to doing the same themselves.

'No . . . er . . . you were talking about this note from him?'

'Yes, yes, of course. As I said, it seems to be an attendance note. His writing is terrible – as you know – but I did my best to try and decipher it.'

He reached inside his pocket and took out a folded piece of paper on which he had written down his understanding of the words.

'This is what it seems to say,' he said, handing her the piece of paper.

Hilary read it.

'Doesn't make much sense to me,' she said after a while.

53

'Nor me. That's why I asked you to make a copy of the file note.'

Hadfield opened the envelope Hilary had given him, and handed her one of the copies.

'You would know A.T.'s writing better than me. See if it makes any sense when you read it.'

Hilary read the page a number of times, and compared it with Hadfield's own note. After a while, she said: 'There are a few words here which might have another meaning.'

'Like?'

'Well, I'm not sure that the word in the first line is "affiliated".'

'Oh?'

'Looks more like "agitated".'

'Well, that does make sense, I suppose.'

'And the second line probably reads "About Robert".'

'I see – and the third?'

'"Client" doesn't look right. I think it's "check". . . but I'm not sure about "backyard". Maybe "background" . . . or possibly "backfired".'

'Hmm. "Check background" seems more plausible than "Check backfired". It's definitely more plausible than "Client backyard".'

'To be fair, James, his writing is appalling. Or should I say *was*. I'm sure A.T. wouldn't mind me saying it: he knew it himself. Sometimes he couldn't read his own notes if he hadn't looked at them for a while.'

'Yes. They say it's common amongst solicitors – myself included, it has to be said. Apparently only a doctor's writing is worse. What do you make of the next one?'

'That's difficult. He seems to have written it very quickly. I think there might be more letters than we can see.'

'I have to admit I was a bit stumped there – although, on reflection, "Farm mates" was a pretty poor stab at it. Does that even mean anything?'

'Don't know. My guess is that the first word is "Firm".'

'And the second?'

'Hard to say but, at a guess, maybe "matters".'

'Hmm. "Firm matters." What does that mean?'

'Don't know . . . and I don't know what the next line means either. The first word is probably "Refers": I think that's an "s" at the end. But the rest could be anything.'

'How do you mean?'

'Well, you have it down as "5120" – all numbers. But it could be all letters. Maybe "size" – although the last letter does look like an "o". And the second letter could be an "l".'

'So it might be a word . . . or . . . maybe each letter signifies a word.'

'Or it could be a mixture of numbers and letters.'

'Right. This is going nowhere fast.'

'I wouldn't disagree with that. Why so interested anyway?'

'Well, at the Manor that day Lydia did say in front of everyone that she did not believe that Rob had murdered her husband. And that she had an idea who did. She then went out to discuss matters with A.T. Perhaps she told him something in private that he was going to look into. About the murder.'

'And this note is a summary of that?'

'Yes. Or something to do with it – if it wasn't for the fact that we can't make head nor tail of it!'

Just then, a young waitress arrived with the tea and sandwiches, and set about laying the table. No sign of Hugh, Hadfield noted. After pouring the tea and tucking in to the first sandwich, he asked: 'And the last line? Did I get that wrong too?'

'Er . . . only slightly. "Wills" seems right, but I think that's an "n", not an "r".'

'So: "Wills change"?'

'Probably. Not that that means anything in particular either!'

'Agreed,' he replied, taking back his piece of paper.

After polishing off a second sandwich, he took a pen from a notebook he carried in his pocket, and jotted down Hilary's suggestions opposite his own, now discredited, scribblings:

Lady B agitated –
About Robert –
Check background –
Firm matters –
Refers **** –
Wills change

After looking at it for a while, he handed it to Hilary.

'I suppose,' he said, 'it does indicate some concerns Lady Barrington had in relation to Robert.'

'And that Mr Timmons was looking into it in some way or other,' Hilary replied.

'But apart from that – what does it tell us?'

'That Rob is in trouble?'

'Yes – I see what you mean.'

'Should we give it to the police?'

'I . . . er . . . I'm not sure. It's not really evidence of anything – even if we have decoded his writing correctly! Perhaps we should wait and see where the police get to with their investigations first.'

'Perhaps you're right.'

'Let's finish up and get back to the office – before Mick thinks he's running the place.'

'OK . . . actually . . . about that, James.'

'Yes,' Hadfield replied, looking at Hilary with a worried expression. When a woman starts a sentence like that, warning bells should ring.

'Do you have any plans to change personnel at the office?'

'No! Er . . . not at all. Whatever gave you that idea?'

'Well, you mentioned changes at the Riverside Inn.'

'I was only trying to . . . er . . . quieten Mick down. I have no plans at all!'

'So, both our jobs are safe?'

'Well, as safe as any job can be,' said Hadfield, trying to restore a bit of authority to what had been a fairly panicked reply. 'Of course, if the workload increases, what with all the recent activity, we might need more assistance. A newly qualified, maybe – if we're that busy.'

'And can afford it.'

'Yes. We'd . . . er . . . have to look into the whole financial side of things.'

'Work in progress, cashflow, debt recovery – that kind of thing?'

'Absolutely. All of that. Now . . . er . . . I might see if I can get the bill here.'

Hadfield turned around, to find the slim, dark figure of Letitia approaching him, with Clarisse at her side.

'Ah, Mr Hadfield. How very opportune. I had planned to pay you a visit shortly.'

'Oh?'

'Yes. About Lydia's will.'

'Her . . . eh . . . will?'

'That's right. The one your firm prepared for her, and which she signed that . . . tragic evening.'

'You know it was signed?'

'Of course. Clarisse witnessed it herself. Isn't that right?'

'Yes, that's right,' replied Clarisse.

'I see,' said Hadfield, stalling for time, and wondering how to deal with this unexpected enquiry.

'I assume it was with Mr Timmons's . . . effects?'

'Well . . . I . . . erm.'

'We are still going through that process,' intervened Hilary. 'There is a lot of paperwork to be reviewed. And grief to come to terms with.'

Letitia turned her piercing gaze to Hilary. 'Who are you?'

'Hilary. I work in the office too. And speaking of which, we should be getting back there now. James?'

Hadfield understood, and called out to reception: 'Beatrice, could you manage to send the . . . er . . . young waitress over. To pay the bill. Need to get back to the office . . . .'

'You can pay for it here if you wish. Tea and sandwiches for two? I'll print the bill now.'

Hadfield stood up. 'Well . . . er . . . nice to meet you both again.'

'Indeed. Make sure to get in touch as soon as you have any news. We'll be at the Manor.' She paused, before adding: 'If there is any change in our accommodation arrangements, we will let you know.'

*

After an afternoon's work in the office, Hadfield decided to ring Charles FitzHerbert.

Hadfield and FitzHerbert had become close friends in college at Trinity, where they had both studied law and boarded. FitzHerbert had fought valiantly to stay single but had succumbed to the charms of Florence, an estate agent who had sold him the property they currently occupied near the centre of Dublin. They were a little over three years married now, Hadfield having been best man at the wedding. There had been no patter of tiny feet, and FitzHerbert had confided in him recently that, having each had the necessary fertility checks, it was unlikely that this situation would change.

FitzHerbert was a senior counsel who specialised in criminal law. While this was not as lucrative as the commercial cases on the civil side, he had a busy practice which 'kept the wolf from the door', as he liked to say when quizzed on the subject.

Hadfield left a message on his friend's mobile, asking him to ring back in the office when he was free. Having a mobile was unusual, but FitzHerbert was always at the forefront of technology, despite his profession. Hadfield had not yet taken the plunge.

Within the hour, Hilary put FitzHerbert through.

'Afternoon, Charles. How are you?'

'Can't complain – and no one would listen if I did.'

'How's business?'

'Kept busy – still keeping the wolf from the door!'

'Good to hear – and Florence?'

'Very well, thank you. She's off to Cork for a cookery course this weekend with a couple of pals – looking forward to that.'

'She is, or you are?'

'She is, of course. I'll miss her terribly.'

'So, you're around for the weekend?'

'I am indeed. Coming up?'

'Yes. I might stay in the club on Saturday. Will I book a table for dinner?'

'Absolutely.'

'Eight PM – meet in the bar at 7.30?'

'Agreed.'

'I'll organise that.'

'Good. How are things settling down after the . . . er . . . recent events in your neck of the woods.'

'Hard to say. Police still doing their investigations. Plenty of rumours doing the rounds.'

'Yes. Sorry I couldn't make it to Timmons' funeral.'

'Thanks. I got your message. The Four Courts wait for no man, I suppose.'

'This is true. How are things in the office? Everything under control?'

'Quiet enough – although it turns out I'm executor of each of the wills of Lord and Lady Barrington.'

'That should be interesting. And Timmons' will?'

'Do you know, I'd never even thought about that.'

'Any chance you're executor there too?'

'No idea. He never mentioned being executor to me. He never mentioned a will, even.'

'I suppose you should make some enquiries – to make sure it's not overlooked.'

'Yes, of course. I'll look into that.'

'I'm sure Hilary might be able to help. Still as wonderful as ever, I take it?'

'I guess . . . .'

'Listen, I have to go into a consultation now: crime never sleeps. See you at 7.30 on Saturday.'

'See you then.'

Hadfield put the receiver down slowly. He had been a little taken aback by the reference to his boss's will. It hadn't occurred to him that this might be his responsibility too. But more worryingly, what might Mr Timmons have provided for in his will – assuming he had even made one! It was only now occurring to Hadfield that Timmons would have had assets of his own to deal with. Including the business – and the office itself!

He now realised he may have been a bit rash in assuming a simple transition to 'Timmons Hadfield & Associates'. Could somebody else take over the business? Who would own the offices? While he was the only practising solicitor remaining in the firm, he had not been a partner, and had no automatic claim to the firm's clients, or its assets.

He rushed out to reception.

'Hilary – we never thought about A.T.'s will!'

'I was wondering when you'd get round to that.'

'Does he have one?'

'I'm not sure.'

'What do you mean? Either he has one or he doesn't.'

'Well, he doesn't have a will here in this office.'

'So that's that, then.'

'But he may have made a will with another firm, and left it with them.'

'And do we know who that might be?'

'On his personal matters, he tended to use an old Dublin firm: Montgomery Darley. It may be with them.'

'I see. Do we know who he dealt with there.'

'I can check the files: I think any relevant ones would be in storage.'

'Let's do that.'

'Or you could just ring them and ask?'

'Er . . . maybe we should just check the files first. Get what information we can. Maybe there is a copy of the will there somewhere?'

'OK, I'll check. But it's unlikely A.T. would have left a copy of his will on a file for general viewing. Should be able to get the name, though.'

'Thanks. Let me know what you find.'

CHAPTER 9

Hadfield took the train up to Dublin the following Saturday. It was much more relaxing than travelling by car – and parking wasn't an issue. He enjoyed the views as the countryside passed by – provided he was facing forward. He'd found a suitable seat, and was settling in for the pleasant scenery ahead.

As it turned out, Albert Boyd was heading up to Dublin too. He was hard to miss, in his baby blue suit and yellow dickie bow.

'Mind if I join you?' he said, placing his suitcase on the rack just above Hadfield's head.

'No, not at all.'

'Glorious morning, isn't it?'

'Yes, indeed it is.'

'Off to Dublin?'

'Yes, I am.'

'Business or pleasure?'

'Having dinner with a friend this evening.'

'Business for me – big banking conference today at the Four Seasons.'

'I see.'

'Connecting with the Customer.'

'I'm sorry?'

'That's the title of the conference. You know: building a bond with the depositors, creating trust with your account-holders. I'm sure you have to brush up on that sort of thing to deal with your clients too!'

'Well . . . we tend to brush up on the law at those type of events.'

'The customer is king. That's the most important principle in our line of business. And yours too, I'd say.'

'Well . . . yes . . . I suppose.'

The conversation eventually turned to the recent deaths.

'I suppose you were interviewed by the police too?' asked Albert.

'Yes. I was. But I had nothing to say, really. Just what I heard that afternoon, same as everyone else. And the altercation with Armstrong at the entrance.'

'Those hooligans. What exactly happened?'

Hadfield told of the run-in.

'Well done, Andrew. Principled to the last . . . .' Albert's voice trailed off as he reached for his handkerchief. 'We'll miss him.'

'We will.'

They both went silent with their thoughts for a while.

'Actually, I didn't see any protestors when I came back to the Manor that evening. Were they there when you arrived?'

Albert replaced his handkerchief. 'Er . . . let me see. There were a number. But not Armstrong, as far as I can remember. I think the police asked about that.'

'Did you have much to tell the police?'

'Not much more than yourself at the Manor that afternoon. The same people were there when I came back in the evening. Except Andrew and Lydia, who were in the study. And yourself. People were in and out, of course. I told them what I remembered. I was probably more helpful in respect of George.'

'Oh?'

'Yes. You see, I was at the nursing home the day he died. I had an appointment with Miss Greta before she met George. Forms to sign. I drop down quite regularly. Quite a number of the residents are customers, and it's often easier for me to come to them.'

'Of course. And how do you think you might have been of help?'

'Well, I was able to confirm that I saw Robert Staunton at the back entrance.'

'Hmm.'

'And that Lord Barrington was alive and well when he came in to Greta's room. I stayed for a few minutes to exchange pleasantries, before taking my leave.'

'Anything else?'

'Well, I mentioned that there was a new nurse there who I hadn't seen before. They're going to look into that.'

'Of course.'

'Have you looked into the wills yet?'

'Well yes, actually. Yourself and myself are the nominated executors.'

'I assumed so. Andrew asked.'

'And you agreed?'

'Yes. I'm often asked. Always willing to oblige a customer – provided, of course, that the will covers the usual requirements – the expenses, that sort of thing.'

'Of course.'

'What do the wills say? Anything interesting?'

'They are quite detailed. It's probably best if you formalise your consent to acting as executor before getting into all that.'

'Yes. You're probably right. I assume you have no objection to the estate funds being managed through the bank?'

'I don't see why not. Presumably the legal work should continue through Timmons & Associates?'

'That makes sense.'

'Good. I'll call you next week to make an appointment to go through the detail.'

'Fine . . . and Andrew's affairs?'

'We are . . . er . . . looking into that at the moment.'

'You'll be continuing with the practice?'

'Yes. That's very much the intention. Obviously a lot of detail to be worked through but . . . er . . . for clients it should be business as usual.'

Very much the intention, thought Hadfield, *but would it be the reality? That would depend on his boss's will – or worse, the lack of one!*

'Very good. If it's any help, we have the deeds to the office. They are held as security for a mortgage Andrew had with us. We also hold the deeds to his house, although the debt on that was paid off some years back.' Albert stopped for a moment and looked out the opposite window for a while. 'There's an . . . apartment in Dublin as well, but I think the deeds to that are probably in your offices.'

'Thank you, Albert. That is . . . helpful,' said Hadfield, while at the same time thinking: 'God almighty! Now there's a mortgage on the office. What does that mean?'

'Of course, if you need any financial advice yourself – for you or the practice – feel free to get in touch. We would be only too willing to assist in whatever way we can. My stop next.'

'Cheerio.'

*

Hadfield pondered his situation after Boyd alighted from the train. Of course there was every chance he would be calling on him for funds if he had to buy out Timmons' interest in the practice. What would he offer as security? His own house was already charged – although the repayments over the years meant that there must be some equity. And what about the offices? Would he have to buy them? Or rent? And that all depended on the new owner – whoever it might be – agreeing. Maybe they would want to sell. Or *have* to sell – if there was a mortgage on the property. Or maybe the bank would have to sell, if the loan could not be repaid.

These gloomy thoughts went round and round in his head as he got off the train. As he did so, he saw a familiar profile get off from the next carriage up, and walk towards him. He wasn't entirely sure about the person's identity, as the hat he was wearing was firmly pulled down.

'Scott?'

The person he addressed stopped and looked at him. It was indeed Scott Hargreaves.

'Ah, James, old boy. In a bit of a rush. Catch up later.'

And with that, he walked off at a firm pace, with a small travel case swinging awkwardly beside him. There was no sign of Scott by the time Hadfield came out to the taxi rank. *He didn't hang about* thought Hadfield as he looked around. He hailed a cab and asked to be brought to the club on St. Stephen's Green. On arrival he paid the fare, and walked up the steps to the entrance and waited to be let in. The ringing of the bell had no immediate effect. Doubtless the porter was elsewhere, discharging one of his myriad duties – least of which always seemed to be attending the front door.

Eventually the porter arrived and let him in.

'G'day, sir.'

'Hello, Martin. How are you?'

'Very well, sir, thank you. A good trip?'

'Yes, took the train up. No delays.'

'Very good, sir. Your room is ready, if you want to . . . .'

'Yes, please. I'll just take the key and head up myself.'

'Of course, sir. Number 12, as usual,' replied Martin, as he handed over the key.

'Thank you.'

'Sorry to hear about Mr Timmons, sir.'

'Oh . . . you'd heard?'

'Yes, sir. In the news. Murder investigation, it seems. Harcourt Street are on the case now.'

'Ah' was all Hadfield could reply. He'd planned to get a paper on the train but Albert had put paid to that.

'Will I have a paper sent up, sir?'

'No thank you, Martin. I might stretch my legs and catch up with the news on my travels. Am I booked in for dinner at eight tonight?'

'Yes, sir – for two?'

'That's right.'

'Mr FitzHerbert?'

'Yes.'

'Very good, sir.'

The club was housed in a building which was more than two hundred years old. The entrance steps led up to the reception area, and this floor included the grand dining room, as well as a less ostentatious restaurant, which doubled up as a bar. The next level had the reading room and the members' lounge, both overlooking the Green. The billiards room and smoking area were at basement level, with the bedrooms on the top floor.

Hadfield took the stairs to his room – there being no lift. He unpacked his suitcase – which took all of thirty seconds – and then freshened up – which took even less. He headed out for a brisk walk around the Green, and after a few laps felt it was time for lunch. The plan was a sandwich at O'Nolans – which also happened to serve the best Guinness in Dublin. He picked up a number of the papers en route.

'MURDERS AT THE MANOR' screamed the headline in one of the more sensationalist papers.

'POLICE SUSPECT POISONING IN WICKLOW DEATHS' led the more conservative paper of record.

He settled into the snug in O'Nolans and read all the relevant articles. It was believed that all three had died of poisoning. The toxicology reports showed traces of certain prescription drugs which could be lethal if taken together, as well as traces of rat poison. It appeared that ingestion of a very small amount would have been sufficient to kill any human. There were signs of a break-in to the medicine locker in the nursing home on the day of Lord Barrington's death. The police were following a definite line of enquiry, but no arrests had yet been made. Superintendent Dockrell of Harcourt Street had taken charge of the investigation. He was reported as saying: 'We believe all three deaths were premeditated, and that they are linked. We are continuing our investigations as a matter of priority, and hope to bring the perpetrator of these crimes to justice in the very near future.' Hadfield couldn't help but think that Richard Barrington's few words from the pulpit may have prompted this communication to the media. The papers had nothing more to add, except for background history on the Barringtons, an annoying reference to the fact that Timmons' death left Kilcreddin without a solicitor, and some comments from locals on their shock at the recent events in such a quiet, picturesque and friendly part of the country.

He finished his lunch and decided to return to the club. Dinner with FitzHerbert was likely to take him past midnight, and a short afternoon nap would be good preparation.

*

Hadfield was enjoying a glass of Chablis in the members' lounge when FitzHerbert arrived.

'Evening, James.'

'Evening, Charles.'

'Its been a while. Over three months, I'd say.'

'Yes. I should try to come up more often.'

'Indeed. Florence sends her love.'

'Please pass on mine. She made it down to Cork, then?'

'Yes. She should be tucking in right now to the gourmet dinner she helped prepare earlier today. I'm expecting nothing but "haute cuisine" when she returns.'

'Naturally.'

FitzHerbert eased into the comfortable armchair adjoining his friend. He was a large man, both in height and in girth, but very neatly dressed. He was never seen without a suit, tie and waistcoat – even in the warmest of weather. Exceptions were made only for holidays and when relaxing *chez* FitzHerbert. A striking aspect of his appearance was his head, which seemed a little too big – notwithstanding his full frame. This effect was quite possibly exaggerated by his unruly shock of hair. It always had the appearance of being uncombed – or, more accurately, uncombable. It was also completely grey, having turned so almost overnight shortly after his marriage – although there was no suggestion that the events were linked. His eyebrows were equally unruly, and arguably in even greater need of a comb, but had the added contrast of being jet black. For some reason, the sudden ageing of his hair had not extended to the eyebrows. The overall impact of his appearance could seem comic from a distance, but a closer view would inevitably draw attention to the clear grey eyes which surveyed his environs, indicating a man to be taken seriously – if he should so determine.

'I ordered the Chablis – a bottle. We should be able to get through that.'

'Indeed we will – and before dinner. If we could get hold of Cyril,' replied FitzHerbert, looking around for the barman. Cyril had to look after both bars, which were on different levels – but always seemed to spend more time in the 'other' bar.

'Ah Cyril, good man!' roared FitzHerbert as he spied the barman on the stairs. 'Another glass here. And you might bring over the bottle as well.'

Silence descended while Cyril did the necessary and FitzHerbert gave the wine a good tasting.

'Excellent choice, James,' he declared, as he reclined in his armchair. 'A splendid aperitif.'

'Thought you'd like it.'

'So. Tell me all. How's life been in Kilcreddin the last few months?'

'Pretty quiet – until recent events. You probably saw the papers this morning.'

'I did indeed. Plenty of time to discuss that. How's the love life?'

'Not much happening there, I'm afraid.'

'What happened to that young solicitor you were seeing?'

'Marjorie?'

'The one you met at the Law Society conference in Killarney.'

'That's her.'

'She seemed keen.'

'A bit too keen, to be honest. And a bit too much . . . ' – Hadfield paused as he searched for the right word – ' . . . a bit too much fun.'

'What on earth do you mean?'

'Well, she found Kilcreddin a complete bore, so all traffic was one way: me going to Cork. And every trip involved a ball or a party or meeting up with her friends for dinner or going to a nightclub or . . . .'

'But James, there are people who would pay good money for that! Party all weekend with a good-looking young girl and head back home to bachelordom for the week.'

'Well, you might think so. But it was quite exhausting – to say the least. And after a while, it just became a bit too much.'

'I see. Well, there's no pleasing some people.'

'Maybe not.'

'Is Deirdre still on your mind?'

'Well, I still think of her, of course. But I suppose I should really start to move on now.'

'Agreed. Two years is a long time. *Fugit irreparabile tempus.*'

'What?'

'It's from Virgil's Georgics – one of his book of poems. Literally it means: "It escapes, irretrievable time".'

'I see,' replied Hadfield, a little uncertainly.

'The phrase is more commonly shortened to "*Tempus fugit*" these days. Meaning: "*Time flies*".'

'Ah. Yes. I have you now. Latin was never my strongest . . . .'

'And while we are on the subject: how is the lovely Hilary?'

'She's well.'

'Still got a soft spot for you?'

'What do you mean by that?' asked Hadfield, moving uncomfortably in his chair.

'Oh come on, James. You must know that she has always had a thing for you.'

'I don't know that I'd go that far.'

'She could have had any man in Kilcreddin and beyond. Did you ever wonder why she stayed single?'

'Well . . . .'

'Never tempted to make a move?'

'But we're work colleagues. It's not considered a good idea to . . . fraternise . . . at such close quarters.'

'Maybe for the young. But as time passes . . . .'

'Anyway, it seems she's seeing someone at the moment.'

'Oh?'

'Hugh Stokes. He runs the Kilcreddin Arms with his mother.'

'Pleasant spot, as I remember. Bedroom was a bit basic, but the food decent enough. Think I remember the young chap – dark handsome fellow?'

'You could say that,' he conceded.

'Something of the diva about the mother, as I recall.'

'You could say that too.'

'Well, good luck to Hilary. She could do worse. Let's finish this and head down to the dining room.'

CHAPTER 10

The dining room was in the grand old style, being at least twice as long as it was wide, and with big chandeliers hanging from the very high, ornate ceiling. Large portraits of historic figures lined the walls and various silver pieces were placed on mantelpieces and sideboards throughout the room – all acquired by the club over the years through donations and bequests from members.

Hadfield and his guest took their usual table in the corner by the left front window, perused the menu and wine list, and ordered from both.

'So! Did you find out anything further about Timmons' will?' FitzHerbert enquired as soon as the waiter had left with their orders.

'Well, not really,' replied Hadfield in a hushed tone, being conscious that the room was only half full and FitzHerbert's voice tended to be on the loud end of the scale. 'It seems he didn't keep it in the office, at any rate. Hilary thinks he may have used Montgomery Darley for his personal matters, and it might be with them. She's checking his files to see if there might be anything there to help us.'

'I see. Assuming he made a will at all. You know the old saying: "A cobbler's children are the worst shod".'

'You know, I've been giving some thought to all this, and I'm not really sure where I'll stand – whether he made a will or not.'

'Yes,' said FitzHerbert, putting his fingers and thumbs together in the form of a steeple and looking towards the ceiling. 'I can see there might be a few bumps ahead – depending on how things turn out.'

'I mean, who'll get the offices? And there's a mortgage on that, according to Boyd.'

'Who's Boyd?'

'The local bank manager. Met him on the train on the way up. He's the other executor under the Barrington wills.'

'Ah.'

'And what about the business? How's that going to work? Can Timmons give it to someone without me?'

'Quite possibly – although you would pass with the business as an employee, of course. Along with Hilary . . . and the others.'

'Yippee!' said Hadfield sarcastically. And a little too loudly, as it happened: a few heads turned in his direction. 'Hardly a cause for celebration,' he continued, lowering his voice again.

'No. But it's not all doom and gloom.'

'Why not?'

'Well, whether there is a will or not, the probate will take quite some time.'

'And?'

'You can use that time to get close to those clients which aren't your direct responsibility already.'

'Like the Barringtons.'

'Exactly. All going well, you will be "the business", and there'll be nothing left to sell.'

'But what about the offices? I'm hardly going to run the "business" from home.'

'You set up new offices nearby – renting to start with, most likely. But realistically, any new owner of Timmons' offices should consider granting you a lease first. That probably maximises its value. If they have to sell it, you would probably be best positioned to buy.'

'With a hefty loan from Boyd, no doubt. He was keen to offer his services when we spoke on the train.'

'I can imagine. That is his job, isn't it?'

Just then, the starters arrived, and conversation ceased as the scallops, pork belly and black pudding were dealt with.

'So, what do you make of it all?' Hadfield asked as the empty plates were removed. 'The murders, I mean.'

'I'm not sure what to think. I only know what I've read in the papers. Quite bizarre, really. Likely to do with money, I should say.'

'Yes, quite likely. The wills certainly give a motive to all the family members.'

'How's that?' asked FitzHerbert, pausing to taste the decanted Pauillac which had been brought to the table, and nodding approval to the waiter.

'Well, obviously this is confidential . . . .'

'You can consider me retained counsel – in case barristerial assistance should be required.'

'Yes. Good. Anyhow . . . . Lord Barrington had provided for all the family . . . .

'The *family* being . . . ?'

'His sister: Greta. His eldest, Richard, who gets the manor house and the estate. His daughter, Samantha, who is next in line, and the youngest, Jasmine. There is also a bequest to another chap, Robert Staunton, who is close to the family but not related.'

'Staunton being the prime suspect, I take it.'

'The only suspect. At least that's what the papers seem to think. And the locals, needless to say.'

'And Lady Barrington's will?'

'Well, that's where it gets quite bizarre.'

Hadfield recounted the details of her will and also the drafts on file.

'So, even Lady Barrington could have had a motive for killing her husband.'

'Perhaps,' pondered Hadfield, just as the main courses arrived. As with the starters, they had chosen similarly – this time fillet of steak. They waited patiently while the vegetables were dispensed, taking the opportunity to cleanse their palates with the full-bodied claret.

'So much for motive,' FitzHerbert said after a few mouthfuls of his medium-rare fillet. 'What about opportunity?'

'I don't really know. I suppose the police are investigating all that.'

'Well, what are the facts – as you know them. Chronologically.'

'Let's see, today is the twenty-fifth of October. Lord Barrington, George, died on Friday the tenth. At the nursing home – before lunchtime.'

'And where's that?'

'It's about halfway between Rathbawn to the east, where Richard Barrington lives, and Rathmore to the west, where his sister Samantha lives. Staunton lives in Rathbawn too. It's about a mile each way. Kilcreddin is about three miles north of the home.'

'And the Manor?'

'It's about half a mile further east of Rathbawn. Although there is a separate road to the nursing home from the Manor, which would be a shorter route. Obviously George and Lady Barrington – Lydia, that is – lived there. As does Jasmine, when she's not in Dublin.'

'Very good. Please continue,' prompted his companion.

'Well, George was visiting Greta Barrington at the home, as he did regularly. It seems that Boyd dropped in just before him, to have some papers signed by Miss Greta. He noticed Staunton at the back entrance, for staff – sometime before lunch. Apart from that, all we know is that George died from poisoning. It seems it was the tea delivered to the room that did it. Miss Greta only drinks warm water, so she was spared. And the medicine locker was broken into. That was mentioned in the papers.'

'And then?'

'Well, there was a bit of a delay before the funeral could take place: autopsy, I suppose. George's body was in repose at the Manor in advance of the funeral, and there was to be a dinner on the evening of the second murders. The family and some friends and relatives. The local priest, Devereux. Boyd too.'

'And Timmons joined them.'

'Yes, after he had been to the office. He went back before dinner to meet privately with Lydia.'

'And Lady Barrington and Timmons both died from the same poison as Lord Barrington.'

'So the papers say. Seems it was the sherry, or something. And the medicines stolen from the nursing home were found at Staunton's cottage later that evening.'

'Nothing found after the first murder?'

'Apparently not.'

'Why did you mention Timmons going back to the office?'

'Well . . . interestingly, that's where I might have some additional information,' Hadfield replied conspiratorially.

'Oh? Pray tell.'

'Well, it seems he went back to the office to do up the will, which Lydia signed. But by chance, when reading up on Timmons' recent files, I came across an attendance note which was written by him, and which I think was done just before he left the office.'

'I see,' said FitzHerbert, perking up in his chair and fixing Hadfield with his clear grey eyes, 'and what did it say?'

'Unfortunately, it's hard to say. It was handwritten and barely legible.'

His guest slumped back in his seat.

'But,' continued Hadfield, 'myself and Hilary made a good stab at it. She's quite familiar with his handwriting. Here's what we reckon he was trying to say.'

He handed FitzHerbert a copy of the file note, as well as their translation – which the latter slowly read out.

Lady B agitated –
About Robert –
Check background –
Firm matters –
Refers ****
Wills change

He rubbed his chin ruminatively. 'Why the four asterisks?'

'Oh, sorry. We just couldn't work out what he meant. It could be four numbers, like "5120", or four letters, like "SIZO", or a mixture of both, like "51ZO".'

'Right. Did you give this to the police?'

'No,' replied Hadfield, a little guardedly. 'Not yet, anyway. I only came across it the other day. And I'm not sure if it's of any help. Does it even mean anything?'

'Well, it must have meant something to Timmons.'

'I suppose it could be viewed as unhelpful to Staunton – that Lydia was worried about him.'

'Or that she was worried *for* him. And that Timmons was to look elsewhere.'

'Yes. She said as much at the Manor in the afternoon.'

'Were you there?' said FitzHerbert with a quizzical expression.

'Yes. I drove A.T. to the Manor and he made me come in. I was invited to the dinner, but the police had already arrived when I got there.'

'Can I keep this for a while?' said FitzHerbert, waving the papers.

'Certainly. They're spare copies, so you can do what you like with them,' he replied, before quickly adding: 'While keeping it confidential, of course.'

'Of course.'

Their conversation was interrupted while plates were cleared and dessert ordered – along with another bottle of red.

'You can't beat a good claret,' sighed FitzHerbert as the second bottle was commenced.

'You can't. Only Burgundy comes close.'

'A decent Italian now and then does no harm.'

'A good Spanish can go down well.'

'No time for that "New World" stuff.'

'Agreed.'

They polished off their desserts and sat back in a postprandial lull, the larger of the diners discreetly unbuttoning his waistcoat.

'I suppose,' FitzHerbert opined, after getting himself comfortable, 'you'll be having the usual gawkers down your way now that all this is front-page news.'

'Quite likely.'

'Nothing like the whiff of murder to attract the lunatic fringe.'

'What did you make of the papers? Dockrell seemed to be indicating they knew who they were after. Presumably Staunton.'

'Hmm. I wondered about that. If they are so certain, why mention it at all?'

'I think I might know the answer to that.'

'Oh?'

'Yes,' replied Hadfield, with a slightly self-satisfied air. 'I think it might have been to placate the Barringtons. Richard gave the police a bit of a roasting in his eulogy for Lord Barrington.'

'That might be it,' replied his companion doubtfully. 'Bit unlike Superintendent Dockrell, though. Not one to give anything away unnecessarily.'

'Actually, speaking of Richard,' said Hadfield, somewhat tangentially, but seeking to get a little legal assistance from his friend, 'I forgot to mention that he pretty much accused Staunton of the murders during his speech.'

'Did he, now.'

'Well, he didn't actually name him. But he looked at him directly when he said everyone knew who did it.' Here Hadfield paused, and with a degree of nonchalance asked Charles: 'As a matter of interest. Do you think that would constitute slander? Where the person isn't actually named? But most people know what was meant.'

'If he did commit the murders, it can't be slander. But if he didn't, he could have a cause of action. He didn't have to be named. He just has to show that some, but not all, of those present reasonably understood that he was being accused of murder.'

'Yes, that's what I thought myself. Just wondering. Very good. Will we . . . er . . . have a glass of port with a little Stilton?'

'Absolutely!'

The cheese had to be followed by a cigar, so they found themselves finishing off the port in the smoking area.

'So. How's married life treating you, Charles?'

'Couldn't be better.'

Fortified by the wine and port, Hadfield ventured: 'And the . . . er . . . medical tests . . . that's all . . . er . . . .'

'Yes. We've accepted all that. We looked at IVF, but that can be difficult. Very difficult. We're happy as we are. Why take a chance of jeopardising that?'

'I can understand.'

'Of course, adoption is a possibility. We haven't really looked into that. We'll let things settle for a while and see where life takes us.'

'Fair enough,' replied Hadfield, slowly turning his near-empty port glass while pondering where life was taking him.

'Time for a brandy?' asked FitzHerbert, with a raised eyebrow.

'Why not?'

CHAPTER 11

Hadfield could hear a distant tapping, but couldn't be sure what it was, or where it was coming from. After a while, the tapping was accompanied by a muffled voice. It seemed to be saying *slur* or *shmur* or something along those lines. Gradually, a foggy realisation developed inside his head. He was in the club. He was in bed in his room. The noises were coming from the doorway.

'Hello,' croaked Hadfield, inaudibly.

There was more tapping.

'Yes. Hello?' he replied, a little more clearly and loudly.

'Morning, sir. Your breakfast.'

'Oh . . . I see. One moment. Just, er . . . .' he mumbled as he tried to get his bearings. The sounds were coming from the door on the right, and he turned out of bed in that direction. As he gingerly approached the door, it occurred to him that engaging with staff in his boxer shorts was best avoided.

'One moment please,' he called out, as he headed for the bathroom, and the safety of a bathrobe.

'Very good, sir.'

Hadfield eventually opened the door suitably attired, to be greeted by Martin, the porter.

'Morning, sir. Lovely day today. I'll leave your breakfast here, sir?' said the porter as he approached the only table in what was quite a small room.

'Yes. That'll be fine. Erm . . . what time is it, Martin?'

'9.15, sir.'

'Oh. Did I . . . er . . . order breakfast for now?'

'No, sir. You didn't order breakfast at all.'

'Ah,' replied Hadfield, somewhat perplexed, but unable to formulate a sensible response.

'Mr FitzHerbert ordered it for you, sir. He says you have an appointment at 10.30 on Harcourt Street. He asked you to join him in the reading room at 10.15.'

'Yes, of course. Thank you, Martin. I'll be down shortly. You . . . er . . . you wouldn't be able to muster up an Alka-Seltzer, by any chance?'

'I'll see what I can do, sir.'

Hadfield crashed back on to the bed as soon as Martin had closed the door. He had no idea what was going on. He'd planned for a late lie-in, followed by a bite of lunch. He could ask FitzHerbert for some clarification, but that would mean getting dressed. If he didn't get dressed, he could miss the appointment – whatever that was! After a while, he accepted there was only one option. A cold shower.

At 10.10, he headed down the stairs to the reading room. He'd only been able to manage a slice of toast and the orange juice, but thankfully this had been supplemented by a strong dose of Alka-Seltzer. Martin had come up trumps.

'Morning, James,' bellowed FitzHerbert, as he entered the room.

'Morning.'

'How's the head today?'

'How do you think? I'm totally hungover. I could still be drunk!'

'Nothing like a full breakfast to cure that.'

'So I shouldn't expect much from the slice of toast I managed to nibble on, then?'

'I had the benefit of the full menu downstairs. The fried liver was particularly good. And of course it wouldn't be Sunday morning at the club without kippers!'

FitzHerbert's constitution was legendary. No amount of alcohol got him inebriated, and no matter how late he had been imbibing it, he rose without fail at 6 AM each day.

'What's this appointment about?' asked Hadfield, anxious to move off the topic of food.

'Well, after our discussion last night, I thought it might be worthwhile to have a word with Dockrell.'

'What?'

'Yes. Having spoken with him, he thought it might be a good idea to meet to have a little chat.'

'This morning?'

'*Carpe diem, quam minimum credula postero.*'

'Huh?'

'It's Horace, a contemporary of Virgil, from his "Odes". It means: "Seize the day, put very little trust in tomorrow", or something like that. More commonly shortened to: "*Carpe diem*".'

'Seems a bit like *tempus fugit*, if you ask me,' replied Hadfield, who was in little mood for old Latin phrases.

'Well, I was going to use another quote from the "Odes", but thought better of it.'

'Oh?'

'*Nunc est bibendum.*'

'Meaning?'

'*Now is the time to drink.*'

'Very funny.'

'Come on. We'd better get our coats and head over. He's not a man to be kept waiting.'

It was a fresh morning, with a hint of dampness in the air. As they walked through the Green, Hadfield picked up the scent of decaying leaves. This was normally a pleasant, thoughtful experience, but today produced feelings not unlike nausea.

'Where are we actually going?' he asked.

'The Special Branch offices. At the top of Harcourt Street. I felt even you could manage such a short trip this morning,' replied his companion.

'You're too kind.'

They exited the Green and headed up Harcourt Street, until they reached a nondescript high-rise building entirely out of character with the rest of the Georgian road. FitzHerbert led the way in through the reception area, and walked up to the public counter.

'Good morning,' he said, addressing the person behind the counter. The officer was slowly turning the pages of a folder he was holding, and was seemingly disinclined to engage with them until this painstaking task was concluded – however long that might take.

'We have an appointment with Superintendent Dockrell in one minute,' continued FitzHerbert, raising his voice somewhat, 'and I am loath to ring him myself and request that he fetch us from the reception area of his own offices.'

This had the desired effect. The all-important folder was quickly closed, and the two of them were promptly brought up a flight of stairs and left in a small, bare room with a table, four chairs and a single window, covered by a set of slightly ill-fitting blinds.

'I'll tell the Super you're here,' said the officer, as he exited the room.

'Thank you, much appreciated,' replied FitzHerbert, adopting a more gracious tone.

It wasn't long before there was a short, sharp knock, and the door was quickly opened.

'Morning, Charles.'

'Morning, Bernard. You know James Hadfield, of course.'

'Yes indeed. We've met at his offices a few times. When dropping in to see Lucinda. And at the Manor, of course. When he gave his statement.'

'Morning, Superintendent,' was all Hadfield could muster in response.

Dockrell went over to the window, to adjust the blinds and let in some fresh air.

He was of medium height and build. His hair was a little unusual, in that it was jet black but slicked back, and slightly to his left, with what seemed to be copious amounts of oil. Either way, his hair was shiny and flat. His face was very white, as though he had not seen the sun in a long time, or was deficient in some vitamin or other. Hadfield could not help but feel that if he sported a short, square moustache, he would look strikingly similar to a certain leader of the Third Reich! His eyes were not so striking however, being slightly watery and red-rimmed. You could be forgiven for thinking that he neither slept nor went out. He wore a brown suit, well used, and a pair of shoes which, although also brown, somehow managed through the difference in shade to clash badly with his outfit.

'So, Mr Hadfield. I understand you have some information which may be useful to our inquiry.'

'Er . . . .'

'The file note,' suggested FitzHerbert.

'The . . . erm . . . file note?'

Dockrell looked at Hadfield a little suspiciously.

'You came across a note from Timmons on one of his files which might be relevant,' continued the Superintendent.

'Well . . . there was a handwritten note on one of Lord Barrington's files. Written the day Mr Timmons died. Bit cryptic, really. Can't say I . . . .'

'Do you have it with you?' interrupted Dockrell.

'Well, I should have a copy somewhere . . . ' he replied, as he began to search his pockets. 'Now, let me see . . . ' he continued, becoming a little agitated as it became clear he was not in fact in possession of the document. 'I'm pretty sure . . . .'

'Here it is, Superintendent,' said FitzHerbert. 'Mr Hadfield asked me to hold on to it last night, so that I could contact you in the morning on it. It's just James's assessment of what Timmons wrote, and a copy of the note itself. The original, barely legible, remains on the file – for safe-keeping.'

'I see,' said Dockrell, giving Hadfield a quizzical look before reading the papers which had been handed to him.

The Superintendent had remained standing the entire time, and walked slowly towards the window again while he considered the note.

'Hmm,' he said eventually. 'Not much to go on there.'

'No,' confirmed FitzHerbert.

'And the missing word?'

'It seems,' he replied, 'that it could be a word or a set of numbers or a mixture of both. Isn't that right, James?'

'Er . . . that's right. We couldn't work it out. The writing is very bad. In fact, the words we have put down may not even be exactly right.'

'We?' asked Dockrell, with an intense look.

Hadfield froze, not sure if he had perhaps committed some offence by showing the note to Hilary.

'Mr Hadfield needed Timmons' secretary to review the handwriting,' interjected FitzHerbert again, 'as she was the person best placed to assist in making sense of the note – which meant nothing to James when he came across it first.'

'All right. We'll need to see the original, obviously. I'll arrange for someone to drop in to your offices to attend to that tomorrow.'

'Of course, Superintendent,' replied Hadfield hastily. 'No problem at all.'

'Now, I understand you have some other documents which may be relevant to our investigations.'

'Er . . . other documents?' he began, before his friend cut in.

'The wills of Lord and Lady Barrington, James. You mentioned them to me as part of our consultation.'

'Oh, of course. The wills.'

'Perhaps you could summarise the bequests in each, for the benefit of the Superintendent,' sighed FitzHerbert. 'It may assist him in establishing motive.'

Hadfield went through the principal terms of each will as best he could, although a short break was required to fetch him a glass of water at one point. This was requested under the pretext of a slight cough, but was almost certainly more related to the effects of dehydration.

CHAPTER 12

'So,' began the Superintendent, after Hadfield had concluded his summary of the wills – albeit speaking more to himself than to the others present – 'plenty of motive there.'

He turned to Hadfield, and continued: 'And when were they signed?'

Hadfield looked at him blankly, as he felt a rising panic take over.

'The . . . er . . . wills?'

'Yes, the wills.'

'Let me see. Lord Barrington's was over a year ago. After his first wife died, but before he married Lydia.'

'I see. And Lady Barrington's?'

'Er . . . The day she died.'

Dockrell stared at him.

'The day she died?'

'Yes.'

Dockrell paused, his eyebrows coming together slightly.

'And where did she sign it?'

'At the Manor, I think.'

The Superintendent took a deep breath.

'I don't recall you mentioning that when we last spoke, at the Manor.'

'Well, I didn't know then. I only found it the other day, in the briefcase.'

Dockrell looked to the ceiling, as if seeking to suppress a strong emotion. Hadfield looked to FitzHerbert for support.

'James. Perhaps you could go through everything as you told me, including the draft wills on file. You will understand, Bernard, that James wanted to consult with me first before taking any further steps with the information he had.'

Hadfield took another sip of water, and told what he knew.

'So, the will was in Mr Timmons' briefcase. The one we returned to your office.'

'That's right, Superintendent.'

'To be fair to whoever checked through that,' interjected FitzHerbert, 'it was in a somewhat secretive pouch. James only knew to look because he has exactly the same type of briefcase himself.'

'I'm sure,' replied Dockrell – who didn't seem too sure at all. 'Needless to say, I'll be looking into that.'

'It was a present from Andrew,' added Hadfield.

'What?'

'The briefcase.'

'Ah,' the Superintendent replied – rather vaguely – before walking towards the window once more, seemingly lost in thought.

'Were there any other bequests, apart from the ones to the family and Staunton?' he asked eventually.

'Well, there were quite a few charities mentioned. Mainly local ones. The only one I can recall specifically was the Annual Fête Trust.'

'Why that one?'

'Er . . . it got quite a large bequest and . . . er . . . .'

'Yes. And?' pressed Dockrell.

'Well, it's just that the church got quite a sum under Lord Barrington's will. And . . . er . . . the church is one of the main recipients of the funds from the annual fête.'

'Reverend Devereux's church, I take it.'

'Yes.'

'Anyone else of note?'

'Not that I can think of.'

'Hmm. We'll need to take those wills tomorrow as well.'

'Of course. If . . . er . . . you have to.'

'What do you mean: *If you have to?* Don't you know . . . ?'

'No issue with that, Bernard,' interrupted FitzHerbert. 'It's just that the originals will be needed for probate purposes.'

'I see. We'll take copies for the moment, so. But the originals may be needed in due course for evidentiary purposes.'

'Understood.'

'Any benefit to Mr Boyd,' enquired the Superintendent, turning his gaze again to Hadfield.

'Er . . . Albert Boyd?' he replied, a bit taken aback by the question.

'Yes. That bank-manager fellow.'

'Well, no. I don't believe so. Not as a beneficiary. He is . . . er . . . he is executor under each will. But that's only an administrative role. No bequest involved there at all.'

'I see. Any other executors?'

'Well, Mr Timmons was named as the other executor.'

'And in his place?'

'Actually, as it turns out . . . it's . . . er . . . me.'

'Did you know of this?'

'No. I didn't.'

'You mean you were given the important role of executor of the wills of Lord and Lady Barrington without having any knowledge of the appointment?'

'That's right.'

'Does that not strike you as strange, Mr Hadfield?'

'Well . . . yes. But actually, now that I think of it, Mr Timmons did ask a number of years back if I had any objection to being named as replacement executor in client wills.'

'And you had none.'

'Well . . . no. You see, you don't have to accept being executor if you don't want to.'

'So you won't be accepting your appointment under the Barrington wills.'

'I . . . erm . . . .'

'Superintendent,' interrupted FitzHerbert, 'it's not unusual for the family solicitor to be named as one of the executors in a will. Timmons, as an elderly practitioner, would have felt it prudent to allow for another lawyer in the firm to take on the role, should he be 'incapacitated'. As the junior, and only, solicitor in the firm, Hadfield was the logical person to name as his replacement. As James has indicated, this did not need a specific consent, but of course it would generally be considered disrespectful to the deceased client's wishes to turn down such a responsible position.'

'So you will be accepting the appointments, Mr Hadfield.'

'That would be my intention, Superintendent. As a matter of precedent. And to respect the wishes of the deceased.'

'And Mr Boyd?'

'Eh?'

'Is he accepting the executorships?'

'I . . . erm . . . I believe so.'

'What makes you say that?'

'Well, he told me he had no objection. If the usual provisions applied. Expenses; that kind of thing.'

'When was this discussed?'

'I met him on the train on the way up here yesterday. Purely by chance. I thought I might mention it to him.'

'And was he surprised?'

'Not really. I think Mr Timmons might have asked him. Mr Boyd mentioned that it's not uncommon for a bank manager to be made executor.'

'What about Timmons' will?' continued Dockrell, keeping his eyes firmly fixed on Hadfield.

'I don't know.'

'Don't know what?'

'I don't know anything about his will. It seems he didn't keep it in the office.'

'So he made a will?'

'We don't know.'

'We?'

'Well, Hilary, Hilary Byrne, his . . . er . . . my . . .er . . .the firm's secretary thinks he may have used a different firm of solicitors. She's checking the files.'

'And did Timmons ever enquire about your willingness to be executor under his own will?'

'No. Not that I recall. I think he only mentioned client wills.'

'And the ubiquitous Mr Boyd. Has he any role in Timmons' affairs?'

'Not that I know of.'

The Superintendent turned away again, tapping his lips with his finger.

'Mr Hadfield,' he said, after a short while, 'can you account for your whereabouts on the day of Lord Barrington's death?'

'My whereabouts?'

'Yes. Your whereabouts.'

'Well . . . I was in the office in the morning. I had been out for dinner the previous night – quite late, as I recall. I may have left the office a little early and had lunch at home. And . . . er . . . maybe a short nap.'

'How long were you gone from the office?'

'Perhaps three hours. From about 12 until 3 or so.'

'And your office colleagues could confirm that?'

'Er . . . Hilary, our secretary, would have been there when I left. And when I returned . . . I think.'

'And can anyone confirm you were at home the entire time?'

'Well, I was on my own in the house. So . . . er . . . no.'

'And the evening of the deaths at the Manor?'

'Well, I left early from the office to get changed for the dinner. About five, I suppose.'

'And you arrived after the murders.'

'Well, yes. The police were already there.'

'Can anyone vouch for you between five and eight that evening?'

'Well, I was at home.'

'Alone?'

'Yes.'

'I see,' said the Superintendent meditatively, walking slowly back to the window.

'Surely you don't suspect James here of any involvement in these matters?' enquired FitzHerbert.

'No. I wouldn't say that. Just a matter of confirming everyone's movements at the relevant times. We've had to ask the same question of quite a number of people. All part of the job.'

Dockrell paused for a moment and looked intently at his shoes while rubbing his chin. He seemed to be weighing something up in his mind. Eventually he looked up and addressed Hadfield.

'As solicitor with responsibility for the wills of Lord and Lady Barrington, I take it you will be approaching the beneficiaries directly yourself with respect to the bequests.'

'Well, yes. That would be normal.'

'Individually, or as a group?'

'Either is permissible. It's not cast in stone.'

'All right. Now I'm going to take you both into my confidence to some extent here.'

Dockrell proceeded to sit down opposite them both, and continued: 'You see, we've done our preliminary investigations, and while we have a prime suspect, it's by no means a foregone conclusion.'

'That would be Staunton, I take it,' suggested FitzHerbert.

'Yes. He had the motive. And the opportunity. And some corroborating evidence. Empty medicine containers, likely the ones stolen from the nursing home, were found at his house. But he is far from the only one who could be in the frame. Not one of the family members have an alibi for the time of Lord Barrington's death, and all were present at the Manor at the time of the death of Lydia Barrington and Andrew Timmons.

'Greta Barrington and Robert Staunton were both at the nursing home at the relevant time on the Friday. Lady Barrington was riding alone on the estate. Richard was attending to paperwork at the estate offices but wasn't seen.

Richard's wife was at home, having dropped the kids to school and collected some messages. Samantha Barrington had left her surgery early to do some shopping in Kilcreddin and meet a friend for a late lunch. Her husband stayed at home, reading the papers, until she got back. Jasmine was in transit from Dublin, with that fellow Scott and his girlfriend Penny. Lady Barrington's sister and her friend were in their rooms at the Manor the whole afternoon. Nobody can actually independently vouch for their whereabouts at the estimated time of death of George Barrington.'

Superintendent Dockrell sat back in his seat and looked at the ceiling, with his fingers intertwined.

'Now,' he continued, 'Staunton is actually placed at the scene of the crime, which of course is a fact which very much goes against him. He claims he was there to see one of the nurses, Sarah O'Doherty, with whom he has a relationship, and this was confirmed by Ms O'Doherty. His intention was to drop in to see Greta Barrington after that, but the commotion following the death of Lord Barrington intervened. The note on Timmons' file could be viewed as a suspicion on the part of Lady Barrington in respect of Staunton's involvement in the murder, but equally it could be viewed as pointing responsibility elsewhere. Another factor concerns the medicine cabinet which was broken into at the nursing home. The autopsy shows that the poisoning contained traces of prescription drugs which, if taken together, are considered highly toxic. However, traces of strychnine were also noted – although this would not necessarily have been found in the medicine cabinet.'

'I can see how things might not look good for Staunton,' FitzHerbert commented, 'but surely his relationship to Lydia makes him somewhat unlikely as a suspect.'

'And his relationship to George,' added Dockrell.

'Go on,' prompted FitzHerbert.

'We've been looking into his background. Just got an update on Friday. He was adopted. The paperwork was handled through Barton, Harvey & Cobb here in Dublin. It's been confirmed that George Barrington was the father.'

'Good Lord!' exclaimed Hadfield. 'So it's unlikely he was involved in the first murder either.'

'Yes. Unless he didn't know they were his parents. We haven't put that to him yet. Or he was enraged by the delay in telling him. We'll have to tread carefully here. As I say, he does have clear opportunity on both occasions.'

'How about Greta Barrington?' asked FitzHerbert. 'She was there too.'

'True. She had the opportunity. But the motive is not so clear. Herself and Lydia Barrington were longstanding friends, and there had been no indication of a falling-out. Of course, the will might have given reason for that, but as I understand it, Greta was quite well off in her own right, and would not have been in any great need of additional funds. As against that, I understand that Staunton's financial position may not have been so stable. Also, Ms O'Doherty mentioned in her interview that he was keen to start his own business, if finances could be arranged. Of course, Greta Barrington and Staunton could have been in it together. It seems they were quite close, and perhaps his need for funds precipitated some sort of joint enterprise. Perhaps O'Doherty was assisting Staunton. There are quite a number of possibilities.'

'And the evidence is a bit circumstantial, whichever way you look at it, wouldn't you say?' queried the barrister.

'Yes. And that's maybe where Mr Hadfield might be of some assistance.'

'Oh?' croaked Hadfield, whose mouth had dried up again. 'How could I be of help?'

'Not entirely sure if you can. But as solicitor to the estates of the Barringtons, you could approach the beneficiaries individually to discuss their bequests. Keep an ear out for anything that might be of interest to our investigations. Perhaps mention that Mr Timmons left a note with his papers. Reservations about Lord Barrington's death. That you passed it on to the police, for what it was worth.'

'And watch out for any comment or reaction that might not quite fit,' mused FitzHerbert.

'Exactly. It may not be immediate. It may produce nothing at all. A shot in the dark, really, but what harm?'

Hadfield was inclined to say that there could be any amount of harm. To him! Presumably one or more of the beneficiaries was the killer. How would they take the news that he'd passed a suspicious note to the police? He was starting to feel very queasy indeed.

'Now,' continued the Superintendent, rubbing his hands as he warmed to the plan, 'you might include Reverend Devereux on your list. He was at the nursing home just before Lord Barrington died. And Boyd too. His motive is not so clear. Unless being executor can be considered advantageous.'

With this, the Superintendent looked at Hadfield with a raised eyebrow, as if Hadfield might be in a position to answer such a question.

Hadfield coughed momentarily and continued: 'Superintendent, I'm not quite sure how helpful I'm likely to be in all this. They may just want to know the terms of their bequest, and leave it at that. Even if they want to talk further – about Mr Timmons' note, or whatever – I'm not going to know if it means much – good, bad or indifferent.'

'I understand that, Mr Hadfield. I'm not expecting any great miracles here. Just note down whatever is discussed afterwards. What I will do, though, is have

Detective Sergeant Forde run through the witness statements, to give you some background. We could do that now, or leave it until tomorrow, when he drops in to your office to pick up the file note and the wills.'

'Er . . . tomorrow might be best, Superintendent,' replied Hadfield, as he fast ran out of energy or enthusiasm for anything but the comfort of his own bed back in Kilcreddin. Which seemed an eternity away at the moment.

'All right, we might leave it there so,' said Dockrell, as he stood up briskly and opened the door, adding: 'Thank you for your cooperation, gentlemen. Give my best to Lucinda, Mr Hadfield. I'll see you down to reception.'

After perfunctory farewells at ground level, the two men headed back down Harcourt Street towards the Green.

'Well, thanks a bunch for that appointment!' said Hadfield, just as soon as he was safely out of earshot of the Special Branch premises.

'Not at all,' replied FitzHerbert, with a hearty laugh.

'For a while there, I thought I was becoming the chief suspect. To be honest, I'm still not entirely sure where I stand.'

'No need to worry there, James. He was just making you more pliable for the role he had in mind.'

'The role of trying to trip up some kind of serial killer! I mean, what kind of danger is he exposing me to here? Do I really have to do this at all?'

'Of course you don't. But really, you are being a little bit melodramatic. He's just asking you to keep alert when doing your job. In case someone might say something that might be of help to the investigation. Nothing more than that.'

'Why don't you do it? As "special counsel" on the case. You know as much about it as me.'

'I'd love to, James. But that might look a little unusual, don't you think? No, you should view this as a little adventure. An opportunity for a bit of excitement while plying your trade as a stuffy professional. Who knows where it might lead?'

'I don't want it to lead anywhere,' replied an exasperated Hadfield. 'I'm more than happy to just do my stuffy job!'

'And that's all you have to do. You are under no obligation to the Superintendent. Or to the Special Branch.'

'Glad to hear it,' he replied, beginning to relax a little.

'Although,' responded his companion after a short pause, 'you might consider you owe it to old Mr Timmons to try and assist the investigation as best you can.'

'Well . . . yes . . . perhaps . . . I suppose,' was as much as Hadfield could muster in reply.

'I'll leave you here,' said FitzHerbert, as they crossed into the Green. 'I have to get a few things down town. Make sure to keep me up to speed on any developments. I may even pop down to see you, if I get a moment.' And with that he was off in the direction of Grafton Street.

Hadfield slowly walked his way back to the club. He was too tired to think of anything much apart from collecting his suitcase, getting the train and heading straight back home. Except for one further nagging thought. Maybe FitzHerbert was right about his obligation to Timmons.

CHAPTER 13

Hadfield arrived at the office a little late the next morning, having failed – or perhaps not caring – to set the alarm when he took to his bed the previous night.

'Good morning James,' said Hilary, greeting him brightly. 'And how was your weekend?'

'Bit like the curate's egg, I suppose: good in parts.'

'Can an egg be partly good? Surely it's either good or bad.'

'Oh I don't know,' he replied, a little gruffly. 'That's the phrase people use, isn't it? Maybe it doesn't make sense.'

'That's all right, James. Don't worry. Which parts of the weekend did you enjoy?'

'Well, obviously the dinner with Charles. Enjoyed it a bit too much, truth be told. Still feeling it today.'

'And the bad?'

'You won't believe it, but Charles arranged a meeting with Superintendent Dockrell!'

'Why?'

'Because he felt that note of A.T.'s that we looked at might be helpful to their enquiries!'

'That must have put a dampener on the evening.'

'Far from it. He didn't arrange it until the next morning, even though we were up half the night putting a dent in the club's best Cognac. He had the porter wake me first thing to say we had an appointment at Harcourt Street at 10.30!'

'Oh dear!'

'Oh dear is right! It was a bloody nightmare. I don't know how I got through it.'

89

At this stage, Mick's interest had been piqued, and he came into reception from his office.

'How's that, Mr H.?'

'Well, apart from the fact that I had the mother of all hangovers, it seems the Superintendent may be considering me a suspect in all this!'

'In the murders?' Mick asked

'Yes! The murders! He wanted to know where I was. It seems I might have no alibi in either case.'

Both Hilary and Mick looked at him with concern.

'And what's more,' he continued, 'he seems to be trying to establish a motive for me. Through the wills.'

'But you didn't receive anything under the wills,' Hilary mentioned hopefully.

'I know. But being executor. He seemed to think that might be a benefit. And he's wondering about Timmons' will too. Christ, I hope there's nothing in that!'

'Now James, you seem to be a little over-anxious on this,' replied Hilary soothingly. 'He's a detective. I'm sure he was just going through the normal procedures for people who are close to the deceased.'

'That's what FitzHerbert said. In fact, he thinks he was just buttering me up to help the police with their enquiries. I'm not so sure. I had plenty of time to think about it on the way back on the train. I think I'm on his list of suspects, at the very least.'

'Crikey,' interjected Mick, with a somewhat worried expression. 'If you are, maybe we are too.'

'Don't be ludicrous, Mick,' replied Hilary. 'If they suspected us, surely they would have interviewed us by now.'

'But they only interviewed Mr H. yesterday.'

'James,' Hilary continued, ignoring Mick's response, 'how did the Superintendent think you could help him with his enquiries?'

'All the family, as well as Staunton, seem to be suspects. So he wants me to meet them individually to discuss the wills and note down our discussions afterwards, in case it might help the case. I said I didn't think I'd be of much help, as I wouldn't know if anything they said meant anything – unless it related to the bequest. So he is sending up a Detective Sergeant to take me through their statements.'

'When?' asked Hilary.

'This morning. I don't know exactly when. He also wants to take away the original note from A.T.'s file.'

'What note is that?' asked Mick.

'It's an attendance note that Mr Timmons put on Lord Barrington's file the day he died,' replied Hadfield in an exasperated tone. 'It's barely legible, and makes no sense any which way you look at it. I wish I'd never seen it.'

'I better take it from the file and have it ready to hand over,' said Hilary.

'Yes. And you might make a copy of each of the wills. He wants them too.'

'Jeepers, it's all getting a bit close for comfort,' said Mick. 'Maybe they will want to talk to us too. You know, now that I think about it, I'm not sure that I have much of an alibi myself. I left shortly after you on the Friday. I'd be relying on the missus to confirm I was at home for lunch.'

Mick's demeanour indicated such support might not be a foregone conclusion.

'And on the Wednesday evening, I was looking after the kids. They're probably too young to be relied on in evidence.'

With this, Mick began to bite his nails, intently considering his difficult position.

'Mick,' replied Hilary, 'you are completely overanalysing this.'

'Well, do you have an alibi if the Detective Sergeant comes asking?'

'As it happens, no. But I'm not the slightest bit worried.'

'Why's that?' enquired Mick.

'Because I didn't do it. I wasn't there. At the nursing home or the Manor. I'm innocent.'

'So am I. But I don't fancy being Kilcreddin's first miscarriage of justice.'

'It's not going to come to that,' replied Hilary.

'Well, if Mr H. can be a suspect, why can't I? Or you, for that matter.'

'Mick might have a point,' interrupted Hadfield before Hilary could reply. 'It seems Reverend Devereux might even be on the Superintendent's list of suspects. And Boyd too!'

'Why Boyd?' asked Mick.

'Who knows. Just because he's executor, it seems.'

'Hardly the strongest of evidence,' suggested Hilary.

'Well, he was also at the nursing home just before the poisoning,' Hadfield admitted.

'Ah. That might explain it. How did you know that?'

'He told me. On the train. He was going to Dublin at the same time.'

'And the police asked you about that too?' piped up Mick.

'Of course not,' replied Hadfield. 'Superintendent Dockrell already knew it. Boyd had told him.'

'Oh' was all a relieved Mick could say in reply.

'Yes. Albert saw Staunton at the back entrance of the nursing home. And noticed a nurse he didn't recognise. All hugely helpful to the enquiry, no doubt.'

'And are you going to help the police, as they've asked?' queried Hilary.

'Well, I don't have to, it seems. But I suppose if it could go some way to finding out who was responsible for Mr Timmons' poisoning, I should probably do what I can.'

'Very decent of you, James,' commented Hilary appreciatively.

'Well, to be fair, it was FitzHerbert who mentioned that to me yesterday. But I'm sure I would have seen it from that point too, once I'd settled the nerves. Probably no harm to keep in with the Special Branch either.'

'Agreed,' said Mick enthusiastically.

'But I won't be putting my life in danger, that's for sure. Don't forget, any one of these people could be the killer.'

'Very sensible,' said Hilary. 'Just do your job as usual and there should be no risk involved at all.'

'Let's hope so,' he replied, a little gloomily.

'Morning all,' said Lucinda, coming into reception. 'Busy morning ahead in Kilcreddin.'

'Why do you say that?' asked Hadfield.

'Just been speaking to Uncle Bernard. DS Forde should be here shortly. In connection with the murders. He said you are expecting him.'

Hadfield nodded unenthusiastically.

'He's on his way to the Manor first, though,' she continued. 'To arrest Scott Hargreaves.'

'For the murders?' exclaimed Mick.

'I'm not sure. He said they had just received some information and were taking him in.'

'Maybe they have their killer now, James,' suggested Hilary.

'I very much doubt it.'

'Something we should know?'

'Well . . . er . . . I actually saw Scott in Dublin. Leaving the train. In a hurry. With a suitcase.'

They all looked at him.

'Did you tell Superintendent Dockrell that?' asked Hilary.

'No. But he didn't ask. And anyway, how was I supposed to know they wanted to arrest him?'

'A little suspicious, though, didn't you think?' asked Lucinda.

'Not at all. I didn't know he was the killer.'

'If he *is* the killer,' replied Lucinda. 'In fact, I doubt he is. Where's the motive? Unless he's in it with Jasmine.'

'Or he's a hit-man!' suggested Mick. 'He could be in it with anyone.'

'Listen. Enough of all this. Let's get back to work. Busy day ahead.'

Mick and Lucinda disappeared.

'Back to work?' asked Hilary with a smile.

'You know what I mean. By the way, any luck with A.T.'s will?'

'Yes,' replied Hilary, 'there was intermittent correspondence over the years with Montgomery Darley in relation to various personal matters. Wills were mentioned from time to time but there were no specifics, and certainly no copies of any will on file.'

'A draft will maybe?' he asked hopefully.

'No,' was the firm reply.

'I suppose I'll need to get in touch. Just to make sure they are even aware of his death.'

'Yes, I suppose you should. All correspondence was with a Leonard Darley. He's the Senior Partner on the letterhead.'

'I might ring him tomorrow. Or maybe later in the week. I'm not sure if I'm ready for any more surprises just yet.'

'Perfectly understandable,' said Hilary sweetly.

'I think I might try and get through some normal client paperwork,' he said as he headed into his office. 'Any chance of a cup of tea, Hilary? And some biscuits?'

'No problem. I'll have them in to you shortly.'

Hadfield closed the door and sat behind the desk, determined to try and get stuck into some run-of-the-mill legal work to take his mind off things. And to start some forward momentum with the practice. He'd have to knuckle down and concentrate on consolidating existing clients and bringing in new business.

The first item in front of him was the six-page letter in relation to Lord Barrington's shop unit in Dublin with detailed comments on, and amendments to, the draft lease Timmons had prepared. He held it for a while, slowly turning the pages, before leaving it carefully to one side. Definitely not a job for today.

He was about to turn his attention to the less taxing agricultural letting agreements, which were next among the papers in front of him, when Hilary knocked and came in with the tea and biscuits.

'Your tea, James.'

'Thanks, Hilary,' he replied, starting to feel a little more upbeat.

'And a Detective Sergeant Forde is in reception for you.'

'Already?'

'I'm afraid so.'

'God!' he said, as he slumped back in his chair. There was a pregnant pause as he considered his plight. 'All right. Tell him I'll see him in five minutes. I'm definitely having my tea and biscuits first.'

'I'll let him know.'

*

'Please come in, Detective Sergeant,' he said as he opened his office door exactly five minutes later.

'Thank you, Mr Hadfield,' was the reply.

'Take a seat, won't you,' he continued, as he pointed to a chair beside the round meeting table.

'Very kind of you,' said Forde as he eased his large frame into the chair and took in his surroundings. His gaze quickly alighted on the empty tea tray on Hadfield's desk, and lingered there for quite a while.

Hadfield took the hint. 'Some tea, perhaps?'

'That would be lovely,' DS Forde replied, with a bit of a cough, and a look that seemed to be directed at the empty biscuit plate.

'And some biscuits too?'

'Yes, please.'

He stuck his head out the door and asked Hilary for the necessary, taking a seat at the table when he returned – albeit at a decent remove from the Detective Sergeant.

'So, I believe you met Superintendent Dockrell yesterday.'

'That's right.'

'And you have a file note from the deceased, Mr Timmons, that may be of interest.'

'Yes. My secretary has the original. And the copies of the wills of Lord Barrington and Lady Barrington. I'll ask her to drop them in when she brings your tea.'

'Very good' was all the Detective Sergeant replied, before going silent and looking into the middle distance. He had a chubby but plain face, which didn't seem to change its expression at all. Hadfield didn't know if he was expected to say something, but if he was, he didn't know what it was he was supposed to say. He couldn't help but think that DS Forde would make a handy poker player – if detectives were allowed to get involved in that sort of thing. The silence was becoming a little awkward.

'Is that the famous briefcase?' he said eventually.

'That one there? That's Mr Timmons'.'

'A couple of heads rolled yesterday over that.'

'I see.'

Silence descended again.

Finally there was a knock on the door.

'Kettle's boiling,' said Hilary as she came in. 'Thought you might want the file note and copy wills. The draft wills are there too.'

'Yes. Thanks, Hilary. You can give them to Detective Sergeant Forde here. I mentioned you had them.'

Hilary took her leave and DS Forde started reading the file note.

'Interesting' was all he said before putting it back in its cover.

He then commenced reading the wills, and did so very slowly. Hilary came with the tea and left, and the reading continued, with a short stop to pour the tea and munch the biscuits. After what seemed like an eternity, he finished reading the wills and put the copies on the table.

'Yes. Very interesting' was the jewel of information which came forth on this occasion.

There was another pause, at which Hadfield began to think he might be stuck here for the entire day – lunch included, no doubt.

'I understand,' DS Forde finally stated, 'that you will be meeting with each of the beneficiaries to discuss the bequests under the wills. As part of your role as solicitor to the deceased and executor of the wills.'

'Er . . . that's right. The Superintendent suggested I meet them individually.'

'And that it might be useful to have some background to the case, from our own enquiries, to enable you to make any useful . . . ' – there was a further pause, before he added – ' . . . comparisons.'

'That seemed to be the idea.'

'That perhaps you would discuss the bequests. And maybe the case more generally, to get their view on matters. And possibly mentioning the file note of Mr Timmons, and that this had been handed to the police.'

'I think that's what the Superintendent had in mind.'

'And making notes after each meeting, summarising the discussion, in case they might be of help. For us, and as an aide-memoire for you.'

'I suppose that would make sense.'

'Good. Now let me take you through what we have established to date. Feel free to take notes if you wish.'

Hadfield had no interest in taking notes, but felt it prudent to go along with the suggestion. Accordingly, he made a bit of a show of taking a pad and pen from his desk and resuming his position at the table.

CHAPTER 14

'As best we can establish them, the facts can be summarised as follows,' started Detective Sergeant Forde, settling back into his chair and looking up at the ceiling.

'The death of Lord George Barrington occurred at the Rathmore Nursing Home at approximately 12.45 in the afternoon of Friday October the tenth. Death was by poisoning, with a combination of powdered prescription drugs and strichnyne present in Lord Barrington's tea, which was served in Greta Barrington's room shortly beforehand. It's not certain that the drugs on their own would have killed His Lordship but the strichnyne was lethal.

'Mr Boyd had an appointment with Greta Barrington to sign some papers and arrived about 11.45. He says he noted Robert Staunton at the rear entrance at approximately the same time as he went in to Greta Barrington's room. Lord Barrington arrived just after noon and Mr Boyd left approximately ten minutes later. He mentioned seeing a nurse on the corridor as he left Ms Barrington's room, but didn't recognise her as one of the usual staff. It seems that a short time later a nurse arrived at Ms Barrington's room and asked would they like some tea and sandwiches. Ms Barrington didn't recognise her either but assumed she was new, and confirmed the request, but with hot water only for herself.

'Shortly after this, Reverend Devereux called in to Ms Barrington's room. It was an impromptu call, and he only stayed a short while, seeing as Lord Barrington was paying a visit. He recalls it was exactly 12.30 when he left the room.

'It seems that between five and ten minutes after the Reverend's departure, the same nurse returned with the refreshments.' DS Forde paused here, and added: 'Although the word "refreshments" might not be the best description – all things considered.'

This moment of levity passed quietly.

'In any event,' he continued, 'George Barrington quickly took a turn for the worse, and Greta Barrington called out for help and pressed the assistance button in her room.

'It seems Robert Staunton visited nurse Sarah O'Doherty when he arrived. They confirmed that they are seeing each other. Nurse O'Doherty can't vouch for Staunton the entire time, as she was called away for a period. Staunton claims he waited in the staff-room until she returned. He says he didn't call in to Greta Barrington at that stage, as he knew Lord Barrington was visiting. The staff-room is quite close to Ms Barrington's, and both Staunton and O'Doherty were there when they heard her call.

'Both ran into the room, and found George Barrington in serious pain, and having difficulty breathing. Nurse O'Doherty left the room to ring for the ambulance, and tried to locate an inhaler, thinking that an asthmatic attack might be the problem. It was at that stage that she noted that the medicine cabinet had been broken into. By the time she returned, Lord Barrington had passed away.'

Hadfield's hand was getting tired at this stage from his note-taking, and he decided a few questions might slow things down, particularly if he knew the answers already.

'And Miss Greta was unharmed?'

'Yes. As I mentioned, it was the tea that was poisoned. Greta Barrington drank only hot water. Apparently tea or coffee does not agree with her.'

'I see. Yes. And the medicine cabinet. Do we know what was stolen from that?'

'No. Unfortunately the nursing home did not keep very detailed records of what was kept there from time to time. Seems primarily to have been the prescription requirements of the residents, as well as more general over-the-counter medicines. Some of the prescription drugs were noted missing when residents sought their usual medication. Traces of some, but not all, of those missing drugs were identified in the toxicology report.'

'So the murderer breaks in to the medicine cabinet, steals a number of medicines, mixes them up and poisons the tea.'

'That's one possibility.'

'I see. Please continue.'

'Well, the upshot of all this is that we know the cause of death. Now, as to who had the opportunity, it seems that those who were in the nursing home at the time could have managed it. Staunton, obviously. Nurse O'Doherty, possibly. Greta Barrington, maybe. Even Reverend Devereux. Or Boyd. Or any two of them. Or perhaps all of them. Based on the wills, and the relations between the parties, all could be attributed motive. Except perhaps Boyd – but the case isn't closed on potential suspects yet.'

With this, DS Forde looked meaningfully at Hadfield, who wasn't sure if this was a reference to Boyd being executor, or to Hadfield himself.

'And . . . er . . . the rest of the family,' he interjected quickly. 'Their move-ments on the day. Any . . . erm . . . information there?'

'Well, a somewhat similar scenario there. All had a possible motive, cer-tainly if the terms of these wills are anything to go by. As to their whereabouts at the relevant time, not one of them has a cast-iron alibi.

Lydia Barrington was last seen leaving the manor house shortly after 11 o'clock to go riding on the estate. Staunton says he met her briefly up at the wood before departing to the nursing home. She returned just after 1.30 for lunch. Nobody can vouch for her movements during this time.

Lady Barrington's sister Letitia and Clarisse Benoit were in their own rooms, reading and resting, at the time. They have each confirmed the other's alibi, but there is no independent confirmation.

Richard Barrington claims to have been at the estate offices during the rel-evant time, going through the accounts. His jeep was seen arriving there by an employee a little after 11, but it seems he saw no one until he arrived for lunch at the Manor Inn in Rathbawn at about 1.45. That time has been confirmed by the landlady. It's close by the estate, and he's a regular there.

Richard's wife dropped the children to school as normal and had morning coffee in a neighbour's house in Rathbawn at 10.30, staying there for about an hour. She returned home after that and remained in the house alone until pick-ing up the children at 3 o'clock. Plenty of time to get to and from the nursing home there.

Samantha Barrington Russell has a surgery practice in Rathmore. She left early that day, heading off around noon to go 'window shopping' in Kilcreddin, but there are no witnesses to confirm this as yet, save confirmation of the time she left from her receptionist and her husband. She met a friend, Mrs Stafford, for lunch just after 1.30 at the Orchard Tree coffee shop in Kilcreddin, and this has been verified with her.

The doctor's house adjoins the surgery, and her husband, Denis Russell, was there from the time his wife left to when she returned at about 3. He had lunch at home and read the papers until it was time to collect their young son from school – which he did at 2.30. It seems he's a house-husband. A retired solicitor, I gather. The school confirmed he generally drops off and collects the young fellow, and did so on the day. So, opportunity there too, for either or both.

Jasmine Barrington returned from Dublin on Friday morning. She claims to have left around 11.30, but there is no one to vouch for her movements at all until she arrived at the Manor at approximately 1.30 – about the same time as Lady Barrington. So a diversion to the nursing home on the way cannot be discounted. Her friends, Scott and Penny, say they were with her. But again, no independent confirmation on that.'

DS Forde paused, let out a sigh and put his hands on his stomach, before continuing. 'And that accounts – or doesn't account – for the movements of the other family members on the date in question. Nothing really to add until the next Wednesday evening. At the Manor. Except perhaps Simon Armstrong. Bad blood between him and Lord Barrington, I gather. No alibi for the time of death at the nursing home. Not sure how he had the opportunity at the Manor, though. Everyone else did. If we start with . . . .'

Hadfield was flagging once again, and concerned that the DS was about to embark on another lengthy soliloquy.

'Er . . . perhaps some fresh tea? And some biscuits?'

The Detective Sergeant's poker face seemed to brighten up ever so slightly. 'That would be nice.'

'One moment,' replied Hadfield, moving quickly to the door and opening it. 'I'll just see if I can locate my secretary,' he continued, while closing the door quickly after him.

Hilary was sitting in her usual place in reception, facing Hadfield, with a questioning look.

'You can locate me right here,' she pointed out.

'Shh. I just need to get out for a few minutes. I'm taking notes of everything, and my hand's wrecked. And my brain. You might give it a minute or two, and take out the tray and tell him the tea is on the way. I'll pop in to Mick's room and go back in with you when the tea is ready.'

'All right.'

He headed in to the adjoining office, closed the door behind him and stood against it.

'How's it going there, Mr H.?'

'Painful. He's giving me a summary of what they know, and I have to write it all down. I think my hand's going numb.'

'Any mention of us yet?'

'No, thank God. But Boyd is still in the frame – even though he's only executor. He says they are still looking into that.'

'Looking into what?'

'Damned if I know!'

There was a glum, worried silence.

After a while, Mick whispered: 'What are you doing in here?'

'I'm waiting for the tea to be ready. Giving my hand a break. And I don't want to give him a chance to ask me too many questions,' he whispered back.

Mick nodded. 'Good thinking,' he said, and fell silent again. Eventually there was a light tap on the door and Hilary stuck her head in.

'You can come out now if you want,' she said.

'Oh. Right. Hold on. I'll open the door for you.'

Hilary placed the fresh tea tray on the table in front of DS Forde, and exited quietly.

'Sorry about the delay. Hilary was . . . er . . . looking for a file. Just gave her a hand with that.'

'Will I do the necessary?'

Hadfield, a little unsure, just looked at the Detective Sergeant blankly.

'Will I pour the tea?' he explained.

'Oh, yes please,' replied Hadfield. 'So. Er . . . you were mentioning the Wednesday evening, at the Manor.'

'That's right,' said DS Forde, pausing while he finished his third biscuit from the plate and taking in a good slurp of tea. 'Of course, you were there that afternoon, so should know the details of that.'

'That's right.'

'Well, from what we can gather, the poison had to be administered some time that day. Most likely between when Lady Barrington left the room to speak to Mr Timmons and before she saw him again that evening at 7.30. All the guests would have had the opportunity to access the study at some point during that period.'

'Where was the poison?'

'In the decanters. It seems they each had a sherry which contained the poison. The same poison as was used at the nursing home. Sherry was Her Ladyship's favourite evening tipple. The staff confirmed she had taken one from the decanter the previous evening, so the poison had to have been applied at some point after that.'

'So Andrew had a sherry too.'

'Yes. But the murderer was taking no chances: the poison was applied to the whiskey and brandy decanters as well. Likely they wanted to get rid of your boss too, and weren't sure what he might take.'

'And anyone could have got into the study to do it?'

'Seems so. Those in the house had ample opportunity. And those who came separately – Reverend Devereux and Mr Boyd – would have passed by on their arrival, or while using the facilities.'

'So who discovered the murders?'

'The butler, Carston, was proposing to announce dinner for 8, and entered the study to consult with Lady Barrington.' The Detective Sergeant paused, to consume the final biscuit, and continued: 'As we know, that proved impossible. They were both dead by then.'

'Who was the last to see them alive?'

'Carston. He brought Timmons into the study.'

'How about Clarisse?'

'Clarisse?'

'Clarisse Benoit. She witnessed the will. Look.'

DS Forde inspected the will where it had been witnessed.

'I see. Hmm. Might need to ask about that. Bigger worries at the moment, though. That fellow Scott Hargreaves. He seems to have bolted.'

'Oh?' replied Hadfield, a little awkwardly.

'Yes. I was due to pick him up at the Manor. Unannounced, of course. But he's gone. No one seems to know where.'

'I . . . er . . . might be able to help . . . .'

'How's that, Mr Hadfield?'

'Well . . . .'

Hadfield slowly divulged what he knew.

'I see,' said the Detective Sergeant. 'You might give me a moment.'

DS Forde produced a mobile phone and exited the room. He returned about a minute later. 'I had better be on my way. Any questions before I go?'

'No, I don't think so. Except the items found at Staunton's cottage. What about them?'

'Obviously we searched his house after the first murder. But found nothing. We decided to revisit after the murders at the Manor, and found various discarded medicines in his rubbish bin, which was due for collection the next day. They corresponded with some of those stolen from the nursing home, as best we could tell. However, we found others in the neighbouring bins as well, which also match. No fingerprints, I'm afraid.'

'I see. A little inconclusive, perhaps.'

'We shall see. Now, tell me. How long had you known Mr Timmons?'

'Erm . . . since I joined as an apprentice – over fifteen years ago.'

'And the others in the firm?'

'Well, Hilary has been here even longer. About twenty years. And our law clerk, Mick, joined maybe eight years ago. Why do you ask?'

'Standard practice to ascertain the people the deceased knew. Did he have any family?'

'Not now. He had a sister, but I believe she died a little over a year ago.'

'And friends.'

'I couldn't really say. Quite a wide circle. Mainly office-related. His work was very important to him.'

'I see. Any word on his will?'

'Not yet. We have the name of the firm in Dublin he dealt with for personal matters. We're following up on that.'

'Good. You might let us know what transpires there.'

'Yes, Detective Sergeant. Of course.'

Hadfield escorted DS Forde to reception.

'Thank you for the tea and biscuits, Ms Byrne.'

'Not at all.'

Hadfield noted that Mick's door was firmly closed.

'Here's my number,' said the Detective Sergeant, turning to Hadfield. 'Feel free to contact me if you have any questions. Or *further* information.'

'Thank you, Detective Sergeant, I will be sure to do that.'

Whereupon Hadfield closed the front door and peeped through the curtain of the adjacent window. After a while he turned to Hilary and said: ' I certainly hope that's the last visit we'll ever have from him!'

CHAPTER 15

As DS Forde's departure coincided with lunchtime, Hadfield suggested a bite to eat – and all four promptly crossed the road to the Riverside Inn. Business was quiet, and they took the same table as they had the previous week. Morton greeted them from behind the bar, saying he would be with them in a minute.

'So,' whispered Mick, 'what had the DS to say?'

'Quite a lot, actually,' replied Hadfield. 'Mainly filling me in on what they know. My head's spinning, to be honest, but I think I got it all down.'

'But what about us? Any questions there?'

'Well, he wanted to know how long we've been with the firm.'

'Oh God. I knew it. When is he going to interrogate us?'

'He didn't mention that. I think he's waiting to hear what's in A.T.'s will. He seemed keen that we follow up on that.'

'I'd be keen that we *don't* follow up on that.'

'Now Mick,' interjected Hilary, 'that would only be increasing any suspicions they have. Assuming they have any suspicions at all.'

'Hilary's right. I'd better get in touch with Montgomery Darley. Before the police start doing it themselves.'

'Did you mention seeing Scott Hargreaves?' asked Lucinda.

'Indeed I did. He was on his phone in a flash.'

Just then, Morton arrived. 'Afternoon all. What can I do you for?'

'Just a ham sandwich, on white,' replied Hadfield.

'Same here,' added a despondent Mick.

'Chicken on brown for me, Peter,' said Hilary.

'And me,' added Lucinda.

'Tea all round?'

They nodded their assent, except Hadfield. 'Not for me, Peter. Had enough of that this morning. Some coffee to keep me going, I think.'

'Was that the police with you earlier?' Morton enquired.

'How the heck did you know that?' squawked Mick – before realising he'd given away the answer with his question.

'I saw the car pull up. A dead giveaway. And the burly chap getting out had Special Branch written all over him.'

'As it happens,' responded Hadfield, 'he was a detective sergeant from Harcourt Street. We had made arrangements to meet him to make available some information that might be relevant to the case.'

'Must have been a lot of information. He was there a good while.'

'Nothing you need concern yourself with, Peter,' replied Hilary. 'Entirely confidential, as I'm sure you would appreciate.'

'Of course,' said Morton with a smile, as he headed back to the bar.

'Sorry,' groaned Mick. 'Now the whole parish will know we're suspects.'

'We are not suspects,' replied Hilary, 'and it doesn't matter what people think. James just needs to concentrate on what he is going to do next.'

'You're right,' he replied. 'I need to get stuck into proper client work. We won't be in business for long at this rate.'

'Actually, James, I meant: what you intend to do to help the police, as the Superintendent requested.'

'Oh. Yes. I suppose I had better send a letter to each of the beneficiaries proposing a meeting. The same one should do for each, I think.'

'Will I do a draft for you?'

'Please Hilary, that would be great.'

'No problem.'

'And actually, would you mind typing up the notes I wrote this morning with the DS. In case they are needed. I can't read my own writing if I leave it too long.'

Mick had been fidgeting the whole time during this discussion, and finally interrupted. 'What I don't understand is why the police are interested in Mr Timmons' will at all. What has that got to do with anything?'

'Well,' replied Hadfield, 'I suppose the wills of Lord and Lady Barrington have provided motive for a number of people in respect of their deaths. They might think A.T.'s will could establish further motive.'

'But who would want to kill Mr Timmons?' asked Lucinda.

'Nobody,' replied Hilary, 'unless they benefited from the will. Or thought he knew something.'

'But nobody knows what's in the will. Or even where it is,' replied Mick.

'True,' said Hilary. 'As far as we know. But the police can't be sure, so they have to consider it.'

Just then Fiona, the waitress, arrived with their order. 'Afternoon,' she said, as she put down the tray. 'How are we all today?'

The four of them confirmed they were well.

'Didn't see you around this weekend, Mr H. Away, were we?'

'Just up in Dublin.'

'Business or pleasure?'

'Er . . . just visiting a friend, Fiona.'

'She wasn't all business, I hope.'

'*He,* actually,' replied Hadfield, becoming a little flustered. 'An old friend from college. We had a very enjoyable dinner.'

'I hear the police are after you.'

'No, Fiona,' interrupted Hilary, 'the police are not after James, or any of us. They were checking some of Mr Timmons' papers, in case they might be of help in their enquiries. You seem to have forgotten the salt and pepper. And some mustard would be nice with the ham. While the tea's hot.'

Fiona sought out the requested items, and placed them on the table.

'Enjoy . . . *while you can,*' she said, smiling sweetly as she left.

'Oh, great. Look who's just arrived,' said Mick.

'Who are they?' asked Lucinda.

'Simon Armstrong. And two of his cronies. Trouble usually follows him.'

'Ah! There they are!' exclaimed Armstrong from the bar counter. 'The great defenders of the privileged.'

'What the hell?' started Hadfield.

'Just ignore him, James,' interrupted Hilary.

'In league with the police as well, I see. Don't think we'll be pushed around that easy. The Barringtons have to learn to respect the law. Just like everyone else. You'll find out soon enough . . . .'

'Now Simon,' interrupted Morton. 'Pipe down there. I've told you many a time. Don't bring your causes in here. It's a hostelry. Not a courthouse.'

Armstrong turned away to converse with his colleagues.

'What's up with him?' asked Lucinda.

'The usual,' said Mick. 'He's had it in for the Barringtons for years. The latest is the tree-cutting at the estate near Rathbawn. Richard is starting a stud farm there, and Armstrong and his lot have been objecting.'

'Hmm. Could he be a suspect? You know, I'm pretty sure I've seen him speaking with that fellow Hargreaves.'

'DS Forde mentioned him, all right,' replied Hadfield. 'Seems he has no alibi for Lord Barrington's death. But said it was difficult to see how he could have got in to the Manor.'

'Maybe there are two different murderers,' suggested Lucinda.

'Except the same poison was used,' replied Hadfield.
'Maybe he was in cahoots with Scott Hargreaves,' countered Mick.
'Maybe let's have lunch,' said Hilary.
They all agreed.

*

Hadfield had been working steadily at his desk for about an hour after lunch, when Hilary knocked on the door and came in.
'Reverend Devereux is in reception. He says he'd like a word if you are free. He was just passing by, and understands if you are too busy.'
'Did he say what it's about?'
'No. It might even just be a social call. I couldn't be sure.'
'Better see him, I suppose. Tell him I'm just finishing something here, and will be with him in a few minutes.'
'Tea and biscuits?'
'If there's any left!'
He finished dictating the letter he was working on, tidied his desk, and brought the Reverend in to the office.
'Good afternoon, Reverend. Please take a seat.'
'Thank you. You're very kind. This was Andrew's office, wasn't it?'
'That's right. I've had to take over the files, so it made sense to. . . .'
'Of course, of course, my good fellow. How have you all been getting on without dear old Mr Timmons?'
'It was a terrible shock, of course. And the place will never be the same without him. But client requirements remain the same.'
'Very true, very true. The show must go on – in life and in death.'
Just then, Hilary knocked on the door and brought in the tea.
'Oh, lovely. Now tell me, Miss Byrne, have you managed to find a decent Protestant chap yet. There are a few still left in the area, you know.'
'Not as yet, but I'll let you know first thing. They'd have to convert to Catholicism, of course.'
'Surely a matter for some debate, at least. In the interests of spiritual harmony.'
'All hypothetical at the moment, Reverend, but God works in mysterious ways,' she replied, leaving the room as expeditiously as etiquette permitted.
'You're a Catholic too, I believe, Mr Hadfield.'
'Yes, although not perhaps the most ardent of the parishioners.'
'Any chance of converting you, then?'
'I'm not that unconvinced just yet.'
'Of course, Timmons had a strong belief. A great supporter of the church down the years. He'll be greatly missed. Both personally and . . . er . . . financially.'
'Yes, he was a good man.'

'We would very much hope,' said the Reverend, adopting a solemn pose, 'that the firm could continue its generous support, as before.'

'Well, we'd have to give some thought . . . .'

'Of course all the local parishioners, particularly the Barringtons, were very appreciative of all the contributions made. As I used to say to Andrew, it was as good for his business as it was for his soul.'

'I see. Obviously I have just got my feet under the desk, so to speak. I'll need to do a full review and try and get an overall picture of the practice. I'll ask Hilary to look into the charitable side of things.'

'I'll drop in a list to her in the morning. Church repairs, the annual fête, that kind of thing.'

'That would be . . . er . . . helpful.'

'Actually, on the subject of the annual fête, I was hoping you could assist me with a little query I have.'

'Er . . . If I can.'

'Well you see, Lydia, God rest her soul, was very dedicated to the fête. Long before she became Lady Barrington. It was the most important event of the year for her. There were differences of opinion of course, particularly with Miss Greta, but thanks to her tireless efforts, success was always guaranteed. Of course, Lady Barrington could never be replaced, but we must strive to ensure that standards are maintained at the highest level.'

At this point, Reverend Devereux paused and leaned towards Hadfield with a conspiratorial demeanour. 'A greater concern, I have to say, is the financial side of matters. As I've mentioned, Lady Barrington was very generous with her time. She was also very adept at obtaining donations from others. I often wondered, sometimes openly to her, how we could continue our great tradition without her. She of course dismissed these concerns, and was fond of saying that the fête went on before she came, and would continue to go on without her.'

The Reverend sat back in his seat, smiling vacantly, as if in a reverie.

'Yes, Reverend,' began Hadfield, who was starting to think that this reminiscence might never end. 'I just wonder how I . . . .'

'Sorry, please forgive me. Got lost in thought there. Now here's where I'm hoping you can help me. You see, Lydia mentioned during one of our more recent discussions that she had in fact addressed my financial concerns directly herself. Of course, I had no idea what she meant, but after a little probing, she indicated that she would make provision for the continued running of the fête. In her will.'

Reverend Devereux paused at this stage, to see if his disclosure would elicit any response. Hadfield said nothing, so he continued.

'Now I'm sure that the beneficiaries will all be contacted in due course. But I was very much hoping that you might be able to confirm the bequest – and perhaps the amount – just so that we could plan accordingly. For the future, of course. It would be very helpful.'

The Reverend was leaning very close to Hadfield at this point, with an imploring expression which was no doubt well practised – although today it seemed genuine.

Hadfield leaned back, before saying: 'Well, formalities have yet to be completed, of course.'

'Of course.'

'But I can confirm that Lady Barrington made a will. And that she made a significant bequest for the benefit of the fête.'

'Yes!' interrupted the Reverend. 'Thank you, Lord. You've answered my prayers. And thank you, Lady Barrington. I knew you would not fail us. This is wonderful news, Mr Hadfield. The . . . er . . . amount.'

'A quarter of a million, actually.'

'Splendid. Splendid.'

'There are a few conditions, of course.'

Reverend Devereux shifted a little in his chair.

'Conditions?'

'Yes. Any decisions on use of the funds have to be by agreement.'

'Whose agreement?'

'Well, yourself obviously.'

'I see. Good. And . . . .'

'Miss Greta.'

'Oh.'

'And Albert Boyd.'

'Ah.'

A somewhat deflated Reverend sat back in his seat.

'Not uncommon, Reverend. Especially with such a large sum.'

'Of course. Yes. Quite right. 'He paused, before adding: 'Do we all have to agree on any . . . er . . . expenditure, then.'

'Yes. A unanimous decision would be needed.'

'I see. I had thought . . . .' His voice trailed off as he fell into contemplation as to the ramifications of these details on the most important event in the calendar.

Silence reigned for a while. It occurred to Hadfield that the bequest in Lord Barrington's will might cheer him up.

'Of course, Lord Barrington's will may be of interest to the church.'

The Reverend perked up somewhat at that. 'Oh?'

'Yes, he made a number of specific donations. Most of them small, but in one case the sum is quite significant.'

Reverend Devereux's interest was certainly piqued now.

'Yes, yes, please go on.'

'The larger donation is for the benefit of the church.'

'Excellent! Good old George. You couldn't be sure, but I always felt he wouldn't let us down. How much . . . er . . . how much would we be talking about. Approximately.'

'It's not that straightforward, actually. A lump sum is to be invested in low-risk securities. These monies may be drawn on from time to time, but only where required for repairs to the church and maintenance of the graveyard. Again, three trustees are nominated to oversee all this, and of course you yourself are one of those named.'

'Ah yes. Very good. Most generous.' Reverend Devereux's responses lacked a certain enthusiasm.

'You weren't expecting this, I take it.'

'No . . . er . . . great news of course. Very thoughtful of Lord Barrington to look after the church like that. You didn't mention the figure . . . .'

'Fifty thousand pounds.'

'Ah. Wonderful news. Obviously I'll need to get in touch with my fellow trustees, I suppose. Well, that has been very helpful, Mr Hadfield. Thank you for seeing me.'

'A word of warning, Reverend, if I may.'

'Oh?'

'This is highly confidential.'

'I see. Understood, my good fellow.'

'The police have been showing a keen interest in the wills. And in particular the beneficiaries of the wills. It seems that anyone who received a bequest is a potential suspect.'

'Suspect? Why?'

'Well, it seems nobody has an alibi for the time of Lord Barrington's death.'

'Who are we talking about?'

'They are not just considering Staunton. The children and their spouses could be suspects. The others staying at the Manor too.'

'And they think one of them killed George?'

'They aren't excluding the possibility until they find the murderer.'

'I see.'

'They aren't the only ones on their list, though. Unfortunately, you may be there too.'

'What! Good heavens! Why would I be a suspect?'

'Because of the bequests under the wills.'

'But I didn't even know they had given anything!'

'But you perhaps expected them to do so.'

Reverend Devereux went silent for a while, coming to terms with this turn of events.

'I thought it was Rob Staunton they were investigating.'

'They seemed to have widened that. The terms of the wills, I suppose. They were here today to take copies. And a note which Mr Timmons had left on his file the afternoon he died. I'm just warning you that anybody who is seen to benefit from the wills and doesn't have an alibi is under suspicion.'

'I see.'

'If it's any consolation, I might be on their list too, even though I didn't get a bequest. It seems just being an executor is enough to raise their suspicions. So myself and Mr Boyd haven't been excluded from their enquiries.'

'This is all a bit far-fetched, surely?'

'Agreed.'

'I mean, I saw Lord Barrington alive before I left the nursing home.'

'But can you prove that you didn't administer the poison?'

'I was doing my round of visits. First in the nursing home, until about 12.30, and then back at Rathbawn. I was on the move the whole time, and headed back to the rectory just after 2 o'clock.'

'But can anyone account for your movements the whole time?'

'Well, the people I visited, obviously. Oh, and actually I saw Margaret Barrington driving towards her house about then. I beeped the horn, although I can't be sure if she noticed me.'

Hadfield was surprised by this, as he knew Richard's wife, Margaret, had said she was in her house from about noon until 3, but made no mention of a drive during this time.

'I think the police are more interested in your whereabouts up until 12.45, when, they estimate, Lord Barrington died.'

'Well, I was in the nursing home, of course.'

'But were you with someone the whole time?'

'Of course. Except when I was arriving and leaving.' With this, Reverend Devereux paused. 'Ah. I see your point. *I* might know I didn't do it, but do the police?'

'I think you will find, Reverend, that we are all in a similar position.'

'Dear me. Does this mean we can't use the money?'

'Well, we have to go through probate first – which will take a while. I'm sure matters will be resolved long before then.'

'Yes, yes. Let's hope so.' The Reverend seemed quite drained as he said this. 'I had planned to make a few more visits, but I might just head back to the rectory and have a rest.'

'Of course. Now, if there is anything else I can do to help . . . .'

'Thank you. You've been most kind. . . . You mentioned a note from Mr Timmons . . . .'

'Yes, couldn't really make much sense of it. Seems Lady Barrington may have wanted him to look into a few matters for her.'

'In relation to the murders?'

'Most likely.'

'I see. . . . Well, better be on my way.'

Hadfield escorted the Reverend to the door and bade farewell, although Devereux managed to recollect himself sufficiently to say he would try and have his 'charitable' list dropped in the next day.

CHAPTER 16

'Well,' enquired Hilary, 'what had the good Reverend to say?'

'Quite a bit, actually.'

'I suppose he was hinting at continuing donations.'

'More than hinting. It seems it might be bad for business if we don't live up to Mr Timmons' generosity. He's going to drop in a list of the worthy causes tomorrow, to save us the trouble of checking our files!'

'How thoughtful.'

'Yes, wasn't it. I suspect, though, that the real reason for his visit was to find out what was in Lady Barrington's will. She had led him to believe that she might make a significant bequest for the benefit of the fête.'

'So the Reverend could be said to have a motive for killing Lady Barrington.'

'Exactly. But he didn't seem to know anything about Lord Barrington's will, so it's hard to see why he might have bumped him off.'

'Assuming the murderer is one and the same.'

'True. Actually, on the subject of motive, the Reverend made some interesting points during our little chat. It seems that Lydia and Miss Greta didn't always see eye to eye on matters relating to the fête.'

'A motive for Greta Barrington, then?'

'Possibly. Although the good Reverend is a little more concerned for himself at this stage. When I asked him about an alibi for his movements on the Friday, he couldn't really say he was in the clear.'

'The plot thickens.'

'Well it does, actually, because when he was trying to remember his movements, he mentioned he'd seen Margaret Barrington driving towards her house at about 2 PM.'

'When she should have been at home until about 3.'

'Exactly!' Hadfield paused at this point, before adding: 'How did you know that?'

'I've just typed up your notes. Here they are.'

'Oh, thanks. I'll have a look through them now. Hopefully the writing wasn't too bad.'

'No worse than usual.'

'Actually, I think I'll dictate a little note of my meeting with Reverend Devereux, to put with these.'

'Not a bad idea. Obviously DS Forde wasn't aware of *all* her movements on the Friday. I'm sure he'd be interested in that.'

'Very likely,' Hadfield replied, a little gloomily, as the prospect of a further meeting with the Special Branch hoved in to view.

'I have also prepared a draft of that letter to the beneficiaries. It's with the notes.'

'Thanks. I'll look at that now as well.'

He retired to his office and sat back at his desk. The paperwork he had put aside when Reverend Devereux had dropped in was not calling to him as strongly as it had after lunch. The six-page letter on the Henry Street store would have to be deferred to another day.

He read through Hilary's transcript of his notes first, before dictating a summary of the salient points of his discussion with Devereux. He then turned to Hilary's draft letter to the beneficiaries, which read as follows:

Dear   ,

I am writing to you in connection with the estates of Lord and Lady Barrington, who both passed away so tragically earlier this month. Please accept my condolences.

It should of course have been Mr Timmons' duty to make contact with you in these circumstances but, as you doubtless know, our esteemed partner was taken from us in a similarly tragic manner, and it has fallen to me to take on the responsibility of managing the legal issues now arising.

As the terms of the wills may have some consequence for you, I believe it would be helpful if we were to meet to discuss these matters directly in private. This might also present an opportunity for me to address any queries you may have in relation to the process generally.

If in order, please contact our offices to make an appointment to meet with me at a time that is convenient for you.

I look forward to hearing from you.

Yours sincerely,

James Hadfield

Timmons & Associates

He read the letter through a couple of times but decided he couldn't put it any better himself. His mind turned to Hilary. Was she actually seeing Hugh Stokes? He was surprised to find that the thought of this irked him a little bit. Or possibly even more than a little bit. It shouldn't, of course, as there had been various suitors over the years, and he had never given any indication to Hilary of any interest himself. He had always thought that one's work life and personal life should be kept separate. Were his feelings changing, now that circumstances were different in the office? Or because FitzHerbert had mentioned that her single status might be down to him? Or because over two years had passed since Deirdre had died? He wasn't quite sure what to think. One thing was certain, though: Hilary was a vital part of the office, and it would suffer badly without her.

'They're all fine,' said Hadfield, as he went back out to reception with the notes and the draft. 'You might do up letters for each of them: Richard, Samantha, Jasmine, Greta and Robert.'

'No need for one to go to Reverend Devereux, I suppose?'

'No. I think we've covered the ground there. Don't want to give him the chance to come back on another charity drive.'

'I can understand that. And Letitia too?'

'Hmm. I guess so. I'll sign them in the morning, and Mick can deliver them by hand.'

'What was that, Mr H.?' said Mick, popping his head around his office door.

'I'm sending letters to each of the beneficiaries to arrange individual meetings. Can you drop them round by hand in the morning?'

'No problem. I hear Reverend Devereux is in the frame. With Miss Greta. And maybe Margaret Barrington too.'

Hadfield looked at Hilary, who just raised an eyebrow.

'I wouldn't put it as strongly as that.'

'It might take the heat off us, at least.'

'Well, it might give the police a little more to think about, at any rate,' he replied. 'Just make sure to bring your moped with you in the morning.'

'Will do,' said Mick, closing his door – although, as usual, not entirely.

'I think I might call it a day,' Hadfield said to Hilary. 'The weekend catching up on me a bit at this stage.'

'I can imagine.'

'Did you . . . er . . . did you get up to anything interesting yourself over the weekend?'

'Nothing out of the ordinary. Just a bit of horse-riding on Saturday.'

'Ah. The Horse Club.'

'Well, I'm not actually a member of the club. I've only taken it up recently. There is an annual fee to be a member. And you would have to apply to a committee to join. I just book a spot when it suits, and pay for it on the day.'

'Do you go anywhere afterwards, as a rule?'

'Usually the Manor Inn in Rathbawn. They section off an area for sandwiches and drinks. And they have a separate function room they use for Socials.'

'Sounds like fun.'

'It is. You should try it some time.'

'Perhaps,' he replied doubtfully, remembering his one – painful – experience at horse-riding a number of years previously. 'What kind of people go along?'

'Mixed bunch in our group. We ride out separately from the members. But we join up in the bar afterwards. Turned into a bit of a sing-song on Saturday. Richard was in flying form. Buying drinks all round. You'd never think he'd just lost his father and stepmother.'

'Pretty bad form.'

'Yes. And he was giving more and more attention to Katherine Rennick as the night went on. Although she didn't seem to mind.'

'Is she the one who was widowed last year? Lives the Dublin side of Kilcreddin.'

'That's her. Pleasant enough – if a bit snooty.'

'I take it Margaret wasn't there.'

'No. It seems she has no interest in horses.'

'And . . . er . . . you mentioned . . . what was it?' he continued hesitatingly – although knowing exactly the word he was looking for – 'er . . . "Socials". I think that's what you called it. What are they like?'

'I haven't been. But I gather they are a little more formal. About once a month. Sit-down dinners. For members only, but they can bring a guest.'

'I suppose the Barringtons would be a big part of all that.'

'Yes. I gather they are all keen horse-people.'

'And the Stokes.' Presumably they're . . . er . . . fully involved too.'

'Well, yes. But Lord Barrington was President, or Captain, or whatever they call it. The rides all took place on the estate, with his permission. I suppose Richard has his eye on running the show now that he is getting the estate.'

'Hmm. Another motive to throw in to the pot, perhaps.'

'Maybe,' replied Hilary dubiously.

'And maybe not. I know what you mean. I think I've had enough detective work for one day. I'm heading off.'

'See you tomorrow.'

Hadfield took his coat, left the office and headed homewards, back up the hill. It was starting to get dark, and a full moon was clearly visible high

115

in the sky. The effect was eerie, but at the same time felt curiously romantic. He was relieved to know that Hilary had not yet been to any of the Horse Club Socials – either with Hugh Stokes or anyone else. But he couldn't help feeling that he might have to get a move on himself. And preferably before the next Social.

CHAPTER 17

Hadfield arrived early the next day, determined to put a dent in the paper-work on his desk. He also wanted to follow up with Montgomery Darley in relation to Mr Timmons' will. He finished up the files he had been working on the previous day, and also dealt with some miscellaneous correspondence that had recently been received. It was approaching 11 AM as he put the Henry Street file in front of him. He decided that a call to Timmons' solicitors should be dealt with first. He got their number from the Law Directory, and placed a call.

'Montgomery Darley Solicitors. Good morning,' a pleasant female voice responded, after a few rings.

'Good morning. My name is James Hadfield, of Timmons & Associates. I was hoping to speak with Mr Darley.'

'I'm afraid that will not be possible, sir.'

'Oh?'

'Mr Darley passed away last June.'

'I'm sorry. I didn't know.'

'Could I ask what you were calling about.'

'Actually it was about Mr Timmons himself, who was the principal of this firm. He ... er ... passed away too quite recently. I was making enquiries about his will.'

'I see. I think Mr Timmons' matters were taken over by Ms Curtis. I'll just check if she's available. Could you wait one moment.'

After a short interval, the pleasant voice returned: 'I'm putting you through now.'

'Thank you.'

'Good morning, Mr Hadfield. Violet Curtis here.' A not-so-pleasant and very business-like voice took over.

'Good morning. Thank you for taking the call.'

'I understand you were enquiring about Mr Timmons' will.'

'That's right. He passed away quite recently, and I was just following up to see if people were aware of the situation. In case there was a will. The files indicated he dealt with Leonard Darley.'

'Yes, we check the death notices, and were aware of his passing. Please accept our condolences. He did make a will, and we have it here. As a matter of fact, we sent a letter to you on Friday, advising the position, and suggesting a meeting at our offices at a suitable time, to review matters.'

'Oh. I see. It may be in this morning's post. I haven't checked it yet.'

'I would be available at 3 PM this Friday, if that suits.'

'Well, let me see. . . . I think I'm free that day. I'd have to get the train up, so . . . .'

'Very good. Three PM Friday it is, so. Any problems, please let us know.'

'Er . . . OK.'

'Goodbye.'

The phone had clicked before he had a chance to reciprocate the farewell.

Hadfield headed out to reception.

'Just spoke to Montgomery Darley,' he said to Hilary.

'And?'

'They have the will all right. Leonard Darley's dead, but there's a pretty efficient Ms Curtis looking after it now.'

'I see.'

'She says they sent me a letter on Friday.'

'This might be it,' replied Hilary, handing him a letter marked 'Private and Confidential'. 'It came in this morning's post.'

He took the letter, opened it, and read it through quickly.

'Listen to this,' he said, and read the letter aloud:

Dear Mr Hadfield,

It is with great sadness that we must inform you of the death of Mr Timmons, late of Hillside Lodge, Hillside Lane, Kilcreddin and formerly the principal of Timmons & Associates, High Street, Kilcreddin.

As solicitors attending to the probate of the deceased's will, we are contacting you as a person who may be concerned with the administration of his estate. To enable us progress this administration we would ask that you contact our offices at your earliest convenience to arrange a meeting to discuss matters and deal with any queries that may arise.

Yours sincerely,
Violet Curtis
Partner
Montgomery Darley

'What do you make of that?' said a wide-eyed Hadfield.

'The same as I made of this,' replied Hilary, handing him a letter from the same firm, in the same terms, addressed to her.

'Good Lord!'

'I got one too,' piped up Mick, from behind his door.

'What does it all mean?' asked Hadfield, to no one in particular.

'What it usually means, I suppose,' said Hilary.

'A bequest!' said Mick, coming into the reception area.

'Do you think so? I suppose it must. Unless they just want information. Or documents. Or there are executor provisions. Or . . . .'

'Only one way to find out,' interrupted Hilary.

'Actually, I've already made an appointment for 3 PM this Friday, at their offices. Or should I say, Ms Curtis required that I be there at that time to see her.'

'Should we all go together?' asked Mick.

'I don't know,' he replied, thinking over the suggestion for a moment, but not seeing any obvious objection to it. 'I don't see why not. Better check with Ms Curtis, I would think.'

'We'd have to close the office for the afternoon,' mentioned Hilary.

'Let's do it. Lucinda can keep an eye on things if necessary. We might as well find out what it's all about sooner rather than later.'

'I'm not sure whether I should be excited or worried,' said Mick, as he thought about the consequences for the police investigation. 'Will we have to report back to DS Forde?'

'I suppose so,' said Hadfield, as he rubbed his chin and considered the possibilities.

'Do you want to sign those letters now?' Hilary asked.

'What?' he replied, somewhat lost in thought.

'Your own letters to the beneficiaries.'

'Oh yes! Of course. I'll sign them now, and Mick can deliver them before lunch.'

He signed the letters, made himself a strong cup of coffee, and headed back into his office.

*

Hadfield sat back in Timmons' old chair, drinking his coffee and thinking about his boss's will. Could it just be a bequest? He'd never been that close to him. The relationship had always been one of master and servant. They had got on well, but socialising together was not a regular occurrence. Was he an executor? This seemed unlikely, as Timmons had used Montgomery Darley to make the will. If he wanted an executor with a legal background, surely he would have gone with Darley or someone in that firm. Maybe they wanted to track down the title documents for the office. And the house. But a written request for that should have sufficed. And why letters to Hilary and Mick too? Probably just some small bequests. But why bring them all the way to Dublin for that? Was there some other purpose?

Eventually he finished his coffee and gave up on the analysis, having formed no firm view on the subject. He turned his attention to the Henry Street file, and the six-page letter from McGuigan McGuirk & Mooney. He noted that, in addition to the six pages of queries and comments, they had also sent on a document with about forty questions on title and planning matters. And returned the twenty-page lease Timmons had sent out, with dozens of handwritten amendments on each page. He sank back into his chair. This case was going to be painful.

He was about halfway through the letter when Hilary knocked on the door and came in.

'There's someone here to see you.'

'What? Did they make an appointment?'

'No.'

'Well I can't see them then. I'm trying to get through this damn Henry Street drivel.'

'I think you will want to see her.'

'Her? Why?'

'It's Jasmine.'

'Oh God! Has Mick delivered the letter already?'

'No. He just left, about ten minutes ago. She seems to have called in off her own bat.'

'Better show her in, so.'

Hadfield barely had time to put the Henry Street papers and file to one side when Jasmine swanned into his office, looking particularly attractive. She was wearing a very fine mink coat, which he offered to take, and placed on his coat-stand. This revealed an eye-catching red dress with a plunging neckline. On anyone else, it might have been considered less-than-ideal autumn wear. The mink doubtless kept out the cold. A matching pair of high heels and clutch-bag were offset very fetchingly by a string of pearls.

She must have just come from the hairdressers, as her raven black hair had been stylishly coiffured. The make-up hadn't been overlooked either. Mascara, rouge and a full, bright red lipstick. In short, a look that was guaranteed to catch attention.

'Very good to see you, Miss Barrington.'

'Oh, please call me "Jasmine".'

'Well . . . er . . . yes, Jasmine. Can I get you some tea?'

'No thank you. It's a bit close to lunchtime.'

'Of course. Of course.'

'Actually, I was hoping maybe you could take me for a bite to eat after our little meeting,' she continued with a demure smile and a slight flutter of her eyelashes, which highlighted her striking blue eyes.

'Oh. I see. I . . . er . . . don't have anything planned. So . . . er . . . .'

'Wonderful. That's settled then. Now. The reason I dropped in, of course, was to discuss Daddy's will.'

'Ah,' began Hadfield, as he tried to adopt a business-like tone. 'If I can be of any assistance, of course I would . . . .' He was cut off by Jasmine mid-flow.

'I'm fairly sure I know what I'm getting, as Daddy mentioned it before, but I wanted to check with you first.' She paused, smiled sweetly at him, and added: 'To be certain it's all legal.'

'Well, yes, I can confirm your father made a will, which we have here. As did Lady Barrington.'

'Oh, I've no interest in that. I'm sure she left me nothing.' There was a slight pause, before she added: 'Or did she?'

'Er . . . no.'

'I'm not surprised. Anyway, Daddy's will.'

'Well, the manor house and estate is given to Richard, but you have a right of residence there until you marry.'

'Yes, Daddy had said that. And the monthly allowance?'

'Er . . . what allowance is that?'

'From the estate fund. That Daddy gave me. I get that too, obviously.'

'I think that probably ended with your father's death.'

'What?'

'Well, the estate has passed to Richard now.'

'So Richard has to pay it to me.'

'Er . . . that's not what the will provides.'

Jasmine tossed her head. 'Well, we'll see about that. I presume the Henry Street property is mine?'

'Yes.'

'And what about the rest?'

'Well, the Cork property goes to Samantha. And there is a bequest to Miss Greta and Robert Staunton. And the church.'

'But everything else is shared three ways.'

'Yes, but only after accounting for Lydia's portion. She would be entitled to a third of the whole estate.'

'Even though she died before getting it?'

'Yes. That's the law.'

'Hmm. How much is each share worth?'

'I don't know yet. We have to make the necessary enquiries to make sure we have got in all the assets, and then carry out a valuation.'

'But at least a million surely.'

'Er . . . yes, I would think so. There is quite a valuable office property on Merrion Square included, which should sell for a good price.'

'But I don't have to wait for all that, do I?'

'Well, yes. And there are quite a few other steps too.'

'How do you mean?'

'Well, the wills have to be put through probate. And then there's the revenue forms, and dealing with capital acquisitions tax, and all that. And then the collection and disposal of assets. And the formal transfer of the properties, and the distribution of . . . .'

'But I need money now. I want to get a new apartment in Dublin. There's a lovely one in Milltown that I've just put a bid on.'

'Unfortunately there won't be any funds available for quite a while, Ms Barrington – I mean Jasmine.'

'But Mr Boyd said there would be no problem.'

'Oh?'

'Yes. He'd be happy to give me the money. He just needs a letter from you confirming what's in the will.'

'I'd be surprised if it's quite so simple. Banks usually want a little more security than that.'

'That's not what he said to me. He said that if you undertake to send him a portion of what I am due from the will, then he saw no difficulty in giving me the money for the apartment.'

'An undertaking? From me?'

'That's right. And the deeds would be held for the bank until the money comes through to pay them back.'

'I see. Well, I had better talk to Mr Boyd, to see just what he has in mind there.'

'Please do. But hurry. I'm expecting to hear back from the agents very soon.'

'Of course. I'll follow up on that.'

'Can I get the rent from Henry Street now?'

'Well, no.'

'Why not? It's mine.'

'You see, the same principles would apply there as I mentioned in relation to the residue.'

'The probate, and all that?'

'That's right.'

'And how long will that take?'

'Hard to say. Anywhere between six months and a year.'

'What?' replied an incredulous Ms Barrington.

'Well, yes. Your father left a substantial estate. There is quite a lot of preparatory work to be done, and valuations, and we are very much in the hands of the Probate Office and the Revenue Commissioners in terms of the timeframe for the process.'

'What happens to the rent, then?'

'The executors will hold that in trust for you until the formalities are concluded.'

'That's you and Mr Boyd?'

'Er . . . that's right.'

'Well then,' responded Jasmine, rediscovering her winning smile, 'can't you give another one of those undertakings to Mr Boyd for that?'

Hadfield hesitated. This was all new territory for him. 'I don't know. It would be most unusual. I'd have to look into that. And discuss it with Mr Boyd. I'm not sure how . . . .'

'Anyway, you talk to Albert. I'm sure there'll be no problem. It's silly to have the money just sitting there until the paperwork is done. I have my own expenses, you know. I can't call on Daddy any more.'

'Of course, of course. I'll look into all that too.'

'Good. Actually, on the subject of Henry Street, one more thing.'

'Yes?'

'Well, the ground and basement has been vacant for a little while, but we agreed terms with a new tenant some time ago. Very high-profile. An English PLC. We were thrilled with the rent.'

'You mean the retail unit?'

'Yes. Is it signed up yet? The agents are worried that they might go further down the street if we don't pin them down quickly.'

'Well,' he replied, as he began to experience a sinking feeling, 'Mr Timmons would have been handling that, of course.'

'But you're looking after it now.'

'Yes. In fact, it was one of the files I was reviewing when you came in.'

'So. Have they signed?'

'Er, no. Mr Timmons had sent a lease out for execution, but the tenants' solicitors have come back with quite a lot of comments and queries,' he replied, picking up the letter he had put aside with the file.

'When was that?'

'Let me see,' said Hadfield – his sinking feeling turning to outright panic – 'the letter is dated the tenth. Probably arrived on the thirteenth, maybe the fourteenth.'

'That's over two weeks ago!'

'Yes. Of course, recent events intervened somewhat.'

'But we may have lost the tenant already! What will they think? No contact for two weeks. Can we get a response to them today?'

'Well, I'm only in the middle of reviewing it myself. There's quite a bit involved.'

'Tomorrow, then.'

'Well, I can see if . . . .'

'Good. But ring their solicitor now. Explain the delay. Timmons' death, and all that. We have to get them signed up straight away. Now I'm going to powder my nose. You make that call, and I'll see you in reception in a minute for that lunch you promised me.'

CHAPTER 18

A bewildered Hadfield was left alone in the office to recover. Jasmine wasn't just a pretty face. She was hard work too! He took the Henry Street letter, and rang the offices of McGuigan McGuirk & Mooney. It seemed that a Ms Philippa Mooney was dealing with the matter for the tenant, but she was otherwise engaged at that moment. He left a message apologising for the delay in responding, and expressing the hope that he could revert 'ASAP'. With that, he put on his coat and took the mink out to reception, where Jasmine was waiting on the couch, reclining in such a way as to reveal her legs (and no little thigh) to good effect. He helped her into the mink, had a slightly confused discussion with Hilary about where he was going and when he'd be back, and headed out the door onto High Street.

He found himself, at Jasmine's suggestion, at a cosy table for two in the dining room of the Kilcreddin Arms Hotel.

Mrs Stokes was quickly by their side, curious no doubt as to the reason for this unprecedented pairing.

'Good afternoon, James. Good afternoon, Jasmine.'

After pleasantries were exchanged, Mrs Stokes turned to the recently bereaved Ms Barrington.

'How are you holding up, dear? After all the tragedy.'

'As best I can, Beatrice. Life must go on.'

'It's a pleasure to see you here again. Haven't seen you for a couple of months now, when you were with . . . .'

'Yes,' Jasmine interrupted quickly, 'how time flies. I've just come into Kilcreddin to discuss Daddy's estate with James.'

'Of course. There must be a lot to get through.'

'It certainly seems that way.'

'I remember having to go through the same when Edward passed on. Of course, Mr Timmons dealt with all that. Very efficient. All done and dusted in under three months, as I recall.'

'Is that possible?' enquired Jasmine of Hadfield, with something approaching a frown.

'Well, of course, it depends on the estate. And the terms of the will. There are a lot of variables but . . . er . . . I suppose it might be possible in some cases.'

'You'll probably be spending more time in Dublin now,' Mrs Stokes suggested, continuing her quest for information.

'I haven't decided. I can always stay at the Manor, whenever suits.'

'I see,' said Mrs Stokes, giving away her surprise with a slightly arched eyebrow. 'I certainly hope you'll keep up with the Horse Club, at any rate. It wouldn't be the same without you.'

'You're very kind,' replied Jasmine, in a manner which indicated the fact-finding mission was over.

'An aperitif, perhaps?' asked Mrs Stokes, who was quick on the uptake.

'A glass of Champagne for me, Beatrice.'

'A sparkling water for me,' answered Hadfield.

'Certainly not. James will have a glass of Champagne too.'

He meekly nodded his agreement to Mrs Stokes, who quietly disappeared.

'So,' began Jasmine, with one of her bright smiles, 'have any of the others been in to see you?'

'How do you mean?'

'Richard and Samantha. And Robert. About the will.'

'No. Not yet. I have sent a letter to . . . .'

'I'm surprised Samantha hasn't been on to you. She wasn't happy about her share in the will.'

'Why's that?'

'The house in Cork. She wanted Henry Street. Or at least Merrion Square. And she was worried about Lydia getting rights over Cork.'

'I see. So she didn't get on with Her Ladyship.'

'Far from it. If you ask me, the police should be questioning her, not Robert.'

'About the murders?'

'Well, about Lydia's at any rate. They never got on, but Daddy mentioning her being a part owner of Cork was the last straw.'

Just then a waitress came with the Champagne, as well as menus.

'Cheers,' said Jasmine, as she clinked her glass with Hadfield and began to peruse the menu.

'Might I ask how you got on with Lady Barrington?' he enquired, knowing that this was a little impertinent to ask of a client, but finding it hard to resist his undercover-detective role. Particularly while sipping Champagne.

'Erm . . . ' replied Jasmine, looking quizzically at him, and pausing, as though she might not answer the question, 'not at first. But I learned to live with her. Or at least learned how to avoid her. Why do you ask?'

'Well . . . .' It was Hadfield's turn to pause: he didn't quite know how he should respond. This detecting lark wasn't easy. 'You see, it seems the police aren't just treating Robert as a suspect. All the beneficiaries may be in the frame.'

'Including me?'

'And Samantha. And Richard. Even Aunt Greta.'

'How do you know that?'

'Well, as half the village seems to know, I suppose I can tell you too. The Special Branch called into the office yesterday and took some papers. Copies of the wills. Some notes Mr Timmons made on the day he died. The detective sergeant told me the police have an open mind on the murderer at this stage. It seems that nobody has an alibi and everyone has a motive.'

The waitress returned to the table, and jotted down their requests for starters and mains.

'You might order some wine, James. White for me,' suggested Jasmine, once the food order had been taken.

'The wine list, please?' he asked the waitress.

'I'll arrange that now, sir'

'What do you mean, no alibis?' asked Jasmine, as soon as the waitress had left.

'Well, it seems that the police estimate the time of death of Lord Barrington at somewhere between 12.30 and 1 PM on the Friday. And nobody can establish an alibi for that time of the day.'

'But I was driving down from Dublin then.'

'With Scott and Penny?'

'Yes. How did you know that?'

'Oh . . . er . . . the police mentioned it. But I'm not sure that they consider that . . . erm . . . independent enough.'

'What do you mean?'

'Well, they might not be looking for one murderer. There may be two, or more, involved. Did anyone else see you?'

'Well, the staff at the Manor can confirm it. I was there at about 1.30.'

'But does that cover the time of the murder?'

'No. But wait a minute. Richard was in front of me for most of the way from Kilcreddin to the Manor. I couldn't get past his stupid jeep. He wouldn't move, even when I beeped him. That proves I was there.'

'At what time?'

'About 1.15, I suppose.'

'Might not put you fully in the clear. Can Richard confirm he saw you?'

'He must have. He continued on to Rathbawn when I turned into the Manor. But he knows my car. And he'd remember the beeps!'

Hadfield was just considering how this did not tally with Richard's account of his movements that day, when Hugh Stokes approached the table with the wine list in his hands.

'Good afternoon, Jasmine. Good afternoon, James.' His greeting seemed a little stiffer than usual.

'Good afternoon,' replied Jasmine, with a slightly strained smile.

'Afternoon, Hugh,' added Hadfield, who couldn't help but feel that his own smile might be a little strained too.

'You wanted to order some wine?' Hugh enquired, handing the list to Hadfield.

A slightly awkward silence ensued as he viewed the list.

'You didn't make it to the Horse Club on Saturday,' Hugh finally commented.

'No. I was in Kilkenny. Attending a ball.'

'You missed a good ride out. And the afters too. Your brother was in good form.'

'So I heard. As were you, I gather.'

'Meaning?'

'I am reliably informed that yourself and Hilary had a good singalong too.'

Hadfield coughed at this point, before saying 'We might have the Pouilly Fumé' and handing the wine list back to Hugh, who promptly retreated, with a 'Very good'. It occurred to Hadfield that the person Mrs Stokes was about to mention before Jasmine cut her off was Hugh himself.

'Does Samantha not have an alibi then?'

'It seems not. She left the surgery around noon and went shopping, before meeting a friend for lunch here in Kilcreddin at about 1.30.'

'Knowing Samantha, she didn't buy anything.'

'That seems to be the case. There don't appear to be any witnesses to confirm she was there.'

'She should be the prime suspect, if you ask me. She's a doctor after all. She'd know about drugs and poisons and that sort of thing.'

'Yes, it seems the poison used was a mixture of prescription drugs and rat poison.'

'Well, there you are. And of course, her insinuating that Robert was responsible because he needed the money. We all know it's Samantha who's stuck.'

'But would she have killed your father for it?'

'I don't know. But the surgery hasn't been doing well. She invested a lot in new beauty treatments and staff, but it's not paying its way. And she was never happy with the Cork property. It's a worthless holiday home. And of course, Denis lives the life of a lord without earning a bean. Daddy was not impressed.'

'I gather he wasn't too impressed with Scott either.'

'Just not Daddy's type. Very few were.'

'I understand the police were hoping to . . . er . . . speak with him yesterday,' Hadfield enquired tentatively.

'How come you are so well informed?'

'Oh, the detective sergeant was very talkative. Pretty much ran through the whole case while he was in the office.'

'Scott left at the weekend. Some business or other in England, I think. Or maybe France. I'm not sure. Penny is in touch with him. Nothing to do with me.'

Jasmine did not appear to have any interest in pursuing this topic of conversation, and thankfully Hugh returned with the wine at this point. He limited his engagement to a perfunctory discharge of his sommelier duties, and departed.

'Er . . . ' began Hadfield, in an effort to steer the conversation to a new subject, as well as eliciting any gossip that might be of interest, 'did you mention that Hugh and Hilary might be an item?'

'I'm not sure. I just said it to annoy him. He has definitely been chasing her. Invited her to the last Horse Club Social, but she didn't go.'

'Why would you want to annoy him?'

'Because he was annoying me! Now enough of that. Let's talk about you. How's your love life?'

'Fairly quiet at the moment,' he replied, somewhat embarrassed by this new turn in the conversation.

'I find that hard to believe. A good-looking lawyer like yourself.'

'Well, it has been very busy in the office.'

'You need to get out more, James. You should join the Horse Club. Then you could ask me to the Social.'

He had no idea what to say to that, but as luck would have it, the waitress arrived with the starters.

He made sure to avoid the subject of romance for the rest of the meal, although Jasmine became more flirtatious with each glass of wine.

'Oh, let's have another bottle,' she said, as Hadfield suggested calling for the bill.

'I'm not sure that would be a good idea.'

'Don't be such a spoilsport. I'm only beginning to have fun!'

'But I do have to get back to the office,' he replied, becoming a little concerned as to where all this was leading.

'What's so important back at the office? Aren't you having fun too?'

'I am. Of course. It's just . . . er . . . it's just . . . .' As he struggled to think of a reasonable response, he got a moment of inspiration. 'The Henry Street file! I have to work on that, to get a response out tomorrow. Another bottle of wine wouldn't be recommended for that.'

Jasmine sulked for a bit, but could see that it was in her own interests to agree. 'I suppose so. But I expect you to take me for a proper outing next time.'

'I'd be more than happy to,' he replied, as he signalled for the bill.

As they left the hotel, he suggested a taxi. Jasmine said she would do a little shopping first, before heading back to the Manor. Mrs Stokes bade them farewell as they left, but Hugh was nowhere to be seen.

Jasmine placed a big kiss on his cheek, as they went their separate ways on High Street, saying she expected to hear from him soon on the matters they had discussed at the office. And their next 'date'. Whatever she meant by that.

As he walked back to the office, he wondered what Jasmine's intentions were. Did she just want to keep close and put the pressure on to get her hands on her inheritance and some advance funds from Boyd? Or did she want to make Hugh jealous? Or maybe she had taken a shine to him. Or just wanted a free lunch: she was obviously a bit short of hard cash. Any which way, he'd no choice now but to get on with the Henry Street file. As he opened the front door to the office, it occurred to him that it could be a long night.

CHAPTER 19

It was after 10 AM the next morning when Hadfield got in to the office.

'You must have been working late,' said Hilary, taking off her earphones as he came through the door. 'There's a lot of dictation on this Henry Street file.'

'Too bloody right! It was nearly midnight when I left here. Ms Jasmine Barrington is on my case about it. Wants it signed up urgently. She knows the letter was sitting there for the last two weeks.'

'Hardly your fault, James.'

'No. But it's my problem now. She's worried the tenant might take a different property.'

'I see. Well, it will probably take a couple of hours to get through it. And there's another tape there as well. Is that urgent too?'

'No. That's just some notes on my discussion with her yesterday.'

'Oh. Anything of interest?'

'Well, she must be broke. Mad keen to get her hands on some money. Didn't seem too fond of Lady Barrington either. Or Samantha, for that matter: she thinks her sister is a more likely suspect than Staunton for the murders.'

'Why's that?'

'Money, it seems. Bit short, by all accounts. Not happy about the will. Thinks she was short-changed with the Cork property.'

'Unhappy enough to kill?'

'Who knows. Jasmine seems to think she's capable of it.'

'Your detective work seems to be raising more questions than it's answering.'

'You're right there. Actually, she said something else that was interesting.'

'What was that.'

'Well, it's in relation to Richard. You know that he said he was in his office on the estate from about 11 until about 1.45, when he headed to the Manor Inn for lunch?'

Hilary nodded.

'It seems Jasmine saw him in his jeep on the road from Kilcreddin to the Manor before 1.30. She turned in to the Manor but he went on: presumably to Rathbawn.'

'That *is* interesting. Now we have both Richard and Margaret Barrington spotted where they shouldn't be around the time of the murder on Friday.'

'Exactly. Could they be in it together?'

'It's possible, I suppose. Anything else?'

'No. That was it. Apart from the frosty exchange with Hugh Stokes.'

'Oh?'

'Yes. It wouldn't surprise me if they were an item at one stage.'

'I think they were. She ditched him a couple of months back.'

'Why was that?'

'Not sure. Think she may have been trying to get him to move up to Dublin, but he wasn't too keen.'

'I see.'

'Is she making a move on you?'

'I hope not. Have enough on my plate just dealing with her legal requirements.'

'By the way, Miss Greta called first thing. In relation to the letter. She'd like you to drop round to the nursing home before lunch to discuss matters. I think that defamation thing is still on her mind.'

Hilary turned towards Mick's door and called out: 'Mick, I think you said you'd looked into that defamation question.'

'That's right,' said Mick, coming into the reception area. 'I have a note here on it. No need for a person to be actually named to constitute a defamation.'

'Actually,' replied Hadfield, as casually as possible, as he recalled FitzHerbert's advice, 'I managed to have a look into that myself. In the case of Richard slandering Staunton, I believe all that is required is to show that some of those present reasonably understood that Robert was being accused of murder.'

'Ah,' replied Mick, a little disappointedly, 'that pretty much sums it up. Here's my note, anyway.'

'Thanks.'

'Of course, if he *did* commit the murder, it couldn't be defamation,' added Hilary.

'Very true,' replied Hadfield.

'Morning all.'

'Morning Agnes,' was the general reply.

'Things hotting up at the Manor.'

They all waited for Agnes to divulge the latest gossip.

'I'm sure you know that that fellow Scott has scarpered. Now Penny has gone too. Left without a word, yesterday lunchtime. Something definitely afoot there. And Richard has told Letitia to move out. Looks like he's going to move into the Manor sooner rather than later. Word is, he took his shot-gun down to the gate and threatened the protesters. Even fired it a couple of times.'

'Nobody injured, I hope,' replied Hilary.

'No, they were just warning shots, apparently. And I gather he's fallen out with Denis.'

'Why's that?' asked Hadfield.

'Money, of course. As the new lord of the manor, Denis felt Richard should be contributing to the latest Rathmore production. Short of funds, with only a few days to go. Richard sent him packing. I hear it has been busy enough here too. Police stayed the whole of Monday morning.'

Agnes waited for a fair exchange of information.

'Nothing too dramatic, Agnes,' replied Hilary. 'They just needed to see the wills, and some notes Mr Timmons had made the day he died.'

'Notes? What kind of notes?'

'Not entirely clear, Agnes,' said Hadfield, 'but the police took them away, in case they might help with their enquiries. Now I need to head over to see Miss Greta at the nursing home.'

'Best of luck,' said Hilary as he headed back out.

*

Hadfield went to his house to collect his car, and headed for the nursing home. It was a short drive from Kilcreddin, as the two were connected by a direct by-road. The autumn leaves had begun to fall, making conditions a little tricky, particularly with the narrowness of the road and the density of the trees overhanging the route. This road led to a T-junction with the main road: Rathbawn was to the left, and Rathmore to the right. The nursing home was almost directly ahead: a right turn on to the road, and a left turn in to the home. There were in fact two entrances, the first being the trade entrance, and the second for visitors. He took the latter, which involved a somewhat winding driveway, before reaching the car park at the front of the home.

After making enquiries at reception, he was given directions to Greta Barrington's room. As he approached, he heard voices.

'So, if we leave everything as is, you won't be hearing from me again.'

'But that's blackmail, and you know it.'

'Call it what you will, Greta, but the facts are the facts.'

'In that case, I have nothing more to say.'

Hadfield was on the point of returning to reception when Letitia strode out, stared at him for a moment and walked on without a word. He waited a few moments before entering the room. It was quite spacious. In fact, there seemed to be other rooms as well: there were two further doors off this first room, which was evidently Greta's living area. She was seated in a large armchair near the artificial fire, which was flickering in the old fireplace.

She was dressed splendidly in a long, flowing, brightly patterned dress. Almost hippie-ish, you could say. And her hair had been tied up with some type of light scarf, which added to the bohemian effect. Her nails were painted a deep purple, and she had a number of rings, bracelets and necklaces to finish it all off. The birds in the trees outside – which could be heard raucously crowing, as well as being visible through the window – created a slightly spooky atmosphere.

'Come in and sit down,' she said, pointing to a chair on the other side of the fireplace. She looked at him closely. 'You weren't eavesdropping, were you?'

'No, no. Not at all.'

'You saw that woman leaving, I take it?'

'Letitia?'

'That's right.'

'Yes . . . er . . . just in the corridor on the way to reception.'

'Her day will come, I tell you.'

'You are not on best terms with her, then?'

'That would be putting it mildly. Now, some tea perhaps?'

'Thank you,' he replied. She pressed a bell beside her.

'I presume you wanted to talk about the defamation question when you sent me that letter.'

'Well, actually, it was more to discuss the provisions of the wills. That kind of thing.'

'I know all about the wills. It's that good-for-nothing Richard I want to hear about. He accused Robert of murder, in front of the whole church! He can't be allowed get away with that. I hope you have been looking into all this for me.'

'Indeed I have, Miss Barrington. I managed to have a brief word with Senior Counsel on the subject.'

'And?'

'Well, it could be defamation, if some of those present in the church reasonably understood, from what Richard Barrington said, that he was accusing Robert Staunton of the murder.'

'Of course they understood it. He couldn't have meant anyone else.'

'You'd have to prove that in court. Get a representative number of people who were in the church to testify to all that.'

'I'm sure I can. You just leave that to me! I'll have a busload available if needed.'

Just then, a nurse popped her head around the door.

'You called, Miss Greta?'

'Oh. Some tea please, Sarah. And some biscuits for Mr Hadfield.'

'Coming right up,' replied the nurse, who slipped away again down the corridor.

'Lovely girl, Sarah. I hope it all works out with Robert.'

Hadfield wasn't sure if Miss Greta's last two statements were linked, so he simply enquired: 'Er . . . works out?'

'Yes, as a couple. All these accusations would put a strain on any relationship.'

'Ah. I see.'

'That's why we have to get these proceedings under way. Clear this whole thing up.'

'Actually, that's another aspect to any litigation on this. It might make sense to wait for the police to complete their investigations.'

'Why would we do that?'

'Er . . . to avoid the possibility of any defence being raised by Richard.'

'And what kind of defence would he have?'

'Maybe that the police were interrogating Robert, and that it was reasonable for Richard to consider him a suspect in the murders.'

'Rubbish. Richard's the much more likely suspect, if you ask me.'

'Why would you say that?'

'He hasn't a red cent of his own. And anything he does get, he drinks. He's always resented George for not letting him run the show. And that stupid stud-farm plan of his. That will prove a waste of money. George was definitely having second thoughts about all that. And Richard knew it.'

'So you think Richard could have poisoned Lord Barrington?'

'He could have got someone to do it for him. That nurse people are talking about. Maybe he paid her to do it.'

'Er . . . what nurse is that?'

'If we knew that, I'm sure this business would have been cleared up long ago. Isn't that right, Sarah?' Miss Greta added, as Sarah came into the room with a tray of tea and biscuits.

'Sorry, Miss Greta?'

'I was just talking to Mr Hadfield about that new nurse. Who delivered the poisoned tea. If they could locate her, all this terrible business with Robert would be over, I'm sure.'

'That would be a relief,' replied Sarah.

'Did you not get a look at her when she came in with the tea?' Hadfield asked.

'Unfortunately not. I was having a bit of an . . . ' – Miss Greta checked herself before continuing – ' . . . a discussion with George after Reverend Devereux left, and I didn't particularly pay attention when she asked about tea, or when she came back with it. I just know I didn't recognise her. Seemed to have a lot of make-up. And possibly not the youngest.'

'Did nobody else notice her?' he continued.

'I think Boyd may have noticed there was someone new on the corridor, but I don't think he got a very good look. You saw her too, Sarah, didn't you?'

'Well, I didn't actually get a look at her, but I did notice that the uniform was different. I assumed she was a new member of staff, or maybe a locum. It's not uncommon, so I didn't think too much more on it. Expected to bump into her later, at some point.'

'Unfortunately, that seems to have been the last that was seen of her,' added Miss Greta.

'Robert didn't notice anything?' suggested Hadfield.

'No,' replied Sarah, 'he was in the staff-room at the time. Er . . . anything else you need, Miss Greta? I've left your medication on the tray beside your water.'

'No, that's all, Sarah. Thank you.'

'Such a nice girl,' she repeated, as the nurse left the room.

And a pretty one too, thought Hadfield. A petite but full figure, with the curls of her blonde hair peeping out from under her nurse's cap. Dyed blonde probably, judging by the shade of her eyebrows, but not unlike one of the screen sirens of times past. Staunton had landed on his feet there.

'Tea, Mr Hadfield?'

'Oh, er . . . yes,' he replied, slightly startled, as he brought his attention back to the matters in hand.

As she was offering him milk and sugar, and he was reaching for a biscuit, it suddenly occurred to him that the scenario being played out before him was not dissimilar to the last time Lord Barrington had a cup of tea. The very last time he had a cup of tea.

'You mentioned you know the terms of the wills,' he said, to divert attention from her litigious wishes – and the tea – 'so you will be familiar with your own bequests.'

'Yes. George had provided an income for me. I didn't ask about the fine print. I suppose you might as well tell me about it, now that you're here.'

'Yes, a bond is to be put in place which will ensure an annual payment to you of IR£50,000, index-linked.'

'And IR£250,000 to Robert?'

'That's right.'

'George never got to change his will, unfortunately. He'd meant to have Robert treated as equal to the others.'

'Oh. Why was that?' replied Hadfield, who was not sure how much he should say.

'Because he was his son. With Lydia. There's no need to hide that any more. Lydia was going to tell Robert just before dinner that night.'

She reached for her handkerchief.

'Poor Lydia. I had to tell Robert myself.'

'You were obviously very close to her.'

'Yes. Although . . . there had been a bit of a falling-out over the fête. A few differences of opinion. And Devereux with a few ideas of his own, of course. Relations were a little strained.'

'And Lady Barrington's will?' he enquired after a moment. 'Are you interested to know of your bequest there?'

She seemed surprised by this, slowly replying: 'She made a bequest?'

'Yes. A number of items of jewellery. I have the list here. These were her personal items. The majority of her bequests would have been dependent on Lord Barrington predeceasing her.'

She again went silent, and looked down at the list of items he had handed to her. She seemed to take a moment to collect herself.

'Well, that's all that dealt with. Now I want to get back to this defamation matter. It's not just Richard who's been making accusations, you know.'

'Oh. Who else is there?' he replied, becoming a little worried about where this was all headed.

'You should know. You were at the house that afternoon. Richard, of course, started it off. With Samantha and Denis chiming in. Nobody had the nerve to disagree. Including, I might say, the lawyers present. Of course, Margaret wouldn't agree with Richard if she was paid. They haven't got on for years. I'm sure she knows about Kathleen Rennick: most people around here do. Scandalous behaviour. Anyway, when can we issue proceedings?'

'Well, as I've said, it might be a little early for that,' he replied, becoming increasingly worried.

'Nonsense! The sooner we start, the quicker we'll have our day. I know these legal processes. They can take an age. We need to get moving now. Issue a writ, or whatever it is. Let Richard know we mean business!'

'Er . . . ' he stalled, before deciding he had no option but to be forthright on the whole defamation debacle. 'If you are really intent on taking such a step at this stage, I suppose I should mention a further matter that arises.'

'A further matter? What do you mean? How difficult can all this be?'

'Well you see, the position of Timmons & Associates has to be considered. The firm has acted for the family for many years. It can't act for both sides in a litigation matter. It's against the profession's code of ethics.'

'Well, just act for us, then.'

'I'm not sure that would be the proper thing to do, Miss Barrington.'

'What? You want to act for Richard and the others instead?'

'Not at all. We couldn't be seen to be taking anyone's side in a matter like this, where we have traditionally represented both parties.'

'So you don't want to act at all?'

'Well, that's how the Law Society approaches it. And I have to say . . . . '

'I think you've said enough, Mr Hadfield! There's to be no case at all, because you can't act for anyone.'

'Of course you can still bring a case, Miss Barrington. And Richard can defend that case. It's just that both parties will need to get separate representation. With separate firms.'

'And who would you recommend for that?'

'It probably wouldn't be right of me to make a . . . . '

'Because you want to recommend to Richard instead, no doubt!'

'Not at all. There would be no question of favouring one client over the other.'

'Then who the hell *is* going to do it?'

'Well, if you don't know of someone yourself, or can't get a recommendation from someone else, you can always call the Law Society. They could recommend a number of solicitors who would specialise in this kind of case.'

'I see. So this has all been a complete waste of time.'

'I hope not, Miss . . . . '

'Why didn't you tell me this at the church?'

'It didn't seem quite the place to get into the finer points of the matter.'

'Finer points, my eye. We've lost a whole week, thanks to your meddling. Don't think you'll get paid a penny for any of this.'

'Of course not, Miss Barrington.'

'Run along now. I have to take my medication.'

'Very good. Any questions, don't hesitate . . . .'

'Hold on. You haven't touched your tea!'

'Sorry. I must have got distracted. It might be a little cold now.'

'Good Lord. What's the point of bringing a pot of tea if you are just going to leave it there untouched?'

'I should probably get on my way at this stage, Miss Barrington.'

'You're probably right. Goodbye.'

CHAPTER 20

When Hadfield was a safe distance from Miss Greta's room, he stopped and leaned against the corridor wall. He was practically punch-drunk from the interrogation. Definitely not the best client meeting he'd ever had. And possibly the last with Miss Greta. He'd have to have a discussion with Richard about the whole defamation business, just so that he could prepare for what was to come. But that might be a breach of confidentiality with Miss Greta and Robert. He'd have to look into that a bit more. All very awkward.

Just as he was gathering himself to head out to his car, Sarah called out to him.

'Mr Hadfield?'

'Yes,' he replied in a low voice, not wanting to attract Miss Greta's attention.

'Everything all right?' she whispered as he came up to her in the corridor.

'Fine, fine. Just don't want to disturb Miss Barrington. She's . . . er . . . taking her medication.'

'Get a bit of an earful?'

'Er . . . how do you mean?'

Sarah motioned him into what seemed to be a private room off the corridor, and continued. 'She can be terribly cantankerous. Finds it hard to hold a conversation without having some argument or other.'

'Well, she definitely wasn't best pleased with what I had to say.'

'About Robert's defamation case, I suppose.'

'How did you know that?'

'It's her hobby-horse. She thinks everyone should be sued for thinking Robert is involved in the murders. Of course Robert has no interest in taking the case at all.'

'Why's that?'

'He doesn't care what people say. Anyway, he thinks it would be a waste of time.' Sarah paused at this point, before adding with a frown: 'And money.'

'So why let Miss Barrington think there will be a case?'

'To keep her occupied, I suppose. It keeps her mind off things.'

'Of course. It must be very difficult losing her brother like that. And Lady Barrington, a long-standing friend, I believe.'

'Yes. Although . . . .'

'They'd fallen out somewhat, perhaps?'

'Well, yes, I think. There had been a lot of arguments of late whenever they met. Over the fête, I think. But maybe there were harsher words than usual this time. They didn't seem able to forgive and forget, as they had done before.'

'And too late now for that.'

'I suppose,' replied Sarah, before wearily sitting down in a nearby chair. She seemed to be on the point of tears as she said: 'Oh, Mr Hadfield, I don't know where to turn.'

'What's the matter?'

'It's Robert. He's so stubborn. He's been arrested twice but still won't see a solicitor. He says he can't afford one, but I think he just doesn't want to take advice.'

'I see. Well . . . .'

Sarah burst into tears at this point. 'Oh please, can you help him? He didn't do anything. I'm sure he just needs a good solicitor to prove all that. Surely you could at least speak to him. Or explain things to the police for him.'

'I'd very much like to help, of course, but . . . .'

'Oh, thank you Mr Hadfield. I knew you would. You seem so kind.'

'Perhaps I should explain, Ms O'Doherty.'

'Please call me "Sarah",' she replied, as she began to recover her composure.

'I need to explain, Sarah, that any advice to Robert, or any engagement with the police, in relation to these murders, would be . . . er . . . .'

'Yes,' she replied expectantly.

'Well, any such advice would be of a criminal nature.'

'I see,' said Sarah – who clearly didn't see at all, but instead looked a little confused.

'And my firm, Timmons & Associates, only deal with civil matters.'

She looked back at him blankly. 'Civil matters?'

'Yes. Conveyancing, probate, employment. You know: buying houses, wills, people being fired. That type of law. We don't deal with criminal law at all. I wouldn't know the first thing about it.'

She started to cry freely now. After a while, between sobs, she managed to say: 'What are we going to do?'

Hadfield placed a hand gently on her shoulder. 'Well, there are a number of solicitors who specialise exclusively in criminal law. I know a few of them myself. I'm sure I can have someone speak to Robert about all this, and give the necessary advice.'

'But how are we going to pay for this? Won't it be expensive?'

'Not necessarily. If he can't afford it, Robert may qualify for legal aid. I'm sure the solicitor can explain all that to him.'

She started to calm down now, taking her hands from her face and rubbing her eyes with a tissue she had taken from her pocket.

'Thank you, Mr Hadfield. You're very kind. I'm sorry to have been such a bother.'

'Not at all. Glad to be of help.'

'You'll have a word with Robert, then. Explain all that to him.'

'Actually, I sent him a letter yesterday, suggesting we meet to discuss the will. I'll follow up and discuss the . . . er . . . police-investigation side of things as well.'

'Thank you so much. Sorry to be such a nuisance. I'm sure you'll want to be getting back to your office now.'

'Yes, I probably should. You stay here and take a little rest. I'll make my own way out.'

And with that, he headed straight for the front door, and the sanctuary of his car.

*

'How did that go?' enquired Hilary.

'Er . . . I think "Not well" might be a fair summary.'

'Oh dear.'

'Yes. She's determined to start a case against Richard for his outburst in the church. And maybe against those who supported him when he made his accusations at the Manor. I had to tell her we couldn't act for her. Not at all pleased with that. I should probably let Richard know we can't represent him either.'

'Would that be wise?'

'I'm not sure. Could be a breach of Miss Greta's confidence to alert him to the case.'

'Assuming she does actually take one.'

'She seemed fairly determined. But maybe your right. Robert's not that keen on it. He mightn't let it get that far.'

'How do you know that?'

'His girlfriend, Sarah O'Doherty, the nurse, collared me as I left. Bit of tears, I'm afraid. Wants me to advise him on his position with the whole police thing.'

'And you couldn't do that either.'

'No, but I said I would have a word with him: recommend a few criminal specialists.'

'That seems sensible.'

'Did you manage to get the Henry Street response done?'

'Yes. It's on your desk. And the notes on your discussions with Jasmine. And the post.'

'Thanks. I should probably dictate a summary of this morning's meetings, in case Detective Sergeant Forde comes calling.'

'Anything of note?'

Hadfield mentioned the overheard conversation between Greta and Letitia.

'That *is* interesting. What could be going on there? I'm sure the police would be interested in that.'

'Might put me in an awkward situation.'

'Hmm. Anything else?'

'Not really. Miss Greta thinks it's more likely Richard did it. Seems he was resentful of Lord Barrington for holding on to everything for so long. And didn't get on with Lady Barrington either. Short of cash too.'

'Not exactly a smoking gun.'

'No. Actually, what's probably more interesting is Miss Greta's relationship with Lydia. It seems they argued quite a bit, usually over the fête. But Sarah seemed to think they may have argued a little more seriously in recent times. In fact, Miss Greta seemed a little taken aback when I mentioned the terms of Lydia's will. She knew everything about her brother's will but didn't seem to know much about Lydia's. Or maybe didn't *want* to know. She was quite distracted when we discussed it.'

'Not quite the basis for murder.'

'Maybe not. ... Although there is the strange nurse to consider.'

'What about her?'

'Not much, unfortunately. Nobody seemed to get a good look at her, except maybe a brief look from Miss Greta, who didn't recognise her. Sarah said her uniform was different from the nursing home's. That's about it. Miss Greta thinks Richard probably hired her to carry out the poisoning for him.'

'It is possible, I suppose.'

'Well, one thing's for sure: the killer is still at large. You can't be too careful. Miss Greta ordered a pot of tea for me while I was there. I couldn't touch it.'

'I'm sure that didn't go down well.'

'No . . . . I don't think I'll be having tea with her anytime soon. Anything to report at this end?'

'I rang Montgomery Darley. Ms Curtis has no difficulty with meeting all three of us this Friday at 3, so I've booked the train tickets.'

'Very good. Any calls?'

'Just a few. I've left them on your desk as well. Nothing too urgent. Except maybe Samantha Barrington. She rang earlier, in relation to the letter. Seems keen that she meets you this afternoon.'

'Oh. Did she mention a time?'

'She has surgery until 4.30 and asked if you could drop by then.'

'Why couldn't she drop by here?'

'I think she wants her husband to be there too. And they don't want to leave their little boy on his own.'

'Oh, all right. Might as well make the effort.'

'They are a potential new client, I suppose.'

'That's true. Having lost a client and turned down two cases this morning, it's probably the least I should do!'

*

Hadfield collapsed into his chair. He was feeling exhausted, and it wasn't even lunchtime! Eventually he forced himself to check through the drafts that Hilary had prepared. He decided to read through the post before returning the calls. The last one he looked at was a little unusual, in that it was a small red envelope. When he opened it, he found an even smaller piece of paper doubled over inside. The letter read:

WATCH YOUR STEP HADFIELD! HELPING THE POLICE TO HELP THE BARRINGTONS MAY NOT BE GOOD FOR YOUR HEALTH

It was written in various capital letters, clearly taken from newspaper clippings. He stared at it for a while, before a knock on the door made him jump. Lucinda popped her head around the door.

'A word, James?'

'Yes. Yes, of course. Come in.'

'You look a little unwell. Are you all right?'

'To be honest, I'm not exactly sure. Just received this in the post.'

He handed the note to Lucinda.

'Oh my God. James, your life could be in danger.'

'Seems so.'

'Who do you think it is?'

'I don't know. That fellow Armstrong, possibly . . . .'

'Would he take things that far?'

'Why not? If he's involved with the murders.'

'Or someone who is worried about your contact with the police.'

'Such as . . . .'

'Well, anyone who might be a suspect, I suppose. They must be worried about the police arriving here on Monday. And what you might have said. Or given them. Mr Timmons' file note, perhaps.'

'Perhaps.'

'Either way, you need to be careful. I might mention it to Uncle Bernard. I told him about seeing Armstrong with Hargreaves. He said to tell him of any developments.'

'You might do that, Lucinda. Actually, you might also mention something else I heard this morning.'

He repeated the conversation he had overheard at the nursing home.

'That certainly raises a few questions,' said Lucinda.

'Not many answers, though. Maybe Letitia knew about Robert's parentage.'

'But wasn't that going to be announced anyway? I should think Letitia knows something else. And it must be something that Greta does not want disclosed.'

'You're probably right. You know, I'm feeling a little bit tired after all this. I think I might head home for a bit of a rest before I take on anything else.'

'Understood. Be sure to look after yourself.'

'I'll try. By the way . . . you dropped in?'

'Oh. Just to say this Friday. If you are all going to Dublin. Happy to look after things. Answer the phone, take deliveries, deal with people dropping in. If you want.'

'That would be great, Lucinda. Thanks.'

CHAPTER 21

Hadfield got into his car just after 4 PM and headed for Rathmore, which, like the nursing home, was no more than a ten-minute drive away – albeit by a different road. It occurred to him that he was doing a lot of running around, and a lot of talking, but he wasn't sure if it was helping very much with the murder enquiry.

Richard was saying Robert did it. Jasmine thinks it might be Samantha. Miss Greta believes Richard could be responsible. Lady Barrington arguing with Miss Greta. Reverend Devereux in the thick of it. And Richard and his wife not being where they said they were: if Jasmine and the Reverend are to be believed. Scott and Penny on the run, and Armstrong in contact for some reason or other. Letitia potentially involved in blackmail, and Clarisse witnessing Lady Barrington's will just before she died. And then the whole business of the nurse. Resolving that conundrum seemed to be the key to all of this, but nobody could say who it might be. And now a threatening note warning him to stay away from the police investigation. Maybe that was the wisest course of action.

These thoughts were going round in his head as he approached Rathmore, a picturesque village split in two by a narrow but steep-banked river. The old mill, from which the village grew, was still standing, just below the bridge which crossed the river. He continued across the bridge and headed a little further along the main street, before stopping in front of a large grey Victorian stone building, which was set in its own, quite substantial, grounds. This was the family home of Samantha and Denis but included, as a separate wing, a doctor's surgery, from which Samantha carried on her practice.

He parked his car as near as possible to the surgery entrance, which was separate from the entrance to the main house. As he was a few minutes early,

146

he walked along the footpath, taking in the view of the building. It was certainly impressive – without doubt the finest in the village. It had been in the Barrington family since it was built, and formed part of the larger Barrington estate at one time, which had included the entire lands making up Rathmore. The other properties in the village had since been sold, or land had been parcelled off and developed. The old mill, as well as some common areas and some small tracts of land, were still in the ownership of Lord Barrington, forming part of the estate. The house itself had been transferred to Samantha a number of years previously, by way of a wedding gift from her father. He had intended it as a family home, but was rumoured to be a little disappointed with the outcome – one grandchild, a doctor's surgery, and a thespian husband was not what he'd had in mind.

As Hadfield walked through the entrance to the surgery, he noticed quite a number of advertisements for different treatments, as well as a list of therapists who were responsible for the various options. He advised the receptionist of his appointment, and that he was a little early. He sat down, alone, in the waiting area.

Eventually a nurse came into reception, and said: 'Please follow me.'

He was led through a veritable labyrinth of little corridors and rooms, until they finally reached another, smaller reception area, where he was asked to take a seat.

'Dr Barrington Russell will be with you shortly. Can I get you a cup of tea?'

'Er . . . no, thank you.'

'Coffee?'

'No thanks. Maybe just a glass of water.'

The nurse returned with a glass of water, and left him again. The reception was really only a small room off the last corridor of the surgery. There were two doors off this room, one with 'Dr Barrington Russell' written on it, and the other unmarked. He was just about to pick up one of the papers on the low table beside him when the door to Dr Barrington's room opened, and Samantha herself came out.

'Sorry for keeping you. I just had to tidy away the files for the day.'

'Not at all, it's only just gone 4.30.'

'We might go into the house. Denis should be able to join us there shortly,' she said, while at the same time locking her office door. She then opened the other door, which appeared to be an entrance into the house, and locked it again once they were inside. He was led through more corridors until being brought into what appeared to be a drawing room, and invited to sit down. He had noted that the inside of the house was on a much grander scale than the surgery but was nonetheless quite sparsely decorated. And colder.

'Denis must not be back yet. He's picking Bartholomew up from his speech-and-drama class, which he has after school every Wednesday. Very important for the development of young children.'

'I'm sure. What age is your son?'

'Seven. Eight next January.'

Samantha took a seat opposite Hadfield without saying anything further. He wasn't sure if she intended to wait for her husband before continuing with the conversation, so decided to try and carry on with the small talk.

'The . . . er . . . practice keeps you busy?'

'Keeps *me* busy, anyway. Can't really say the same for the rest of the staff at the moment. I'm working on that, though. It's our only source of income, of course, so I have to give it my full attention.'

'Your husband retired some time ago, I believe?' he replied, knowing the answer, but wanting to keep the conversation moving along.

'That's right. He was a partner in one of the larger law firms in Dublin. But he gave it up soon after Bartholomew was born. We'd got this house, and I'd started the surgery. Denis preferred the idea of the country life to a daily commute. And it meant we didn't have to hire a nanny.'

'Your husband looks after all the domestic matters?'

'We have a housekeeper who cleans and brings in provisions. But Denis looks after Bartholomew during the day. And he likes to cook. He's quite a decent chef. Ah! I hear Denis. We are in here!' she called out after what sounded like the closing of the front door.

A young boy in a smart school uniform and strong spectacles soon entered the drawing room but stopped just inside the door when he noticed Hadfield.

'Good afternoon, mother.'

'Good afternoon, Bartholomew. This is Mr Hadfield. He's the family solicitor. He has come to talk about your grandfather's will.'

'Good afternoon, Mr Hadfield. I'm pleased to meet you.'

'Good afternoon to you, Bartholomew. Your speech-and-drama class went well?'

'Very well, thank you.'

'Good afternoon, James,' said Denis, entering the drawing room and adjusting his spectacles – which, Hadfield noticed, were almost identical to those of his son, notwithstanding their sturdy 1950s style.

'Good afternoon, Denis,' he replied.

'Bartholomew, there is a fruit snack on the kitchen table for you, which you can have now, before starting your homework. And after you give your mother a kiss.'

'Good of you to come by,' continued Denis, after the boy had kissed his mother on the cheek and left the room. 'It can be difficult for both of us to get away from the house at short notice.'

'No problem at all. I can imagine the difficulties. Your wife was just telling me how the surgery is keeping her occupied.'

'Yes. And a house-husband's work is never done, too. Can I offer you a tea or coffee?'

'No, thank you.'

'Something stronger, perhaps?'

'No, I'm fine.'

'Down to business, so. You wrote to Samantha, saying you wanted to meet?'

'Well, I have written to all the beneficiaries, suggesting a meeting to discuss the wills.'

'Wills?' queried Samantha.

'Lord and Lady Barrington's.'

'I assume Lydia's doesn't concern me.'

'Er . . . no. I suppose it doesn't. But Lord Barrington has made a bequest in your favour, and I thought you might wish to have the details confirmed directly.'

'I'm sure I don't want to hear. That useless holiday home in Cork. And a third of whatever's left after anything of value has been given to the others.'

'Well, I can confirm . . . .'

'Would you have a copy of the will for us?' interrupted Denis.

'I just have my own copy here. It's not a public document yet, as the probate will have to be processed first.'

'Perhaps you could summarise it for us, so.'

He ran through the principal terms of the will, which seemed to come as no surprise to either of them.

'Needless to say, Mr Hadfield, I am not at all satisfied that my father has dealt with this matter fairly.'

'I'm not sure that I understand.'

'Richard gets the manor house and estate. Jasmine gets the Henry Street property. Even Robert Staunton gets a big lump of money, and he's not even family. It's just not acceptable.'

Hadfield was a little taken aback by this, as he assumed she would have known of Robert's parentage at this stage.

'I can see that there may be different views on the bequests, but unfortunately the division of the assets was a matter entirely for your father, Dr Barrington Russell.'

'Not so! There are rules on this kind of thing. The children of a deceased have to be treated fairly. Isn't that right, Denis?'

149

'Well, I haven't practised for a while, and it's not really my area. But I do think the law puts a duty on a parent making a will to make proper provision for the children. Wouldn't that be right?'

Hadfield had never come across this in the office, but had a vague memory from his law studies that there was some such concept under an old Act from the 1960s.

'Er . . . yes. I believe there is such a law in one of the older statutes.'

'There you are,' interjected Denis. 'Perhaps we should be challenging the will on the basis that there hasn't been fair treatment of the children. What do you think, James?'

'We'd have to have a close look at that. I'm sure there must be criteria that have to be met to bring a case. Maybe earlier gifts, like this house, might be relevant?' This was as much as Hadfield could think to say, in the absence of any concrete knowledge on this particular area of the law. He decided to take the plunge and mention Robert's parentage as an additional factor.

'Of course, there is one issue which could be relevant. I had assumed you knew. About Robert?'

'What about him?' asked Samantha.

'His parents.'

'You mean the Stauntons?'

'Er, no. It transpires he was adopted.'

'And his real parents?' asked Denis.

'Lydia. And Samantha's father.'

They both looked at him, speechless.

'So, for the purposes of a court challenge to Lord Barrington's will, Robert Staunton might have to be considered one of the children.'

Samantha collapsed back into her chair.

'A drink, dear?' suggested Denis.

It took a few sips of brandy for Samantha to recover.

'Sorry to surprise you like that. I thought you knew.'

'I certainly did not. How did you know?'

'Well, the wills made mention. And Miss Greta told me herself. I had assumed . . . .'

'Why would she tell you that?'

'Well, I was with her this morning, to discuss the wills. As I am with you now. She told me then.'

Samantha went silent and took another sip of her brandy. Denis spoke up.

'And Lydia's will. What did she provide?'

Hadfield was reluctant to impart this information, as neither of them were beneficiaries, but he didn't have the resolve to make the point, and it was sure to come out sooner rather than later.

'She split it fifty-fifty between Robert and her sister Letitia.'

Samantha rolled her eyes.

'Letitia?' said Denis. 'I didn't think they even got on.'

'Does anybody?' said Samantha, knocking back her brandy and indicating the need for a refill.

'Any other bequests?' asked Denis, as he returned to the decanter.

'A substantial sum for the annual fête.'

'Devereux will be pleased. A drop of brandy yourself, James?'

'No, thank you.'

'Any mention of the Rathmore Players at all? Lydia was a keen attendee.'

'Afraid not. The only other significant beneficiary was Greta.'

'Greta?' queried Samantha, in a startled tone. 'Are you sure?'

'Yes. All her jewellery. You seem surprised?'

'Well, it's just that there had been a falling-out a little while back. A tiff over the fête, of course. Lydia was going to sell one of her pieces to make up a shortfall, even though she'd told Aunt Greta they were being given to her. Aunt Greta wanted her to ask Daddy, but Lydia was afraid to ask, as she'd already touched him for the original budget.'

'Lydia said the jewels were hers to do with as she wished,' continued Denis. 'Aunt Greta told her she could sell them all, as she didn't want them. Lydia said she might just do that, but one way or another Aunt Greta wouldn't get them.'

'I see,' said Hadfield, beginning to understand Miss Greta's behaviour that morning on the subject.

'Relations were a bit frosty for a while, but they had to keep meeting up for the fête. Lydia's stance must have thawed.'

'That stupid fête,' said Samantha. 'I suppose Devereux will be on to you straight away about that!'

'Well, he dropped in on Monday . . . .'

Samantha rolled her eyes again and sat back to sip her replenished brandy.

'Not the only one who dropped in to you on Monday, I hear,' Denis mentioned, with what seemed to be a slightly amused smile.

'Er . . . yes. Special Branch had arranged to drop by. They were looking for information on the wills. And some notes on Mr Timmons files, which he made on the day of the murders at the Manor.'

'Why would they want that?' asked Samantha

'To assist with the case, I suppose,' replied Hadfield.

'They must be building a case against Staunton,' added Denis.

'Not necessarily. It seems the police have quite an open mind on it. I had a few words with the detective sergeant while he was there.'

'An open mind on what?' asked Samantha.

'Well, the murders. It seems from the wills, and from their interviews, that all the beneficiaries had both the motive and the opportunity.'

'Including me?' asked Samantha, in a high-pitched tone.

Hadfield just nodded.

'But I wasn't anywhere near the nursing home on the day. I was in Kilcreddin. The police know that.'

'Well, that's what you told them, but it doesn't seem to be proof that you could not have got to the nursing home at the relevant time.'

'But that's ridiculous. I have to prove that I wasn't at the nursing home in order not to be a suspect!'

'Agreed. Believe it or not, I'm a suspect myself, because I don't have an alibi for the Friday afternoon.'

'And what could your motive be?' asked Denis incredulously.

'Being executor of the wills, it seems. Even though I don't get anything.' *There's also the possibility of Timmons' will*, he thought, but he didn't feel like mentioning that.

'Who is the other executor?'

'Albert Boyd.'

'That could put Boyd in the frame too, surely?'

'It could and it does. He was in the nursing home before the poisoning, and has no alibi for after that.'

'And not one of the beneficiaries can establish an alibi?' continued Denis.

'No. Lady Barrington claimed to be out riding. Richard claimed to be in his office. Jasmine was driving up from Dublin with Scott and Penny. But no one can corroborate it. Same with the others at the Manor. In fact, the only one who can offer an alibi is Staunton himself. His girlfriend says she was with him most of the time in the nursing home when it happened.'

'Good Lord!' exclaimed Samantha.

'Miss Greta is on their list too. And spouses as well.'

'What? Denis has to have an alibi too? I don't believe it.'

'And Richard's wife. As I understand it, both were by themselves at the time: him in his office on the estate, and her at home.'

All this seemed too much for Samantha, who fell back in to her chair.

CHAPTER 22

'Might have a brandy myself,' suggested Denis. 'Shouldn't really, of course, what with the opening tonight. But needs must. You'll be there of course, James.'

'Er . . . the opening?'

'Yes, *The Mikado*. You said you'd put it in the diary.'

'Ah. Yes.'

'Good. Should be close to a full house.'

'Enough of that bloody play,' said Samantha. 'We are suspected of murder! I tell you what: if Robert didn't do it, I think I have a good idea who might have.'

'Might I ask who that could be?' enquired Hadfield.

'Jasmine, of course. She never really got on with Lydia once she moved in to the Manor. Cramped her style.'

'And Lord Barrington?'

'Who knows. She certainly needed the money. Putting in bids for fancy apartments in Dublin without a penny to her name. Expecting her father to fund it all – which I'm sure he had no intention of doing. He gave her a perfectly good apartment as it is. They'd had a number of arguments over that. And God knows what she was up to, with that pair staying at the house. Both since disappeared, I'm told. I'd suggest the police should be looking closely into all that.'

'Indeed, my dear,' replied Denis, as he savoured his brandy. 'James, you mentioned that Staunton's girlfriend is giving him an alibi for the murder?'

'Yes,' replied Hadfield, 'at least for Lord Barrington's murder. She works at the home, as a nurse. She says she was with him in the staff-room pretty much the whole time.'

'Hardly the strongest of alibis, your own girlfriend. Can anyone else confirm that?'

153

'Not that I know of.'

'They could be in it together, of course,' suggested Samantha, who seemed to be recovering, having emptied her second glass at this stage. 'In fact, it wouldn't surprise me at all,' she added, indicating to Denis at the same time that a further brandy was required.

'Very possible,' agreed Denis, getting up again to do the needful. At the drinks cabinet, he stopped for a moment, and seemed to be giving some thought to a puzzling concern. As he returned to his wife with the third Cognac, he addressed Hadfield.

'Did you say Margaret Barrington had no alibi because she was at home the whole time?'

'Yes. Apparently she had coffee with a neighbour mid-morning and returned home. She was there until about 3, when she picked up the children from school.'

'That's strange. I'm fairly sure I saw her driving through here around then.'

'What time was that?'

'Just after 12. I was in the front garden. I'm pretty sure the church bell had just gone.'

'Which way was she going?'

'Towards Kilcreddin.'

That is strange, thought Hadfield. *She should have been at home from 11.30 until 3. Now she was at Rathmore at noon and Rathbawn at about 2.*

'I see. . . . I'm sure there is a good explanation for it.'

'There had better be,' Denis replied. 'For her sake.'

'Up to no good in any event, I'd bet,' added Samantha, who was becoming quite loquacious.

'Let's not jump to conclusions, dear . . . .'

'I've never trusted her,' she cut in, warming to the subject. 'There's something sly about how she carries on. Too quiet for my liking. Remember the time . . . .'

'Now, I'm sure Mr Hadfield is much too busy to be hearing about our family foibles. We've taken up more than enough of his time already. Unless there is anything else?' Denis enquired, as he rose from his seat and gestured towards the drawing-room door.

'No, I just wanted to let you have the details of the bequest. We'll obviously be moving the probate along. Er . . . goodbye, Dr Barrington Russell.'

'Goodbye, Mr Hadfield. And I'll expect to hear back from you about my share under the will. Not happy about that at all.'

'Er . . . yes. I'll certainly be looking into that.'

Denis escorted Hadfield through a further corridor leading to a high-ceilinged hallway, and opened the large, wooden-arched front door.

'Don't really expect to hear too much on the old will challenge,' commented Denis, as he stood on the doorstep, 'but probably best that it comes from the horse's mouth, so to speak.'

'Yes. Of course. I understand. You . . . er . . . don't miss the law game yourself, I suppose,' queried Hadfield. With the week he was having, Hadfield was starting to feel as though he wouldn't mind swapping places with Denis himself. *Wouldn't want the wife, though. And probably not the son.*

'Not in the slightest. Time's my own now. Plenty to keep me occupied here. And the commute would have been hell.'

'Where did you work?'

'Barton, Harvey & Cobb. One of the larger firms. Corporate, primarily. M&A, that kind of thing. Quite dull, really. You can't beat the stage. Nothing like the roar of the greasepaint and the smell of the crowd. Now, there's two tickets for this evening. You can fix up with me another time.'

'Oh. Very kind. I . . . er . . . .'

'You mentioned some notes on Timmons' file. The day he died. Why would the police be interested in that?'

'Not entirely sure. His note was a bit cryptic. But it seems Lady Barrington wanted him to look into some background issues. Probably related to Lord Barrington's death.'

'I see. Well, best left to the boys in blue, I suppose. See you tonight.'

And with a cheery wave, he closed the door.

*

Hadfield decided to take a slight detour on the way back to Kilcreddin. It was getting dark now, but he wanted to have a look at the tradesman's entrance to the nursing home. If the mysterious nurse had got into the home on the Friday, it was unlikely she had come through the main entrance. He drove up the secondary entrance, which was a winding, tree-covered roadway that led to the rear of the building. It had a number of lay-bys, as well as some additional laneways, which seemed to serve an adjoining farm. The roadway itself led to a discreet car park at the rear of the main building; the car park was not immediately visible from the principal rooms of the home.

He parked the car and followed the signs to the rear entrance. He found himself at a door which opened directly into the corridor which led to the staff-room and on to the resident rooms, the nearest being that of Miss Greta. *This must have been where Albert saw Staunton*, thought Hadfield. He tried the door but found that it had a combination lock. He looked around to see if there were any alternative entrance points, but none were evident. It seemed that the mysterious nurse could have easily got access to the home unnoticed – but how did she get in? Did someone open the door for her? Or did she know the code?

'Hello! What brings you back here?'

Hadfield turned, with a start, to see Sarah O'Doherty approaching him.

'Oh. Er . . . I was just wondering about that nurse nobody recognised.'

'Wondering what?' Sarah asked, a little dubiously.

'Well, how she actually got in. If she wasn't a member of staff. There's a combination lock.'

'They've only just put it in. After Lord Barrington's death. I think the police may have commented on it to management.'

'So there was no combination lock on it at the time of her murder.'

'No. It only went in last week. Bit of a nuisance, really. Have to open the door every time there's a delivery. There used to be a normal lock, which we could leave open during the day.'

'I suppose it would have been easy enough for someone to come in unnoticed at the time.'

'I suppose. How come you're taking such a keen interest in this? Not really your job, is it?'

'No. I guess I feel I've become a little involved. Being so close to the whole thing. Through the wills and all that. It does seem to me that the unknown nurse may be the key to solving all this.'

'So you don't think Robert had anything to do with it?'

'Well, that's really a matter for the police. But if this nurse is responsible, it's difficult to see how Robert could be involved. He'd hardly deliberately come to the home at the same time as the murderer, if he knew it was going to happen.'

'I hope they find out who she is. I . . . er . . . I have to go in now. I was just taking a smoke-break in my car. Goodbye.'

'Goodbye.'

Hadfield returned to his car and drove back to the office. Hilary and Mick were just getting their coats as he came through the front door.

'Evening all,' he said.

'Evening,' they both replied.

'How did that go?' asked Hilary.

'Becoming a bit predictable at this stage. Samantha has her own view on who the murderer is. And she also wants to challenge the will.'

'Tell all.'

'Well, she assumed Robert did it. But if he has an alibi from his girlfriend, then she thinks Jasmine probably did it. Says Jasmine didn't like Lady Barrington being in the Manor. And needed the money for a property in Dublin she had already put a bid on. And she thinks the will was unfair. Wants to bring a case to force the courts to vary the terms. She thinks the holiday home in Cork isn't worth anything like the manor estate or the Henry Street property.'

'Can she bring a case like that?' asked Hilary.

'I think there might be some section in the Succession Act dealing with children's rights. Mick, could you have a look into that? I'm sure it's only for special cases, but we'd better find out. She'll be on to us again about it, no doubt.'

'Will do.'

'Of course, she has completely ignored the fact that Lord Barrington gifted her a beautiful big Victorian property only a few years ago.'

'Bit of an ungrateful bunch all round,' added Mick.

'I wouldn't disagree with that,' he replied.

'Anything else to report?' asked Hilary.

'Well, one thing maybe. When I mentioned that none of the beneficiaries or their spouses had alibis, the husband, Denis, said that he'd seen Margaret Barrington in Rathmore at about noon. Heading towards Kilcreddin. She was supposed to be at home then. And Reverend Devereux saw her near the rectory in Rathbawn at about 2.'

'Her story doesn't seem to be standing up,' commented Hilary.

'No. It doesn't, does it. Actually, I dropped by the nursing home again on the way back, to check something.'

'Oh?' queried Hilary.

'Yes, I noticed a separate tradesman's entrance this morning when I was meeting Miss Greta, so I decided to investigate it on the way back from Rathmore. It occurred to me that Margaret may have accessed the nursing home that way on the Friday.'

'Dressed as a nurse?' queried Hilary, raising an eyebrow.

'Well, yes. I drove up the roadway. Plenty of places to leave your car unnoticed along the way. It could even go unnoticed in the tradesmen's car park, if it was busy enough. I checked the back door. It leads straight into the corridor where Miss Greta's rooms are.'

'Are you sure that was wise?' asked Mick worriedly.

'What do you mean?'

'Well, someone might have seen you.'

'What's wrong with that?'

'We are all still suspects, you know,' replied Mick. 'If the police found you returning to the scene of the crime just to have a look around, they might ask questions.'

'Did anyone see you?' asked Hilary.

'Well, I bumped into Sarah O'Doherty, Robert's girlfriend, who I'd met earlier today.'

'A witness!' exclaimed Mick. 'She might go to the police. Did she seem to be suspicious of you?'

'No. Of course not! As a matter of fact, she wants me to try and help Staunton in all this. She was able to confirm that the door was not usually locked during the day. They only put a combination lock on after the murder.'

'So,' Hilary mused, 'you think Margaret Barrington may have put on a nurse's uniform, hidden her car on the tradesmen's side, got through the rear door, taken the tea order from Miss Greta, made the tea, served it, and left. All without being recognised.'

'Er . . . I suppose that's the . . . er . . . logic of it.'

'And what's her motive?'

'Well, I . . . erm . . . haven't really thought too much about that. Maybe she wanted to make sure that Lord Barrington didn't dilute her husband's share of the estate. Or maybe she's in it with Richard.'

'Maybe,' replied Hilary.

'And maybe Sarah O'Doherty will tell the police that you were tiptoeing around the back of the nursing home, looking to solve a crime that shouldn't have anything to do with you,' added Mick.

'I very much doubt she will do anything of the kind,' replied Hadfield, while simultaneously doubting whether he should have gone near the home at all.

'I'm sure not,' Hilary said soothingly, before adding: 'Let's hope the CCTV doesn't raise any alarms.'

What a fool! Hadfield thought to himself. It had never occurred to him that there might be cameras in situ. And if they weren't there at the time of the murder, they surely were now.

'We were going to pop across for a drink. Want to join us?' asked Hilary.

'Er . . . better not. Actually, Denis twisted my arm and made me take two tickets for tonight, the opening night of *The Mikado* at Rathmore.'

He looked at Hilary before adding: 'Anyone interested?'

'No thanks!' they both said, as they headed for the door.

'You might ask Lucinda,' suggested Hilary as they left.

'OK. See you in the morning.'

'See you then,' they both replied.

The door closed after them, leaving a rather forlorn-looking Hadfield heading slowly back to his office.

CHAPTER 23

Hadfield and Lucinda entered the Rathmore Theatre in time for a drink before the show. It was a small venue, but pretty, and done in the old style, with velvet and drapes. No boxes, just seats in a single auditorium.

The reception area, which included the bar, was quite full, and Hadfield tried to catch the barman's eye.

'James! Would you be a darling and get me a G&T while you're there. I'm just going to powder my nose.'

It was Jasmine, of course. Hadfield noted Richard at the far end of the bar holding court, Katherine Rennick amongst them, with Margaret a short distance away, looking distinctly cheerless.

'I'll help,' said Lucinda, as he got the orders and sought out a secluded spot.

'For God's sake, Richard, could you get me my drink!' said Margaret.

'Coming, my dear, coming.'

'Ah, thank you, James,' said Jasmine, with a coquettish smile as Hadfield handed her the requested G&T. 'You're very good.'

She eyed up Lucinda carefully. 'And who have we here?'

'I'm Lucinda Dockrell. An apprentice with Timmons & Associates.'

'Any relation to . . . ?'

'I'm Superintendent Dockrell's niece.'

'I see. How . . . interesting. Oh, there's Wanda. Must have a word. Back in a sec.'

'That was short and sweet,' said Lucinda.

'Very. Look, here comes Letitia. With Clarisse.'

'Good evening, Mr Hadfield. I got your letter. Presumably you can confirm that the terms were as witnessed by Clarisse. One half to me and one half to Robert – subject to the specific bequests.'

159

'Well, yes . . . .'

'Good. I've moved out of the Manor. Staying at the Kilcreddin Arms. You can get me there as soon as you have moved things along. I'll be in touch if I need anything.'

'I should perhaps mention that the police were in the office on Monday. Looking at the papers. They were a little surprised to see Clarisse's signature as witness to Lady Barrington's will.'

'Why would they be surprised?'

'Because it probably meant she was the last person to see Lydia and Andrew alive. But never mentioned it.'

'I wasn't asked,' said Clarisse.

'Anyway, we've told them everything,' added Letitia. 'They came around on Monday afternoon. Some chap called Forde. Timmons asked her in, to be an independent witness. She signed and left. Now we'd better go and find our seats. Goodbye.'

'She's a cool character,' said Lucinda.

'Agreed. What did you think of her explanation?'

'Not sure. Could make sense. But a witness to a will doesn't have to be familiar with all the terms. It's just the signature she's witnessing. Perhaps she was chosen specifically to confirm the details of the will.'

'How do you mean?'

'Maybe Letitia needed confirmation of her bequest. She couldn't witness it herself, as a beneficiary. Maybe it is all related to the blackmail Miss Greta mentioned.'

'Hmm. Interesting. Speak of the devil . . . .'

Just then Miss Greta arrived, with Robert behind the wheelchair and Sarah beside them. Almost immediately, there seemed to be some kind of disturbance. Somebody was trying to push their way through. Eventually Samantha appeared, with a glass of brandy in her hand and looking a little unsteady on her feet.

'How dare you!' she shouted at Greta. 'Tell half the world about Robert, and not your own family.'

'That's not fair, Samantha. It had to be kept quiet while Phoebe was alive. And Lydia wanted to announce it only after all the legalities had been finalised. Obviously that wasn't possible.'

'Then why didn't you tell us yourself? Instead we have to hear it from our bloody solicitor!'

There was an awkward silence as eyes turned to Hadfield.

'I assumed the wills would make that clear. I only told Robert myself. Maybe I should have . . . .'

'Oh, this family!' cried Samantha, throwing her glass to the ground and running out of the theatre.

'Sarah, you might . . . ' said Greta, indicating that she should follow Samantha, to look after her. Assuming that would be possible. Or welcome.

'Greta. What's this all about?' asked Richard, approaching from the bar.

'Yes. What's going on?' added Jasmine.

'God damn it. I thought you'd know by now. George and Lydia were Robert's parents!'

All went silent. A bell rang to announce the start of the show, and people moved quickly to take their seats, whispering furiously as they went.

*

The crowd filtered out at the interval.

'Quite enjoyed that, I have to say,' said Hadfield to Lucinda.

'Yes, not my usual cup of tea. But good entertainment. Mr Russell is very good, isn't he?'

'He is, actually.'

Hadfield surveyed the reception area, and decided it might be better to avoid any public questioning.

'Might go out for a breath of fresh air. Want to join me?'

Lucinda nodded, and they both walked out – only to be greeted by Superintendent Dockrell.

'Uncle Bernard!'

'Hello, Lucinda.'

'What brings you here?'

'Business, I'm afraid. Evening, Mr Hadfield.'

'Good evening, Superintendent.'

Hadfield looked around, and noticed a policeman and policewoman standing a little distance away. DS Forde was also there, and slowly approached. Dockrell gave him a nod, following which the burly detective walked through the front door.

'What business exactly, Superintendent?' asked Hadfield.

'The police in France have just apprehended Hargreaves. His girlfriend Penny was with him. There are some outstanding offences there. Drug-related. He's being quite cooperative on that.'

'So why are you here?' asked Lucinda.

'Need to speak to Ms Barrington. Armstrong too. We're trying to track him down at the moment.'

'Are they involved?'

'Seems so. According to Hargreaves.'

161

Just then, DS Forde came out through the front door, with a clearly hysterical Jasmine.

'Get your grubby hands off me! What do you think you're doing? I've done nothing wrong. James! Why are you here? Tell them to let me go.'

'Now, miss, if you will just follow me to the car here. Nothing to do with Mr Hadfield.'

DS Forde managed to get her in to the car, and all four of them sped away.

'Do you think they could be involved in the murders?' asked Lucinda.

'Maybe. We'll be bearing that in mind during the . . . questioning.'

'There was a bit of activity before the opera started too.'

'Oh?'

Lucinda related the incident with Samantha.

'I see. So nobody seemed to be aware of Robert's real parents.'

'That's how it appeared.'

'Hmm.' Dockell turned his attention to Hadfield. 'Lucinda told me you received some kind of threatening letter today.'

'Yes. Actually, I have it here.'

He handed it over to the Superintendent. The detective looked at it closely. 'Might hold on to that. You'll need to be careful for the next while. But don't worry. We have surveillance around all this. We won't be far away.'

Hadfield wasn't sure how much comfort to take from that. What was the point of nearby surveillance if you were actually *with* the murderer!

'Thanks for the information on the discussion between Greta and Letitia. Very interesting. We are following up a few lines of inquiry on that.'

Dockrell looked to the ground while placing his hands on his coat-lapels.

'Anything else of note?'

Hadfield recited the discrepancies in Richard and Margaret's accounts, and the various suspicions of each of the individuals he'd spoken to.

'Very good. We'll look into that. All right, better be on my way. Keep up the good work, Hadfield. And I'll be in touch with you soon, Lucinda.'

Dockrell walked away to his own car, and Hadfield and Lucinda turned, to see a group of people still standing at the entrance, watching out for any more drama. It occurred to Hadfield that it might not have been entirely wise to be seen standing side by side with Dockrell as Jasmine was taken away. *Nothing to be done now*, he thought, as the bell went again and everyone headed back in for the second act.

'Never a dull moment with you, James,' said Lucinda, as they sat in their seats again.

'Not by choice, I can assure you,' he replied, feeling a great deal of attention being directed his way rather than to the stage.

He settled back as the opera recommenced, and decided to try and enjoy the rest of it. Denis, as Nanki Poo, was certainly talented, and very much enjoying his role on stage. Perhaps he was better off in the theatre than back working in a law firm in Dublin. Hadfield wondered if he had any acting talent himself. Although he couldn't sing, he knew that. As his mind wandered along these lines, something began nagging at him. About solicitors. What was it? There was some link he hadn't quite joined up. Just as he was about to let it go, he remembered that Denis had said that the firm he worked with was Barton, Harvey & Cobb. Specialising in corporate work. Mergers and Acquisitions, was what Denis had said. Was that the same firm as Dockrell had said looked after Robert's adoption? He was fairly sure it was. Did Dockrell know? Maybe he should mention it, just in case.

He turned his attention back to the show. The second half went down as well as the first, and the cast was given a standing ovation at the end. A beaming Denis took numerous bows, although he seemed to become a little distracted as he looked through the audience. Presumably he was hoping to see Samantha amongst the crowd, in his moment of glory.

Hadfield suggested a quick departure, and they went straight to his car.

'Actually, Lucinda,' said Hadfield, as they were driving back to Kilcreddin, 'you might do something for me tomorrow.'

'If I can.'

'It's just in relation to Denis. He mentioned that he used to work for a law firm in Dublin called Barton, Harvey & Cobb. On the corporate side. Mergers and Acquisitions. That kind of thing. Now when I was speaking with your uncle last weekend, I'm fairly sure he said the same firm dealt with the paperwork for Robert's adoption. By the Stauntons.'

'I see.'

'Perhaps you could give him a call tomorrow, just to check I got that right.'

'Of course. Although would it be a bit unusual for a law firm to do corporate work and adoptions at the same time?'

'I suppose it would be. But back then, maybe practices weren't so specialised.'

'Or Denis is embellishing his time there.'

'That wouldn't surprise me.'

'This is me here. I'll call Uncle Bernard first thing on that. Thanks for a very entertaining evening.'

She undid her safety belt and gave him a kiss on the cheek. Hadfield was a little taken aback.

'Er . . . see you tomorrow, so,' he said.

'See you then. Goodnight.'

CHAPTER 24

Hadfield found Hilary and Mick a little subdued the following morning.

'Late night?' he asked.

'Bit later than planned, anyway,' replied Hilary.

'I forced her to go to Bellamy's on the way home,' added Mick. 'We fell in with a bad lot.'

'I can imagine,' said Hadfield, who had fallen similarly before.

'How was the opera?' asked Hilary.

Hadfield recounted the evening's highlights.

'Maybe should have gone after all,' said Hilary.

'Would have been feeling a bit better today, that's for sure,' added Mick.

'I'll leave you to suffer the consequences.'

He went into his office, deciding to ring FitzHerbert to see if he was around the following evening.

'Morning, James, how are you?' was the cheery reply.

'Good, thanks. Yourself?'

'Could be worse. Although I have been better: had a dinner in the King's Inns last night.'

This was a regular event in the calendar of barristers and judges, and seemed designed to test their drinking stamina. He could be sure FitzHerbert didn't stint in his efforts.

'What time did you finish up at?'

'About 2. What has you calling at this hour?'

'I'll be in Dublin tomorrow. Just seeing if you're around.'

'I am indeed. What brings you back so soon?'

'Timmons' will, actually. Montgomery Darley have it. So we're meeting Ms Violet Curtis at 3 tomorrow.'

'Violet? Wouldn't mess with her.'

'You know her?'

'I've dealt with her a few times. A bit serious, but not immune to the humorous side of things. You mentioned "we"?'

'Yes. Hilary and Mick are coming along too. It seems the will may have some relevance to them too.'

'How intriguing.'

'Yes, I suppose it is a bit.'

'How's the detective work going?'

'To be honest, I've been doing little else all week. I had Detective Sergeant Forde first thing Monday.'

'Hmm. Not a man to hurry himself.'

'You're right there. I thought he'd never leave! Anyway, then Reverend Devereux dropped in that afternoon. Jasmine Barrington, the youngest of the children, came in on Tuesday, and took up most of the afternoon. I had to drop out to Greta Barrington at the nursing home yesterday morning, where I was collared by Staunton's girlfriend, Sarah, who works as a nurse there. And I was summoned to Rathmore in the afternoon for a meeting with Samantha and her husband. Then Dockrell turns up at the theatre last night to take Jasmine away!'

'I see. Any information worth passing on, at this stage?'

'I'm not sure really. Jasmine thinks Samantha did it. Greta thinks Richard did it. Samantha thinks Jasmine could have done it. Jasmine saw Richard's car where it shouldn't have been. Reverend Devereux and Samantha's husband saw Richard's wife's car when she was supposed to be at home. Greta had a recent falling-out with Lady Barrington. If Sarah is to be believed, Robert Staunton is the only one who didn't do it!'

'So you're clearing things up nicely.'

'Oh! And I overheard Miss Greta accusing Lady Barrington's sister of blackmail.'

'How interesting.'

'Of course, I've managed to upset Miss Greta, because I can't act for her in the defamation case she's determined to pursue. Jasmine wants to force Richard to keep making the payments which fell away when Lord Barrington died, and Samantha wants us to challenge the whole will on the basis that it wasn't fair! Oh, and Sarah wants me to advise Robert on how to get the police to drop the case against him.'

'Hmm. A few tight spots there. A good dinner is what you need, to see your way through all this. I'll book an early table at the club. Let's say 6.30. I'll meet you in the Shelbourne for 6.'

'Sounds good to me. Will Florence be joining us?'

'Afraid not. She's visiting her mother this weekend. I'd go too, but we have an understanding that myself and Sabine meet only on festive occasions – when there are plenty of other people about.'

'Sounds a sensible arrangement.'

'So weit, so gut!'

'What?'

'It's German, like my mother-in-law. "So far, so good." I take it you've been keeping notes of your meetings.'

'I have.'

'Bring a spare copy of them along with you tomorrow. Better run along: Judge Grattan is not known for his patience!'

Hadfield put down the phone, and was just on the point of picking up one of the employment files when Hilary knocked on the door.

'Sorry, James, but while you were on the phone there, Richard called, and asked that you drop out to him. He'll be at his house until 11 this morning.'

'The Barringtons clearly don't make advance appointments!'

'No. It doesn't seem to occur to them that the firm might have other clients. It's always been like that.'

'I guess I'd better go. He's likely to be our main client when the will has been sorted.'

'That's true. Cup of tea before you go?'

'Please.'

*

Hadfield returned home for his car at about 10, and headed for Rathbawn. It was a short trip, but a tricky one. As well as being narrow, the road was still wet from the thawing of the early-morning frost, and the fallen leaves added to the hazard. As he negotiated one of the bends, he noticed a small sports car hurtling towards him. There was barely enough room for the two of them, and any sudden braking would almost certainly result in dangerous skidding. As the car approached at speed, he spotted a slight indentation to his left, where a farmer's gate was situated, and pulled in immediately, as tight as was possible, breaking his wing-mirror in the process. The Mini Cooper Sport sped by without even slowing down. He saw that Jasmine was behind the wheel. She was looking straight ahead, and seemingly oblivious to the danger that had just been averted. Her sojourn with the police had clearly not enhanced her respect for the laws of the land.

After collecting himself, he inspected the car. It seemed that the wing-mirror was the only damage done, apart from a lot of mud caked on the front. He continued carefully on his way until arriving at Rathbawn. This was a smaller village than Rathmore, but possibly even prettier, with quaint houses and cottages on either side of the road that passed through it, and on the little laneways off it. The two main buildings were the rectory and Richard's house. There were a few shops, as well as a café and the Manor Inn. Richard's house was not as large as Samantha's but looked more homely, with its Elizabethan style. He turned into the driveway and parked in the first available spot on the gravelled area to the front of the house.

As he was getting out of his car, he was greeted by Albert Boyd, dressed as usual in a garish suit and dickie bow.

'Morning, James.'

'Morning, Albert.'

'Got the summons to Richard?'

'Yes. He rang this morning. Presume he wants to talk about the will.'

'And getting access to some monies, I should think.'

'Hmm. Possibly. Actually, on that, I had Jasmine in with me earlier this week. She seemed to think that you would be in a position to advance her some funds. Before the probate is completed.'

'That's right. Nothing unusual there. Probate can take time. We try to facilitate our most trusted clients. Between you and me, she's very short on funds; always has been: Lord Barrington kept a tight rein on the finances. Richard's been finding things a bit tight too: that's why he called me. If the bequest is clear and the assets confirmed, there should be no difficulty in making a little bridging available, to tide them over.'

'She mentioned some kind of solicitor's undertaking.'

'Well, of course we'd have to have the legal side of matters confirmed. To be sure the bequest will come through. You could deal with all that. Set out the terms of the bequest, and confirm you'd hold it for the bank as security – with Jasmine's and Richard's written authority. Don't see any issue there.'

'But can we be sure of any bequest while a murder enquiry is under way?'

'That's only Staunton's concern, surely. The other bequests won't be affected.'

'I'm not so certain about that. The police were in earlier this week as well – looking at documents. I think the suspect list has more than one name on it.'

'Oh? How many?'

'To be honest, just about everyone who benefitted from the wills. And us.'

'What do you mean "us"?' a startled Boyd replied.

'I mean you and me. As executors. They seem to think that might serve as some kind of motive.'

'But that doesn't make any sense. We don't get any bequests.'

'I know. I explained that, but it seems we can't be "eliminated from their enquiries" until we can prove we couldn't have done it.'

'I see . . . .' Albert paused for a while, as he thought about this new information. 'Might have to hold off on this bridging business until things are a little clearer.'

'Might be best.'

'We won't be too popular, I'm afraid.'

'I'm getting used to that,' said Hadfield – more to himself than anyone.

'What?'

'Oh, nothing. Just that the wills aren't proving as straightforward as I'd expected.'

He suddenly remembered he was supposed to call Boyd this week, to make an appointment to discuss the executorships and the processing of the wills.

'I had planned to call you later to make that appointment to go through things on the executor front. To move the wills along. Perhaps some day next week?'

'No problem. I'm around generally. Give me a call whenever suits.'

'Will do. I'd better go in: I think Richard has to leave by 11.'

'Right-o. See you next week. And take care: he's not in the best of moods.'

*

The front door was opened by a fully proportioned middle-aged woman, who seemed to be the housekeeper. She brought him in to one of the front rooms, which doubled up as a drawing room and office.

'Ah, Hadfield! The very man. Take a seat there. Can I get you something?'

Richard was pouring himself a glass of whiskey as he asked this.

'No, thank you. A bit early for me.'

'Me too, as a matter of fact. But it's just that bloody Jasmine. She's impossible to deal with!'

'Oh. I did pass her on the way up here.'

'She has some crazy idea that I should be making payments to her from the estate. What does the will say about that?'

'Well, nothing actually.'

'So she's not entitled to anything?'

'That would be a literal interpretation of the document. Jasmine seems to think that Lord Barrington would not have intended the payments to stop if his death was untimely.'

'Well, she can think all she likes. She won't be getting a penny from me unless the will absolutely requires it. You'd think she would have more pressing matters to deal with – like keeping out of prison.'

'Is there . . . er . . . some risk of that?'

'Very likely. Mixing with that Hargreaves chap was never going to end well.'

Richard walked towards one of the side windows of the room, taking a good shot of the whiskey as he did so. Hadfield noticed that the window gave a clear view of the manor house itself, which sat atop sloping green fields leading all the way down to Rathbawn.

'What a lovely view of the Manor,' he said, hoping to move the conversation on.

'Yes. Now on that, I need to have a clear understanding of Jasmine's right of residence. I presume the will did provide for that.'

'Yes, it did. Until such time as she should marry.'

'I see. Now what exactly does this right of residence mean?'

Hadfield hadn't given very much thought to this, but was immediately conscious that it could become a serious source of argument.

'Well, it means she can live there.'

'All the time?'

'If she wishes to, yes.'

'What rooms can she use.'

'All of them, I should think. It's a joint use.'

'What? She can go where she likes? To the library, or the drawing room, or the kitchen, no matter who's there?'

'I don't see why not.'

'And sleep in any bedroom, whenever she wants?'

'Well, I'm not so sure about that. There would have to be a degree of reasonableness in the exercise of the right.'

'And who's going to decide all that?'

'A court, I suppose. In the event of a dispute.'

'We can't have that. She'll have to agree arrangements so that there is as little contact as possible. You'll have to draw up some document to cover all that.'

'I'll see what can be done. Although it will of course need input from Jasmine to be effective,' he replied, thinking at the same time that the chances of getting agreement between the two must be slim.

'Do what you have to do. Just make sure she doesn't disturb us. Now, more importantly, when can I move in?'

'Move in?'

'To the Manor. And the estate. It's mine now, isn't it?'

'Your father did bequeath them to you. But there is the process of probate to go through first. To prove the will. And then make the formal transfer. It takes a little time.'

'How long?'

'It depends. Could be six months. Something of that order.'

'Six months! Are you mad? Who looks after the house and the estate during all this?'

'That would be the personal representatives. The executors under the will.'

'You and Boyd!'

'Yes. How did you know?'

'Boyd told me, of course. But what the hell do either of you know about running an estate.'

'Very little, to be honest.'

'And the house just lies idle while we await the wonders of "probate" to be dealt with.'

'Obviously the executors would need to ensure that the assets are managed during that time.'

'And what, might I ask, are the executors doing about that?'

'I . . . erm . . . I'm meeting with Mr Boyd next week. We will discuss what needs to be done then.'

'You'd better bloody get on with it. This is my property you're talking about. Why can't I just look after everything until your legal stuff is done.'

'I'll discuss that with Mr Boyd. It might be that a caretaker's agreement would be appropriate, in the circumstances.'

'With full rights to the income, of course.'

'We can look at that. I'm sure we can maintain the status quo, at least.'

Richard's reply to that was a grunt of some kind, followed by the downing of the remainder of his whiskey.

'Er . . . was there anything else you wanted to see me about?'

'Well, I suppose you had better confirm the terms of the will. I know about the estate, obviously. Assume the Cork house went to Samantha. Jasmine told me about Henry Street. I presume the rest has been split up equally.'

'Yes. There was an annuity to Miss Greta, and a lump sum to Robert Staunton.'

'How much?'

'Er . . . IR£250,000.'

'God damn it. But he won't get any of it if he's convicted, will he?'

'No. If he's guilty.'

'He's guilty all right. I don't know why the hell the police are taking so long about it. Didn't they find poison in his bin? What more do they want? He should have been locked up and charged long ago. And to think he's bloody well related to me! Is there anything we can do to speed it up?'

'A criminal case is a matter entirely for the police,' he replied. 'Obviously they need to establish all the evidence before taking a prosecution.'

'But they have all the evidence they need. He was at the nursing home and at the Manor. Nobody else was.'

'And the motive?'

'He needed the money, of course. He'd fallen out with George. Wanted to leave the shoot and start his own business. A shoot of his own. And some sort of bed-and-breakfast business – with that young one from the nursing home. Very probably in it together, if you ask me. Staunton wanted an advance to help him on his way.'

'From Lord Barrington?'

'Yes!' replied Richard with a snort of laughter. 'You can imagine the reaction to that. There was talk of changing the will for a while.'

'But he didn't.'

'Well, obviously not. Unless you know better,' said Richard, with a glare fixed on Hadfield.

'No, no, not aware of anything like that,' he replied.

'So, there you have it. The opportunity and the motive,' continued Richard 'What more do they need to put him away? There's nobody else who could have done it, is there?'

'I suppose the police do need to conclude their investigations. As a matter of fact, they came to our office the other day to check some papers.'

'Oh? What papers?'

'Just the wills.'

'I see.'

'And some of Mr Timmons' notes from Lord Barrington's files.'

'What would that have to do with anything?'

'Not sure. But the police didn't seem to be confining their investigations to Robert Staunton.'

'Who else are they investigating?'

'Well, it seems none of the beneficiaries have been eliminated from their enquiries as yet.'

'Why's that?'

'I believe it's because they don't have any alibis for the times of death.'

'Are they saying that one of the family could have done it? That I could have done it?' roared Richard.

'No, no, of course not,' Hadfield replied. 'It's just that the family members don't seem to have anyone to confirm their whereabouts at the time of Lady Barrington's murder. That doesn't mean they did it.'

'Should certainly think not. Load of nonsense. They should be looking at the people who were actually there!'

'I'm sure the police will get to the bottom of it eventually,' said Hadfield, in as soothing a voice as possible, seeking to calm the situation as best he could.

'They'd better. Or I'll be looking to you to force things along.'

He didn't know how to reply to this suggestion. Taking on the guards for tardiness of prosecution in a murder enquiry did not strike him as the wisest of moves. Fortunately, Richard had moved on to a further concern.

'Which reminds me. I hear Aunt Greta is trying to get Robert to bring some kind of defamation action against me.'

'Oh?' replied Hadfield blankly.

'Yes. It seems she wasn't happy with my eulogy at the funeral.'

'I see.'

'Now, I want you to send her a letter on my behalf, saying that she can sue me all she likes. I'll defend it to the hilt. I was entirely justified in every word I said, and won't retract a jot of it.'

'There might be a slight difficulty there.'

'What difficulty?'

'Well, you see, both yourself and Aunt Greta and Robert are all clients of Timmons & Associates. It wouldn't be possible for us to act for each side, and we shouldn't be seen to be favouring one client over another.'

'Who the hell does act, then?'

'The recommended practice in such a . . . .'

'Christ, here's Margaret!' exclaimed Richard, looking out the front window. 'It must be after 11. We'll have to discuss this later. I'll go out the back way. You can see yourself out.'

And with that, Richard was gone, leaving Hadfield alone in the room.

CHAPTER 25

Hadfield looked out the front window and saw a car pull up at the front of the house, with Margaret Barrington inside. He picked up his briefcase and headed towards the front door. He didn't know whether to open it or wait for Margaret to come in herself. He picked the worst option, which was to dither first and then quickly decide to turn the latch, finding himself face to face with Margaret.

'Good Lord!' she cried, jumping back.

'Terribly sorry. Didn't mean to startle you.'

'You gave me an awful fright.'

'I'm sorry. I was just meeting your husband. He had to leave in a hurry. Asked me to let myself out.'

'Sloping off before I came in, no doubt,' she replied, recovering her breath and her composure at the same time.

Just then, Richard's jeep sped out from the side of the house and past them both, accompanied by a brief wave from the driver.

'Mr Hadfield, isn't it?'

'That's right.'

'Discussing the will, I suppose.'

'Yes. Richard asked that I drop by.'

'All is in order, I trust.'

'Well, I was able to deal with his queries, in any event.'

'Actually, I have a query or two of my own. You might come inside.'

Margaret led him back into the same front room, and closed the door behind him.

'I've been meaning to consult a solicitor on this for some time.'

'Hopefully I can help.'

'I'm going to need a divorce.'

'Oh.'

'Yes. Now that Richard has the estate, he can afford it. He can live at the Manor. I'll stay here with the children.'

'Well, he doesn't have the estate just yet. There's a process.'

'But he's entitled to it, is he not?'

'Yes. Under the terms of the will.'

'And he has a share in the other assets?'

'Er . . . yes.'

'There you are. It's just a matter of time. Now, what do I need to do to get things moving?'

'I think I'd better stop you there, Mrs Barrington.'

'Oh! Why?'

'You see, your husband is a client of the office already. If this were to be a contentious matter, we wouldn't be in a position to act against him.'

'Contentious? Of course it will be contentious! But he doesn't know anything about it yet. I've had to wait until he actually had some money of his own to even let myself think about it.'

'I see.'

'So you can't act against him. Does that mean you can't act *for* him?'

'Er . . . we would have to consider that but . . . er . . . not necessarily. Provided you had separate representation, of course.'

'So you can look after him, but not me?'

'Well, he is a client. We have been retained by him historically.'

'I am too!'

'Oh?'

'Mr Timmons did my will at the same time as Richard's. Does that not make me a client?'

'Er . . . perhaps it does.'

'Now that I think of it, I'll need to change all that now. I suppose you can't look after that either!'

'Well, if the matter is contentious, it may be that you will both have to take separate legal representation.'

'So, I need to talk to someone else then?'

'Might be best.'

'Well, in that case, not a word to anyone about this. I don't want Richard knowing anything until he has to.'

'I understand. I'd . . . er . . . better be on my way.'

'Yes,' replied Margaret, 'I think you already know your way out.'

Hadfield took his leave, got in the car and disappeared down the driveway almost as fast as Richard had a little earlier.

*

'I'm not sure I can take any more of this,' said Hadfield, in reply to Hilary's greeting on returning to the office.

'What's up now?'

'The usual. Richard wants to know exactly what Jasmine's right of residence is. And he wants to take control of the estate straight away. And he wants me to write to Miss Greta and Staunton to tell them we'll defend any proceedings they bring.'

'Hmm.'

'Oh, and he might want us to take proceedings against the police if they don't hurry up with their enquiry.'

'No problem to you.'

He paused and checked Mick's room – which was empty – before continuing. 'It gets better. Richard scarpered out the back to avoid his wife, who then cornered me to ask about getting a divorce.'

'That could be tricky!'

'Exactly. We mightn't be able to act in any of that either. And by the way – not a word to anyone. Not even Mick.'

'Understood. Why is she looking for a divorce now?'

'Seems she was waiting until Richard had something to divorce with. She's suggesting he move into the Manor and she'll stay in Rathbawn with the children.'

'Bit of a motive for the murders there, wouldn't you say?' suggested Hilary.

'Crikey, you're right!' he responded, before adding, while stroking his chin slowly: 'And her alibi doesn't stand up if Reverend Devereux and Denis Russell are to be believed.'

'True.'

'It doesn't look so good for Staunton either, though. Richard says he had a falling-out with Lord Barrington. Wanted to set up his own shoot and was looking for an advance. There was a suggestion that George might change his will as a result.'

'An even stronger motive for Robert, then.'

'Yes. And it seems he wanted to start a B&B with his girlfriend, the nurse. So she might have a reason for being in on it too.'

Just then Mick came through the front door.

'Getting some fresh air?' Hadfield enquired.

'Getting something a bit stronger than that,' said Mick, holding up a box of Solpadeine.

'How did your visit to Richard go?'

'Definitely a pattern developing in all this. Everyone has an opinion on the murderer and everyone has an opinion on how the will should be. We'll have our hands full dealing with this.'

'Or not,' added Hilary.

'By the way,' said Mick, 'I looked into that question you had on Samantha Barrington challenging the will. The Succession Act 1965 has a specific section dealing with it. Hold on, I'll get the papers.'

He went into his office and returned with a number of books with pages marked in various places.

'Here, Section 117 of the Act. Basically the court can order a change to the will if it feels proper provision has not been made for a child.'

Hadfield read through the section. 'Pretty broad, isn't it?'

'There are quite a few cases on it. I've marked them out here. The courts won't change a will just because the children have been treated differently. Usually has to be a hard case. And earlier gifts can be taken into account.'

'That's great. Thanks. I'll look at those later. I'd better dictate my notes on my visit to Rathbawn first.'

After dictating his notes and grabbing a sandwich, Hadfield settled back into his chair to read the papers Mick had pulled together. You could nearly say it was a pleasure to be reading the law again, in comparison to the work he had been undertaking of late.

As he read through the case law, he noted that Mick was right. The courts had developed principles in their interpretation and application of the section. They could have regard to previous gifts, such as that given to Samantha. They could take account of the financial position and prospects of the children as at the testator's death. In one case, it was held that the child's behaviour towards the parent could be a factor in the determination of the application.

Hadfield was intrigued by this, and couldn't help reading the unusual details of the case, in which a son had illegally worked the father's farm for his own benefit, despite objections and litigation. At one stage, matters became so violent that the police were involved. Even with an injunction requiring that the son vacate the property, he continued to work it for his benefit. On the father's death, the son got a small legacy, with the remainder going to another relation, who had looked after the father during his last years. The son took a case under Section 117. The judge considered the son's farming of the land which seemed exemplary. But at the same time all the evidence reflected the 'appalling behaviour' of the plaintiff towards his father. Hadfield was glad to see that no change was made to the will.

As he read the judge's reasons, he noted the fact that a child was precluded from taking proceedings in certain circumstances. Reference was made to Section 120 of the Act: 'A sane person who has been guilty of the murder, attempted murder or manslaughter of another shall be precluded from taking any share in the estate of that other, except a share arising under a will made after the act constituting the offence, and shall not be entitled to make an application under section 117. . . . Any share which a person is precluded from taking under this section shall be distributed as if that person had died before the deceased.'

It occurred to Hadfield that all this could be very relevant to his own case. If Samantha was guilty of Lord Barrington's murder, then she could not take a case under Section 117 and her share would go back into the residue, to be divided between the remaining residual beneficiaries: Richard and Jasmine. And Lady Barrington, in respect of the one third share she was entitled to as the spouse of the deceased. Of course, the position would be likewise if one of the other beneficiaries was found to be the culprit.

As he was considering all this, it suddenly struck him that the reference to Section 120 might have another meaning: could it be the S120 in Timmons' file note? He took out his own notebook, where he had jotted down his, or rather Hilary's, 'translation', which now read:

Lady B agitated –
About Robert –
Check background –
Firm matters –
Refers Section 120 –
Wills change

He sat back and contemplated this interpretation of his old boss's notes. 'I wonder . . . .'

CHAPTER 26

'What do you think?' asked Hadfield of Hilary, as they sat in the alcove of the Riverside Inn having tea and a sandwich for lunch.

'I can see how it might mean Section 120. But what did A.T. mean when he referred to it?'

'Well, when I was at the Manor, Lady Barrington did indicate that she had an idea who Lord Barrington's murderer was. And she took Andrew aside to discuss matters with him in private. Maybe she thought that Robert was being set up so that he could be disinherited for the crime. So that the bequest to Robert would go back into the estate.'

'Seems a drastic step for IR£250,000, when you think what the other beneficiaries got.'

'Or maybe the real guilty party knew of the proposed change to George's will, which was going to give Robert an equal share.'

'Now that might be a reason all right.' Hilary paused for a moment, before adding: 'Except, who knew about that, apart from Lydia?'

'Hmm. See what you mean. Letitia, maybe. Greta, possibly. Apart from that . . . .'

Just then, Morton approached their table. 'Everything alright for you there?'

'Yes, thanks,' they both replied.

'Hear you are up to Dublin tomorrow.'

A perplexed Hadfield looked at Morton and then at Hilary, whose head was now down and focused firmly on her teacup.

'For the reading of Timmons' will,' continued Morton. 'I gather all three of you are going.'

'Who told you that?' replied an incredulous Hadfield.

'Common knowledge in Bellamy's, apparently.'

'Oh?'

'It wasn't me,' Hilary said meekly.

He paused while he took all this in.

'I think I know where this story may have originated. For the record, we are not attending a reading of Mr Timmons' will. Mr Timmons' personal solicitor has simply contacted us in the usual way, as part of normal legal process, to assist in the administration of the deceased's estate.'

'And you all have to go together?'

'Well, of course, that was . . . er . . . to . . . er . . . facilitate the solicitors. Much more efficient to meet the three of us at the same time. Now if you don't mind,' he said, as he reached for his wallet, 'we need to be getting back to the office. That should cover it. You can hold on to the change.'

'Very kind of you,' replied Morton, with a little chuckle which he didn't try very hard to repress.

'Let's go,' said Hadfield, as soon as the proprietor was out of earshot. 'We'll talk about this back at the office.'

*

As soon as they got back to the office, Hadfield called Mick into the reception area.

'What were you telling people in Bellamy's last night?'

'About what?'

'About our going to Dublin tomorrow.'

'Nothing. Just that we were going there. One of the lads wanted to drop in to swear a declaration on Friday afternoon. I said we wouldn't be here.'

'According to Morton, all of Bellamy's think we are going to a reading of Mr Timmons' will.'

'But we are, aren't we?'

'We don't know for sure. Either way, we shouldn't be disclosing that kind of information to anyone.'

'But I didn't say anything about reading the will.'

'Well, what did you say?'

'I probably mentioned the letter I'd got from the solicitors about the will.'

'And that we'd all got a similar letter?'

'Maybe,' said Mick, a little defensively.

'Well, of course they are going to start speculating about his will with that kind of information. We won't hear the end of it now until the will is made public.'

'Sorry. I didn't think . . . .'

Just then the doorbell rang. Hilary opened the door, to find Robert Staunton on the step.

'I was looking to see Mr Hadfield. He sent me a letter.'

'Come in, Rob,' she replied.

'We'll discuss this later,' Hadfield said, sotto voce to Mick, by way of dismissal.

'Is now a good time?' asked Robert.

'Er . . . not a problem,' Hadfield replied. 'Just back from lunch. Perhaps you could wait in reception here for a couple of minutes, and I'll just tidy away a few things in the office.'

Staunton took a seat while Hadfield returned to his office and cleared the meeting desk. He also took the opportunity to pace the room a number of times, in an attempt to calm himself. Eventually he called Robert in.

'Can I get you a cup of tea?' he asked, as he ushered Robert to one of the seats at the meeting desk.

'No, I've just had lunch myself. . . . I got your letter, and I have a few questions about the wills and that.' Robert looked directly at him before adding: 'As long as it doesn't cost me anything.'

'No, don't worry about that. The purpose of the letter was to let beneficiaries ask any questions that might be on their mind. If more work is needed, we can deal with that separately.'

Robert looked at him a little suspiciously but said: 'All right then. He took out a piece of paper with some handwritten notes on it, and continued. 'I suppose the first question is: what does the will say? About me?'

Hadfield noted that Staunton seemed a bit uncertain of the answer. 'Well, there is a bequest to you under Lord Barrington's will. Quite significant, actually: IR£250,000.'

Robert didn't give any particular reaction to that, just asking: 'And when can I use it?'

'Well, as I have explained to the others, there is a probate procedure to go through. About six months, I would say, in an estate of this kind.'

Robert groaned. 'I thought it would be quicker than that. I want to start a business.'

'What business is that?' Hadfield asked innocently.

'I want to run my own shoot. And a B&B.'

'By yourself?'

'No, of course not. My girlfriend, who works in the nursing home, would run it with me. I discussed all this with Timmons.'

'I'm sorry, I wasn't aware of that. Perhaps you could summarise the proposal for me – from the beginning?'

Robert let out a slightly frustrated sigh, and continued: 'Greta told me about the bequest some time ago. It got me thinking. I run the shoot at the estate but report to Richard. It's no secret that we don't always see eye to eye. With Lord

Barrington overseeing, it was always manageable, but I had to think ahead. If Richard had complete control, the likelihood was that I'd be looking elsewhere for employment. I mentioned this to George. I was happy to continue running the shoot at the estate with him in charge, but needed to plan for the future. Also, my girlfriend had in mind a switch from nursing to managing a B&B. I thought that if we could buy a suitable property, Sarah could look after the B&B side of things, and I could build up a small shoot as part of that in my spare time.'

'And what was Lord Barrington's reaction to that?'

'Not very good . . . particularly when I suggested an advance to get things started. That was probably a mistake. He thought myself and Richard should be able to work out an agreement in relation to the estate shoot. And he said he had no intention of paying a penny towards a competing shoot. I tried to explain that it would be aimed at a completely different type of customer: novices and passing tourists. But he wouldn't listen.'

'So that was the end of that, I take it.'

'Well, no. Obviously I mentioned it to Greta. She didn't see the difficulty with what I had suggested. Unfortunately, she also told George what she thought.'

'Which was?'

'That all the children had received advances of some kind or other to set them up, and that a small loan, to come out of my share under the will, would not prejudice anyone. A bit of a rant followed that.'

'I can imagine.'

'He said she was trying to make him rewrite his will. And that he had a good mind to do just that.'

Robert paused, before adding: 'That's one of the reasons I came today. To see if he had.'

'No. It seems not. Both your bequests remain unchanged.'

Robert thought about this for a while.

'So we might have to go back to our original plan: the one I discussed with Mr Timmons.'

Hadfield gestured to the effect that this meant nothing to him. Robert took a deep breath and continued. 'After Greta's discussions with George, she was a little concerned about the possible outcome. She suggested the possibility of selling her cottage, where I stay, and using the proceeds to buy a suitable property for myself and Sarah. I spoke to Timmons on the phone about it. We discussed setting up a company, with the shares divided between the three of us, or maybe divided equally between myself and Sarah, with a loan from Greta secured on the property.'

'And what happened?'

'Not much, I'm afraid. Mr Timmons suggested getting some tax advice. And maybe a business plan. And a valuation on the cottage. And identifying the availability of a suitable property. That slowed things down a bit . . . .'

Robert shrugged his shoulders. Hadfield recognised that Staunton's talents lay in the running of the shoot, not in the practicalities of setting it up.

'I'll probably have to start looking into all of that now. Sarah's anxious to move on from the nursing. But without any actual money, it's hard to know where to begin. You're the new solicitor: what should I do next?'

Hadfield was conscious of Sarah's concerns on the criminal side of matters, and saw an opportunity to steer the discussion in that direction.

'Well, it is going to involve quite a deal of work. In the first instance, you should probably talk to an accountant. As Mr Timmons said, you need to form a business plan and agree a tax structure. You will have to do costings and projections, to make sure it is a viable proposition. That will all involve quite a bit of time – and money. You will need to engage agents to deal with valuations on the properties and the marketing side of things. Again, time and money. We can get involved when you have finalised a plan: forming the company, conveying the properties, drawing up agreements to regulate matters between yourself, Sarah and Greta. Needless to say, that doesn't happen overnight, and we do charge for our services.'

Robert was becoming glassy-eyed as Hadfield spoke, and leaned back in his seat without saying a word.

'A project like that will need your full attention. And funding. Perhaps it might be best to concentrate on more . . . er . . . immediate matters.'

Robert looked up at him with furrowed eyebrows. 'What do you mean?'

'I mean the police investigation. I happened to meet Sarah briefly yesterday. She's very concerned about that whole side of things.'

'What were you doing meeting Sarah?' asked Robert in a slightly querulous tone.

'I was visiting Miss Greta at the nursing home,' he replied hurriedly. 'I had sent her a similar letter to the one I sent you, and she asked me to come over yesterday morning. Sarah called me aside for a word as I was leaving.'

'I see,' responded Robert gruffly.

'Yes. She's worried that you have been interrogated twice but refuse to seek any legal representation.'

'But I haven't done anything wrong.'

'But the police don't know that.'

'They do. I told them.'

'What did you tell them?'

'That I didn't poison anyone.'

'But you were the only person at the nursing home who might have had a motive.'

'I was with Sarah the whole time. She confirmed that.'

'Then who *did* administer the poison?'

'I don't know! It could have been anyone. Even Richard. Or Samantha. Or Jasmine. Who knows?'

'But they weren't there.'

'Maybe nobody saw them. Or they got someone else to do it. Like that nurse that Sarah saw. All I know is that it wasn't me.'

'Yet you are still the police's main suspect.'

'That's their problem.'

'But it could become yours. If you are innocent, wouldn't it be best to have someone represent you who can argue your case for you?'

'Why would an innocent man pay someone to prove he's innocent? Anyway, I couldn't afford it.'

'Well, if you can't afford it, the state may cover the cost. There is a free legal aid scheme, which may apply.'

Robert thought about this for a moment.

'If it doesn't cost me anything, maybe there's no harm in it. But they haven't charged me with anything yet.'

'You could consult with a specialist criminal solicitor in advance, so as to be fully prepared for that.'

Robert thought again for a moment.

'No. Unless the police charge me, I don't want any advice. If they do, I might consider it then.'

'Are you sure about that?

'Certain.'

Hadfield leaned back in his chair, somewhat relieved. At least he'd done as he had promised for Sarah. Also, it wasn't immediately necessary to set up a consultation for Staunton. He wasn't too sure who he would call anyway.

'Was there anything else you wanted to ask?' he enquired, hoping to wrap things up.

Robert checked his piece of paper before replying.

'Yes. Greta mentioned the possibility of a payment in advance from the bank. Based on the terms of the will and some kind of undertaking.'

Hadfield resisted the urge to curse and look to the heavens. Instead he looked down at the table, closed his eyes and took a deep breath.

'This question has come up already. It is sometimes possible in an entirely straightforward probate for a bank to lend money in advance of the completion of formalities. This has not turned out to be one of those cases.'

'Why's that?'

'Because the testator has been murdered!'

Robert seemed a little taken aback by the response, and Hadfield realised that he may have been a little vehement in answering his query.

'You see,' he continued, in a more placatory manner, 'the law has certain rules dealing with what can and what can't be inherited. If a person is given a bequest under a will, and is found to have murdered the person who made the bequest, then the bequest is null and void.'

'But I haven't murdered anyone.'

'No, but the bank don't know that.'

'Why do the bank have to know?'

'Because if you want them to give you money before the probate is completed, they will want to be sure that there is no risk of it being taken back.'

'But where's the risk? The money won't be coming back from me. I didn't kill George.'

'I think you will find that the bank won't be making any advances to anyone unless their innocence is proved. And that almost certainly means finding someone guilty.'

'So. No advance then.'

'No.'

There was a moment's silence as Hadfield let the news on the advance front sink in. As he waited, he noted with surprise that he could hear voices from the reception area. This was unusual, as the room was very well soundproofed, to ensure quiet and privacy.

'Anything left on the list?' he asked, as much to distract from the noise as to try and conclude matters.

'Just one more. It's about this defamation thing.'

'Yes?'

'Well, Greta seems determined to pursue it. Although I don't really care one way or another. Do we have a good case?'

'I had a detailed discussion with Miss Greta on that yesterday. I'm sure she can fill you in on all that. There is an arguable case, but it will depend on the witness evidence produced, and how the courts view it. You see . . . .'

He was going to go into more detail, but couldn't help but notice that the noise level seemed to be rising outside the door.

'How much would you charge to take the case?'

Hadfield was finding it difficult to concentrate at this point, but managed to respond. 'Actually, as I explained to Miss Greta, it won't be possible for Timmons & Associates to act for you in such a case. Unfortunately, where . . . I'm terribly sorry. Could you excuse me for one moment.'

The noise had increased again outside. Hadfield felt he had to put an end to it, if he was to have any chance of finishing up with Staunton. And as a matter of observing the professional proprieties. He walked straight to the door, quickly opening and closing it behind him, while turning to Hilary and saying: 'What in God's name is . . . .'

He had been expecting to see Hilary and Mick in the reception area. Instead, he was faced with the back of Richard Barrington, who was standing directly in front of a seated, and exasperated, Hilary.

CHAPTER 27

'Ah! There you are. I've been waiting an age for you. We need to finish our earlier *dishhcushion.*'

Hadfield looked with alarm at Hilary, who just shook her head and motioned with her right hand that drink had been taken.

'I'm very sorry, Mr Barrington. I am not available at the moment. I'm sure Hilary explained all that to you.'

He noticed that Hilary was trying to catch his attention, but Richard was moving closer to him, saying: 'But we never finished our discussion on that . . . ' – there was a pause here, while Richard delivered a hiccup –'. . . that . . . whole defamation thingy. . . . I need you to get that letter *shorted. Shtraight* away.'

'I cannot discuss this with you now. Please, Mr Barrington, you will have to make an appointment. Hilary here can arrange that with you now. There would be no difficulty meeting with you at your house as we did this morning, if that suits.'

Hilary was now making firm pointing gestures with the first finger of her right hand. Hadfield couldn't understand. It seemed to be pointed at him.

'Better not. Her indoors. Need to discuss cash as well. Boyd says shouldn't be a problem. *Jusht* a little note from *yourshelf* and Boydy says Bob's your . . . er . . . .'

'Now really, Mr Barrington. We cannot continue this discussion in the reception area. You are interrupting my consultation with a client. I have to ask you to make an appointment with . . . .'

He noticed that he had lost Richard's attention, which was now focused, though perhaps not firmly, on the door behind him. Hadfield turned slowly, but rather than seeing a pristine white door, as expected, he was faced with the very client with whom he had been consulting. The door was fully ajar.

'What the devil's going on here?' shouted Richard, who was now the person pointing a finger towards the office where Staunton had appeared. 'Why are you having a consult . . . *conshult* . . . having a meeting with him?'

'In response to my letter,' replied Hadfield. 'The same one as I sent you. All beneficiaries got one.'

'Damned irregular! The man's a . . . a *shuspect*. For murder! And you're talking to him about father's will?'

Richard pointed his finger at Robert again, a little unsteadily, and added: 'When everyone knows he did it!'

'That's it. You'll pay for that!' replied Robert.

Hadfield tried to intervene as Robert advanced on Richard. At the same time, the front-door buzzer sounded.

Robert managed to get his hands on the lapels of Richard's jacket, despite Hadfield's intervention.

'It's probably you the police should be talking to,' Robert shouted, as he struggled to get Hadfield out of the way. 'You couldn't wait for him to go.'

'Get your hands off me. I'll . . . .'

'Stop that immediately! All of you!' A familiar voice could be heard crying out above the mêlée.

All three looked around, to see Jasmine standing in reception. As usual, she looked stunning – and would have been suitably attired if she was going to a ball.

'Richard. Your jeep is completely blocking the road. You need to move it. And what are you doing here with Robert?'

'I . . . er . . . had *jusht* come by to . . . .'

'You're drunk!' she replied dismissively, before turning to Hadfield. 'Didn't you notice?'

'He only just arrived,' gasped Hadfield, as he continued to hold Staunton back. 'I was in a meeting with Mr Staunton at the time.'

'But you somehow managed to let them start a fight.'

'I'm trying to prevent it.'

'Not doing a particularly good job, I'd say. Richard, I'm bringing you home.'

'But I haven't finished . . . .'

'Let's go,' Jasmine ordered, 'before you get yourself in trouble.'

Richard slumped somewhat on hearing this. Robert loosened his grip, and Richard swayed slowly towards his sister. 'Not to Rathbawn,' he whispered. 'Margaret and all that.'

'All right. You can sober up at the Manor. Give me the keys to the car.'

Richard fumbled in his jacket pockets, and after a few attempts located the keys for his jeep. He handed them to Jasmine, who threw them to Robert.

'You can leave it at the Manor. He'll need it later.'

Staunton fumed silently, as Jasmine directed her brother to the door.

'By the way,' she said to Hadfield from the doorway, 'did you speak to Boyd about that advance? I really do need to move on the apartment.'

'I . . . er . . . had a brief word. Er . . . .'

Fortunately for Hadfield, Richard tripped slightly at just that moment, and Jasmine's attention was distracted.

'Maybe now's not the time to discuss it,' suggested Hadfield.

'I'll call later on that,' she replied, with a somewhat stern smile. 'And for an update on Henry Street.' She paused, before adding: 'I might also need some advice on a . . . separate matter.'

The door closed, and Hadfield let out a relieved sigh. The relief was short-lived.

'So. What's sauce for the goose isn't sauce for the gander!' exclaimed Robert.

'Sorry?'

'Advances all round for the Barringtons, but not a penny for the person falsely accused of murder.'

'I don't know what you mean.'

'You know exactly what I mean. In cahoots with Boyd. And I see you can act for Richard in the defamation case but not for me. One law for the rich and another for the poor.'

'It's not like that at all!'

'That's exactly what it's like. Didn't I hear it with my own ears!'

'But you didn't hear the full story. You see . . . .'

'I've heard all the stories I want to hear, at this stage. I'll be on my way, thank you very much.'

And with that, Robert left the office, closing the front door with a bang.

'God almighty!' exclaimed Hadfield. 'Just when you thought it couldn't get worse!'

'All a bit unfortunate, I'd have to admit,' replied Hilary, suppressing a laugh. 'Although in time I'm sure you'll see the funny side of it.'

'In the funny farm at this rate! I'll have all the time in the world to laugh then.'

'Is it safe to come out now?' enquired Mick, sticking his head gingerly around the door.

'Completely safe. Not a client in sight. The way things are going, we won't need to worry about anyone darkening our door.' Hadfield retreated towards his office. 'I need to sit down.'

He had hardly collapsed into his office chair when Hilary rang through.

'Sorry to disturb you so quickly, James, but Samantha is on the line. From her mobile.'

'Christ! What does she want?'

'She just passed the office in her car and saw Richard, Jasmine and Rob outside. She seems to think there is something afoot. Wants to talk to you about it.'

'To be honest, I don't think I could handle that right now. Could you just tell her I'm engaged? And . . . er . . . if you wouldn't mind . . . er . . . perhaps explain to her what really happened? So that she doesn't need to worry.'

'Or drop in.'

'Exactly.'

'I'll try.'

'Thanks.'

Hadfield waited for a short while in his office. He rang Hilary's number but it was engaged. He waited a little longer, and tried again. Still engaged. He went to the door, but could only hear the muffled voice of Hilary speaking intermittently. He opened the door slightly, so as to hear what seemed to be the ending of the call.

'That's right.'

'Exactly.'

'Entirely coincidental.'

'Of course.'

'Not at all.'

He stuck his head out.

'Sorted?'

'I think so. Glossed over Richard's inebriation, but she may well have guessed.'

'She doesn't want to meet?'

'No. Not at the moment, anyway.'

'Great. You're a star. Now, if anyone calls, I'm out of the office for the afternoon. And no appointments until Monday.'

'Understood. Oh, Lucinda mentioned she might have a word when you're free.'

'I'll drop up.'

Lucinda's room comprised the loft which made up the upper floor of the offices. It had been used as a storage space before she had joined as an apprentice, but room had been made for a desk and a couple of chairs. A bit cramped, but she didn't seem to mind. The stairway was quite steep and tight, and Hadfield bent his head as he entered the room.

'Hilary said you wanted a word?'

'Yes. I checked up on Barton, Harvey & Cobb. It seems Mr. Russell was a solicitor with the firm at the time of Robert's adoption.'

'As a corporate lawyer?'

'Not sure. It was very much a private-client firm back then. Conveyancing, probate, family law. A bit of litigation. There would have been some corporate advice needed, no doubt.'

'But Mergers and Acquisitions might be gilding the lily a bit.'

'Quite a bit, I'd say. But whatever he may have been doing, he could have known about the details of Robert's adoption.'

'And if he did?'

'Well, maybe he told Samantha, who realised that Lord Barrington might change his will to everyone's detriment.'

'Hmm . . . . If she did, she certainly put on a good show of not knowing, when I told her at the house. And an even better one at the theatre.'

'Very true. Did you mention this to your uncle.'

'I did. Spoke to him about Jasmine too.'

'Oh, tell all.'

'Well, you know they arrested Hargreaves in Paris. Uncle Bernard had Penny followed when she left the Manor. That's how they got him. He's deny-ing any involvement in the murders but is admitting to drug-possession and a limited level of dealing. The French police are doing further investigations into that. Penny doesn't seem to know a whole lot about it, but has admitted to using whatever Hargreaves may have had with him. They took in Simon Armstrong as well, on the basis of Hargreaves' statement. Seems he may have been dealing too.'

'And Jasmine?'

'Hargreaves claims he organised drugs for her, and that she owes him money for that. Uncle Bernard thinks the debt is probably a lot greater than Hargreaves is saying, but that he's afraid to say the full amount because of the consequences in relation to the charges against him. Of course Jasmine is denying all of it. She says she may have shared some of the drugs with Scott and Penny, but that she never bought any, and never intended to.'

'Will that stand up?'

'Bernard seems to think so. Unless some better evidence is found. He thinks Hargreaves could have been blackmailing too. Making threats unless Jasmine paid up her debts.'

'Another possible motive for Jasmine, then.'

'Exactly.'

'And possibly Hargreaves too.'

'Hmm . . . .'

*

Hadfield emerged wearily from his office at 5 PM.

'That's enough for me. I've left a couple of tapes inside. Including today's exciting instalment. Charles wants to have a look at them, so you might print an extra set of the lot. I'll bring them with me tomorrow. Is the train booked?'

'Yes. Three open tickets. We can collect them at the station. Train leaves at 12.30. Arrives 2.30.'

'Great. Leave here around 12?'

'Should be plenty of time,' replied Hilary, as she sifted through some papers in front of her.

Hadfield dawdled for a moment.

'Might . . . might go for a pint.'

'Not surprised. You've had a challenging day.'

'Do you want to . . . ?'

'Better not. Should try and get a head-start on the dictation. But . . . er . . . .'

Hilary looked up at Hadfield and across to Mick's door, which was shut.

'Mick's a little upset about the Bellamy's incident. Might be no harm to take him with you for one.'

'Maybe you're right. I might have been a bit harsh earlier.'

He knocked on the door and looked in on a dejected figure behind his desk.

'Fancy knocking off early and going for a pint?'

'Is the Pope Catholic?' was the quick reply.

A reanimated and relieved Mick left the office with Hadfield, leaving Hilary to lock up after her.

'Where are we off to?' asked Mick, once they were out on the street.

'We could go to Bellamy's,' said Hadfield, with a straight face.

'What?' was the slightly worried reply.

'For the hair of the dog . . . ' – he paused momentarily, before adding – ' . . . that bit you!'

Mick got the joke and laughed, albeit a little nervously. 'Maybe not,' he suggested.

'No. Maybe not. And not Morton's either. We might let him sit for a while.'

'The Arms?'

'Good idea.'

Hadfield was greeted by Mrs Stokes as usual in the foyer.

'Dining with us this evening, Mr Hadfield?'

'No, just an after-work drink, actually,' he replied, as he headed into the bar which adjoined the reception area.

'Very good.'

191

'I'll get these,' suggested Mick, as they took a table near the bookcases along the right-hand side of the room.

'A pint?'

Hadfield nodded, and waited while Mick ordered the two pints of stout.

'Ah. Mr Hadfield. I thought it was you.'

He looked around to see Letitia. He had forgotten she was now staying at the Kilcreddin Arms. Was anywhere safe these days?

'Good evening.'

'Seeing you pass through reminded me of something.'

'Oh?'

'You mentioned at the Manor that Lydia would be entitled to a third of her husband's estate if she received less than that under his will.'

'That's right.'

'I think you mentioned that some kind of election has to be made.'

'Yes.'

'And the persons to make that election are now you and Mr Boyd.'

'I . . . er . . . suppose so.'

'Presumably you will be getting on with that. Obviously as a beneficiary under Lydia's will, it would be important for me that you attend to that as expeditiously as possible.'

'Yes. Of course.'

'I might just drop you a note confirming that. As an aide-memoire. We wouldn't want your dealings with the police to distract you from your client responsibilities. Good evening.'

Hadfield just stared as she glided away.

'Crikey, who was that?' asked Mick, as he returned with the drinks.

'Letitia. Lady Barrington's sister.'

'Something a little scary there. Not sure I'd want to have too many dealings with her.'

'Not sure I'd want any at all.'

'Anyway. Cheers.'

'Cheers.'

There was a short pause while they both made a decent dent in their pints.

'Sorry about Bellamy's last night. I didn't think that . . . .'

'Don't worry too much about it. You just need to be a little more careful in what you say in public. Especially about office matters. People talk. You know what they're like around here.'

'I know. They'll be plaguing us about Mr Timmons' will now, I suppose.'

'For sure.'

They each took another swig. Although the room was empty save for the barman, Mick made a point of carefully surveying their surroundings.

'Speaking of Mr T.'s will,' he whispered conspiratorially, 'what do you think the solicitors want us for?'

Hadfield sat back in the comfortable armchair and thought about his reply. Just then, he heard Mrs Stokes from the reception area.

'Good evening, Jasmine. How are you?'

He straightened up in his seat. 'Very well, Beatrice. And yourself?'

It was Jasmine Barrington all right.

'What's wrong?' asked Mick.

'Shh!' whispered Hadfield, putting his index finger to his lips.

'Can't complain. Off to the fund-raiser tonight?'

'Yes. Meeting Hugh for a drink first. Is he here?'

'Should be. I'll check.'

'Thanks. I'll just go to the powder-room for a moment.'

Hadfield hid as best he could behind the side of the armchair, and saw Jasmine pass by the entrance area to the bar.

'Quick! Knock that back! We have to get out of here.'

They both did the necessary, and headed straight back out.

'Going so soon?' enquired Mrs Stokes.

'Yes, just a quick one Beatrice. Have to be on our way.'

'I see' was the short reply, accompanied by a dubious look over her spectacles.

'Evening, James. Mick.'

Hadfield turned, to be greeted by Hugh coming through the front door.

'Er . . . good evening,' they both replied.

'Hilary not with you?'

'No,' replied Hadfield. 'She's . . . er . . . just finishing up in the office.'

'Is she going to the quiz tonight?'

'Quiz?' he asked.

'At the Manor Inn. Fund-raiser for the Horse Club.'

'I . . . er . . . I'm not sure.'

'Probably not. I hear you're all off to Dublin tomorrow. For the reading of the will.'

'That's right. Or rather we're off to Dublin. But not . . . .' Hadfield was conscious of the possibility of Jasmine's return at any moment. 'Anyway. We'd better be on our way. Couple of thing to organise. Enjoy your evening.'

Hadfield exited the hotel at speed, followed by Mick. As they approached the office, he slowed, to catch his breath.

'That was a close shave,' he said.

'Avoiding Ms Barrington, I suppose.'

'Correct. She wants me to arrange an advance on the will – which won't be possible. I couldn't face an interrogation in the reception area of the Arms Hotel!'

'Don't blame you.'

Hadfield sighed. Even a relaxing quiet pint was proving difficult to achieve. 'Better call it a day, I suppose,' he said.

'Fair enough,' replied Mick. 'See you tomorrow.'

'See you then.'

Hadfield turned away and headed up the hill towards his cottage. As he passed the office, he could see Hilary through the curtained window, typing at speed. He very much hoped she was going straight home when she finished.

CHAPTER 28

The train journey to Dublin the next day was subdued. Nobody seemed inclined to discuss the likely outcome of the meeting with Timmons' solicitors. Depending on how things went, they could be out of business – or persons of even greater interest in the police investigation. They would all know soon enough.

The weather disimproved steadily as they approached the capital. A stormy night had been forecast, and for once it looked like the experts might be right.

A few stops from their destination, a group of schoolboys got on, and bedlam ensued as they moved from seat to seat through the carriage, all shouting and laughing at the same time. Hadfield was on the point of intervening to quieten things down when they moved on down the carriage. He assumed they were planning to torment the next group of traingoers, but it seemed they were in fact getting off at the next stop: they congregated at the exit as the train slowed down.

As the boys got off the train, there was a loud bang just in front of their seats, followed by another, and then a third. Both Hadfield and Hilary practically jumped out of their skins. Mick didn't flinch.

'Bangers,' he said. The other two looked at Mick as if he had taken a turn.

'It's Halloween. Didn't you know?'

'Er . . . no.'

'I totally forgot,' admitted Hilary, letting go of Hadfield's arm, which she had grabbed in fright.

'I saw the boys getting them ready. Sure the kids are at it at home as well. Big night tonight. At least the weather might help keep the lid on it.'

The rest of the journey passed off without incident, and the train arrived at its final destination on time. By this stage, the storm was well under way, with heavy rain adding to the increasing gusts of wind. As they left the station, they noticed that no taxis were waiting – and there was a queue ahead of them. They waited fifteen minutes before a taxi arrived. People started to leave the queue.

'We might have to walk,' suggested Hadfield.

'I think you're right,' replied Mick.

'Not a chance!' said Hilary. 'In this? You must be joking. People will get fed up waiting. We'll be all right.'

Sure enough, the queue dwindled as people took their chances in the rain. At 2.50, they were the first in the queue, and a taxi pulled up. It was just after 3 when they arrived at the front door of Montgomery Darley and hurried inside.

The receptionist took them straight into what she called the 'Boardroom'. It was an impressive old high-ceilinged room with a large mahogany table and ten chairs around it. A glass bookcase spanned the width of one end of the room, containing various Acts of the Oireachtas and case-books stretching back many years, as well as some very old texts whose usefulness was likely to have long since passed. There was a sideboard at the other end of the room, on which tea, coffee and some small buns had been set out. Two high windows looked down on the street.

They were helping themselves to the refreshments when the door opened brusquely and a petite middle-aged woman entered the room, carrying a slim file and a writing pad. She had very dark hair, which was tied back tightly, making her look almost Spanish. Her complexion was very pale, possibly aided by some kind of powdered make-up. Her lips were thin, although the red lipstick seemed to extend slightly beyond, so as to alter the impression. Hadfield thought her quite good-looking but in a severe, even scary kind of way.

'Good afternoon. I'm Violet Curtis.'

'Good afternoon,' they all replied, taking turns to shake hands and introduce themselves.

'Please take a seat,' she said, pointing to the end of the table nearest the sideboard, as she placed herself at the top of the table at the other end.

Likes to keep her distance, thought Hadfield. *And no rings either*, he noticed, as she opened her file and writing pad.

'Thank you for making the journey to Dublin. And for all coming together. My condolences on Mr Timmons' passing. A terrible tragedy.'

Ms Curtis put on a stylish pair of reading glasses, which had been discreetly hidden somewhere in her tight-fitting pencil skirt and jacket.

'Now I have here his will, which is dated the twenty-fourth of July, 1975.'

She inclined her head and looked over her glasses, to see the three others exchanging confused glances. She continued to read from the will: 'This is the last will and testament of me, Andrew Timmons, of Hillside Lodge, Hillside Lane, Kilcreddin and I hereby revoke all former wills and testamentary dispositions heretofore made by me.

'I hereby appoint Leonard Darley of Montgomery Darley, Solicitors and Bruce Ridlington of Campbell Purvis, Chartered Accountants to be the executors of this my will.

'I give devise and bequeath all my property of every nature and kind whatsoever and wheresoever situate unto my sister, Felicity.'

Ms Curtis paused once more, to survey three now quite bemused-looking individuals.

'Any questions?'

'I have one,' piped up an exasperated Mick. 'Did you need to bring all three of us up from Kilcreddin just to tell us that?'

Hadfield cut in before Ms Curtis could respond, while frowning sidelong at Mick.

'Of course it's of interest to us all to hear the terms of Mr Timmons' will. We are very grateful that you could make yourself available to communicate this to us. It has greatly clarified the situation.'

Ms Curtis smiled primly, although it wasn't clear if this was in appreciation of Hadfield's gallant response or in recognition of Mick's obvious disappointment.

'Didn't Felicity pass away last year?' This question came from Hilary.

'Yes indeed. In January.' Ms Curtis paused for a moment. 'She had never married.'

'How's that relevant?' blurted out Mick, unable to keep his thoughts in.

'Well, it is relevant in that it seems to have prompted Mr Timmons to have a codicil drawn up. Which I have here – dated eighteenth March of this year.'

There was a stunned silence.

'The codicil makes a number of amendments to the earlier will. Firstly, it allows for alternate executors for both Mr Darley and Mr Ridlington, should they predecease Mr Timmons. As Mr Darley passed away in June, I have taken on the role of executor jointly with Mr Ridlington.'

'Of course,' interjected Hadfield, 'I should have said when we spoke before. Our condolences on Mr Darley's passing.'

'Yes, our sincere condolences,' added Mick breathlessly.

'Thank you. He was a sad loss to the firm.' She paused momentarily, before continuing 'Now the codicil acknowledges the untimely passing of his sister and directs that his assets be redistributed as follows, and I quote:

'Firstly I give, devise and bequeath unto my loyal and trusted secretary, Hilary Byrne, my house and lands at Hillside Lodge which I know she will care for as I have always done myself.

'Secondly I give, devise and bequeath unto James Hadfield the offices and business of Timmons & Associates on High Street, Kilcreddin in the hope that he can continue the best traditions of the firm from the same premises. This bequest is subject to the mortgage outstanding at the time of my passing but I have every faith in Mr Hadfield's ability to meet this obligation from his running of the practice.

'Thirdly I give, devise and bequeath to Michael Flanagan the vintage Harley-Davidson which I know he has always appreciated together with the sum of IR£20,000 to assist in its maintenance and to avoid its sale.'

Ms Curtis paused – primarily to allow Mick's low whistle to fade away.

'The codicil also provides that certain other assets are to be sold to ensure that sufficient funds are made available to each beneficiary so that the tax costs of the bequests can be met.'

'How very thoughtful,' said Hilary. 'Just like Mr Timmons to consider that.'

'Yes,' replied Ms Curtis, 'testators often overlook the financial consequences of CAT when making their wills.'

There was another pause – this time to signal that the reading had come to an end.

As she began to put the papers back into the file, Hadfield coughed.

'Er . . . are we the only beneficiaries?'

'No. There are three others.'

There was an expectant silence.

'No harm, I suppose. They have already been informed. Mr Boyd was given an apartment here in Dublin. Mrs Goodbody was given a financial bequest. And the residue, after all taxes have been addressed, goes to Mr Timmons' local church, to be administered as Reverend Devereux sees fit.'

Another silence followed.

'Any other questions?'

'Er . . . just one more,' replied Hadfield. 'You don't know how much the mortgage is?'

Ms Curtis couldn't resist a small, high-pitched laugh at that. She recovered herself quickly.

'Mr Boyd is to confirm the exact figure. But he expects it to be no greater than IR£200,000.'

She turned to Hilary and added: 'There's no mortgage on the house.'

Hilary nodded in reply.

'Now I take it I don't have to explain the process and timing of probate.'

'No, not at all,' said Hadfield, who was now anxious to be on his way, 'we're all familiar with that. Thank you very much for your time. I'm sure you'll be in touch when required.'

Farewells were promptly exchanged, and all three found themselves back in the reception area.

'Do you need a taxi?' enquired the receptionist. 'It's still very bad out there. Could be a bit of a wait, though.'

'No thanks,' replied Hadfield. 'I know where we can go.'

*

'To good old Mr Timmons,' said Mick as he raised his hot whiskey.

'To Mr Timmons,' replied the others.

Hadfield had brought them to McTiernans, a small cosy pub just up the way from Montgomery Darley and a short walk from Stephen's Green.

'Who would have thought?' continued Mick. 'The sly old dog! Can't wait to get my hands on that Harley. I suppose you'll keep the house?'

'I suppose,' replied Hilary, holding her hot port contemplatively in both hands.

'And that's you set up for the business,' Mick added, to his new boss.

'Assuming we can make some money from it. Hasn't been the most promising of starts.'

'I'm sure it will be fine.' Mick looked around surreptitiously. 'What did you make of the Dublin apartment? To Boyd!'

'I didn't know he had one,' said Hadfield.

'Do you think there was something going on there?'

'What do you mean?'

'You know. Mr Timmons and Boyd. Two bachelors. An apartment in Dublin.'

'How would I know. They might just be friends. Maybe the apartment was just a gift. Like the bequests to us.'

'What do you think, Hilary?' continued Mick excitedly, determined not to be put off his line of enquiry.

'Well, based on your theory, people could say myself and Mr Timmons were having a relationship.'

'But we know you weren't.' Mick stopped, and looked at her for a moment, adding: 'Don't we?'

'Of course I wasn't. But we don't know that he was having one with Mr Boyd, do we? And even if he was, it shouldn't be the subject of idle gossip. If Mr Timmons wanted people to know, we'd know.'

'Fair enough' was all a deflated Mick could muster.

'It would be nice to think, though,' Hilary mused, 'that perhaps he did have some kind of relationship, an emotional one, outside the office. Maybe even a romance.'

'With Boyd?' Mick responded sceptically.

'With anyone, Mick. I don't mind who. As long as it was someone who made him happy.'

Hilary sighed. 'I guess we'll never know.'

'We could ask Boyd,' suggested Mick mischievously.

'No, Mick, we won't be asking Boyd. Or anyone else.'

Hadfield decided to divert the conversation. 'I'd say Reverend Devereux will be happy with his lot. Money pouring in all around. Should keep the fête going and the church in ship shape.'

'Hmm . . .' responded Hilary. 'I wonder what the police will make of that.'

'I was thinking about that all right. He seemed to be surprised at Lord Barrington's bequest, but if you assume that was an act, you could say he's the only one who had a motive for all three murders.'

'Apart from yourself,' added Mick.

'What?'

'Well, you said before that the police had you on their list already. For being executor. Now you're a beneficiary under Mr T.'s will as well.'

'On that basis, you can add Mr Boyd to the list too,' said Hilary.

'That's true,' replied Hadfield. 'I suppose I'll have to include all this in my report to Detective Sergeant Forde.'

'Er . . . all of it? Surely they wouldn't be interested in my small bequest,' Mick enquired tentatively.

'A vintage Harley-Davidson and IR£20,000 is hardly a "small bequest",' responded Hilary. 'And anyway, James will have to make a full and frank disclosure. To be seen withholding that information would be serious for him. And raise even more questions about you.'

'Even more questions? What do you mean by that?'

'Well, if, hypothetically, you are currently a suspect – which was a concern you said you had after the Sergeant's visit – then deliberately holding back the fact of your bequest is going to look very suspicious. Don't you think?'

'Er . . . yes. I see. I think,' said Mick, knocking back the rest of his drink.

'Anyone for another?' proposed Hadfield.

'Better not,' said a worried-looking Mick. 'Have to catch the early train back. For Halloween at home. It leaves at 5.30.'

'Hilary.'

'Same again, please. I'll catch the later one.'

'When does it leave?'

'Half past eight.'

'I'll head off,' said Mick. 'See you on Monday.'

'See you then.'

Hadfield headed to the bar and returned shortly with another round. There was an awkward silence for a moment, as if both of them had questions on their minds but were reluctant to voice them.

'Mick mentioned,' Hilary began, 'that . . . er . . . Jasmine was in the Arms last night.'

'Yes! It was a close shave, I can tell you. We had to finish our pints in double-quick time while she went to the ladies'.'

'You didn't want to see her?'

'Certainly not. Why would you think that?'

'Well, after lunch on Tuesday, I thought maybe . . . .' Hilary paused, and shrugged her shoulders.

'Thought maybe what?'

'That maybe you might meet up again. You know . . . socially.'

'Not a chance. She just wants to keep me sweet so that she can get her hands on some money as soon as possible. I intend to keep her very much at arm's length – as much as that is possible with a client. It was a lucky escape at the Arms, I can tell you. It was straight home for me after that – well out of harm's way.'

'I see.'

Hadfield paused, took a sip of his drink and then asked: 'Er . . . did you get out yourself last night?'

'No. I stayed late to finish off the dictation, and went home. Microwave dinner in front of the TV.'

'Like myself.'

She took a sip of her drink, looking at Hadfield while she did so. 'Why do you ask?'

'Oh . . . it's just that . . . erm . . . I hear there was a quiz night for the Horse Club. Last night. At the Manor Inn.'

'Oh that. No. With the trip up to Dublin today, I decided not to. How did you hear about it?'

'Actually, it was Hugh Stokes. I bumped into him on the way out of the Arms. He was wondering if you were going.'

'Ah . . . .'

'Are you . . . er . . . interested in . . . er . . . Hugh at all? Socially.'

'Hmm. He's good company. But I think I might be a temporary interest only. To catch Jasmine's attention.'

'I don't know about that. He seems pretty keen on you of late.'

'Maybe. But no. I don't think he's the one for me.'

He fought back the urge to shout: 'Yes!' It was probably best to change the conversation before he said something foolish.

'Needless to say, he had heard all about the big trip to Dublin. For the "Reading of the Will", as he said himself.'

Hilary laughed.' Poor old Mick. The whole of Kilcreddin and beyond will be waiting to hear the result of our day out.'

'You're right there.'

'I suppose we'd be better off just coming straight out with it. To avoid the prying.'

'And false speculation.'

'Yes. That too.'

'Just tell Mick that it's OK to mention it, I suppose. Then it's sure to be all over the town in no time.'

She laughed again, and settled back into her chair. 'That's true. It would probably be the easiest way to spread the news.'

Hadfield sat back in his chair too. He was thinking about Hilary's bequest.

'You . . . er . . . didn't seem absolutely sure when Mick asked about keeping the house.'

'No, I guess not.'

'Can I ask why?'

'It's quite a big house. For one person.'

'Mr Timmons didn't seem to mind.'

'No. But he had people who looked after it. The maintenance. The grounds. I'm used to managing on a smaller scale. And there'd be the costs as well. I'm still in the same job.'

'I see what you mean.'

'Of course,' she continued with a coy smile, 'you could always give me a raise. I'm sure that would help.'

'Well, obviously,' he began, becoming a little flustered, 'I'll have to familiarise myself with the whole financial side of the business first. The accounts, the work in progress, the borrowings. All that kind of thing.'

'Of course, James, it was just a little joke. I know you'll need time to get on top of all that.'

'Exactly.' He noticed that both their drinks were nearly finished. 'Erm . . . . Actually, I'm meeting Charles for a drink in the Shelbourne at 6. Plenty of time before the train leaves, if you want to . . . .'

'I'd love to. Haven't been in the Shelbourne for ages. It's always nice to see how the other half lives.'

Hilary stopped herself, and thought for a moment. 'Although thanks to A.T., maybe I'm a bit closer to the middle.'

CHAPTER 29

The rain had eased off, so both of them were able to walk directly to the Shelbourne. On arrival, they found the place heaving.

'You got your wish,' said Hadfield.

'Hmm?'

'Half of Dublin seems to be here.'

'James!' a voice boomed to his right.

He looked over, and saw FitzHerbert gesticulating from a corner of the 'Lord Mayor's' lounge. He seemed to have secured a table for two.

'Ah, Hilary! Lovely to see you again. Looking as radiant as ever. Please, take a seat. James: you sit here. Drop of white? Or perhaps the occasion merits some Champagne?'

Hilary nodded. 'Some Champagne would be nice.'

'Good, I'll be back shortly.'

After a while, a waiter arrived with their drinks and an additional chair.

A few minutes later, FitzHerbert joined them.

'So, I take it the visit to Ms Curtis was a worthwhile one? Go on, tell all.'

Hadfield told him the details of their meeting.

'Excellent,' he exclaimed. 'Definitely a cause for celebration. Here's to Mr Timmons.'

They raised their glasses in unison to toast the testator.

'Of course, you'll join us for dinner in the club, Hilary. I've booked an extra spot at the table.'

'Well, I have to get the 8.30 train back.'

'No problem there. We'll look after you. By the way, did you bring those papers, James?'

'Yes, I have them here.'

Hadfield opened his briefcase and took out the spare copies of his reports, which Hilary had handed to him that morning.

'I'm not sure how much light they might throw on this whole business. If anything, it's getting less clear with every day.'

'*Nil desperandum*. I'm sure all will be revealed in due course.'

'I suppose I should contact DS Forde to send him a copy of his own.'

'You leave that to me. I'll look this over tomorrow, and let the Super know how matters stand. Tonight we pay homage to the generosity of Andrew Timmons. Bottoms up!'

'Cheers,' they both replied.

'So, Hilary. It's been a while since I've seen you.'

'Yes, last summer in Kilcreddin, I think.'

'I'd swear you've got younger since then.'

'It's all the fresh country air.'

'Undoubtedly. And the healthy lifestyle that goes with it, I'm sure,' said FitzHerbert, pursing his lips in mock-seriousness.

Hilary giggled, before adding: 'Actually, I've taken up horse-riding recently. That does get me out and about. I suggested James do the same, but he seems reluctant.'

'I tried it once. Not really for me,' said Hadfield.

'I remember that. You had difficulty walking for days,' chuckled FitzHerbert.

'A few lessons is all he needs, I should think,' said Hilary, trying hard not to laugh too openly.

'Maybe' was Hadfield's noncommittal reply.

'No doubt you have all the horsey set chasing after you,' FitzHerbert suggested to Hilary.

'I wouldn't say that. But there is a good social side to it.'

'You don't fool me for a second. I'd bet . . . .'

'Er . . . don't you think . . . ' – Hadfield interrupted his friend mid-flow, concerned as he was with the direction the conversation was taking – ' . . . that we'd need to be moving on to the club? It's just coming up to 6.30.'

'You're right. Let's finish this off and make our way down.'

*

The club was only a short walk along the Green, and all three were soon seated, with the food and wine ordered.

'A little quiet, isn't it?' mentioned Hilary. They were the only ones in the dining room.

'Yes. But it will pick up later. Most don't come in until after 7. I booked early because I thought James would only be loitering after his visit to Montgomery Darley.'

'Probably wise,' she admitted.

'So!' exclaimed FitzHerbert. 'The Manor murders. What's the state of play?'

'Getting less clear by the day, I'd say,' replied Hadfield. 'Anyone could have done it. I've met them all now and I'm none the wiser.'

'No new information, then?'

'Well, yes. But probably confuses more than clarifies.'

'Let's take them in order. As you met them . . . but after this.'

The wine had to be tasted and the starters served. FitzHerbert partook in a little of both the white and the red, and made some approving noises before resting back in his chair.

'Now, where were we? Yes, who did you meet first, following your letter.'

'Erm . . . .' Hadfield couldn't immediately recall.

Hilary came to his aid. 'Reverend Devereux, wasn't it? Although he managed to call in even before the letter had been sent.'

'That's right, yes. He was very keen to see how the church had fared. Lady Barrington had obviously told him of her intended bequest. Wasn't too happy with the trustee situation. Seems Greta might curtail his plans. I told him about the bequest from Lord Barrington too. Hard to know what he made of that.'

'I see,' said FitzHerbert, 'so the good Reverend had a motive to kill all three of them, as it turns out.'

'Yes,' said Hadfield. 'And he *was* in the nursing home at around the time of death.'

'Food for thought,' said FitzHerbert. 'Speaking of which, let's finish these starters and refill the glasses.'

He waited for the table to be cleared, before picking up the conversation again.

'Who did you see next?'

'Let's see. That would have been Jasmine. On Tuesday morning. Definitely needs the money. Got the impression she didn't get on too well with Lydia. Seemed to think Samantha was a more likely suspect than Staunton. Nothing much else there.'

'Except,' added Hilary, 'that she spotted Richard's car at about 1.15 on the way from Kilcreddin to the Manor. When he was supposed to be in his office at the estate.'

'Oh yes, that's right.'

'I see. Anything else to report?'

'I don't think so,' said Hadfield.

'Apart from her drug-dealings,' suggested Hilary.

'Oh. Of course. Lucinda was speaking with Dockrell. It's in the notes there.'

Hadfield summarised his discussion with Lucinda.

FitzHerbert nodded. 'Next?'

'Miss Greta,' said Hadfield. 'The next morning, at the nursing home. I met Sarah O'Doherty there as well: Staunton's girlfriend. She's a nurse there.'

'And what had Miss Greta to say?'

'A lot. But mainly about the defamation case. Mad keen to get proceedings under way. I did get the impression, though, that she might have had a falling-out with Lydia. And Sarah separately confirmed that.'

'And,' added Hilary, 'it seems that she wasn't too happy with Lord Barrington either.'

'Why was that?'

'Because Robert wanted an advance from George to start a new business, but he wouldn't entertain it. Miss Greta had got on to him about it, but he wasn't for turning.'

'In fact,' Hadfield interjected, 'there was even a suggestion that George might change his will because of it.'

'To cut Staunton out.'

'That seems to have been the thinking, anyway.'

'Hmm. What did you make of his girlfriend?'

'Pleasant girl.' Hadfield shot a look at Hilary. 'Quite pretty, you could say. Very concerned for Robert. Wanted me to get him to take some legal advice about his position. With the Guards.'

'I see. And her relationship with Greta Barrington?'

'Seemed to be fairly close. Why do you ask?'

'No particular reason.'

'Apart from the possibility that all three are in some way involved?' suggested Hilary.

FitzHerbert did not get the opportunity to respond, as her question coincided with the arrival of the main courses.

'Yes, that is a possibility of course,' continued FitzHerbert as the waiter retreated.

'What is?' asked a confused Hadfield.

'That Greta, Robert and Sarah are all in it together,' replied Hilary – to save FitzHerbert the bother.

'Ah. Interesting theory.' Hadfield nodded sagely. 'Miss Greta had fallen out with both Lydia and George. Staunton was afraid of a change in the will. Sarah wanted to get a move on with the new business. They worked it together, to give each other alibis.'

'It can't be discounted,' agreed FitzHerbert.

Hilary wasn't so sure. 'But there is the question of the mysterious nurse.'

'That Sarah claimed to see. Perhaps she made it up.' Hadfield wasn't letting go of the latest theory without a fight.

'And Mr Boyd too?' was her quick retort.

He paused. 'Hmm. He's hardly in on it as well.'

'You never know,' interjected FitzHerbert. 'Any other information of note?'

'Well, let's see. I had to go out to Samantha's house that afternoon. Bit of hard work. Don't envy the husband. She didn't have a good word for anyone. Thought that if Robert didn't do it, Jasmine was the most likely candidate. She wants to challenge the will as well, of course.'

'On what basis?'

'The Succession Act. Failing to make proper provision. Even though she already got a gift of the house they live in.'

'Best of luck with that.'

'To be fair, the husband seemed to agree. He's a retired solicitor. Actually, the same firm as handled Robert's adoption. Maybe they knew about it and were worried Lydia would convince George to change his will to benefit Robert.'

'Interesting.'

'Also . . . . He did mention one thing: that he saw Margaret Barrington, Richard's wife, passing by his house, when she was supposed to be at home.'

'And don't forget,' added Hilary, 'Reverend Devereux saw her driving in to her house later on as well. So her alibi has been disproved by two separate sources.'

'So both Richard and his wife have been telling porky-pies about their movements that day. Discover anything in that neck of the woods?'

'Not really. Except that Richard can't wait to get his hands on his inheritance. He seems desperate for money. And desperate to avoid his wife. He went out the back door as soon as she came up the driveway during our discussion. And of course she wants a divorce, now that he's coming in to some loot. Er . . . that's highly confidential, of course. I told her she may have to go elsewhere to deal with that. Not best pleased, I can tell you.'

'I can imagine. So that leaves Staunton then.'

'Yes, he was in yesterday. Didn't seem too sure of what the will might say.'

'Because George might have changed it?'

'Exactly. He was clearly relieved that it hadn't. But he wasn't too pleased about having to wait to get it. It turns out he had already discussed with Mr Timmons the possibility of selling Miss Greta's house and using the money from that to start his new business with Sarah. And with Miss Greta being involved in some way too. I suggested he concentrate on clearing his name first.'

'Very sensible. He didn't have anything to say to help clear himself?'

'No. Except to say that he didn't do it.'

'Hmm. Anything on Letitia?'

'Plenty.'

Hadfield recited the overheard conversation and his various run-ins with her. He also mentioned the threatening note.

'The plot thickens,' said FitzHerbert.

'Murkier by the day,' said Hadfield.

'I see. So that's the lot, then.'

'Oh! Except for one thing,' Hilary added. 'James thinks he may have worked out the note from Mr Timmons. Isn't that right?'

Hadfield made a poor attempt at disguising his pride at what he considered to be an important bit of problem-solving. 'Well, yes. I have to admit it took a bit of time, but I think I know what he was referring to.'

'In the Section 120 note?' replied FitzHerbert.

'Yes. We think what he was referring to was . . . er . . . hold on. Did you just say Section 120?'

'I did.'

'Eh . . . well, that's what I was going to say.'

'Glad to hear it. Seemed the logical interpretation.'

Hilary couldn't resist a giggle at Hadfield's deflated demeanour. Their companion did his best not to laugh too loud.

Hadfield remained a little crestfallen as the plates were cleared and the dessert menus arrived.

'Cheer up, James. You're doing sterling work. I'm sure that Superintendent Dockrell will be very impressed with progress to date. Now, what are we having for dessert?'

'Actually, Charles,' said Hilary, 'I should probably get going. I have that train to catch.'

'Not at all. No point in going now. You can stay at the club tonight. I checked earlier, when I rang. They have spare guest-rooms available.'

'Well, I suppose . . . .'

'That's settled. Sure where would you be going on a night like this.'

Hilary looked at Hadfield briefly. 'Absolutely. I . . . er . . . I was going to suggest it myself, in fact. And it's Halloween as well. Better off staying right here.'

'Agreed,' added FitzHerbert, without allowing any further opportunity for discussion. 'Now, a light dessert, I think. Followed by some cheese.'

'And port?' responded Hadfield.

'*Res ipsa loquitor.*'

Hilary looked quizzically at the barrister.

'A popular phrase among barristers, Hilary. It means that something is so obvious you don't even need to say it.'

*

A leisurely hour or so was spent in the dining room, before FitzHerbert suggested retiring to the members' lounge.

'Now tell me, Hilary,' he continued, settling back into one of the armchairs in the corner, and warming a brandy with his right hand. 'What do you make of it all? The murders, I mean. Have you formed a view on them yet.'

'Like – who did it?'

FitzHerbert's shrugged response was hard to read.

'Well, no. I don't know that it's possible to say yet.'

'What, then, do you think are the salient features which might point the way?'

Hilary thought for a moment. The alcohol had long since taken effect, but she decided to proceed anyway. 'I suppose the note from Timmons must mean something. And the unknown nurse.' She looked sidelong at Hadfield. 'If there was one, of course. And the break-in to the medicine cabinet. When the strichnyne on its own would have been enough.'

'My thoughts exactly. That's where we need to look, to get to the bottom of this.'

'And Richard and his wife lying about their whereabouts,' added Hadfield. 'That must mean something. Maybe they're in it together. And only pretending to want a divorce.'

'And his affair with Katherine Rennick is just a ruse?' suggested Hilary.

'Er . . . yes. I guess so. If it *is* an affair.' Hadfield's initial enthusiasm subsided somewhat.

'Of course,' she continued, 'there is the possibility of any combination of people being involved.'

'Such as?' enquired FitzHerbert.

'Well, there's Greta, Robert and Sarah – as James already mentioned. Richard and Margaret have to be considered' – Hadfield nodded gratefully at this – 'Samantha and her husband, perhaps. Or Jasmine and Samantha – accusing each other as a cover. Maybe even Reverend Devereux and Greta.'

'Not exactly separating the wheat from the chaff here, are we?'

'No,' conceded Hilary, 'I guess not. . . . What's your own view?'

'I have an idea but it's not fully developed yet. I'll look over James's notes and have a word with Superintendent Dockrell. A little more investigation might be needed.'

'I take it *we're* in the clear, anyway?' asked Hadfield with an unconvincing laugh.

'Hmm?' replied FitzHerbert, a little distractedly.

'Me. Hilary. Mick. Suspects?'

'Oh, I see what you mean. No, I don't think Special Branch will be doing any investigation in that direction.'

'Thank goodness for that.'

'Now, I'd better finish up.'

'What?' he replied. 'So soon? But it's hardly ten.'

'I know, but I have to chair a legal conference tomorrow in Blackhall. Need to put together an opening speech. Now you two stay and have another. *'Nemo saltat sobrius.'*

They both looked at him vacantly.

'It means "Nobody dances sober." It's the shortened version of *"Nemo enim fere saltat sobrius – nisi forte insanit."* The longer version being far superior, of course, containing as it does an important qualification.' He paused, before adding: "Nobody dances sober – *unless they are completely insane!"'*

And with that gem of knowledge satisfactorily imparted, FitzHerbert finished his digestif and bade farewell with an 'All the best, and see you soon!'

'What was all that about?' asked Hadfield, after his friend left the room. 'He hardly thinks we're going dancing, does he?'

'I don't think that's quite what he meant. But I'll have another glass of wine . . . .'

Two hours later, they found themselves alone outside the lounge, on the landing between the reception area below and the bedrooms above. They looked at each other, and then looked away.

'Thanks for a lovely evening,' said Hilary.

'I enjoyed it too.'

They looked at each other again. Hadfield could not stop himself. He leaned forward to kiss her, and Hilary closed her eyes as their lips met. Her bag slipped to the carpet while they embraced.

'I have my key here,' said Hadfield after a while. 'I can go down and get yours.'

'Do you want to?'

'Er . . . no.'

CHAPTER 30

They both got the Sunday afternoon train back to Kilcreddin and went their separate ways at the station.

Hadfield arrived at the office just after nine the following morning, to find Hilary in her usual place.

'Hi, gorgeous,' he said.

'Now, James. We agreed to keep our relationship professional when in the office.'

'That's true. Sorry. Is Mick in yet?'

'No.'

He bent over the reception area to kiss her. There was no resistance.

'See? It's not that easy.'

Hilary laughed before replying. 'Well, let's at least try.'

'OK. Anything from Friday?'

'Jasmine called: Lucinda took a long-winded message.'

'Let me guess. Getting an advance. Her claim for payment from Richard. Henry Street. And some personal advice. Would that sum it up?'

'That's about it. Actually, there's a reply in from McGuigan McGuirk & Mooney on the lease.'

'Just my luck. Anything else?'

'A letter from Letitia "confirming" what you discussed on Thursday.'

'I was expecting that.'

'And a couple of progress calls from your "regular" clients. I've left them on your desk.'

'Thank you, my dear.'

Hadfield leant forward for another kiss, just as the front door opened.

Mick walked in. It wasn't clear if he had noticed anything untoward, as they hadn't quite made contact, but he had a quizzical expression on his face.

'Morning all.'

'Morning,' they both replied.

'Good weekend?'

'Yes,' they said together.

'Didn't see either of you about.'

'Stayed in Dublin,' said Hadfield.

'I made a long weekend of it too,' added Hilary.

'Where did you stay?'

Hadfield held his breath as he waited for Hilary's reply.

'With an old acquaintance. How was your weekend?'

'Fine. Good night on Friday, when I got back.'

'How did Bridie take the news?'

Hadfield noted with relief that she was skilfully deflecting the conversation away from the weekend's sleeping arrangements.

'Thrilled, of course. Won't be much left to look after the Harley, though – if all her ideas are put into action. Actually, on that: do you think you could argue that the will requires at least some of the money to be used for the bike?'

'I think it was more a wish than a condition,' Hadfield responded.

'Perhaps, James,' suggested Hilary, 'it could be said that to avoid any question over it, a basic minimum amount should be expended on maintenance for its useful life?'

'Perhaps. At least to Bridie.'

'That'll do me,' said Mick, with a wink.

'All right. Let's get on with the day-jobs. I'd better read that Henry Street stuff and get back to Ms Jasmine Barrington. I think it's about time I got a little firmer with her.'

Hilary laughed.

'You know what I mean. We discussed it yesterday . . . .'

Hilary's eyes widened, and Mick's narrowed.

'Er . . . myself and Boyd. Which reminds me, actually. We . . . er . . . we are to meet this week. To discuss the executorships, and to stop this whole "advances" nonsense. Can you see if he's free to drop in tomorrow?'

'I'll ring him now. He's an early starter.'

Hilary picked up the phone and Hadfield went straight to his office, leaving Mick with no opportunity to test his growing suspicions.

*

Hadfield came out of the office mid-morning with a broad smile on his face. 'Well, that's that dealt with, anyway.'

'Oh?' replied Hilary.

'Yes. Just rang Jasmine there. Told her the bad news on the advance. Sent her back to Boyd if she wants to query it any further. He started it, after all.'

'Fair enough.'

'And I told her the claim for payment from Richard wouldn't stand up.'

'Very good. And Henry Street?'

'Well, I read the correspondence from McGuigan McGuirk & Mooney. They're digging in: it will be a painful negotiation. So I told her I would need to set up a meeting with solicitors and principals to trash the thing out.'

'How did she take that?'

'Not well. Especially when I told her it would take half a day of her time. Actually, would you mind setting that up with the other side?'

'No problem.'

'Er . . . and with Jasmine too?'

'Fine.'

'She's a little worried about Dockrell. Had to tell her criminal law is not my area, but I did say I'd try and find someone to represent her if the need arose.'

'Maybe Charles would know someone?'

'Good idea.'

He looked towards Mick's door, which was shut. He lowered his voice.

'Bit of a close shave earlier. Well done on steering the whole thing away.'

'Hmm. I'm not sure that we're above suspicion there.'

'Maybe not. Let's try and keep him in the dark for as long as we can, anyway. If Mick has his suspicions confirmed, it won't be long doing the rounds.'

'Agreed.'

'Although I'm not sure how we're going to keep everything under wraps. If we're going to see each other.'

'A step at a time, I guess. Cup of tea?'

'That would be great.'

He blew her a kiss, furtively, and returned to his office. He was pleased with the outcome of his direct approach to Jasmine, and decided that it might be worthwhile to adopt a similar stance with the other beneficiaries. A formal letter setting out the position to each was perhaps the best option.

He'd write to Jasmine first, so as to confirm their earlier discussion. A letter to Reverend Devereux should spell out the obligations with respect to the trustees. He'd have to clarify for Miss Greta that she and Robert would need to go elsewhere to pursue any defamation action. And a similar letter to Richard on that. And telling him to agree the residential situation with Jasmine himself – if he wanted to avoid a court case. The letter to Samantha would confirm that the prospects for a successful claim under Section 117 were slim to none – and that if she still wished to pursue it, Timmons & Associates would not be in a position to act. He'd reply to Letitia when he'd spoken with Boyd.

However, all that would have to wait for the moment. He had been prioritising the Barringtons and their business, to the detriment of his own existing clients. He was determined that the rest of the day was to be dedicated to dealing with their neglected requirements. As soon as he had his tea. And maybe a private moment with Hilary.

*

Hadfield arrived early on Tuesday to keep up the pace in clearing the backlog, dictating and making calls as necessary. He worked through lunch, until 2.30 – the appointed time for his meeting with Albert Boyd. At precisely 2.30, Hilary announced Boyd's arrival, and Hadfield brought him through to the office.

'Afternoon, Albert.'

'Afternoon, James.'

'Thanks for dropping in.'

'No problem. All part of the job.'

'Now, first things first. You might just sign these forms. Accepting the executorship for Lord and Lady Barrington. And then we can get down to the business of the probate itself.'

The best part of an hour was spent going through the estate, and the various forms and correspondence that would be required. Albert proved very helpful, having detailed knowledge of the assets and their whereabouts. And who might be contacted to get them in. He wasn't short of suggestions on who might be called to value and sell them either.

Hadfield mentioned his discussions with Letitia and produced the letter she had sent.

'Cold fish, that one,' said Albert. 'You'd think she would still be grieving for her sister rather than chasing her estate. But she is right, though.'

'Yes. We do have a duty as executors to maximise the assets. Better press on with that, so.'

As they concluded their business, Hadfield decided to broach the subject of Timmons' will. 'We . . . er . . . met Mr Timmons' solicitors on Friday.'

Albert became unusually tight-lipped. 'I see' was all he could manage.

'I don't mind saying: he's been very generous.'

Albert hesitated for a moment before saying 'Oh.'

Hadfield decided to press on. 'Yes, he's given me the office.'

This was greeted by silence.

'And Hillside Lodge goes to Hilary.'

A slight twitch, but nothing said.

'Even Mick benefitted. He gave him his old Harley-Davidson.'

'Hmm.'

He decided on a different tack. 'Of course, there is the downside that the police might see these bequests as giving the three of us motives in the murders.'

Albert thought for a moment before speaking. 'I suppose you better include me in that.'

'Oh?' he replied innocently.

'Andrew gave me a bequest too. I was at Montgomery Darley myself earlier this week. He left me his Dublin apartment.'

'How very kind.'

'Yes. Very kind. It's a lovely spot by the canal.' He seemed to choke for a moment, before continuing. 'But how could they even think that I would have anything to do with his murder. We were such longstanding . . . friends.'

His eyes had begun to well up at this point, and he looked down at his folded hands.

Hadfield, caught a little off guard, stood up. 'Now, Albert, I'm sure there's no need to worry on that score. I'll . . . er . . . just get some tea. I'll be back in a moment.'

He was glad to see that Albert had collected himself by the time he returned with the refreshments.

'It doesn't make any sense to think that any one of us would have had any part in this,' he said, as comfortingly as possible, as he laid down the tray. 'And if they did, how would they decide one from the other? We're all in the same boat in that respect.'

'Except I was at the nursing home near the time of Lord Barrington's death.'

'But you've confirmed he was alive when you left.'

'With nobody to witness me leaving. I saw Robert but he didn't see me.'

'Hmm. But you noticed that nurse that seemed out of place.'

'That's right.'

'And Miss Greta and Robert noticed something odd about her too.'

Albert began to perk up. 'Did they?'

'Yes. Which certainly points the finger away from you,' he replied – although he couldn't help thinking: *Unless you were in on it with them!*

Albert sat back, considerably relieved by this analysis.

'So you think this nurse may have been the culprit?'

216

'Well, it's a good possibility,' Hadfield replied, looking sideways at Albert, before adding: 'if everyone's account is to be believed.'

Albert didn't flinch.

'I think you mentioned before that you didn't get a good look at her,' he continued.

'That's right. She was a little way down the corridor when I saw her.'

'What made you notice her, then?'

'Well, her uniform didn't look quite right. I've an eye for that sort of thing. I had a brief glimpse of her profile as she turned off the corridor, and didn't recognise her as one of the regular staff. I explained all that to the police when I spoke with them.'

'Of course. I'm sure that's where they are directing their enquiries. The bequests from Mr Timmons shouldn't change any of that.'

'Hopefully not.'

'So . . . er . . . what do you plan to do with it?'

'With what?'

'The apartment.'

'Oh.' Albert's demeanour drooped somewhat at that. 'I . . . erm . . . not too sure really. Probably keep it. It . . . er . . . could be useful. For trips to Dublin. Conferences. That sort of thing.'

Albert was obviously reluctant to dwell on this too much further.

'Of course, the bequest of the office means we can continue the business here. For the foreseeable future, at any rate.'

As Albert nodded in reply, Hadfield recalled the exact terms of the bequest. 'Actually, Albert, there was one aspect to the bequest we might discuss. Mr Timmons indicated that the mortgage on the office would pass with it, to the beneficiary. I was . . . er . . .just wondering . . . .'

'No problem there, James,' replied Albert, glad to be reverting to his normal sphere of discussion. 'As soon as the probate is through, we can refinance with a new loan. I'm sure I can get you similar terms. Leave all that to me.'

'Thanks, Albert, I'd appreciate that.'

'Not at all. That's what I'm here for. Anything else?'

'No, I think that's it. Except . . . er . . . this business of the advances. I explained to Jasmine this morning that we would have to hold off on all that until this whole police investigation gets resolved.'

'Of course.'

'I did mention that she should get in touch with you if she wished to clarify that any further.'

'Understood. I'm sure funds must be tight there. I'll see if I can organise some kind of facility to tide her over.'

'I've had to make the same point to Richard. And Robert.'

'I'll speak to Richard. We should be able to come to some short-term arrangement there. Robert might be a different matter – but leave that with me.'

'Thank you, Albert. That would be very helpful.'

'Anything else?'

'No, I think that's it. At least for the moment, anyway.'

'Very good. I'll be on my way, so. Thank you for the tea.'

'Not at all.'

'And we might keep the apartment bequest between ourselves. At least for the moment.'

'Of course, Albert. Strictly confidential.'

CHAPTER 31

'How did that go?' asked Hilary, after Albert had left through the front door.

'Very helpful on the executor front.'

'And on A.T.'s will?'

'Not so forthcoming there. He wasn't even going to mention the apartment after I'd told him about our bequests. It was only talk of the possible police interest that got him going.'

'What do you make of it? Were they an item?'

'Hard to know. He seemed a little emotional. Referred to A.T. as a "long-standing friend". Wants it all kept confidential, though.'

'I see.'

'Better let Mick know the position before he starts blurting.'

'Will do.'

'Anything while I was inside?'

'Just a call from Charles. He asked that you ring him as soon as you were free.'

'Hmm. What could that be about? Better ring him now.'

Just then, Agnes came in, carrying some fresh flowers.

'Afternoon all. Enjoyed the trip to Dublin? I'm told you were getting details of the will. I suppose you were happy with what you heard.'

Hadfield and Hilary exchanged resigned glances, and disclosed the details of their own bequests. It was probably safer to give the exact details than let Chinese whispers develop.

'Of course, Mr Timmons was very generous to me as well. I was up in Dublin earlier in the week to meet the solicitor, Ms Curtis. Very efficient, so she was.'

'Any news from the Manor?' asked Hilary.

'Well, Jasmine has been quite on edge. Ever since her little chat with the police. Richard seems to be half drunk most of the time, and Samantha hasn't been at the surgery since the opening night. Letitia has moved in to the Arms, of course. But her friend Clarisse has gone back to Paris, I'm told. There are those who think it might have something to do with that Hargreaves fellow and the French police. Of course everyone's talking about Robert. I had my suspicions, of course . . . .'

'I might leave you there, Agnes,' interrupted Hadfield. 'I have a few calls to make.'

'Of course, Mr Hadfield, of course. Don't let me detain you.'

He returned to his office, and got FitzHerbert at the first time of asking.

'Ah, James! How are you?'

'Very well, thanks.'

'How did Friday go?'

'Er . . . you were there, weren't you?'

'I meant, after I left. I take it a guest-room wasn't needed?'

'No. We got by without it.'

'Excellent. You both stayed Saturday too, I suppose?'

'Yes we did, as a matter of fact.'

'Thought so. Would have called you to join me with Superintendent Dockrell on Sunday morning but it occurred to me you might be otherwise occupied.'

'Thank you for sparing me that!' Hadfield paused for a moment, before adding: 'Why were you meeting him?'

'Well, after the conference I came home and read those notes you gave me in a bit more detail. They confirmed what I had been thinking, and suggested a few definite lines of enquiry. Some of them a job for the Guards, so I thought I'd update Dockrell. He was very appreciative of your efforts.'

'Glad to hear it. Does it mean I'm not on his wanted list?'

'I think you would be very far down at this stage.'

'And who's at the top?'

'Better not say. Dockrell is still running a few things to ground. Shouldn't take long though.'

'How exciting. What are they looking at?'

'He wants that kept quiet at the moment.'

'So, I do all the leg work and now I can't be told anything?'

'*Tempus omnia revelat.*'

There was a silence as Hadfield waited for the translation. After a sigh, FitzHerbert continued: ' "All will be revealed. Or, strictly speaking, "Time reveals all". '

'I see. Can I even ask when?'

'Yes, you can actually.'

'Oh good. When?'

'This Friday.'

He had a suspicion he was at the receiving end of one of his friend's wisecracks, and responded in kind: 'All sounds a bit vague to me. When exactly on Friday?'

'Shortly after 11 in the morning.'

Hadfield couldn't resist a little snort of laughter at this. 'I see. And I suppose you know where, as well.'

'As a matter of fact, I do. Your office.'

That stopped him in his tracks. 'My office?'

'Yes. That's why I'm ringing you.'

'You'd better explain.'

'I've agreed with Superintendent Dockrell that you'll arrange a meeting of all the relevant parties there next Friday. At 11 o' clock. As a follow-up to your earlier correspondence. To clarify a number of legal issues arising from the wills, and your discussions with the parties.'

'Actually, I was going to write to them myself shortly, to deal with their various queries.'

'You might hold off on that. I've drafted the letter you can send. It should go to each beneficiary and their partners. Mr Boyd should be asked to attend also, as executor. Any queries to be deferred until the meeting.'

'And what happens at the meeting?'

'Leave that to me. I'll take matters from there.'

'You're coming to the meeting?'

'That's right.' There was a muffled sound, as FitzHerbert seemed to talk to somebody with the phone covered. After a moment, he continued: 'Sorry about that. Can you make sure those letters are all delivered first thing tomorrow, and I'll see you there on Friday. Have to run.'

'Just spoke to Charles there,' Hadfield said to Hilary, as he stood in reception, stroking his chin with a perplexed look on his face.

'Anything to report?'

'Quite a bit, actually.' He thought on that for a while, before adding: 'But not a lot, really.'

'I see. Care to elaborate?'

'Well, after reading my notes, he decided to meet up with Superintendent Dockrell. It seems they have an idea who did it. But won't say who it might be. Or why.'

'Need to get more evidence, maybe?'

'Yes. It seems there is a bit more police-work needed. But the funny thing is, Charles reckons they'll have it cracked by Friday.'

'How does he know that?'

'No idea. But he wants me to send a letter to all the beneficiaries, and have them meet me here at 11 that morning.'

'To do what?'

'He didn't explain. Just wants the letters delivered tomorrow and he'll see us here on Friday.'

'All very mysterious. What are you going to say in the letter?'

'He said he'd drafted it and was sending it through.'

'Hold on. I'll check if anything has come through on the fax. . . . Yes. There we are. I'll make a copy.'

As Hilary organised this, he checked again that Mick's door was closed.

'He seemed to know about us, as well.'

'What's that?' replied Hilary, who couldn't quite hear over the sound of the photocopier.

He waited for the copying to finish before answering, in a low, whispering voice. 'You and me. Charles seemed to know.'

'Yes. He suggested as much to me when he rang earlier.'

'How did he know?'

'Intuition. Or more likely rang the front desk to see if I had booked in.'

'Of course!'

'Now. There you are,' she said, as she handed him the printout. 'Do you want to read it out?'

He nodded.

Dear   ,

Following on from recent meetings with the intended beneficiaries of the wills of Lord and Lady Barrington, a number of legal issues have come to light in the administration of the estates of the deceased.

Having considered the matter in some detail, I determined to engage the services of Senior Counsel who has advised a general meeting of those affected by these matters.

Senior Counsel has made himself available for this purpose at 11 AM this Friday, here at our offices in Kilcreddin, where the issues can be explained in more detail and advices furnished as to their resolution.

Senior Counsel has stressed the importance of all invitees attending, and accordingly I would be grateful if you could contact our offices as soon as possible to confirm your availability.

Yours sincerely,
James Hadfield
Timmons & Associates

'How extraordinary,' said Hilary.

'Yes. Hard to know what to make of it.'

'And who are we to send the letters to?'

'Actually, he's listed them here. Richard and his wife. Samantha and her husband. Jasmine. Robert and his girlfriend. Miss Greta. Reverend Devereux. Letitia.'

'Curiouser and curiouser,' she replied, just as Mick was opening his office door.

'Oh. What's so curious? Or . . . er . . . maybe I'm interrupting.'

She looked at Hadfield, who decided it was probably better to put Mick in the picture.

'I've just been talking to FitzHerbert. He wants me to convene a meeting of everyone involved in the Barrington wills for this Friday morning.'

'Why?'

'We don't really know. Here's the letter we are to send. And the addressees.'

Mick read through it himself. 'Curious is right. Is it anything to do with the murders?'

'Could be. But as Charles said himself: *"Tempus omni . . . ."* Hadfield struggled as he tried to recall the exact words. 'Er . . . that's Latin for "All will be revealed in . . . er . . . due course".'

'Those Latin guys had a succinct way of putting it,' mused Mick.

'Sounds a little like "time will" to me,' added Hilary with a laugh.

'I think it was the abbreviated version. "Time will tell." Something like that. Anyway, Charles wants them delivered first thing tomorrow, so maybe you could do them up before we go. I'll sign them and Mick can take them home and deliver them before coming to the office in the morning.'

'I'll get going on that now,' she replied, still smiling at Hadfield's dubious explanation of his Latin translation.

'Oh. And can you see if Boyd can attend the meeting also. In his capacity as executor. Keep the details brief. Just a meeting with Counsel to discuss a few issues.'

*

It was just after 5.30 when Hilary finalised the letters for signing.

'Now, straight home with those,' Hadfield said to Mick, as he handed the envelopes to him for delivery in the morning.

'Will do. There's quite a few, isn't there? Do we have enough seats for everyone?'

'Good point,' replied Hilary 'We might need to get some chairs in from Morton.'

'Will I go over now and ask?' asked Mick.

'Better leave it for the moment,' replied Hadfield. 'If he gets wind that there is a big meeting, it will be the talk of the village in no time. We'll ask for them on Thursday night, so he has no chance to spread the word too far.'

'Fair enough. I'll be on my way so,' replied Mick, as he headed out the door. Hadfield looked out the window.

'Fancy a drink?' he said, when he was sure Mick was gone.

'That would be nice.'

'And a bite to eat afterwards?'

'Where did you have in mind?'

Hadfield frowned as he thought about this. 'I guess choices are pretty limited if we are to stop tongues wagging.'

'A case of your place or mine, then?'

'For the moment, anyway. I suppose we'll have to own up at some point.'

'But not tonight.'

'No. Maybe my place tonight. I think I could rustle up dinner for two, if you're not too fussy.'

'Let's go.'

Just as they were leaving, Lucinda came down the stairs. 'I gather congratulations are in order.'

The couple looked at each other. How could Lucinda possibly know? Had FitzHerbert been spreading the word? Or had Mick jumped to conclusions.

Lucinda smiled. 'About the bequests. I gather Mr Timmons was very generous.'

'He was, Lucinda,' replied Hilary. 'We're very grateful.'

'And the practice should be safe for a while longer,' added a relieved Hadfield.

'That's good news.'

A thought occurred to Hadfield. 'Actually, speaking of news, Agnes mentioned that Clarisse, Letitia's friend, had headed back to Paris. I'm not sure, but maybe that's something your uncle should be told.'

'I think he's been keeping a close eye on the movements of everyone involved, but I should probably let him know. Enjoy your evening.'

CHAPTER 32

It was a bitterly cold November morning when Hadfield arrived at the office the following Friday.

He was greeted by Hilary at reception – and the sound of cursing from his own room.

'What's going on in there?' he asked.

'Mick is trying to organise the room for the meeting.'

'Is it safe to go in?'

'Probably not. But you'd better anyway.'

He carefully opened the door to his office, and peered inside. A flustered Mick was in the middle of the room with his hands on his hips. He was surrounded by chairs.

'Everything all right, Mick?'

'Not sure, Mr H. Got these chairs from Morton last night. Can't seem to make them fit.'

He noted that there were ten chairs from the Riverside Inn, which Mick was trying to place in the area beside the client table and to the front of Hadfield's desk. It was never going to work.

'I see what you mean. Let's take these four chairs from the client table and move the table to the wall. We can move my desk-chair to the side with the table, and push the desk back a bit. But not too far back: we'll need three places behind the desk.'

'For who?'

'Myself, Boyd and Counsel.'

'Very cosy.'

'Yes. Let's just use three of the client chairs for that. And put the spare beside the wall.'

'And Morton's chairs facing the desk?'

'Exactly. Five on this side of the door, by the window. Five on the other, by the table. In twos, and one at the front.'

After a few minutes' exertion, they had it set up. Hilary entered the room just as they were resting against the client table, contemplating a job well done.

'Looks well,' she said.

'Yes,' replied Hadfield, 'the front seats are a little close to the desk, but I think it's the best that can be done.'

Mick nodded his assent to this analysis, with the air of a man who had given the matter his full professional consideration.

'And Miss Greta?'

'Huh?' was the simultaneous response from both of them.

'Her wheelchair.'

There was a pause as the workmen gave this some thought. A mixture of 'bugger' and 'feck' was the joint reply.

'No need to worry. You don't need the front chair by the window. Just turn the others into a slight arc and there'll be room for her.'

The two workmen decided to think about this, even though it was obvious that the suggestion would work.

'Leave you too it so.'

*

As 11 AM approached, Hadfield sat fidgeting in the centre seat behind his desk. Work had been out of the question that morning. His main concern was where to sit for the meeting: he wasn't comfortable with the middle position, but didn't like left or right either.

'James.'

He jumped as he was brought back from the world of seating arrangements by Hilary. 'Sorry! Er . . . what's up?'

'Reverend Devereux is here for the meeting.'

'Already?'

'He's a little early.'

'Better show him in . . . .'

'Good morning, James!' exclaimed Devereux after Hilary had sent him through.

'Morning, Reverend.'

'Cold one, isn't it?'

'Yes, indeed.'

'A drop of tea would be just the thing.'

'Of course. Just one moment.'

He had completely forgotten about refreshments, and headed for the door just as Hilary opened it, with a smile, to let Mick through: he was carrying a heavy tray with all the necessaries.

'Ah! Here we are.'

Mick and Hilary laid everything out on the client table, and left. He noted the delph and cutlery as that of Morton's. Doubtless Hilary had been thinking ahead.

'Help yourself, Reverend.'

'Thank you.'

Having made his tea and selected a few choice biscuits, he sat down in the front row. On the right, as viewed from the desk, and nearest to the table. And the biscuits.

'You heard the good news, I take it.'

'News?'

'Timmons' will. He's left a tidy sum to the church.'

'I see.'

'And, I might add,' continued the Reverend, looking pointedly at Hadfield, 'I'm advised by his solicitors that its use is entirely discretionary.'

'That is good news.'

'Yes. The fête should be safe for another few years, at least. How about yourself?'

'Er . . . I'm not sure . . . .'

'Andrew's will. I hear you were up with the solicitors too.'

'Oh. Erm. Yes. We . . . er . . . that is I . . . had an appointment . . . .'

Just then, Hilary opened the door: 'Dr Barrington Russell and Mr Russell are here.'

'Show them in, please. Show them in.'

After pleasantries had been exchanged and tea served, Samantha and Denis took the two back seats, on the left as viewed from the desk and on the opposite side from Reverend Devereux.

'Very good of you to come to the office this time,' said Hadfield, determined to avoid giving the Reverend a chance to continue his questioning. 'I know how busy you all are.'

'It didn't suit at all,' replied Samantha. 'Very short notice. Had to rearrange a lot of appointments.'

'I can imagine . . . .'

'This won't take too long, will it?' asked Denis. 'I have a meeting at the theatre at lunchtime, you know. Did you enjoy the show, by the way?'

'I . . . er . . . .'

'Mr Boyd is here,' announced Hilary – to his relief. 'Will I bring him straight in?'

'Please.'

Boyd was wearing a lilac suit with a purple dickie bow, and greeted everyone effusively before helping himself to a cup of tea.

'Where do you want me?' he asked Hadfield, while looking around the room.

'Beside me, I think. At the top there.'

He was still undecided about the seating, but was tending towards putting Boyd in the middle.

'Perhaps in the . . . .'

Too late. Albert had already taken the outside seat facing Reverend Devereux.

Hilary popped her head in again. 'Mr Barrington is here to see you.'

'That's *Lord* Barrington, if you don't mind,' boomed the man himself, as he brushed past her and took the inside seat in front of Samantha.

'Damned nuisance having to come all the way in here.'

'Apologies . . . er . . . Lord Barrington. Counsel suggested . . . .'

'Counsel suited himself, I'm sure. Hopefully Counsel has some answers. I'm none the wiser from our last discussions.'

'Will he be addressing the Section 117 question?' asked Denis.

'I think it's best if we wait for Counsel.'

'Where is he, then?' asked Richard. 'It's after 11.'

'I'm sure he'll be with us shortly.'

Any further discussion was interrupted by something of a commotion in the reception area – the source of which was revealed as Miss Greta appeared in the doorway in her wheelchair, with Robert behind her.

'Not very wheelchair-friendly here, are we?' she scowled. 'Practically impossible to get through the front door. I'm sure there are laws about that.'

'Erm . . . over here, in front of Richard,' replied Hadfield – who had no idea as to his obligations on accessibility. 'We've kept a space by the window for you.'

Robert tried to manoeuvre the wheelchair through the office doorway, with some difficulty: the chairs had to be pulled in quite a bit to let her through. He was followed in by Sarah.

'Such fuss and bother,' Miss Greta continued, once she had been settled in her appointed place. 'What's this all about, anyway?'

'Well, as we said in our letter . . . .'

'The letter said nothing at all. Just wanted us all to meet here. Most irregular. We all know what's in the will. What is there to discuss?'

'Quite a bit, I should say,' interrupted Richard. 'Like, when can we actually start getting the benefit of the bequests? God damn it, Hadfield, life has to go on!'

'Of course, Lord Barrington, I fully understand. We can deal with all that, I'm sure. But best wait until everyone's here. Just Jasmine and er . . . your good lady wife?'

'She'll be along shortly, I expect. Making her own way. Why the blazes does she have to be here anyway?'

'And me,' piped up Denis.

'It was Counsel's suggestion that . . . .'

'Jasmine Barrington is here now. And Margaret Barrington too,' announced Hilary at the door.

A none-too-talkative Jasmine marched through first, barely acknowledging Hadfield. Robert and Sarah had sat in the two free back seats, across from the Barrington Russells. Jasmine sat on the inside seat, in front of Sarah and behind Reverend Devereux. Margaret came in next, and surveyed the room. The only chairs left were those beside Richard and Jasmine. After a slightly disdainful look at her husband, she reluctantly sat beside him. This had the benefit of silencing Richard.

'Ms Cavendish,' announced Hilary.

Letitia walked in and sat beside Jasmine, without a word.

'So where is this Counsel fellow, anyway?' asked Miss Greta, while scowling at Letitia.

'I'll just go out and check.'

'You don't know where he is?'

'He was getting the train from Dublin. I would have expected him here by now.' Hadfield decided to exit the room as quickly as possible, to avoid any further interrogation. 'Excuse me for a moment . . . .'

He closed the door as he left, and looked around.

'No sign yet?'

Hilary shook her head.

'Even a call?'

She shook her head again.

'Where the hell could he be?'

'Hold on. I'll check the train station. See if it's been delayed.'

He drummed his fingers on the reception counter as he waited for the outcome. After what seemed a lengthy wait, and a brief discussion, she put the phone down.

'Arrived on time. Should have been here at a quarter to, if he'd come straight.'

'It's a quarter past now.'

'Problem?' said Mick, as he came out of his office.

'No sign of FitzHerbert, even though the train was on time.'

'Oh dear. What are you going to tell *them*?' asked Mick, directing his thumb at the office door.

'Nothing. And I'm not going back in there without something to say.'

Mick put his ear to the door. 'I can understand that. A difficult crowd, by the sounds of it.'

He jumped back with fright as the door opened quite suddenly. Boyd walked out, and closed the door. He looked a little stressed. 'Getting a bit warm in there for me. Seem to think that, as executor, I should have all the answers. Any word on Counsel?'

'Well . . . ' began Hadfield, just as there was a loud knock on the front door. He didn't wait for Hilary to check on the intercom, but opened the door immediately himself.

FitzHerbert stood outside, his large frame enhanced by an unusual multi-layered coat which seemed designed both for warmth and for protection from the rain. He was carrying an old brown leather briefcase which had obviously seen much of the rough-and-tumble of criminal practice.

'Thank God for that!' said Hadfield. 'We didn't know where you were.'

'Apologies for the delay,' replied the barrister, as he entered the reception area. 'Got a little diverted on the way. Can I give you this?'

Hadfield took the massive coat and put it in the cloakroom behind reception.

'And you are?' continued FitzHerbert, as he smoothed down his immaculate dark navy three-piece suit and adjusted the red handkerchief in the top pocket – which, naturally, matched his tie.

'Albert Boyd, manager at the local bank. Here's my card.'

'Ah, yes. And executor to both of the wills.'

'That's right.'

'Is everybody here, James?'

'Yes. And have been for a while.'

'Very good. Let's not keep them waiting any longer. Just tell me who is sitting where, and we'll head straight in.'

CHAPTER 33

The general hubbub subsided as the three entered the room. Boyd sat back in his seat on the left facing Reverend Devereux, Hadfield took the seat on the right in front of Miss Greta, followed by Counsel, who bent down towards him: 'You might push up there, old boy,' he whispered. 'Bit tight in the middle. Perhaps a brief introduction, and I'll take it from there.'

Hadfield stood up and moved to the centre, clearing his throat. 'Thank you all for your patience. I'd like to introduce you to Mr Charles FitzHerbert, who is the Senior Counsel I retained in connection with the . . . er . . . issues surrounding the wills of Lord and Lady Barrington. Counsel suggested that all the interested parties be asked to attend a general meeting at our offices with a view to . . . erm . . . progressing matters as best we can. So, perhaps I might let Mr FitzHerbert . . . er . . . take it from here.'

'Thank you, James,' replied FitzHerbert, standing up and moving slightly to the side of the desk, to allow some freedom of movement.

'Apologies for the delay. I was obliged to take a slightly circuitous route to get here. Now, firstly, can I thank you all for attending today: I'm sure you are all very busy, and need to get on with your daily obligations. I'll try not to detain you too long. Secondly, you are all doubtless wondering why we had to have a meeting with everyone together to discuss the wills, the terms of which are already known. I shall try and explain that to you now.'

'That would make a change!' piped up Miss Greta. 'Explanations have been slow round here to date.'

'*Paulatim est certe,*' Miss Barrington, 'Counsel replied.

'Hmm?' was the flummoxed response – followed by a stifled laugh from Denis.

'What's he rabbiting on about?' continued Miss Greta – to nobody in particular.

'It's Latin,' explained Denis. 'It means "Slowly, therefore surely".'

Miss Greta made a sort of dismissive snorting sound, and started to rummage in her handbag.

FitzHerbert rested slightly on the corner of the desk, to take some of the weight off his feet.

'Now you have all met Mr Hadfield during the course of last week, and I understand you each had different queries and concerns in relation to the administration of the estates of Lord and Lady Barrington. These matters can be dealt with in turn, but the primary issue which concerns us, and which needs to be addressed before we can move on, is the tragic manner in which the wills have come into effect.'

Counsel paused, and surveyed the room, noting puzzled faces all round – and Miss Greta looking at herself in a handheld mirror.

'I am of course speaking of the murder of Lord Barrington, followed by that of Lady Barrington and our esteemed colleague, Andrew Timmons.'

'What's that got to do with it?' asked Richard. 'That's a matter for the police. If they ever get round to dealing with it.'

'You are right, of course, Lord Barrington. But it is also a matter very relevant to the administration of the estates and the distribution of the bequests. You see, there is a legal principle enshrined in the law, which dictates that the perpetrator of a murder should not benefit from the estate of the murdered party. Where the perpetrator is known, and is a named beneficiary, then his – or her – share is forfeited, and that share falls back into the residue of the estate of the deceased. Now, if the murderer is not known but there are a number of suspects, then the share due to the suspects can be held back pending determination of the responsible party. In the meantime, any beneficiaries who are above suspicion can take their share and the executors can act accordingly. All clear?'

There was a general nodding of heads in the room.

'Of course, that presents quite a difficulty in the present case. I understand from Mr Hadfield's contact with you and with the police that none of the beneficiaries have alibis and that each has a potential motive. Accordingly, at this point in time, it is not possible to distribute any of the assets.'

There was general uproar at this last statement. Richard could eventually be heard shouting above the rest: 'So when in God's name do we get our hands on it.'

'When the identity of the murderer is known.'

'But we already know . . . .'

'Don't you dare say another word!' cried Miss Greta, before Richard could make another accusation.

'But that could take forever!' exclaimed Jasmine, whose heightened colour could be seen through her make-up.

'Maybe not,' replied FitzHerbert quietly.

'How long, then?'

'Not too long at all, in fact.'

'What do you mean: "Not too long"?' asked Reverend Devereux.

'By that, I mean that I believe it is possible at this moment in time to establish the murderer.'

This was greeted by gasps and then silence.

'How the hell can *you* know?' said Robert eventually, from the back.

'Well, thanks to Mr Hadfield's sterling work in reviewing Mr Timmons' files, he stumbled across a note left by the former principal of this firm on the afternoon of his death. This gives us the first clue to the identity of the culprit. The note was quite cryptic – deliberately so, I would think – in order to avoid an outright accusation. I have it here.'

There was an amount of uncomfortable shuffling as Counsel opened his briefcase and produced a sheet of paper. 'It reads as follows:

Lady B agitated –
About Robert –
Check background –
Firm matters –
Refers Section 120 –
Wills change

'And that's it.'

'Well, that settles it,' cried Richard triumphantly. 'Even Mr Timmons thought it was Staunton.'

'That could be one reading of it, Lord Barrington. But another reading is possible. Perhaps Lady Barrington was worried for Mr Staunton, not suspicious of him. In that case, she may have been suspicious of one of the others, who would benefit under the will. The reference to Section 120 was not easy to work out, but thanks to the ingenuity of Mr Hadfield and his most capable assistant, Hilary Byrne, the meaning became clear. Section 120 is the section of the legislation which deals with disinheritance in the event of murder. It also has the consequence of changing the outcome of a will. I think it is clear that Lady Barrington believed that Robert Staunton, her son, was being framed by another so as to benefit from the forfeited share.'

'What are you saying, Mr FitzHerbert?' enquired Samantha. 'That me, or Richard, or Jasmine did it?'

'No.'

'It must be Letitia then,' said Greta.

'Her conduct has been far from acceptable, but I don't believe it stretches to murder.'

Letitia said nothing, but started to look a little uncomfortable.

Albert coughed politely, before saying: 'But if none of the beneficiaries did it, then how can there be a disinheritance?'

'A good point, Mr Boyd. When the true culprit is caught, there will not be any disinheritance.'

'And you know who the culprit is?' asked Sarah.

'Yes.'

'Are they here?' asked Margaret.

'Yes.'

'Who is it?' asked Denis.

'You.'

Everyone turned to look at Denis.

'Are you mad?' he replied, visibly indignant. 'You make an accusation like that based on those nonsensical words?'

'They were the starting point. It seems Mr Timmons had intended to check your background but never got the chance. You mentioned to Mr Hadfield that you were with Barton, Harvey & Cobb. Specialising in company law – corporate M&A, and the like. We checked that, and it transpires that your area of expertise was in fact private-client: wills and that sort of thing, as it turns out. A far cry from the heady world of boardroom battles. What's more, it seems your departure was not entirely voluntary.'

'What do you mean by that?'

'A certain concern in the partnership with the level of expenses being incurred in the course of your practice.'

'I left of my own free will. There was absolutely nothing illegal in anything I did.'

'That's not how the partnership saw it.'

'Is that it? Is that the full basis for your accusation that I'm the murderer?' replied Denis, as he sat back smugly in his chair. 'All I can say is: I hope you are well versed in the laws of defamation.'

'I am, thank you. One of the basic principles of such an action is that telling the truth is a good defence.'

'And you intend to establish that with what you yourself called a "cryptic note", and the moans of a few miserly solicitors?'

'And of course you would have been aware of the details of Robert Staunton's adoption, and his true parentage. On Lydia Cavendish's marriage to George Barrington, you became very concerned as to what that might mean for the Barrington estate.'

'Pure supposition. I think you will need a little bit more than that.'

'Agreed.'

FitzHerbert reached down for his briefcase, placed it on the desk and opened it. He took out something white, unfolded it carefully and held it up for all to see.

'Do you recognise this, Mr Russell?' Counsel asked.

'Looks like some kind of uniform. Other than that, I couldn't say,' he replied.

'I recognise it,' said Sarah. 'It's the uniform I saw on that nurse I didn't know at the home the day of Lady Barrington's murder.'

'What nonsense!' Denis exclaimed. 'This is getting more ludicrous by the minute. One nurse's uniform is the same as the next. And why should we believe her? Staunton is the main suspect, not me. She's probably trying to cover up for him.'

'I recognise it too.'

Everyone turned round to look at Albert, who had just spoken.

'Go on, Mr Boyd' said Counsel, with an encouraging smile.

'Yes. I noticed a nurse I hadn't seen before in the home that day too. I didn't get a very good look at the nurse herself, but what caught my attention was the uniform she wore. You see, the uniforms in Miss Greta's home are plain white, with a little blue monogramme on the breast pocket. May I?'

Albert reached over and took the uniform FitzHerbert was holding.

'This uniform has a green line down each side, and a small decoration on the left-hand waist pocket.'

There was general nodding as Albert showed the detail to those present.

'And you are sure that is the uniform the mystery nurse was wearing that day?' enquired Counsel.

'Positive' was the reply, as Albert handed back the uniform and sat down.

'And what does that tell us, might I ask?' said an incredulous Denis.

'Quite a lot, actually,' replied FitzHerbert.

'What? That one of the nurses wore a slightly different uniform that day? Pathetic.'

Denis was laughing as he made this response. The others in the room shifted in their seats, unsure as to what to make of the latest information.

'What it tells us is that two separate witnesses have confirmed seeing an unknown third party on the premises at the time of Lord Barrington's murder.

And that this third party was wearing a nurse's uniform that is the uniform used in your wife's medical practice.'

A number of gasps were audible in the room.

'Dr Barrington Russell,' continued Counsel, 'can you confirm that this here is the uniform used by the nurses in your practice?'

'It . . . er . . . it looks very similar.'

'I see. So now it's my wife who is implicated in all this,' retorted Denis, with a laugh, which was bordering on the uncontrolled.

'No. I think it unlikely your wife is involved at all. I believe you yourself took one of the uniforms from the surgery and masqueraded as a nurse at the home that day. Your thespian background would have facilitated the change, and it doubtless presented you with an interesting theatrical challenge.'

Denis sat back in his chair and took a deep breath. 'So let me get this straight. You think I murdered Lord Barrington because I retired from legal practice and have an interest in the theatre, dressing up in a uniform obtained from my wife so as to commit the deed?'

'That would be one way of putting it,' replied FitzHerbert.

'What if I put it to you that somebody else took the uniform and committed the crime?' suggested Denis. 'You said yourself that any number of us had a motive. And no alibi.'

'That's true. But . . . .'

'In fact, should you not be looking at those whose statements have been shown to be false?'

'You mean, having seen Margaret Barrington in her car outside your house when she said she was at home.'

'Exactly!'

'To which we could probably add her husband Richard being seen in his car on the road back to the Manor when claiming to be in his office.'

'Well, there you are!' said Denis triumphantly. All eyes turned to Richard and Margaret Barrington. The former looked up to the ceiling, while the latter studied the carpet intently.

FitzHerbert stood up to his full height and moved towards Richard and Margaret in the front row. 'Would it be fair to say that, if it proved necessary to do so, you could each produce a witness to confirm your whereabouts at the time of the murder of Lady Barrington.'

Both looked towards Counsel and slowly nodded.

'That's all very well,' continued Denis, 'but look here, you haven't one shred of evidence that actually connects me with any of this. It's all speculation. This wouldn't get past the DPP – never mind a court of law! You must know that.'

'I do. But unfortunately for you, the trail does not end there. You had to elaborate the murder of Lord Barrington by breaking into the medicine cabinet. This was done to set up Robert Staunton. To make it appear that he had obtained the poison on the premises which he then used to kill Lord Barrington.'

'Ah! So it was me that broke into the medicine cabinet,' interjected Denis, while making a noise that sounded like something between a squeak and a laugh.

'Yes.'

'And while dressed up in a nurse's uniform and without being noticed, I proceeded to put all the medicines together into a lethal concoction and administered it to Lord Barrington with his tea.'

'No.'

'Oh! I see. So now I *didn't* do it.'

At this point Denis turned to his wife. 'All right. Come on, dear. I think we've listened to enough of this nonsense. Time to get back to the real world.'

'I didn't say you didn't do it,' continued Counsel.

'Well, what *are* you saying?'

'I am saying that you broke into the medicine cabinet and stole a number of medicines, and poisoned Lord Barrington.'

Perplexed glances were exchanged around the room. Hadfield began to worry that perhaps FitzHerbert had lost the thread of his argument. Or just the run of himself.

'Er . . . ' began Hadfield, 'perhaps you could clarify the . . . erm . . . difference between the two positions?'

'Of course, James. It's quite simple really. Mr Russell had already prepared the poison before he came to the nursing home. It would take too long, and present too great a risk, if he were to mix all the medicines together at the premises after breaking into the medicine cabinet. The sole purpose of the break-in was to make it look as if somebody on the premises at the time, who would not have access to such medicines in the normal course of events, had used them for the murder. This would point the finger firmly at Mr Staunton.'

Hadfield looked around the room. There was still a degree of uncertainty apparent, which he shared himself.

'And . . . er . . . Mr Russell mixed these medicines himself before he went to the nursing home, having got them . . . er . . . .'

'They were lying around the house, of course,' said Denis, sarcastically finishing Hadfield's sentence. 'We have them everywhere, don't we, dear?' he added, turning to his wife. 'I just put all these drugs together, popped down to the nursing home, stole similar ones from the medicine cabinet, and went on my merry way.'

'Do you keep any drugs in the house?' Hadfield asked Samantha tentatively.

'Absolutely not. Just the normal over-the-counter medicines we all have. For headaches, colds, that kind of thing.'

Denis sat back with a look of feigned surprise on his face. This was not going well, thought Hadfield as he looked around the room. Uncertainty was turning to scepticism.

'Maybe the surgery?' he suggested.

'No' was her immediate response. 'Nothing at all kept there. All medicines must be bought at a pharmacy. Over-the-counter or prescription.'

'I see,' he replied, slowly turning to FitzHerbert with evident anxiety.

'Thank you, James. You have of course put your finger on the key issue here.'

Hadfield kept his head down. He had no idea where this was all leading – and he wasn't sure he wanted to find out. Counsel had been resting against the desk again during the last exchange, but now stood up and took in a deep breath, revealing the full extent of his majestic waistline.

'The key issue, as I am sure you have all realised, is the need for a prescription for the drugs required to make the poisonous cocktail. Mr Russell had access to these through his wife's surgery.'

'Are you saying I signed prescriptions for my husband to kill Lord Barrington?'

'No. Your husband took blank prescriptions from your surgery and forged your signature to obtain the requisite drugs.'

'Oh' was the doctor's quiet reply.

'And I suppose you can prove that?' enquired Denis.

'Yes. The police have checked with a number of pharmacies in the area and located the prescriptions which matched the drugs used for the poisoning.'

'I wouldn't call that proof,' replied Denis, with a more worried look on his face.

'They sent the prescriptions to a handwriting expert, who can confirm that the signatures on those prescriptions match your own handwriting when compared with the signed statement you gave the police at the outset of the enquiry.'

The room went deathly quiet as Denis slumped back in his chair. After a moment or two, he collected himself and turned to his wife. He slowly kissed her on the cheek, saying: 'I did it for us dear.'

He then looked behind him and stood up, addressing FitzHerbert. 'If I might be allowed say one thing,' he began, standing out in the gap between the chairs and placing his hand on his own seat. 'Let the punishment fit the crime!'

And with that he bolted for the door, carrying his chair with him. In a flash he was on the other side of the room, with the door closed behind him. Robert grabbed the handle but could not seem to get out.

'He must have secured it with the chair.'

Hadfield was immediately anxious for Hilary, who might be in danger on the other side.

'We'll have to force it open. Everyone move back.'

'No need, James. Everyone should just sit back down in their seats.'

'What do you mean? Hilary is alone in there with that murderer!'

'Everything is under control. Please take your seats, and allow me . . . .'

As the panic subsided and people sat down again, FitzHerbert walked slowly to the door. After pausing for a moment, he gave it a gentle knock.

A few seconds elapsed, during which some muffled sounds could be heard. Everyone held their breath as the door-handle turned and the door slowly opened, revealing the limp figure of Denis Russell being escorted back into the room by two burly sergeants, with Detective Sergeant Forde and Superintendent Dockrell immediately behind them.

CHAPTER 34

The two sergeants directed Denis back to his chair.

'What do you mean: you did it for us?' asked Samantha, a hysterical note creeping into her voice.

Her husband sighed. 'The wills, of course. You were treated very badly. You said it yourself many times. That useless holiday home was your main bequest. It was only going to get worse. Once Lydia married George, I knew there would be changes, and one person was sure to benefit from that: Robert.'

'But I didn't want anyone to die!' retorted Samantha. 'You only spoke of challenging the will. Section 117 or something. What was wrong with that?'

'I mentioned it to calm you, dear. But it never had a realistic chance of success. The only way to right the wrongs against us was to proceed as I did. I couldn't be sure if and when George would make the changes. And I had to make it look like Robert had done it. To disinherit him if George did increase Robert's share.'

Samantha buried her head in her hands, shaking it over and over. 'No, no, no,' was all she could say.

'Yes, dear. It all made sense. The entirety of his share under the will would be divided between the real family. Now you might argue that there was still a degree of inequality when comparing Richard and Jasmine's bequests to your own, but I felt we could live with that.'

Richard and Jasmine exchanged startled glances, while Miss Greta responded with a sarcastic: 'Awfully decent of you to spare the rest.'

'But not Lady Barrington or Mr Timmons' added Hadfield.

'Yes, that was unfortunate. And certainly not part of the original plan. Lydia seemed to have suspicions, and went to speak with Timmons. My reference to disinheritance at the Manor that afternoon may not have been wise. It seemed to trigger something with Lydia. She must have recalled my being in the same firm as handled Robert's adoption. I couldn't take the chance.'

'So you administered the poison to the decanters in the study before dinner?' enquired FitzHerbert.

'Yes. I put it in before Timmons arrived, while excusing myself to go to the bathroom. I knew that he and Lydia would have their discussion before dinner. She usually drank sherry. Timmons liked a tipple too, but I wasn't sure as to his preference. So I put the poison in all three. Everything went smoothly. The perfect crime, you could say. Except for Timmons' file note. How was I to know about that? I was slightly concerned when Mr Hadfield received a visit from the police. I thought Timmons *may* have mentioned something to him.'

'So you sent a threatening note.'

'Yes – to see whether he knew anything or not. I was aware of Simon Armstrong's views on his involvement with the Barringtons. The note could have come from him, but if he had suspicions about me, it might have given me an indication. But when he came to the house, he didn't show any concern. The letter convening this meeting seemed to indicate it related more to administrative matters. I was looking forward to Senior Counsel's analysis of a Section 117 claim. Of course, my own view on that . . . .'

'All right,' interrupted Superintendent Dockrell. 'I think we've heard enough. Take him down to the station.'

The two guards stood Denis up, handcuffed him and escorted him from the room. At the doorway, he turned back towards his wife. 'Darling. You will let the cast know that I have been unavoidably detained – but that the show must go on. With or without me!'

'Theatre's great loss, no doubt,' replied Miss Greta.

The room went quiet again as the culprit was taken through the reception area and out the front door, with DS Forde and Superintendent Dockrell following behind. The latter turned briefly at the door and gave a brief bow to FitzHerbert, in the custom common among the legal fraternity, accompanied by the barely discernible hint of a smile.

Letitia got up to go.

'One further matter, Ms Cavendish,' said FitzHerbert.

Letitia stopped and stared at him.

'You might like to explain how your sister came to bequeath almost half her inheritance to you.'

'Letitia, you don't have to say anything!' shouted Greta.

'I don't intend to say anything at all,' she replied.

FitzHerbert took a piece of paper from his briefcase. Everyone looked at it intently.

'It is a certificate. Of marriage. From 1965.'

Greta sighed.

'Between Lydia Cavendish and Jonathan Baird.'

'You mean she was married before?' said Richard. 'To this chap Baird?'

'Still is, Lord Barrington,' came the reply.

There was consternation in the room.

'Which of course had consequences for Lady Barrington's inheritance. She would get nothing. Letitia knew this. As did Greta. Letitia was blackmailing her sister, but Greta could not prevent it, as Robert would lose out if the truth were known. It is likely that Clarisse was asked to witness the will, so that she could verify that Lydia had provided for her sister, as required. Of course, as a beneficiary she could not witness the will herself. Isn't that right, Ms Cavendish?'

There was no reply.

'As you wish. I believe Detective Superintendent Dockrell is waiting outside. Do take all the time you need to answer *his* questions.'

Silence descended on the room as Letitia slowly walked out.

'Well, I believe my work here is done,' said FitzHerbert. 'I think a little light refreshment at the Arms might be in order.'

'How about the other issues?' asked Richard.

'Yes,' added Jasmine, 'can we actually get some money now, please?'

'And Robert too,' said Sarah. 'He's just as entitled also, isn't he?'

'Don't forget Richard's slander,' Miss Greta chipped in. 'It's been proven here, hasn't it?'

'And what about Samantha? Can she still take her share? She's married to the murderer.'

This last query came from Margaret. There was a brief silence all round, before Samantha burst into tears and ran from the room.

'Those queries would be very much in Mr Hadfield's bailiwick, and I shall leave him to deal with them as he sees fit,' replied FitzHerbert, gathering up his briefcase and heading for the door. 'Good-day.'

*

It was a good hour later before a tired-looking Hadfield left the office, joined by Hilary and Mick. They headed straight for the Kilcreddin Arms, where they were greeted by FitzHerbert, who was accompanied by Superintendent Dockrell in the lounge area. Lucinda was there too: she had left the office earlier, to meet her uncle.

'Good man!' exclaimed FitzHerbert. 'Thought you might be here a little sooner, though.'

'I was lucky to get away at all,' replied Hadfield, a little sullenly. 'It didn't help that they were expecting "Learned Counsel" to be on hand for their queries.'

'No bother to you. I'm sure you dealt with them all admirably. Important to maintain the solicitor-client relationship, you know. Counsel's role should be an occasional one only. Now! What are we all having to drink?'

He called over the barman, who organised a round of drinks, following which FitzHerbert formally introduced the Superintendent to Hilary and Mick.

'James needs no introduction, of course,' said his friend with a wink.

'We've already had the pleasure,' acknowledged Dockrell. 'Thanks for all your hard work on this. And sorry about the clandestine nature of the operation today, but it was felt best to keep those in the know to a minimum.'

'Of course,' replied Hadfield, somewhat appeased by the Superintendent's remarks. 'These things need to be kept under wraps, I'm sure.'

'How did you know it was Russell?' asked Hilary.

'Well, Mr FitzHerbert put us on to that initially. In fact, he was just about to explain, when you came in. Perhaps . . . ?'

'Happy to oblige,' he responded, settling back into his chair. 'Of course it was Mr Timmons' file note which was the key. It was a little unclear at first, primarily because of the handwriting. It wasn't immediately apparent that Section 120 of the Succession Act was being referred to. But we knew that the Superintendent wasn't convinced that Staunton was the guilty party. If one assumed that the murderer was someone other than Staunton, then other possibilities presented themselves. One point did stand out, in particular, from the discussions at the Manor. It was the comment Russell had made, and Lady Barrington's reaction to it.'

'What comment was that?' asked Hilary.

'Well, mentioning his previous life as a solicitor, and pointing out that the murderer would not gain from the will. Russell's comment was a quite legalistic analysis. It also showed someone who had familiarity with succession law. At that point, the file note of Timmons began to make sense – and point towards Denis Russell as a suspect in the mind of Lady Barrington. Naturally, I passed on my thoughts to the Super here.'

'And of course,' added Dockrell, 'the background checks we carried out confirmed Russell was there when Staunton's adoption was processed. And that he was not known for his honesty. While this was not damning in itself, it did mean that certain avenues of investigation could be pursued.'

'The mysterious nurse, for example,' continued FitzHerbert. 'Russell's enthusiastic references to his involvement in *The Mikado*, when he spoke last with James, opened up the possibility of him acting out the role. The nursing home itself could be easily accessed from the separate 'trade entrance' to the side, without much risk of him being spotted up close.'

'Fortunately for us,' added the Superintendent, 'two separate witnesses noticed the nurse – although without recognising who it was. The descriptions suggested the possibility of a uniform from his wife's surgery'

FitzHerbert nodded. 'And the break-in to the medicine cabinet could be interpreted as an attempt to frame Staunton, of course. As I mentioned earlier, I thought it likely that the poison had been prepared elsewhere. So that the murderer would not have to spend any more time than absolutely necessary in the nursing home, but make it look like someone with fortuitous access had broken in. There was another, perhaps more obvious, factor, which pointed to this.'

'The strichnyne?'

'Exactly, Lucinda. The strichnyne. Why did the murderer add this? Because they wanted to be certain the poison would work. Russell is likely to have had some knowledge from his wife as to the medicines in the nursing home. Mixing various medicines that could be found there might not guarantee death. The murderer just wanted to stage the break-in to point the finger at Staunton, whom he knew would be there. He likely thought the police would not be too interested in the finer detail of the poison itself, once the spotlight was on Staunton.'

'In fact,' responded Dockrell, 'the analysis done in the lab indicated that the medicines on their own, without the strichnyne, would have had a less-than-certain chance of creating a fatality – although serious illness would certainly have resulted.'

'So that all pointed,' continued FitzHerbert, 'to our murderer sourcing the medicines themselves. In the case of Russell, that meant he either had the cooperation of his wife, or he was obtaining them himself, under some pretext.'

'And that gave rise to the possibility of forged prescriptions from Dr Barrington Russell's surgery, which we duly investigated in the neighbouring pharmacies.'

'And what about the stolen medicines that were found in the bins?' asked Hilary.

'An afterthought of Russell's, I should think. Probably done by him at some point, before he returned to the Manor on the evening of the murders. Would you say so, Bernard?'

Dockrell nodded.

'But Russell thought dumping them all in Staunton's bin would be too obvious, and might point to a set-up.'

'That's right, Lucinda,' replied Dockrell. 'And spreading them around the neighbours could be interpreted as a panicked reaction by Staunton before he went to the Manor.'

'So there you have it!' declared FitzHerbert.

'Why did it all have to happen at the office?' asked Mick, a little suspiciously.

FitzHerbert looked at Dockrell, who, after a brief pause, gave a slight nod of approval.

'Well, the first concern was not to alert Russell to our actual suspicions. Of course James had, as agreed, referenced the fact that the police were not treating Staunton as the only possible suspect. It was felt that a meeting of all the parties to discuss the legal situation without any obvious police involvement would help alleviate any concerns on that score. Also, it was the most likely way to get Richard and Margaret Barrington to admit that they did in fact have alibis for their whereabouts at the time of Lord Barrington's murder. There was another, more practical, reason. Super?'

'Yes. We wanted to gain access to the house and surgery while both Russell and his wife were certain to be absent, and unable to know of our presence there. Firstly, to obtain the surgery uniform, to check that it matched the description given – which it did. We also needed to check that the prescription forms at the surgery corresponded with those used by Russell at the various pharmacies to obtain the medicines he needed. In fact, we found a number of blank ones in his office.'

'Apologies, old boy,' said FitzHerbert to Hadfield. 'That explains the delay in my arriving at the office. I had to wait for the search to be completed. And bring the evidence to the meeting.'

'Apology accepted. But . . . er . . . hold on. About those prescription forms. Why did you need to check them? I thought you already had proof that he'd falsified them. From a handwriting expert.'

FitzHerbert looked at the Superintendent again – who simply shrugged his shoulders.

'Well, our handwriting expert was taking a little longer than expected to respond formally. He felt there were differences between Dr Barrington Russsell's signature and those on the prescriptions which we believed were used for the poison.'

'But he hadn't established that the signature was that of Denis Russell,' suggested Hilary.

'Not as of 11 o'clock this morning, no.'

'But,' interjected FitzHerbert, with a dismissive wave of his hand, 'with finding the blank prescription forms in Russell's office, it was decided a calculated gamble was merited.'

'To get him to admit the murders,' said Hadfield.

'Exactly.'

'Could that be entrapment?' queried Mick.

'I doubt it, Mick. For a start, our expert has since come through with the confirmation. And if you were present in the room at the time, I think you will find that my statement was entirely true – the use of the words "can" and "when" being at the crux of the issue.'

'He's also signing the confession freely as we speak,' added Superintendent Dockrell, just as Detective Sergeant Forde entered the room.

'Ah! Forde. Perfect timing. All satisfactorily signed off?'

DS Forde nodded in the affirmative but retained his blank expression.

'What about Clarisse?' asked Lucinda.

'We caught up with her in Paris. No link with Hargreaves, but she has a shadowy enough past of her own, it seems. Embezzlement and the like. We might have some corroboration on Ms Cavendish's blackmail once the local police have processed all that.'

'And Jasmine?' asked Hilary.

'Might leave matters lie there for the moment. Hopefully a lesson learned. Same for Armstrong.'

Dockrell looked at his watch. 'Better be on our way.'

'You won't stay for a bite of lunch, gentlemen?' enquired FitzHerbert.

DS Forde seemed on the point of nodding again – although it was hard to tell.

'No thank you,' replied Dockrell. 'Detective Sergeant Forde has to drive us back to Dublin. Should try and get there while it's bright. We'll pick up a snack on the way.'

The Superintendent departed without delay. He was followed, a little less quickly, by DS Forde, whose demeanour as he left gave the impression of someone who felt that a snack on the way back was somewhat less than his due for the morning's work.

CHAPTER 35

'I couldn't eat another thing,' said FitzHerbert, moving his empty dessert plate away, followed by the necessary unbuttoning of his waistcoat.

'Skip the cheese, so?' enquired Hadfield.

'Alas.'

'But perhaps not a brandy?' suggested Hilary.

'Always room for a digestif. Very important aid to healthy digestion. That's what it actually means, of course. Needless to say, the French invented the word.'

As the after-dinner drinks arrived, the discussion returned to the murders once more.

'So, why did he do it?' asked Lucinda.

'Well, of course he claimed to have done it for his wife,' replied FitzHerbert. 'She felt that Lord Barrington's will was unfair in its distribution. I'm sure Russell would have assisted her thinking in that regard – doubtless ignoring the substantial benefit already conferred by the gift of the property in Rathmore. But I suspect the reasons were more selfish.'

He sat back for a moment, to partake further of the brandy.

'Why do you say that?' asked Hadfield.

FitzHerbert paused to savour the taste, before continuing. 'Firstly, it seemed clear that Lord Barrington had little time for him: retiring from practice and "taking to the boards" is not likely to have gone down well. But Russell also knew of Robert's true parentage, and was concerned when Lydia came on the scene that a far greater share of the estate would go to her son. He was right, of course. Finally, he probably needed Samantha to get her inheritance sooner rather than later. It seems from police enquiries that Russell was very keen to run his own productions, and had been for some time – and substantial sums were needed for that. But his wife's business was in some difficulty: she had overstretched herself with new treatments in recent times. Lord Barrington's passing, and Staunton being held to blame, would have eased matters considerably.'

'I see,' said Hilary. 'So ultimately it was just personal greed that drove him to it.'

'Yes. Filthy lucre to blame at the end of the day,' he replied, adding, as he noted the bemused looks on the faces around him: 'That means money. Middle English phrase. Probably Tyndale who coined it – if you pardon the pun.'

After waiting for the laughter – which didn't come – he continued. 'Of course, he would have probably got away with it if he had just kept his mouth shut in the Manor that afternoon. Either his natural tendency to show off made him respond as he did, or he simply enjoyed the thrill of hinting at what only he knew. He took a few risks along the way – which makes me think the latter.'

He tossed back the last of his brandy.

'Better start thinking of the train back.'

Hadfield understood what was meant, and ordered another round. As the drinks arrived, he recalled something from earlier that day which had seemed a little odd. 'Actually, Charles, do you remember what Russell said just before he tried to make a bolt for it? Something about crime and punishment, I think. What was that all about?'

'Ah yes! "Let the punishment fit the crime." It's from Act 2 of *The Mikado*. The Emperor sings about his intended administration of justice. Russell had to have the last word before exiting the stage. Quite witty, really . . . .' FitzHerbert mused for a moment, before quickly adding: 'If it weren't for the circumstances, of course.'

'So did he think he shouldn't be punished for the crime?' wondered Hadfield.

'Possibly. But it was unlikely he would get far. He may have had a different ending in mind.'

'Committing hari-kari!' exclaimed Mick – which got a good laugh from the table.

'Maybe. Although the correct description is "hara-kiri". "Hara" meaning "stomach", and "kiri" meaning "to cut".'

'Doesn't sound as good,' grumbled Mick.

'No, possibly not. Might explain how the error came about. Anyway, just as well the police were on hand to nab him: *Nemo est supra legis* – as they say.'

'Two questions, Charles,' asked Hilary. 'What does that mean, and why do you always speak in Latin – or whatever it is?'

'The first question is easily answered: it means "No man – or woman, for that matter – is above the law." To answer the second question, I have to refer to that well-known phrase: *Quidquid latine dictum sit altum videtur.* FitzHerbert waited for a moment as he observed the perplexed faces around him, before adding: 'Which is generally taken to mean "Everything sounds more impressive in Latin".'

'I see,' replied Hilary, with a laugh.

'Anyway, enough of all that: I suppose you'll all be happy to get back to the more routine business of running a solicitors' practice.'

'I'll miss the excitement,' said Lucinda.

'I won't', replied Hadfield. 'No doubt about that.'

'You should be able to crack on with administering those wills now, James.'

'Yes – and Albert was in generous mood, now that the beneficiaries are clear. The bank's advances should keep them going until we can get the probate through.' He paused momentarily, as he cast his mind back to the earlier meeting. 'Actually, one point on that, Charles. I assume you heard Margaret Barrington's comment just before you left the room?'

'About Samantha having no entitlement because she is married to the murderer?'

'Yes. Er . . . I suppose there's nothing in that. I mean, if she didn't know . . . .'

'Of course not, James. If she isn't guilty of a crime herself, the law doesn't treat her any differently.'

'Thought so myself, of course. Er . . . didn't seem right . . . .'

'It wouldn't surprise me,' he continued, 'if Russell had considered that too. A calculated risk: if he got away with it, they stood to gain from the disinheritance, but if not, Samantha would be no worse off.'

'He struck me as having an ego that didn't consider failure,' commented Hilary.

'You could be right, Hilary. It's likely that he felt duty-bound to remedy the perceived injustice of the wills. Failure may never have come into the equation.'

'Hard to see Mr T.'s role in the injustice,' added Mick. 'The fellow's just mad, if you ask me.'

'Very likely, Mick,' replied FitzHerbert. 'Definitely not the workings of a normal mind. Poor old Mr Timmons, getting caught up in all that.'

Silence descended for a moment, as they each thought again on the solicitor's tragic end.

'At least today has cleared up any doubts about your involvement in the crimes. Montgomery Darley can get on with their job too.'

249

'Were we really under suspicion?' gasped Mick.

'"Suspicion" might be too strong a word. But the police have to keep an open mind in these situations. Anyhow, I'd better be on my way. Train leaves in fifteen minutes.'

He rose from the table, and rebuttoned his waistcoat.

'Made any plans for Hillside Lodge yet?' he asked of Hilary.

'Not really. Haven't had much time to think about it.'

'It was your boss's wish that you'd look after it as he would. Wasn't that the phrase he used?'

'Yes. But still, it's a big undertaking for one person . . . .'

'Easily rectified!' he replied with a wink.

'Next lunch on me, James,' he added, as he approached the waiter to collect his coat and briefcase.

'See you all soon,' he bellowed, as he left the restaurant with a stately gait.

*

'What a day!' exclaimed Mick.

'Agreed. Let's hope it's a one-off,' replied Hilary.

'Better be,' added Hadfield. 'I don't know how much more of that kind of business I could handle.'

'No. The reputation of Timmons & Associates has to be considered,' she pointed out.

'Or is it Hadfield Timmons & Associates?' enquired Mick.

'Are you changing the name of the firm?' asked Lucinda.

'Just slightly, perhaps. To reflect the new circumstances. I think "Timmons Hadfield & Associates" will do.'

Hadfield's fellow diners looked at each other briefly before nodding their approval.

'Well, that's me done for the day,' said Hadfield, as he finished his brandy. 'The office will still be there on Monday, I'm sure.'

He looked surreptitiously at Mick, who was still nursing his brandy, before adding:

'Er . . . I think we can all take the rest of the day off. Might . . . erm . . . get the bill.'

Mick looked at Hilary, who was busy studying her napkin, and realised it was time to make himself scarce.

'Actually, I . . . left my paper in the office,' he said, knocking back the last of his drink. 'I might just collect it and head on home, if that's all right.'

He gave a gentle nudge to Lucinda as he got up.

'Oh. Yes. I'd better be on my way too.'

'See you Monday,' said Mick.

'Thanks for lunch,' added Lucinda.

'See you Monday,' replied Hilary.

'See you then,' added Hadfield, as they both left the restaurant at a clip.

'They know,' said Hilary.

'So be it,' replied Hadfield, as the waiter came with the bill.

They had to wait for a while as their coats were brought to them at the entrance to the restaurant. As they did so, Jasmine and Hugh came strolling by, arm in arm.

'James! Hilary! Having a late lunch, I see,' exclaimed an ebullient Jasmine, who had obviously come from a lunch à *deux* herself. 'Join us for a drink in the lounge. I've just been telling Hugh all about the morning's excitement. Haven't I, darling?'

'Yes. Extraordinary turn of events. What will you have?'

'Actually . . . we're just . . . er . . . going back to the office,' replied Hadfield.

'Oh, surely that can wait. Do stay for a while.'

'Better not. Best to deal with the paperwork while . . . er . . . .'

'It's still fresh in the mind,' continued Hilary. 'James is a stickler for that.'

'Oh well,' Jasmine replied, with a slightly exaggerated pout. 'Perhaps another time.'

They said their goodbyes to each other in the corridor, before exchanging pleasantries with Mrs Stokes at reception, who seemed to be regarding them with a curious expression.

'By the look of her, she knows too!' said Hadfield, as they stood out on the street at the front of the hotel.

'Quite possibly. She has a sharp eye.'

'I think you were right about Jasmine and Hugh.'

'Yes. We may have been pawns in that particular game.'

'But in a way, I don't mind. It did bring us together. Speaking of which: left or right?'

'How about straight ahead?'

'Hmm?'

'Hillside Lodge. I have the keys.'

'Good idea! It's probably due a house-warming . . . .'